BREAKOUT

Books by Alek L. Cristea

The Fractured Cities Tales

Cornucopia

BREAKOUT

THE ALTAYIH CHRONICLES #1

ALEK L. CRISTEA

Cover design by Rebecca Treadway www.artinkcovers.com

ISBN-13: 9798834789581

DEDICATION

To the misfits and the marginalised who have been waiting to see yourselves as heroes, this one is for you!

AUTHOR'S NOTE

I like to joke this book burnt its way out of me, lighting a fire that burnt bright until I finally put the last word to paper. Born from a song ("Breakout", by Celldweller - give it a listen!), *Breakout* became so much more than I could have expected: it took me on a journey not only through the stars but also through myself.

Until I wrote this book, I wasn't out as trans, and with most people who'd known me pre-transition no longer in my life, I'd spent years passing (more or less well) as a cis guy. But then I wrote Trystan, and realised that I didn't want other trans boys and men out there to just be able to see themselves in him - I wanted them to also know *I* was like them. That *we* can achieve our dreams and be happy, that the experience I wrote about was inspired, in part, by my own life.

This book taught me to accept my transness in ways I didn't know I could, and I hope that - for those who share some of my experience with gender - you, too, can find something good in these pages.

Now I should add a couple of warnings: although the entirety of the cast is queer, and most of the planets and places they exist in are queer-normative, there is one location where that's not the case. There is no on-page queerphobia, but there are many instances of misgendering, since our trans protagonist is still in the closet. That said, *Breakout,* was written to be a celebration of queer joy, and as such, this queerness will never be what brings conflict to the plot or characters.

There are also mentions of grief and mental health issues, as well as physical disability, so if you find some of those topics difficult, know that they are present not as central themes of the story, but rather as part of the characters themselves.

I wrote this book for my teenage self who had yet to discover his own queerness, and for all my queer siblings out there who long to see themselves as the heroes of adventures out there in the impossible, vastness of space. I hope you'll find bits of yourself amongst *Breakout*'s many, many stars, and enjoy the journey you're about to set off on!

HUMAN INTERGALACTIC YEAR 1406

PART 1

TOO LATE FOR A PRAYER

Man was born free and is everywhere in chains.
Jean-Jacques Rousseau

CHAPTER 1
MALEK

Fire.

Explosions.

The breeching alarms.

I feel like I'm running up a hill of shifting sand instead of familiar corridors, each step taking a million years as smoke pours in from everywhere. I'm running away from my room, my bunk, all the things that have defined me for fourteen years.

So many fights expertly fought in the darkness of space, so many careful plans and calculated risks only for it all to end here. With an attack we didn't see coming. I'm running against the current, screaming for amma, scared as my entire world goes up in flames, rocked time and time again by the missiles battering the shields, rending the hull.

The smoke would blind us if not for the red emergency lights piercing through. Red like fear. Red like blood.

The evacuation order has been given, but I can't find amma and she is the only thing that matters. Captain Sabra Sidana, who is probably still on the command deck, standing proud amongst the chaos, head held high even as the Farikhar *goes up in flames around her. I need her right now more than I ever have. More than I need to breathe.*

I scream for her, pushing against the faceless crew making for the escape pods, tearing myself from someone's grip. I'm trying to get through to her, but she doesn't answer the coms and all I can do is keep running, for the lift—no, the stairs—and up towards her.

The ship is too large, too small, put together all wrong. These stairs shouldn't lead me to where I arrive, the corridor to the command deck an endless stretch, the door always too far for me to reach.

I scream for amma again, a cry cut short as a wall panel explodes, sending me flying. I smash into the wall and I'm no longer on the upper decks, but further down, closer to my room, far from everyone.

The fire is in my limbs now, my leg twisted under me. I can't move. Everything hurts so much. Everything is numb. Something sharp drips on my face. A sharpness that burns. A leak. I try to move an arm to shield my face, using the other to drag myself away, and suddenly the explosion is happening again and again in quick bursts, and I'm watching myself caught in an endless wave of flames.

I try to move but every nerve is out of sync, refusing to cooperate. I don't know what's up or down anymore.

The dripping leak becomes a torrent that engulfs me.

The pain is a new level of agony. My vision goes red. Then white. And finally, it all fades to black.

***

HELIOS 2

I wake with a start, gasping the stale recycled air as though I'd been drowning. The darkness of my cell is almost enough to make me think I'm still blind. But beneath my fingers there are no traces of mangled flesh. Only skin grafts and cybernetic eyes.

I take another deep breath, trying to put the images from the nightmare back to where they belong: to four years ago, when the attack that destroyed amma's ship nearly killed me in the process. Four years since a fire tried to eat me alive but only claimed two of my limbs.

In waking moments I've got little more than flashes and hazy memories of the whole incident, aside from the fire that burns bright to this day. Only today, I could swear that instead of haunting my heart, it's taken residence inside my soul, reminding me that I'm alive.

Sitting on top of my prison bunk, Akim snoring softly beneath me, I feel more than I have done in years. I feel so alive, so bright, that I could laugh. The darkness that had swallowed me whole is gone. I smile, for real, for the first time in too long, and I know that today is the day.

Today, we make history.

Today, we escape Helios 2.

***

"I know exactly what we need to do," I attempt to whisper to my friends as we slide into our customary seats in the refectory, the lights overhead flickering ominously.

"You're going to get us in trouble," Nooma hisses, deep brown eyes hard. "Keep your voice down!"

"The whole point *is* to get into trouble," I reply, receiving three concerned looks as a response.

"Getting in trouble is not a plan, Mal," Alta says, so quiet I can barely hear them over the din of breakfast.

I'm about to respond when something casts a shadow over me. I glance sideways at the bulk of a six-foot something bald man glaring down at me.

"Not today," I mutter under my breath, slipping my fork up the sleeve of my overalls as I turn to him.

"You said something?" he asks, getting so close that I have to strain my neck to look up at him—I really should be owed another growth spurt by now.

Behind me I can feel Akim almost wrapping his arms around his tray, whilst I know Alta will be shovelling as much in their mouth as they can fit. This isn't the first time we've danced this dance with Baldy and his friends.

"Yeah." There is a smirk on my lips. "I said, not today."

There is a sharp moment of surprise. We've always given in; handed over our trays to escape the beating. But the fire in my heart is saying no. Enough.

"What are you doing?" Nooma hisses, but at the corner of my eye I catch her hands becoming fists.

Enough.

"You feel like a beating?" Baldy cracks his knuckles.

"Nah, I feel like dishing one out."

He slams his hand on the table next to my tray and I stab the back of it with the fork, my movement so fast I almost startle myself.

He howls in pain, and I stand, punching him in the face hard enough for him to crumple, the fork still in his hand. His cronies step forward, but Nooma stands up next to me. She's tall and muscular, and her strength is legendary amongst the inmates. Nooma doesn't pick fights, ever, but she'll always finish them.

"You're gonna pay for that, you little shit," Baldy snarls as he staggers to his feet, his nose bleeding.

Around us the refectory carries on as normal, pretending nothing is happening, the faceless androids still patrolling the edges of the room. Their only purpose to make sure we don't escape. Everything else we deal with ourselves.

"You want to go again?" I ask, all but bouncing on the balls of my feet. "Because I'm game if you are!"

"Malek," Nooma hisses. "Can you not make this worse?"

I ignore her, watching the men with their narrowed eyes and their faces twisted in anger.

"You better sleep with one eye open," Baldy says, pulling the fork out of his hand and throwing it at my feet. Then he turns away without another word, his cronies in tow.

"What was that about?" Alta asks, their olive skin gone ashen. "Hadn't we agreed it was better to just give them our stuff once in a while?"

"Not anymore," I reply, the fire dancing in my soul as I turn back to my friends. "I'm done not fighting back. I'm too alive to spend the rest of my days bowing to other people."

My friends exchange a look, part worry, part surprise, part something I can't quite read, and then all but Akim are looking straight at me.

"Have you lost your mind? This could have ended really badly," Nooma chastises me, running a hand through the tight coils of her hair, her dark black skin a little gaunt.

I shrug. "But it didn't. Now, do you wanna hear my plan or not?"

CHAPTER 2
TRYSTAN

EDEN ONE

I'm out of the pew the second the priest finishes the service, almost running out of the church. I need to be outside, away from the words that want to make me feel guilty about my existence. A sermon about being good children to our parents, good citizens to our government. A variation on a theme that has framed my entire existence.

My mother calls after me but I don't stop until I've cleared the church gate and emerged into the park beyond, the trees swaying softly in the breeze. It's a beautiful day: too clear, too sunny, and I want nothing more than to get out of the open. I never feel more exposed than in moments like this, in my church best, the skirt grating against my legs, everyone's eyes snagging on me.

My mother grabs my wrist, whirling me around, a look of utter disappointment on her face. Behind her I can see my father lingering by the church talking to senator Pense, his own son by his side.

Once upon a time, Nathaniel and I had fled the church together, laughing. When we'd been children and still allowed to be friends.

"Where do you think you're going?" my mother demands.

I resist pulling my wrist free.

"I needed some air," I say, trying to smooth over the edges of my tone. "I'm sorry."

She looks a little mollified, her blue eyes so dim even with all the bright sunlight. She lets go, fixing her wavy bob in that fussy way she has. I tidy my own hair behind my ears before she reaches over and does it for me.

"You need to have more decorum than that," she tells me, and I cast my eyes down. Better to look contrite than to roll my eyes and get her twice as annoyed. "The daughter of a senator needs to comport herself properly."

"I know, mother. I'm sorry. It won't happen again." I go through the motions, but I don't know if she believes the lie. I've made too many such promises and never kept them, but the dance has been danced and she turns away, looking for my father who is meandering towards us, Senator Pense at his side.

Nathaniel meets my eyes and I look away, feigning shyness.

"Mom, I need to go to Uncle's laboratory," I say, before my father is within earshot. "Would it be a problem if I headed there now?"

"Why do you need to go there on a Sunday of all days?"

"I need to finish some homework. I want to make father proud with my grades."

My life has been a great web of lies and carefully concealed truths for the last three years. I'm practically a pro. Sure, sometimes I fumble my lines, but today my delivery is flawless, my composure impeccable.

"You and this science stuff," my mother sighs. "You realise you will never need this again after school, right?"

"I'm sure it might help me help my husband," I say with a tight smile, my eyes trying so hard to not fall on Nathaniel.

The boy I've been promised to since we turned ten.

The boy I never want to marry.

"Fine, fine," my mother relents. I spoke the right words and I'm free to turn away, to escape an uncomfortable conversation with my father and Pense and Nathaniel. "Go on, I'll tell your father. Be home for dinner, though. No staying out late, young lady!"

"Of course not, mom," I say brightly, although the way she says 'young lady' makes me feel sick to my stomach.

I all but flee towards the automated taxis waiting to take the churchgoers home, not caring that I shouldn't be running, that I should do everything with poise.

***

The city seen from above is almost beautiful. A forest of metal and glass, white concrete decorated with greenery. It glitters like a jewel in the sunlight, clean and perfect, but I know its soul, and the darkness it houses dims its beauty.

I tear my eyes from the view and grab my phone, bringing up the message Uncle sent me during Mass.

Tryst, come to the lab. Project U is ready for testing.

The aura of a migraine blossoms behind my eyes, but I wouldn't postpone this for anything. It's been our little secret for three years: since he came back from his exile following the war with Ishnira.

I didn't just gain an uncle when he did, but words for everything that I knew without knowing about myself. I never believed there was power in words until then. Now I know how much words can empower. And how much they can hurt, too.

Outside the window, the city seems so vast that it's almost impossible to grasp. In the distance I catch sight of the space port, not quite outside the city but almost. I can't see it from here, but I know the sign that greets anyone landing there.

Welcome to Eden One. A new Earth. A new Heaven.

Eden One. My home. My prison. A place that worships an Earth that was already outdated by the time my ancestors left on their generation ships. A place where everyone must fall in line and stay in their place.

I wonder how many out there feel as out of place as I do. Would we outnumber the ones who truly fit this system?

As we descend towards my uncle's laboratory, I watch the quiet street. Not many people work on a Sunday, but my uncle isn't a believer and is old enough to skip Mass without bringing about the wrath of his parents. I'm not quite that lucky yet.

I make a beeline for the lift as soon as I'm out of the taxi, heart racing. The lift is the slowest thing today, and I take a few seconds to lean my forehead against the cool metal, a futile attempt at soothing my headache.

When the doors slide open, I'm greeted by the clean and familiar scent of chemicals and tech.

My shoulders relax even if the migraine doesn't, rendering my thoughts a little fuzzy, but I'm here, in the one place I can be myself, and it's all that matters.

I spot my uncle, hands flying at his holoscreens as he rearranges formulae that are beyond my level. To one side a 3D image of my brain, to another the map of wires and chips that artificially mimic it. Getting the equipment for this without people asking questions hasn't been easy but my uncle is far more cunning than most give him credit for.

"Left," is all he says as the door whispers shut.

I turn, heart stuttering. The android—*my* android—is standing up, eyes closed, features so realistic that it's almost like looking into a mirror.

It's perfect.

*He'*s perfect. Last time I saw him, the synth-skin was missing, his chest cavity revealing the android beneath, cables spooling out his brain, linking him to the computer as I uploaded optional software I wasn't sure I'd be able to use.

Now the illusion of life is almost complete. I reach a hand to his flat chest, almost expecting to feel my heart beating beneath. Before I can stop them, tears roll down my face. The migraine stabs but it can't hurt me, nothing can right now. My uncle wraps his arms around me from behind, giving me the space to pull away. I don't. Today it doesn't matter how wrong this body feels, because I'm looking at something that gives me hope.

"He's perfect," I whisper.

My uncle chuckles. "You make a very pretty boy."

I let out a laugh that is half sob.

It's my face but not my face: same grey eyes but a sharper jaw; my body but not my body: same milky white skin but not even a hint of breasts. It's everything I've ever wanted to see when I look in the mirror.

"What tests do you need to run?"

Soon, maybe, I can feel better.

"Let me show you."

Soon I won't just be looking at my android self.

But through him.

CHAPTER 3
LÀHN

KIRILLION

They say on Kirillion all your dreams can come true.

A planet of trillions, one unending sprawl of a metropolis as diverse as it is old. There is no other known place like it in all the galaxies. It was old when the oldest of the space-faring races took their first steps amongst the stars.

Kirillion is a city of dreams and nightmares, of angels and monsters basking in the latest tech and scientific inventions. A place that doesn't know the word 'impossible'.

I don't remember coming here, but Kirillion took me into its arms and never let go. I'm part of its underbelly: where neon signs flicker, cops don't patrol, and you don't need hovercars to get around. I know Kirillion's dirty secrets, and I love every single one of them as much as I love its flashy face and intoxicating pace.

Purple Gravity is a slice of it all: neon lights, crowds as diverse as their fashion is eclectic, and the ever-present promise of danger and thrill. The anti-gravity dancefloor takes centre stage: dancers whirling to the music, painted in flashing lights. Three floors of lounges with more bars than I can count selling more alcohols than I know the names of. Everyone comes to *Purple Gravity*: from the workers of the lower levels to the children of the elite in their floating glass domes; from the businesspeople in search of a good time to the outlaws who call this place home.

I'm still nursing my first drink, leaning on the bar whilst my mark is on his fifth shot. He's not even close to tipsy yet: Kundar-Human hybrids are a resilient bunch. Hybrids are what happens when science takes over, mixing DNAs that would not naturally work together and creating life out of it—a common sight on Kirillion.

My mark is in his twenties, male—implying a mostly Human physiology as Kundar are genderless—with Human-shaped eyes that are entirely fluorescent purple, the block colour and lack of pupil of the Kundar and Shinarians strange on his face. His skin is a pale off-white, a stark contrast to the black scales that wind down his arms, climbing up his throat to line his jaw and accentuate his cheekbones. He lacks the horns and extra two arms that the Kundar have, but no-one would mistake him for a full-blooded Human.

He makes me wish this wasn't just a job.

He takes notice of me, slamming his eighth shot down and getting up. He's tall, over six foot five, nearly a whole foot taller than me, wearing loose pants and chunky boots with a cropped tank that shows off the scales at his hips. It's easy to forget he's an executive director for Saion Corp.

"You look like you could use the company," he says in the local Human dialect. I lower my eyes, playing coy.

"Just been a long day," I shrug, looking up from beneath lowered lashes.

He meets my eyes, takes in their chemically enhanced gold—a recent birthday present—and then his eyes move down to trace the rest of me. Kundar eyes are hard to track, but I've had practice.

"The kind of long day that leaves you feeling lonely?"

It's almost too easy to get him where I want him, but that's exactly why Zoon sent me on this job.

"I guess," I take a slow drink, dragging my tongue across my lips. He watches every second of it. "I've got a pretty lonely job…"

"Do you now?" He leans forward slightly.

He's moving fast, but he's hot, the beat is deep, and this is the perfect setting for my little game.

"Yeah. So many hours spent all by myself," I say, playfully sad. There is something dangerous about him, and that draws me in.

He motions to the private booths at the edges of the club. "I could alleviate all that loneliness," he purrs, and I close my eyes to collect my thoughts. There is something about his voice that makes me tremble. He must have some top-of-the-line vocal augmentations, which would be dangerous if I wasn't well versed in recognising the effects of such things.

"That doesn't sound like a bad idea."

His hand finds my wrist and he yanks me to my feet. He's strong, the muscles of his chest firm against my hand as I steady myself.

This is always a game with risks, but as my heartbeat ticks upwards, I'm smiling.

No-one notices us as he pulls me after him, his own smile feral. No-one would see even if I struggled to free myself from his grip.

In this city of trillions, we're all tiny, insignificant, grains of sand.

***

The Kundar all but slams me into the padded back wall of the booth, his lips crushing mine. It's a startling kiss, deep and passionate and his hands are roaming up and down my body, searching.

When he pulls away, I'm panting and almost miss the small device blinking in his hand.

"What's that?"

"Needed to make sure you weren't chipped or recording."

"Chipped? What?" I wasn't prepared for him to be expecting trouble.

"I'm someone who has to take precautions. I have enemies in high places," he says with a wolfish grin and an arrogance that suits him far too much.

"Do I *look* like a threat?"

"Whether you're a threat or not doesn't mean you couldn't be used as a spy." A pause as his eyes rake over me again, undressing me with a glance. It's definitely getting hotter in here. "Sorry if I scared you."

"You did," I admit, keeping my gaze locked on his. I know there is danger to these jobs, but I always feel in control behind soundproof curtains and with my smile as my weapon.

Around us the beat of sensual music pounds in rhythm with our hearts.

"I can make it up to you," he promises, and I want to melt into him.

"I wouldn't mind that."

"What's your name?" he asks as he pulls me to him so that I'm straddling him. He's the kind of guy that makes me want to just have a bit of fun before I finish the job. It wouldn't be the first time in a curtained alcove like this one.

"Làhn. You?"

"Shi'lu'Fan."

He slides a hand through my hair, kissing me again. I run my hands over his chest and down to his hips, slipping down over his pockets. He's too distracted by the kiss and where my other hand is headed to notice, and I can feel the tiny data chip beneath the fabric.

My target.

I know nothing about this chip save that Zoon wants a copy made for a client. The rest was on a need-to-know basis and apparently, I didn't need to know.

Shi'lu'Fan is kissing my neck now, one hand in my hair, another running down my back. I can feel all of him under me and I'm almost too distracted to slowly reach inside his pocket. He's so warm under me, like a fever taking over my body.

"Are you even old enough for this?" he asks, laughing softly. My fingers are closed around the chip and my heart is racing.

"Yes," I playfully snap back, feeling a creep of heat on my cheeks. This is, also, not a first.

That wolfish grin on his face again, almost disguising his loneliness. It's the problem with being grains of sand, sometimes it's easy to feel adrift. Only I'm not here to make connections. Not tonight. But as I trail my tongue along my lower lip and allow a soft, mischievous smile to unfurl, it's hard not to want to. I'm not lonely but being close to people like this makes me feel so alive. I move to kiss his neck; he leans back and offers me the perfect angle to pull the chip out. I kiss my way down the scales on his collarbones, even as I slot the chip into the reader in my back pocket.

I slip one hand under his top and he mirrors the motion as his other hand pulls my head back so he can reach my neck again.

A few more seconds and the chip will have copied and then I just need to get it back in his pocket. Easy. What won't be so easy will be leaving. I wouldn't mind letting things run their course, but there is always a risk to lingering.

His lips are trailing down my jawline when the sound from the club pours in. My stomach drops as Shi'lu'Fan's eyes grow wide with surprise.

"Freeze!"

He pushes me off him, toppling me onto the cushions. In the doorway stand four people in full combat suits and visored helmets.

The only distinctive feature is a circle surrounded by flames emblazoned in gold and red on their chest plates.

"What do you want?" Shi'lu'Fan snarls.

"Give us the chip," one of the people says, their voice distorted.

"Password," Shi'lu'Fan demands, unflinching even as the merc raises their gun.

And fires. The laser leaves a deep gouge in the plush upholstery. I yelp, clamping my hands over my mouth too late, and they turn to me, another gun lifting. It's the opening Shi'lu'Fan needed. He charges the mercenaries, pushing them back out into the club.

I take it as my cue, and bolt to freedom.

CHAPTER 4
MALEK

HELIOS 2

Everything is going to plan.

Sort of.

In a loose kind of way, which matches my loose plan. I mean, really, it's more a set of guidelines than an actual plan.

We've been sent down one of the nearly exhausted veins of the mine, near the lifts. Here the okronium is almost all gone and hitting quota will be near impossible. Today, I'm less worried about that than the fact we've been paired up with the three assholes from earlier.

Our collective punishment for disrupting the peace.

I know causing trouble is a part of the plan, but I hadn't intended to start until we were down here. Oh well, it's certainly got the tension in the mineshaft turned up to eleven and the andies around us are more alert than usual.

Maybe that can all work in our favour. I'm pulling out a couple of components from my scanner discreetly when clattering draws my attention. Akim looks two seconds away from a panic attack, one of the men trying to encroach on his personal space.

"Get out of my way, kid," Baldy snarls, ready to push a frozen Akim out of his way.

Alta swears.

I react without thinking, throwing myself between them. "Leave him alone!"

"I wasn't talking to you," he snaps, cronies coming to flank him.

I couldn't have asked for a better opportunity.

"You mess with my friends; you mess with me!"

"You think picking a fight with me is a good idea, you little shit." He shoves me hard in the chest.

Before, I'd have taken the blow. Apologised. But not anymore. I root myself to the spot even though my cybernetic knee twists a little out of place.

He blinks.

I smirk.

"If your quota is not fulfilled because of in-fighting, consequences will be weighed as if you had missed for several days," one of the androids warns in its monotone voice.

"You heard the andies, guess we better get back to work," I offer my most charming smile.

The one amma always said asked for trouble.

Baldy throws a punch and I leap away with a taunting smirk.

"Guess you really should worry more about your quota if you're that slow," I goad.

"You said what, you little shit?"

He pushes his sleeves up, rage warping his features.

"Going deaf as well, gramps?"

I hear Nooma groan as Baldy lunges, fists first. I wish my implants weren't being kept offline by the tech here, but even without the AR display, I know just when to move. Baldy barrels straight into the andie at the shaft's entrance.

His companions rush to him as he sputters about it being my fault. But the warning lights on the andies are on.

"Inmate attack detected. You are all to be taken for disciplinary action. Do not attempt to resist or we will take drastic measures."

"I didn't do anything! That little brat's the one who started this!" Baldy yells, pointing a finger at me.

I greet his glower with a bow.

"Follow us. Now." The andies aren't listening.

We have no choice, not with three of them with weapons pointed at us. I hide the bits of the scanner up my sleeve, catching Nooma's eyes as we're led out of the tunnel, Alta pulling Akim by his sleeve.

We're taken back up to the lift, which is guarded by another two andies and wait in restless silence as the lift descends. Seven of us to three andies get on. Not ideal when I don't trust the three guys, but it'll have to do.

We've not been heading up for twenty seconds when I slam my elbow back into the andie to my right. Nooma moves a beat behind me, slamming the one closest to her into the wall. I whirl, jamming the component I took from my scanner into the andie's neck when a shot goes off. I whirl as my opponent crumples. Nooma is on the floor, a hand to her injured side, a splatter of red on the wall behind her. The third andie has its blaster levelled at us. Set to kill.

I thought we could be quick enough, but I overestimated our capabilities.

I'm wracking my brain for a plan, the three adults still as statues as though they're trying to prove they're not on our side, when something that feels awfully like an explosion rocks the lift, sending us sprawling to the floor.

The overhead lights flicker, and then go dark.

By the time the emergency ones come on, the andies are still. Disabled. Whatever just happened jammed them.

And stopped the lift, stranding us halfway between the mines and the surface.

***

Aside from the creaking of the lift, silence hangs heavy.

Alta is the first to move, rushing to Nooma as she gets back to her feet. The wound seems superficial but the blood on her uniform makes my mouth go dry.

"What the hell happened?" Baldy asks, smashing the buttons as though it's going to help.

"How the flark are we supposed to know?" I snap back, rising to my feet. I can't see an easy way out of our predicament. The ceiling is one smooth sheet of metal, and the lift shaft might not even be climbable.

"From now on, you kids do as we say," one of the cronies declares, now holding the andie's blaster.

"You can't use that," Akim says blandly.

I would have rather kept that knowledge to myself and seen the look on their faces when they realised, but I guess that works too.

"What're you talking about?"

"You can't use that," Akim repeats.

"Of course, I can!" He tries, and of course, nothing happens.

"The guns are keyed digitally to the andies," Nooma explains on a sigh, as though they're complete idiots for not knowing.

I only know because she told me.

The asshole throws the gun down angrily and there is another moment of silence before Alta speaks.

"I think I might be able to reroute the power from the emergency lights to the mechanism. I can't guarantee it, but we need to try something before they come back online and blame us for this shit."

I nod and go to help them pry the control panel open. My left hand is clumsy, a fact that's getting worse by the day: the prosthetic hasn't had maintenance in too long. Without Alta, the whole thing would probably be bust by now.

Once the panel is off and the wires are exposed, I take a step back to let them work. Meanwhile the adults do the first useful thing they've done in a while, caving the andies' heads in with the butts of their blasters.

The tension in the lift is thick, and although I want to ask Nooma how she's doing, I know she won't give me an answer in front of the others. Instead, we exchange a long glance that might as well have been half a conversation: she's hurting but it's not life threatening, and we'll all feel better once we're out of the lift.

Time stretches as Alta works, swearing softly now and then, Akim hovering at the side. The sound of another explosion reaches us from far away, the silence thickening.

When the lights flicker and die, all I can do is hold my breath as fear washes over me.

But then the lift starts moving again and I let out a shaky breath.

Next stop: the surface.

CHAPTER 5
TRYSTAN

EDEN ONE

"Are you listening to me, young lady?" mom snaps, and the word *lady* is enough to make me feel faint. What's not helping is that I am partially controlling my android self and it's tempting to slip away, leave my mother to deal with this me unconscious.

But it won't help, so I mutter a half-hearted: "Yes, mother," which only infuriates her more.

"Don't act like this! I deserve my own daughter," –can she just be done with all the gendered words today?– "to show me some respect! It's not my fault that you're incapable of learning how to behave yourself like a girl your age should!"

All this over how I left church. I should have known I hadn't escaped a scolding when she let me go to Uncle's. I'm so frustrated I drop my concentration, almost falling away from the android. Being split like this: seeing out of two sets of eyes, feeling two bodies, is exhausting. The chip is helping my consciousness expand so I can process the data from two places at once, but it's going to take some getting used to. Now that I've been ambushed by mom, I know the safe thing would be to pull away from my new self, but I'm scared of not finding my way back to him.

"I told you I just needed air! Would you have rather I half fainted in the church?"

My uncle warned me that this would take time, but I wanted it to be easy yesterday.

"I would rather you stopped making a spectacle of yourself! Everyone is whispering behind your back about how improper you are. Do you know how damaging it is for your father? For me?"

I'm so angry I can barely think. "Have you ever wondered how hard it is for *me*?" I snap without meaning to. "I don't care what these people say about me. I'm not some superficial airhead who needs everyone to approve of her!"

I know how mom is going to take this. I know she'll think it's how I see her. And maybe I want her to take it that way so she can feel a portion of the hurt swallowing me whole.

She just stares at me, mouth frozen in a perfect 'oh', tears in her eyes. I bolt out, feeling both awful and vindicated as I run up to my room.

I lock the door and collapse against it. I don't know how to keep being this person I'm not. Only, there are no alternatives: I can't leave the colony unaccompanied until I'm twenty-one and by then I'll be married and ruled by the whims of my husband. If only I had been born a boy for all to see…

Tears sting my eyes and I glare at my room. White walls and pale pink, dainty furniture: the mould I hate and simply cannot fit into. Father likes to say I was born contrary.

I find an escape in changing my holo-walls to a simple forest view, all trees and soft light, making it easier to pretend I'm not trapped at home.

The headache throbs behind my eyes. I'm too unwell to keep my consciousness expanded.

I start crying and in a fit of rage I throw all of myself back into the android.

In this body the headache is nothing but a distant sensation. I know my head hurts, but the feeling doesn't truly register.

In the lab I'm still facing the mirror mounted on the wall. I smile at my reflection, at the faintest hint of hair above my upper lip.

For a little while, I decide to just let myself be Trystan.

***

Being alone here is weird, but my uncle didn't expect me to be doing this until tomorrow after school.

Only, I can't ignore this escape. I should stay in the lab, get used to the split consciousness, mess around to see if I can use any of the software I downloaded. But it's so quiet, so empty.

I'm hyper-aware of every sensation in this body, the world somewhat sharper.

Before I can talk myself out of it, I slip on a spare lab-coat and call the lift. I know I shouldn't do this, but with the headache so distant, I don't see why not to. After all, it's a Sunday and there already was barely anyone around earlier.

I go down to the level with my uncle's office, the butterflies in my stomach as distant as the headache. If anyone sees me—recognises me—this will turn from dream to nightmare.

My uncle isn't in his office. He's probably gone home. I should do the same. But with the place so empty I can't help myself from wandering around, desperate to experience more through this new me.

I walk for a while, letting my fingers trail against the walls, grounding me here. The silence is still unpleasant, but when I hear voices coming from behind the observation bay doors, my discomfort only increases.

I recognise my uncle's voice, and draw closer, intent on eavesdropping, more out of curiosity than anything else, when a second, unknown voice catches my attention. It's male, clipped.

I'm about to lean my ear against the door—time to test my new hearing properly—when the door slides open, and I just about manage to not fall over. My uncle stands on the other side of the door, startled.

"Doctor Johnson," I manage, all too aware of the other set of eyes on me. "There is, er," my eyes slide past my uncle, past the man in the dark uniform, to the machine in the testing bay and the creature attached to it.

My mind goes blank: there is a naked alien in my uncle's lab, having some fluid drained out of them.

"Yes?" My uncle asks, his eyes wide as he takes me in.

But I can't look away from the creature: pale green skin with darker scales—or is it a type of bone growth? —winding about their body in elegant patterns. A creature with four arms and horns curling at their temples where there should be ears.

"What is this about?" the man in the dark uniform asks sharply, and my eyes snap back to him, falling on the insignia at his breast: a B above an arrowhead encircled by a stylised sun.

Somehow, I find my voice. "Doctor Johnson, there is an urgent call for you in your office."

Thank this body for the absence of stuttering. My uncle doesn't miss a beat, regaining his composure as he turns back to the other man.

"Please excuse me a moment, I'll be back shortly."

I walk out, one step ahead of him, and I don't stop until we're safely tucked inside his office.

"What are you playing at, Trystan? I thought I told you not to come back until tomorrow!" There is so much anger in his blue eyes as he grabs my arm that, for a second, he might as well be my father. Even in this body a hundred times stronger, I shrink into myself. He softens at my reaction and somehow that makes it worse.

"I needed some space!" I snap, yanking my arm free. "I needed to be away," I add, hating how easily my voice loses its edge.

"Trystan, do you realise how risky this is? You're not ready to spend this long split, yet. And what if someone had seen you?"

I want to say that it's fine, that no-one is here, but Cat chooses that moment to message asking if I want to hang out, interrupting my thoughts. I'm almost relieved: if I go back, I don't have to think about what I just saw; about all the questions I have.

"I'm sorry..." It's all I can say. "I just... Mom was... She was *mom* and I... I needed to… I don't know. Not be there, I guess." I swallow all I want to ask him, unable to question the only person who has been helping me with my secret. He takes me in his arms, and I wish I didn't feel so uneasy.

"Let's take you back up for now, okay? I promise you can go out soon, but we're still just testing this." He smiles a little sadly. "I don't want you getting hurt, you get that right?"

I nod, and we head back up. As soon as I'm alone again, the tightness in my chest returns, now worse than before. I don't know what to make of what I saw. I can't reconcile what I know of my uncle, of what he's done in the past, with a man who would strap an alien to a table to experiment upon.

I message Cat back, my best friend since I was six, hating how much I need her when there is so much I can't tell her

My head throbs and I take some pills before flopping face first on my pillows, leaving this body to rest.

In the lab I stare at my uncle's computer. The answer to a lot of my questions might be sitting there, if only I'm willing to reach for them.

I slide in his chair, feeling like a traitor as I enter the password I've watched him type a hundred times. But I need to know, and it's not something I know how to ask him.

Like everyone else, he'll lie and say it's to protect me, but I think a lot of people say that when really, it's themselves they're trying to protect.

Maybe if it was just to protect me, I'd let him, but this feels different. And trying to understand this takes my mind away from my parents and the telling-off from my father I probably have coming.

CHAPTER 6
LÀHN

KIRILLION

The club is packed full of people here to have a good time. No-one wants to acknowledge a group of armed mercs. No-one wants to see the boy running away from them, slipping between people, swallowed by the crowd. If the mercs got a scan of me, speed is my only advantage. The emergency door on this level is guarded. They came prepared. Of course they did, it's what they do. The guard spots me through the crowd, and I swerve away.

I glimpse helmets coming after me in someone's reflective dress. The chips: original and copied alike, weigh a ton in my pocket.

I shouldn't have ran. I made myself suspect by doing so. But I panicked when I saw the guns, the uniforms.

I could try and hand over one of the chips but that's still putting myself at the mercy of the enemy.

Whoever the enemy is.

Making bargains with unknown elements is never a smart move. I might well get shot either way.

I break through the crowd, colliding with the railing. On the other side, the anti-grav dance floor is full of people.

I vault over the barrier. I've done it on dares: when a little drunk and out with friends. This time there's a moment of terror as I start to fall before the purple field catches me and I become weightless. My momentum sends me crashing into the inside of the field at the other end, the air knocked out of me, my wrist twisting at an awkward angle. Lucky for me you can't leave the anti-grav field until your feet are on the floor.

I turn, spotting the mercs on the balcony, their guns trained on me.

Panic is spreading through the club now. You can't ignore that many guns and people are fleeing, the dancers manoeuvring to safety. I kick off the barrier and dive for the ground.

The mercs fire.

Without my momentum I'd be dead. I hear a scream: a Vanark teen got hit in one of the tentacles that grow from their heads. Another scream as the man in front of me takes a laser to the chest, dead on impact, his partner screeching in terror. That could have been me. Should have been me.

I don't have the time to dwell as a laser goes straight through my forearm, leaving a cauterised gouge in its wake.

I don't know if I scream, but something inside me snaps, fear shattered by raw panic. I hit the ground, rolling to my feet.

The music still thumps on, the Vhiner'zzi DJ yelling for security.

I run for the main doors, pushing through the escaping crowd. The mercs are coming, shooting, my small stature and speed the only reason I burst out into the street without any further injuries.

The warm, humid air hits me like a slap after the coolness of the club. My arm throbs but my nerves are too fried to register much of the pain.

I throw myself down a side street, layering a map of the city on my ocular implant, even as I send a thought-to-text message to Kode.

Trouble. Being chased. Need a pickup.

I run down another few alleys, aiming for the main thoroughfare of the Phodredy district. And the parade.

When the Wandering Fleet comes into port, no-one wants to miss the party. If not for tonight's job, I would have been right at the heart of it.

The crowd dancing down the avenue swallows me, rendering me just another shape in a sea of bodies. A Mallak planet-side ship hovers a few metres off the ground, music blaring from its open doors, wreathed in smoke from the incense burners dangling at its sides, colourful clan banners snapping in the wind. There are another two ships in front and more behind, with ramps lowered for people to climb on board. I can see parties held in cargo holds, lights flashing with vibrant colours.

The Mallak turn whole cities into clubs.

I wish I could stay here, lose myself in the crowd. Forget everything in that way you can when drowning in music and the press of bodies. But I need to get back to the Guild. To Zoon.

A message from Kode flashes across my eyes.

Can't pick you up from the parade. Get here.

Attached to the message are coordinates to her position in a perpendicular street.

I pull my injured arm to my chest as I push through the crowd. People of all ages, of all races, pressed together, arms raised in the air or wrapped around one another—or both for those that are gifted with more than one pair. Vanark tentacles, streaked in fluorescent paint, are lifted, swaying in time with the music.

I get jostled, and even groped a couple of times, but I keep my head down. I just want to get to Kode. I've lost track of how many times she's dragged my ass out of trouble.

Eventually, I make it to the edges of the parade where Mallak stalls are already set up, small metal booths decorated with bright fabrics, selling foods and trinkets.

Kode is waiting, leaning back, feet up on her bike's control panel, neon green shoes reflecting the light. She sits up when she sees me, motioning for me to hurry before flashing her hands in a question. I learnt the Kirillion Human Sign Language whilst growing up alongside her and I flash my answer back.

Long story, will tell you once we're at the Guild.

She gives me a worried look, her eyes going to my arm as I hop on the back of the bike. A message flashes across my implant.

Your arm?

It's fine, let's just go, I send back.

She slides her helmet on. I twist and grab mine out of the back compartment. The breathing unit inside lowers itself in front of my nose and mouth, the neck guard extending down. We take off the second I'm strapped in, up and away from the Mallak parade, back towards the lower levels and the Guild.

I throw one last glance over my shoulder, but the mercs are nowhere to be seen.

***

Kode parks on the Guild's roof and I let the familiar sounds of our neighbourhood wash over me: traffic and street vendors, hints of music from a nearby club. Shu'a'kash is the very bottom—if you ignore the underground parts—most central level of Kirillion, but the buildings here still reach fifty floors. Before the city spanned the planet and became impossibly layered and impossibly vast, it had been the heart of Kirillion.

Shu'a'kash is home.

Kode looks worried as I wobble off the bike, shaking with shock.

Come on, let me take a look at your arm, she signs, her many coloured rings flashing in the streetlights, and I let her lead me inside.

The light above the entrance is red, informing us that Zoon is out. He set the Guild up a few decades back, claiming the top five floors of an abandoned building as his turf.

Mine and Kode's rooms are next to each other, a pair of windowless boxes cramped with all our stuff.

We go to hers and I plop down on her bed as she rummages about in the stacks of plastic boxes she uses to keep the chaos at bay. A mural I haven't seen before is projected above her bed.

What's that? I sign as she turns back. It's a tree, but unlike the ones here with their flowers big as my face and leaves in bright purple and red, it has small, delicate flowers in pastel pink.

Cherry tree. From Earth, she replies. *I was researching something for Zoon when I found the pictures. It's from Asia, I think. Like my ancestors,* she adds with an almost embarrassed smile.

She shouldn't be embarrassed: of all the things we Humans lost when we took to the stars, we never forgot our birthplaces back on Earth, the countries and traditions and languages that had brought us together as much as kept us apart. I wish I knew how my people came to the stars.

Kode had her parents long enough to know bits. She keeps a miniature version of the shrine they had, high on her wall, and she often leaves little offerings. She doesn't know the right way to do it, but she's learning, making it her own.

My only hint is the tattoo at my wrist. Ancient letters from a language now changed beyond recognition. It took Zoon a lot of research to decipher it.

I don't like to think of what is inked into my skin. Of the things it hints that I have lost. That I could find. Not when I'm happy just being Làhn, here and now.

What's wrong with your wrist? Kode asks when I wince as I brush my fingers against the tattoo.

I smacked it into something, if I explain what I did she's going to be mad. *Probably just bruised it.*

She shakes her head, twin tails dancing. They're neon blue today, yesterday they were silver.

Let me have a look. You can tell me what happened after.

Her small nose wrinkles in that cute way it does when she's concentrating as she takes hold of my arm. The wound on my forearm is small to say how much it hurts. Kode reaches for a spray bottle, and I grit my teeth, the first spray stinging enough that I almost jerk my arm away. Once done, she wraps a length of bandage loosely around the wound and lets it tighten to itself.

Next, she prods my wrist and I yelp, waving to alert her that it hurts. A lot.

I don't think it's broken, or fractured, but let me check, she signs. I cradle my injured arm, and when she turns back with a scanner, she just raises an eyebrow at me.

Did you nick stuff out of the infirmary? I ask. Much like the spray these things aren't as cheap or widely spread as some assume. Even in a city so full of tech, medical stuff is difficult to get hold of. Humans are one of the latest species to join the ever-growing population of Kirillion and medical tech varies from species to species, meaning nothing was ready for us when we got here a couple of centuries back. It's why most Humans live down in

Shu'a'kash. The newest species get the old turf. It's not a bad place, and as long as you're here legally, Kirillion is very good at looking after its inhabitants.

Only neither me nor Kode are here legally. Neither of us have ID. Neither of us *exist*. Life would probably have been very different if we'd been flagged on systems as orphans. I'm not sure I would have liked a life away from the Guild. Away from Zoon. A life in which Kode and I might never have met.

Shuobe gave me stuff, Kode replies.

Where did she get it?

Shuobe is Kode's girlfriend, part Mallak, part Human, who works as a waitress when not acting as a stunt double.

One of her mum's packages. I think the last one only cleared customs because it was from the Wandering Fleet, she explains, grinning. *She sent her some* really *cool stuff!*

The Mallak have a way of getting hold of impossible things. Sometimes even impossibly lost things.

I'll have to thank her, I clumsily sign as she scans my wrist.

It's just sprained. She lets me know after the device beeps. *No fracture or anything. Just take it easy and put a brace on or something.*

Yes mum, I sign back, dodging as she swats at me.

Do you want to talk about what happened? she asks, serious now.

I wonder what happened to the hybrid. Did they shoot him once they realised he didn't have the chip? Did I give away that I had it by running like I did? What happened should be on the news, but I can't bring myself to look.

I can't face it.

I don't know, I admit. A pause. *I don't know if I can tell it twice, and I need to see Zoon.*

She nods but she's playing with her lip ring in a way that tells me she's worried. We know how to give each other space, but it doesn't mean it's easy.

Want me to come get you when he's back? You could do with some rest.

Thanks.

She squeezes my hand briefly, a sad smile on her lips as I leave her room for mine. I don't even bother to kick my boots off as I collapse face first into my pillows. I'm too shocked for tears, too tired for all the fear to catch up with me. Sleep finds me before I realise it's coming.

CHAPTER 7
MALEK

HELIOS 2

As soon as the lift doors open, we're running, the emergency lights casting the grey corridors in sickly hues. No andies stand in our way, and for the time it takes to reach the station, it feels as though all animosity has been set aside. Outside, the sound of fighter ships is unmistakable. A moment of giddy elation washes over me and I almost start laughing as I dash towards the train waiting to make the return journey back to the central complex. I'm yanked back, however, a meaty arm wrapping around my throat as I kick out.

Another crony has grabbed Alta, pressing a sharp piece of metal at their throat.

"What's this about?" Nooma asks, hands raised.

"You kids are gonna help us get the train started," Baldy says. He tightens his grip on me as his crony nudges Alta forward.

"We would have done that without this," I choke out.

If not for Alta being in such a precarious situation, I would smash his nose.

"He's right," Nooma says. "We want to get out of here as much as you do."

"That's the thing," Baldy drawls. I'm getting dizzy from the pressure at my throat. "We're not interested in dragging a bunch of kids with us."

I should have seen this coming.

Baldy's grip relaxes a little as the train door slides open, the lights coming on.

"Okay it's on, let me go," Alta snaps.

Baldy lets out a low laugh. "Nah, we're keeping you sweetheart. You're our little tech whizz from now on."

I hear Alta being shoved inside the train, see Nooma's hands tightening into fists. And Akim… Stars, where *is* Akim?

There's a sudden cry and the sound of impact a second before Baldy releases me. I whirl around, eyes wide as I see Akim brandishing the bloodied tool he just smashed Baldy's head with.

"Behind you!" I shout, as the third guy grabs Akim from behind, wrapping his arms around him, lifting him clean off the floor.

"You shouldn't have done that," Baldy snarls, a hand to the back of his head. "You're gonna regret it."

"Just let them go!" I hate how desperate I sound. But Alta and Akim are in danger, and I don't know what to do. "Just leave, we won't stop you!"

"You and your girlfriend can stay here. We're taking the other two," Baldy declares, his crony dragging Akim towards the train.

To hell with this.

These guys have made our lives miserable for the last couple of years and I've had enough.

I look at Nooma and she nods.

Enough.

"Hey Baldy," I call as he makes for the train.

He glances at me, frowning at the smirk stretching the corners of my mouth. "What?"

"If you mess with my friends, you mess with me," I declare, pointing at my chest for emphasis.

He's so focussed on me he doesn't see Nooma moving, and when his crony lets out a warning, it's too late: Nooma's kick catches him in the side of the head, sending him sprawling.

I vault over him, clamping my prosthetic hand on the forearm of the guy holding Akim. It might be a clumsy hand, but it still has enough strength to crush bones if I put enough force behind it. It's the one benefit of metal limbs. The man screams and pushes Akim into me, sending us both stumbling back.

Baldy pulls himself into the train and the third guy is on his way as it starts.

Alta is still in there.

I don't think, leaping forward and jamming my metal fingers in the doors. They stop and I pull them open with a cry. Baldy yells as Alta kicks their captor in the groin, throwing themself through the doors.

My cybernetic joints aren't happy with me, and I can feel the place where organic nerves join tech straining, so I let go and let myself fall back.

The door slams shut even as the train departs, the four of us left breathless on the platform.

Not a moment passes before we witness the tube being hit, shattering, and vomiting the train out into the vacuum of the atmosphereless Helios 2.

A vacuum now coming for us.

Red lights flash and the emergency doors start to close.

"Out! We need to get out!"

I grab Akim by the shoulder, propelling him forwards as Nooma and Alta run ahead. The doors are closing faster than I want. The few metres to safety feel like lightyears, especially when the sucking sensation intensifies and moving becomes harder.

I throw myself through the closing doors last, falling in a heap as they seal shut, the threat of the vacuum still tingling on my skin.

"Guess we need another way out," I say, panting.

"We can go around," Nooma says. "Get into the next complex and hope we find another train."

"Yeah." I turn to Alta. "You okay?"

"Shaken. But in one piece."

"Akim?"

He's looking straight over my shoulder. "I should have hit harder."

"It's okay," I tell him. "We'll make it out. Come on," I add, motioning for everyone to follow me.

We walk quickly back the way we came, then down the other corridor. I'm not sure where this leads but it's the only choice left.

The corridor stretches on as we walk in heavy silence, the earlier euphoria threatening to turn sour. What if we can't get out?

When we turn a corner and find two andies frozen in front of one another, I am taken over by a childish instinct and I shove the first one hard in the chest, watching it topple back, taking the other one down with it. The clattering noise is so loud but also hilarious and I burst out laughing, ignoring Nooma as she smacks me up the back of the head.

"Why are you the way you are?" she mutters. "Get a move on, Malek!" She pushes me towards the exit, my laughter dying as I see the state of it.

There's a gaping hole in one side of the thick doors, the edges of the metal still incandescent from the blast, the control panel nothing but a sparking ruin. This must have happened during the power cut, and when I look up, I see a matching hole in the ceiling, the stars overhead only slightly blurred by the haze of the forcefield. Had we been out here when this happened, the void of space would have claimed us.

"I can't fix that…" Alta admits mournfully.

I step up to the opening: big enough to fit through but touching the metal threatens severe burns.

Unless…

I grip the edge of the gap with my cybernetic hand, a warning sensation replacing pain. I pull myself up, landing on my prosthetic leg, melting the bottom of my prison shoe, wobbling for a breath before I can safely drop down on the other side.

On this side the door panel is intact, but the mechanism is busted and the door only parts enough to create a squeeze space. Alta is small enough to fit but Nooma doesn't stand a chance, and Akim's expression is clouded.

"I'll try and make it wider," I say, getting hold of the door, bracing myself, so grateful amma paid for such good prosthetics.

"You'll hurt yourself!" Nooma warns as I heave.

The door is heavy, but it starts to shift. My shoulder joint screams and I am all too aware of my leg stump rubbing against the prosthetic casing.

Sweat breaks across my forehead but the door is opening, painful centimetre by painful centimetre. Nooma adds her strength to mine, and soon there's enough space for Akim and her to fit.

I collapse to the ground, my shoulder in agony and my stump raw, months of discomfort finally blossoming into blinding pain.

Pain that must show on my face because Nooma pulls my overalls open at the collar.

And swears.

The metal has bitten deep into my flesh, tearing at synth and real skin, blood seeping slowly into my clothes. I'm so overdue new limbs it's not even funny.

We exchange the same look we did on the lift.

"Where now?" Alta asks.

Two possible ways ahead of us, one heading left and the other right.

"I think left is our best bet," Nooma replies.

"Left is always good," Akim declares.

"Why?" Alta asks.

"It's what my mums always say."

"That seems a little...arbitrary..." I mutter.

"Right or straight would be arbitrary too. My mums say left is always the better option."

"Left *is* the better option here," Nooma repeats, impatiently, and I take a step forward, intent on leading. Pain shoots through my stump and I stumble, a wave of nausea washing over me. Thankfully no-one comments. We don't have time for this.

Nooma takes point, Alta leading Akim, letting me fall behind.

We've been hurrying along for a couple of minutes when a loud noise reaches us from beyond the wall. Nooma blinks in a way I know would activate her implants, but it's useless right now, only a habit neither of us shook off.

"What's going on?" Alta asks.

The question answers itself when the wall ten feet ahead of us bursts apart. As the dust settles, a Shinarian girl steps out: pale pink matted hair pulled back in knots, long pointed ears, and sharp cheekbones, her skin a rich brown covered in golden markings. I'm opening my mouth to speak when she turns to us, her large, block-coloured eyes brilliant gold.

Akim gasps.

Clearly, I'm not the only one aware that gold eyes on a Shinarian are never a good sign.

***

For a moment, no-one moves. She takes us in from head to toe. Then, slowly, she blinks. Once. Twice. The gold of her eyes turns sienna.

"Who are you?"

I'm so grateful Shinarian is one of the many languages loaded on my translator.

"Just people trying to get out," Nooma's tone is cool, even.

The girl nods, her own translation chip must be good because Nooma's Human dialect isn't exactly common.

"I will help. If you take me with you." Her speech is halting, as though she's been quiet for a long time.

"Sounds like a plan," I step forward, Nooma glaring at me. I know trusting someone after what happened earlier might not be the best idea, but she seems okay. "We're heading for the spaceport."

"There's a small hangar closer to here," she says. "I have a map."

I gape. Amma would have said I looked like a fish out of water. Though, honestly, I don't know what a fish out of water looks like apart from cooked.

"How?" Akim asks, not realising that looking a gift ship in the engine is a bad idea.

"The people attacking. They sent me it."

"They're here for you?" I blurt out.

She hesitates, eyes flashing bronze. "Yes. But I'm not going with them. And no, before you ask, it won't put you in danger if I tag along: they won't do anything to jeopardise my safety."

Maybe this could work in our favour.

"Fine," Nooma says, sharing a look with me. "Show us the way."

The Shinarian's eyes turn teal. "We need to hurry. As soon as the androids come back online our chances of escape are going to fall dramatically. And they will come back online," she adds, motioning for us to follow her. "I'm Nephanie by the way."

"I think she's hiding something," Akim whispers to me as Nooma introduces the rest of us.

"Aren't we all?"

He blinks. "I'm not."

"What makes you think she is?"

"Her eyes. Met a Shinarian where I studied so I learnt what their colours meant. Way easier to read than facial expression," he adds, and I'd have to disagree there.

Amma's navigator had been Shinarian, but I never managed to learn. He'd been equally confused by our facial expressions, so I guess we'd been even.

"Well, let me know if anything else seems off, okay?"

He nods.

The corridors are deserted, and the silence thick around us. I can't help but wonder why there is a Shinarian fleet attacking a Helios prison to rescue this girl—against her will to boot. She's either someone really dangerous, or really important.

Or both.

After about ten minutes of endless corridors, and two close calls avoiding other groups of potential fugitives, we reach a set of large, locked doors. They're more than twice my height of reinforced metal.

"I'll hack it!" Alta immediately offers.

"We don't have time." The Shinarian girl steps forward as she speaks, eyes gold.

Gold.

As far as I know, Shinarian eyes only change to gold when they're pushed too far. A shudder runs down my back. Definitely someone dangerous then.

She steps up to the door, wreathed in a golden aura, stretching out an arm, the aura moving to engulf the door. She yanks her arm up, and the door is wrenched from its hinges, metal groaning and wires snapping in a shower of sparks, revealing a small hangar.

A handful of ships are landed there, along with three still-operational mech-bots. They turn as one, arm-cannons loading up with a terrifying sound.

"Take cover!" Nooma yells, bolting forward and skidding down behind a prisoner transport unit. I follow her as Alta pulls Akim to a safe spot the second before the first blast goes off.

It hits the centre of the doorway, where Nephanie is still standing. Dissipating smoke reveals her, shielded by her golden energy.

She darts forward with terrifying speed, barrelling into the first mech-bot, the golden power she wields piercing a hole right through its chest.

"How the hell did they even *keep* her here?" Nooma hisses.

The mech-bots fire again, but the girl has propelled herself into the air, landing fists-first on top of the second one, crumpling its head. The third fires again but this time the girl just stretches her arm out, stopping the laser as it reaches her. All I can do as she reverses its momentum is stare in awe. Seven-foot worth of metal explodes and I dive back behind cover.

"Clear. Now let's get out," she calls.

I stand up, our unlikely saviour now with her hands on her knees, catching her breath. Sweat beads at her brow.

"Which ship do we take?" Alta asks, drawing my attention back. The smallest of them seems the best choice: fast and manoeuvrable.

"That one," I say and Akim nods.

"Good choice."

"Let's hope so."

Akim is the first in, settling into the pilot seat as I slide next to him as co-pilot, Nooma standing behind us. He shakes his head once, firmly, and then his hands are on the control.

"You okay to do this?" I ask. He might be a trained pilot, but I can get us out if needed. Just, probably not as smoothly as him.

He doesn't reply, eyes focussed on the controls, only giving me the slightest nod. I wonder if this could be one of the many ship models he has memorised.

"Let's do this!" I call, as the ship comes to life.

CHAPTER 8
TRYSTAN

EDEN ONE

A knock at my door jerks me awake. I don't remember abandoning my android after looking through my uncle's files, but I must have drifted back here at some point.

"Tris," a cheerful voice calls. "You in there?"

At least with Cat here I won't have to dwell on what I found out. I press the button above my nightstand and the door unlocks.

Cat is everything I can never be, with her long summer dress and light cardigan, and her chestnut wavy hair pulled back in a practical but elegant ponytail.

"What's wrong?" she asks, stepping in.

I rub a hand over my face as I sit up, trying to collect my thoughts.

"I..." I want to tell her everything, but it all gets stuck in my throat. "Stuff with mom."

She pops her bag down and settles next to me. There is the thinnest dusting of eyeshadow on her lids, a blush on her pale cheeks, probably added in the taxi that brought her here. Another of the small rebellions that allows her to breathe in a world trying so hard to choke us.

"What this time?" she asks.

"How I left church," I sigh, trying to run my fingers through my knotted hair and wincing as they catch.

“Migraine?”

“The leftovers.”

“I'll get you a cool patch, it should help.”

Cool patch. Good plan. I hadn't even thought. I'm not good at taking care of myself. Cat digs them out of the mess of my drawers.

We know each other's rooms by heart. We were just little kids when she purposefully sat down next to me, stared at me intensely, and declared, in the most serious tone I have ever heard from her: *"You're always alone and that sucks, so we're going to be best friends, okay?"*

She was already popular back then: extroverted and charismatic, but still here she is. It's hard to imagine a life without Cat in it, be it as my buffer at school from the worst of the bullying, or just as the friend I have spent hours gaming and laughing with.

"Ground control to Tris." Cat waves the cool patch in my face.

I blink furiously, refocussing. "Thanks."

"One day you'll actually learn to look after yourself." She has a kind, sad smile that she reserves for me. I'm still mystified how well we get along, how much we fit together.

She has a subtle kind of spunk that I envy, with her thousand little ways of rebelling. Not like her sister, Shauna, who declared on her seventeenth birthday she would be a lawyer—something that almost caused her father to have a heart attack.

"Do you want to talk about your mom?"

She settles cross-legged on the bed. It reminds me of a simpler time when we were kids and Nathaniel was still allowed to play with us and we'd spend hours here whilst our parents discussed adult things downstairs.

I groan. I hate thinking about Nathaniel, hate thinking about how mom keeps pushing me to start officially dating him before it comes time to announce our already planned engagement.

"Tris?"

I push the thoughts away.

"Not really. I just... I said some mean things to her. And..." I shrug.

"She probably deserved it." Cat is ruthless behind her pretty smiles and innocent green eyes.

"Maybe. Still, I hate doing that to her. At least she'll have calmed down by the time father comes back."

"I'm staying for dinner," Cat declares, ever my shield, pulling me into her arms.

"Thanks," I whisper.

I can taste the words I want to say to her, the secret I want to speak. But there is no-one either of us know who is out as being gay or trans or anything like that. It's too dangerous here, and it makes it hard to know how she'll take any of it.

She is my one and only friend, and maybe this lie is the price for it. Maybe it's even worth it. I can't bear the thought of losing her. I don't realise I'm clinging onto the hem of her cardigan until she gently lays her hand on top of mine.

"I don't know what's going on, Tris, but whatever it is, you know you can talk to me, right?"

I can't respond, only cling harder as she leans her head against mine.

"It's...complicated," I say, and she just kisses my hair.

"I'm here for you. Always."

I want to trust her with this so bad, but I can't risk losing her.

So, I just stay silent, closing my eyes against the tears that threaten to fall.

***

Cat and I settle to game, loading up an RPG we've been meaning to start for forever. We spend far too long in the character creator, as tradition dictates and, against my better judgement, I make a male character. I feel strangely laid bare as I create him. Not another version of me—that feels too close to the truth—but someone I wouldn't mind looking like.

Cat doesn't comment, because it's not like it's strange to play someone of the opposite gender, but I feel like I'm making a wordless statement, nonetheless.

We've just properly gotten started when mom calls us to dinner and Cat quickly helps me look presentable.

My father is back and in a foul mood, and for a terrifying second, I think he might send Cat home. But he's as nice to her as usual. Dinner is tense nonetheless, but Cat, mistress of polite conversation, fills the awkward silences like I never can. I barely feel like eating, the lingering headache a perfect excuse for my lack of appetite and although I know I shouldn't, I let myself slip back to my android self.

The lab is dark, but my night vision adjusts quickly—which feels very cool. I take the lift whilst trying to keep track of the conversation. I should do this later, once I'm alone, but I need to get away from all the tension. I need to find out more about what I read earlier.

I can't believe my uncle would be someone to just carry out such experiments on a sentient being without being coerced into it. Even with how clinical his notes were, I want to have faith in him. I need to believe he's better than this makes him look.

My only experience with aliens has been through media and what I've looked up on the DarkNet—though they never were a priority. This planet only allows Humans, even cyborgs being heavily regulated.

"Sit up straight, young lady," my father snaps and I jolt back into my body, pushing my shoulders back, cheeks growing hot, pinned to my chair by his stare.

"Sorry, father," I manage, hand clenching around my knife. I hate myself for how much power he has over me. But I don't know how to stand up to him, too afraid of the potential consequences.

The silence that follows is so heavy, I want to scream. I can barely breathe. Cat's hand finds mine under the table, squeezing tightly.

The maid is serving dessert by the time I make it to the testing labs. She looks exhausted, the bags under her eyes so visible that I don't know where to look. I know how my parents treat her and I wish I could make things better for her too.

My headache is getting worse again, and I know I should leave adventuring around as my android for the night. But there are too many questions, too much I need to escape from.

The testing lab is dark, the alien nowhere to be seen. The previous nine subjects died upon the third extraction, and I have no idea how long this alien has been here for. I hope they're not already dead, that I'm not too late, even if I have no real idea what I mean to do. Whoever my uncle is working for thinks that Kundar blood could hold the key to eternal youth for Humans. Eternal youth and superhuman strength and resilience, bought at the cost of somebody else's life.

Is my uncle a victim or a co-conspirator in this?

I spot another door out, hardly aware I'm drifting further and further away from my organic body, fleeing the headache as well as my father. The door slides open to reveal a narrow corridor, with two cells on either side, the Kundar laying on their side in one of them.

"Tris, Tris!" Cat's worry snaps me back to myself just as she catches me by the shoulder.

My father is looking at me in utter disgust. I feel too ill to care.

"Tris, is it the migraine?" Cat's words barely reach me, and either way they're meant for my father. A way to remind him I'm not well and that he should care.

He's never cared.

I groan in acquiescence. I'm paying for every second I spent controlling the android. I can hardly think, let alone move. All I know is that I need to get the android somewhere safe, but I don't have the strength to reach him. I feel like vomiting.

It hasn't been this bad in years.

"Mrs Wright," Cat again. "Can you help me get her to her room?"

I'm helped from the chair. My knees buckle, head roaring as I stand. I gag but don't throw up. Someone's hand is on my forehead.

"Oh my, she's burning up."

I did this to myself.

But I can't be trapped in this body, in this family, when there is an escape.

When I finally come around, I'm in bed, the lights off, a painkiller patch itching at my wrist. I don't remember making it up the stairs or getting into pyjamas. Yet here I am, tucked between the sheets, the last dregs of the migraine fading away.

I reach for my phone to check the time.

5 AM.

Without a second thought I throw myself back into my android self.

CHAPTER 9
MALEK

HELIOS 2

"Boys, how are we going to open that?" Nooma asks, pointing at the hangar doors.

Another problem I should have thought of in advance.

Akim is focussed, expression telling me it won't take him long to be ready.

"Mal, there's more of them coming!" Alta calls from the back.

I'm the captain.

The thought is lightning, the jolt I need to move. Elation and fear merge as my mind clears. I'll make amma proud.

"What weapons do we have?"

My crew, my *friends* depend on me.

"Two front laser turrets," Akim responds.

"And a mounted machine gun at the back," Nooma adds, clinging to the back of my seat as the ship lifts off. The radar informs me of the incoming mech-bots.

"Can you work it?" I ask at the same time as Nephanie calls: "I'm going out!"

"Don't be stupid!" Alta cries out.

I lunge out of my seat, but Nephanie is faster. She slams her hand on the ramp control before we can stop her. It opens to a mech-bot firing at us. I yelp as Akim jerks the ship to the side and I sprawl, prosthetic knee twisting. Nephanie doesn't even lose her footing. She leaps down the ramp, wrapped in her gold aura, and I hear the force with which she lands.

Akim exhales sharply as he narrowly avoids another blast.

Nooma buckles up in the rear gun chair, Alta clinging for all they're worth to an emergency grip.

I grew up with tales of brazen and daring escapes, raids, and rescues. Now it's time for my own story.

"Akim, keep us steady, I'm getting the door open!"

Below us the battle between the mech-bots and our superpowered Shinarian rages.

I push to my feet, gritting my teeth through the pain in my stump as I hurry down the ramp. Below me are two disabled mech-bots and two more getting their metal arses handed to them. The fifth one has its arm-cannon pointed at the ship.

I don't stop to think, throwing myself off the end of the ramp. For a few seconds, I'm flying, and then falling straight at the mech-bot.

I grab onto it with my prosthetic hand, yanking its limb down enough that the shot misses. Pain shoots through my shoulder and I feel more sticky warmth against my skin.

The mech-bot shakes me off and I land hard on my back, winded, watching as it readies to gun me down, knowing that with my busted knee there is no way I can get to cover.

High-calibre bullets pierce through the mech-bot. I glance back at the ship and through the tiny clear window I can see Nooma, her face determined.

Nooma, who just saved my life.

I limp as fast as I can towards the emergency controls, grinning as terror and common sense are pumped away by adrenaline. I clumsily leap over containers and stop in front of the panel.

Obviously, that's when a team of androids decides to rush in. There are maybe ten of them, and behind them... Stars, but the mech-bot unfolding is twice as big as the others, its lumbering form filling the ruined doorway. A shipwrecker. Something even amma feared.

I override the door controls, a second before I need to throw myself out of the andies' line of fire. I'm not quick enough, but when I look down and see only the twisted metal of my left hand, a laugh bubbles out.

"Wrong one, suckers!" I yell as I stand, metal hand held up, giddy with being fine. Alive.

"GET DOWN!" Nooma yells over the ship's external coms as she empties another round into the andies.

The doors are cycling through the opening procedure, and I need to get back on the ship before the whole place depressurises. But the shipwrecker is on the move and the andies are closing in on me.

"Malek!" Nooma calls. "On my signal, dodge right! 3—"

Her right or my right?

"2—"

To her right I catch the glimpse of a metal foot. To my right, open space.

"1—"

I hate right and left directions.

"Now!"

I leap away from a flurry of lasers, screaming, rolling behind a different cover, convinced that whatever gods amma worshipped must be looking after me. Nooma mows the androids down without hesitation, but in that moment the shipwrecker reaches the ship.

There is that one second of pause as everyone realises we're screwed. The hangar doors are starting to open, the forcefield still up for now but it's a matter of minutes at most before the vastness of space comes to close its fingers around my throat.

I can't see Nephanie, can't rely on her powers. I'm the captain and like hell is this thing taking my crew down.

I rush to the nearest android, dragging my bad leg behind me, and keeping the andie's fingers on the blaster I point it at the shipwrecker.

"Hey, junkbucket! Why don't you come and play over here?" I yell.

If I'd had the same implants as amma, I could have used them to spot its weaker points. As it is, I can but fire blindly, joined in that process by Nooma.

As the alarm blares, the shipwrecker turns to me.

I swear. Colourfully.

There is no escaping that.

But then, Nephanie reappears. There's no way she could have jumped this high. Yet there she is, coming down foot first onto the shipwrecker's head, crushing it.

"Get back on board, quick!" Nooma orders.

Nephanie leaps off the back of the shipwrecker, landing gracefully on the ramp as the mech topples backwards. She pulls me up and we make it to safety the second before the forcefield vanishes from the doorway. She collapses, Alta there to catch her as I throw myself back into the co-pilot seat.

Seconds later Akim is flying us out of the hangar, and straight into the firefight outside.

***

The Shinarian ships are even smaller than the Helios ones, and so fast that the radar is struggling to keep track of them.

But the numbers aren't in their favour, not with the Helios Surface Defence System on high alert and swarms of android fighters already in the fray. The sky is lit up with lasers and Akim is flying around to try and stay out of the fighting.

"Can this thing even jump by itself?" Alta asks.

"Yes," Akim replies, before I can. A transport like this has to be self-sufficient. "As soon as we're clear of the planet's pull we're good to jump."

"You're sure?" Alta sounds anxious.

"I was the best pilot in my class, so yes, I'm sure," Akim's tone is something in between non-committal and deadpan. I glance at him, his dark, thick hair falling to obscure all but the determined line of his mouth.

He doesn't talk about his past often: not with distant eyes like Alta, or bitter disgust like Nooma. Akim told us only the minimum: he was at a pilots' academy when he spotted an anomaly on the system. A day later Helios troops burst in his dorm to arrest him.

"Malek, can you handle the weapons?"

I glance down at my wrecked hand.

"Malek?"

Pull yourself together! "Yeah!"

My hand shakes as I flick through the switches, engaging the forward lasers, new readings layering in front of me.

We need to make it through, get away from the ground before the SDS gets us.

This isn't the maiden voyage I dreamt of. Go big or go home, I suppose. Or, in my case, go big *and* go home.

To freedom.

To the stars.

"This is gonna be rocky, guys, so hold onto something."

"Mechs incoming!" Nooma yells.

"They fly?" I ask in disbelief.

"No, they're being carried by drones! Of course, they flarking fly!" Nooma shouts back as she opens fire.

Akim banks sharply to the left, nearly knocking Alta off their feet, their hands tangling painfully in my hair as they grab onto my seat.

"Malek, Helios ship at four o'clock."

Helios, and its ships and androids, can go drown in a blackhole.

"On it!"

"Why is it shooting at us?" Alta asks as I adjust the aiming overlay. The auto-lock is smooth, better than the shuttle I learnt to do this on.

"We're probably not broadcasting the frequency they use to recognise each other."

I fire. So does the enemy ship. Akim throws us sideways. The blast glances off our shields.

"Mechs still incoming?" I'm yelling despite the relative quiet inside the ship, my heartbeat loud enough to deafen me.

"Two down. One more on our tail but it's hesitating the higher we get," Nooma reports, calmer than I could ever be.

The Helios ships are still on us, missing thanks to Akim's expert piloting. Amma would be impressed. I've dispatched two of them but more keep coming.

I'm lining up my next shot when Nephanie reaches over me for the coms.

"Do you mind?"

"Shut up and let me do this," she snaps, tapping in a frequency.

"Attention Shinarian fleet." Her voice sounds completely different suddenly, all sharp authority. "This is Princess Nephanie Tia Sha'hira aboard the *Charon 63*, requesting assistance to exit planet's pull. Respond."

"Princess? Why are you aboard a ship? We were coming for you," a gravelly male voice responds. He doesn't sound happy.

"Because I'm getting out, and not with you."

"Princess, you need to come back with us. We will take you to the main ship now."

"You help us get away, and that's all."

A blast hits the ship, and the shields go down, warning lights flashing. I take our attacker down but still more are coming.

"We're coming to escort you to the rest of the fleet."

The Shinarian ships are converging towards us. Nooma dispatches the last mech as I line another shot. Our latest pursuer takes the blast straight on, bulkhead coming apart.

"No, uncle, you'll help us get away and that's it," Nephanie snaps back. "If you try anything else, I will space myself. Good luck explaining *that* to my parents."

Stars but I hope that's an empty threat.

"Princess!"

"I'm serious."

With that she shuts down the coms and pulls away. "Get us out of here."

I have so many questions. Not least of all about the fact she's a *princess*. Stars, but amma would laugh if she were here. Still, now is not the time for questions.

"Akim, follow the Shinarians and let's get ready for a jump." I do my best to keep my voice calm, to sound like I'm in charge.

"To where?" Alta asks.

"A junk colony I've got contacts on."

"Is it safe?" Nooma asks, joining us.

I don't dignify the question with an answer. I don't think Nooma really understands what is and isn't safe out there. Not after what we're about to pull, anyway.

The Shinarian ships are in position around us, turning themselves into a shield, an arrow aimed straight towards our freedom.

CHAPTER 10
LÀHN

KIRILLION

I'm jolted out of bad dreams when someone buzzes my door, and for a beat I can't remember where I am. What happened. In the fading haze of my nightmares, I can still hear gunfire. In my sleep it sounded nothing like what it had at the club. But then I hadn't been in a club, or had I? The memory dissipates like smoke as a second, insistent buzz rings out.

Groggy I fumble for the door remote on my bedside table and narrowly avoid throwing half of its content to the floor.

On the other side of the door, Kode's face is wan under her smudged neon make up. My stomach drops.

What is it?

Zoon's... her hands pause. *He's hurt*. I can see how badly on her face.

Zoon is like our father, and he's supposed to be around long after us.

Where is he?

She turns and I follow her, squeezing her hand as we hurry down the corridor, needing the comfort of her presence. She glances up, squeezing back, brown eyes a little too wide. I'm afraid too. Losing Zoon... Neither of us ever wondered what that would mean for the Guild. For us. It's not supposed to happen. Zoon is a Furakian-Kundar hybrid. Nigh-on indestructible. All but immortal.

We walk hand in hand all the way to the infirmary. Others are already here, crowding around the viewing window to the treatment room. At first, all I can see is the tall, slim shape of our medic—Shey-Roon—hunched over Zoon, his grey skin glistening with sweat.

Then I see Zoon and only Kode's hand is keeping me standing, grounded.

Half of his face is burnt, the scales of his snout peeling back to reveal pale flesh beneath, and there is a hole through his chest, oozing silver blood.

The medic works steadily, the machines moving around him, obeying his every command. Part Human, part Cynen, he moves with an uncanny, mesmerising grace. But watching him dance around Zoon just makes me feel sick.

I turn, bile rising in my throat and bump into Ashya, their narrow eyes on Zoon. They're Ishinmar, emotions rippling across their skin in shifting waves signalling distress and fear.

They've been with Zoon for a long time, something forbidden back on their homeworld, but just another rule Kirillion likes to break.

"He'll be fine," they say, voice halting in the Kirillion Human dialect, their vocal chords ill-suited to it though they insisted on learning. Ishinmars aren't fond of implants. "Furakians are tough, and his mother made sure he got that side of her." A pause as two of their arms wrap around me and Kode, gently guiding us back out in the quiet corridor. With their other two arms, they sign for Kode, which is no small feat given their hands only have two fingers and a thumb each.

They're our other parent, their presence always a little softer than Zoon's. They pull us in close, gently smoothing our hair. Even with worry rippling across their skin, they're still trying to look after us.

We're the youngest members of the Guild, the latest orphans Zoon picked up. I think he's waiting until we're all grown up to start playing father again.

I hope he gets the chance to.

Zoon's a badass that can triumph over anything. I can't understand how he could have gotten hurt.

"He'll be fine," Ashya assures us again, signing the words. Ashya loved learning KHSL with us, although teaching it to a four-armed, two fingered, alien had been a challenge and a half for our teacher.

"Do you know what happened?" I ask, but they only shake their head.

"What happened with you?" They nod at the bandage and support on my arm.

"Job didn't quite go to plan."

Kode signs quickly. *What job was Zoon out on?*

Just a pick-down job. Nothing dangerous. Ashya replies. "What about you?" she asks me, hands still translating.

I still don't want to talk about it. But with Zoon in his current state, I don't think I'm about to tell him any time soon. I sign for Kode as I tell Ashya about the mercs and what happened.

They frown. "Do you know who they were?"

I shake my head.

“Do they know you have the chip?”

"I think so. Maybe if I hadn’t bolted but I… I was scared. I didn’t think. I didn’t want to get shot just for being a witness."

Ashya wraps me in all their arms, and I let them. When they pull away, it’s with a sigh and a shake of their head that sets their grass-like hair to swaying.

“Lay low for a while. Until Zoon is on his feet."

They say it as though it’s a fact. But all I can think about is the seriousness of the wounds. The look on Shey-Roon’s face.

“I want to help,” I say but Ashya shakes their head in a final ‘no’ that I don’t have the energy to argue against.

Ashya will have sent people far more qualified than me by now. They’re head of the Guild until Zoon wakes up. *If*. I can’t get the image of him on that bed out of my head, tubes going in and out of him. Sure, Furakians are tough with their limited pain receptors and their secondary organs. But Zoon isn't *just* Furakian.

Ashya pulls us both in another tight embrace. Yesterday I would have said I was too old for hugs, but today I don’t care. Kode and I melt into it like when we were younger. I’m so scared of losing Zoon, scared of losing the Guild. Of losing home.

The world feels like it’s shifting out from under me. The feeling prods at the places of blank memories I try so hard to never touch.

Kode's hand finds mine as we hug Ashya back, taking all the comfort we can from their presence and the strength of their arms.

***

Kode and I sit on the roof, legs dangling over the edge, a packet of salty snacks in between us.

We silently watch Shu'a'kash's nightlife and the market below. We've walked it so many times, stuffing our faces with food and spending our earnings.

I wish I could be lost in that crowd right now, that everything could be just like it was yesterday.

But something tells me that nothing will ever be the same.

We could have a look, Kode signs.

At what?

Zoon's files.

Zoon is meticulous about keeping records and Ashya made it clear they wouldn't discuss details with us. Kode is the only one I know who could get into his computer. She got her nickname for a reason.

Ashya's gonna be mad if they find out.

Her smile creases the corner of her eyes. Her troublemaker smile, as Zoon calls it. She rolls off the ledge, landing lightly on her feet, a hand held out to me.

There's been a wordless connection between us for so long. When I first came to the Guild we couldn't communicate, but she held out her hand as I cowered behind Zoon and we've been fast friends from then on.

We cross the deserted corridors on quiet feet, and, after a quick stop by Kode's room to pick up her kit, we head to the lowest inhabited level, the only one where outsiders are allowed. Kode hacks the door panel, eyes dancing. This is what she lives for. She's as good with tech as I am with people.

The light turns from red to green and we slip inside.

The office is dark, and I blink my night vision on; no point giving ourselves away by turning on the lights. The office is small: Zoon doesn't try to impress anyone who comes here. They'll know what the Guild can do by reputation.

The art on the wall is stuff he bought at the night market: paintings of landscapes in shades I've never seen. The sky here is a bruised purple from the chemicals cleaning up all the pollution.

The office is neat; in direct opposition to Zoom's cluttered room, full of all the strange things he collects.

I'm restless as Kode works, eyes darting from the holo-screen to the terminal strapped to her wrist. I pace, she ignores me.

What will I do if Zoon dies? Ashya would inherit the Guild but they're not as well-known as Zoon and that means we would lose some status. And that's what keeps us safe, preventing crime lords from bringing us to heel.

Could this be why Zoon was attacked? Is this the beginning of a hostile takeover?

I've stopped pacing, staring at one of the paintings, when something hits me in the back of the head. I whirl to find Kode trying to get my attention.

I think I found something.

What?

She points to the list of appointments displayed on the holo-screen. The first few are names I recognise. But the last, I've not seen before. Kode brings up the search bar and types it in. A second later, the face of the person Zoon was last with stares back at us.

She's full blood Shinarian if the sharp angles of her face and the swirling golden markings on her brown skin are anything to go by, her block-coloured eyes a focussed black. She's wearing a black and purple reinforced body suit uniform in the main picture. Law enforcement. The helmet under her arm with the stripes that mark her rank as a police captain.

Why would Zoon have a meeting with someone from the police?

We're a group of thieves, hackers, and con men who make our living on the wrong side of the law. We don't fight the police. They show up, we disappear. It's the first rule of the Guild: you don't engage.

I don't get it, Kode signs.

Me neither.

Do you think Ashya knows? We should talk to them.

They won't tell us anything. Otherwise, they would have done earlier, I reply, shoulders sagging.

What was Zoon doing? Was this woman the one who hurt him? My hands are trembling fists and when our eyes meet, I see that Kode's just as lost as I am. We spoke of going after whoever hurt Zoon, more daydream than an actual plan but if this woman is responsible then there is nothing we can do.

Against a police captain we're powerless.

I push a hand through my hair, dragging in deep breaths. Kode's still riffling through Zoon's files.

I tap her on the shoulder when another idea hits me, setting the chip down next to her.

You have anything that can read this? I ask.

Is that what he sent you for?

I nod.

Back in my room, maybe. You think it might help?

Zoon was in a hurry for me to get this so… Maybe. Saion Corp info sounds like something the police might have an interest in.

Kode plays with her lip ring for a second, then she powers the computer down and we're off.

CHAPTER 11
MALEK

SAEELSHI SOLAR SYSTEM
CHARON 63

The shuttle rattles down to its bolts as we speed away from Helios 2, the Shinarian ships falling around us, shot down one after the other. The one in front gets blown apart and our shield alarm blares as we're showered by debris. For a second, I wonder if our daring escape is going to end in a blaze of glory.

We pull through into the clear with a final burst of speed, nothing but a thousand stars and the hint of a nebulae to fill the viewing window.

"Inputting coordinates," I say, echoing the tone amma used when on the command deck. "Fixed jump point acquired. Let's go, Akim."

Before he can acknowledge my command, a massive ship materialises, cloaking tech turning off, the hull red in the solar rays. It's all curves, and elegant lines: a Shinarian mothership.

Nephanie swears.

"Malek, they're hailing us." Akim's voice is a dangerous monotone.

I feel the earlier panic returning.

"Don't answer," Nephanie orders.

"Their weapons are locked on us!" I point out, bringing up another display. I reroute all power to the shields, dimming the lights. "I don't think our shields will hold."

"They won't," Nephanie confirms. "But they won't fire."

"You sure?"

Akim pushes forward, blocking the transmission. We need to get far enough from the planet's pull to jump.

"They don't want me dead."

I have so many questions.

"There's something else locking onto us," Akim declares as another reading pops up.

Nooma swears. My mouth goes dry.

"Tractor beam," Nephanie declares. "They want to pull us in."

"Brilliant," I mutter. "Akim, accelerate as much as you can, we need to get to our jump point."

My heart pounds in my ears. Just a bit more and we're good. I feel the force of our speed pinning me to my seat. Attempting a jump at this velocity is going to be dangerous.

"Okay, getting ready to jump in—"

I'm interrupted as the ship is yanked to a brutal stop. I'm thrown forward, bashing my face into my console. *This is why you buckle in, kiddo,* I hear amma's voice. My forehead throbs like hell, my left eye glitching out for a second before coming back on—thank the Stars. Akim is fine, seatbelt holding firm.

"They're pulling us in." His voice is emotionless.

"We need to break free, full speed forward!" My head is spinning.

"We don't have enough power for that," Alta yells from the back. "If you push the ship anymore the engine's going to overheat."

I swear: the distance to our jump point keeps growing.

"Alta, can you do anything?"

Their answer comes muffled, and I lurch to my feet. Akim fights the tractor beam as I stagger into the cargo area, almost falling over as my prosthetic leg gives way.

"Thrusters are starting to feel the strain!" Alta yells.

I see them stumbling about the engine room, tools scattered everywhere.

"Can you fix it?"

"Give me five!" they snap, their brow slick with sweat, eyes wild with panic. I wish I knew what amma would have done. "I can give us some more power but not for long. Akim, if I give you a burst of speed, can you stop it from locking on us again?"

"Now I know what it looks like, yes. But aren't you going to fry the engines?"

"Only the thrusters. We can jump without them."

Can we?

"Ready when you are."

"Everyone, strap in!" I yell. I throw myself back in my seat and buckle up as Nooma and Nephanie secure themselves in the back.

We're too close to the mothership for comfort, its hangar doors opening like a monstrous maw.

"Three," Alta yells.

Akim is flying manually, tilting the ship at the ideal angle to get us out. I'm ready to kick off our jumping sequence as soon as possible. Regulations about safe distance from planets and ships be damned, we're making this jump as soon as we can. I override the system so I'm in manual too. No computer to aid or impair us, only our guts and knowledge.

I hope I don't mess this up.

"Two."

My heart feels like it's trying to break out of my chest.

"One..." A pause. No longer than a breath. Long enough for Akim's knuckles to turn white on the controls. "Now!"

A small explosion goes off in the engine room and the ship leaps forward, away from the beam: free. We're thrown forward. Alta screams.

Warning lights flash everywhere. The right thrusters are gone, the left ones damaged, but Akim is making the best of what manoeuvrability we have left to avoid the beam as I initiate the jumping sequence.

Amma would have loved his flying style.

"Jumping in five—" The tear in space starts to open.

The tractor beam grazes us, sending us off course. We hurtle towards the tear with too much speed and at the wrong angle. This cannot end well. We're going to crash.

I don't want to die.

The ship spins, the motion so sudden that it rattles my bones. I witness the tractor beam missing us by a hair, the Shinarian ship in the distance. And then the tear closes.

Akim lets out a hysterical bark of laughter. I can barely comprehend how he spun us around to compensate for the broken thrusters and managed to aim us through the tear backwards.

Amma *really* would have liked his style.

We're still spinning slightly, but the shift to hyperspace has slowed our momentum considerably.

"Stars, Akim, that was… That was…" I don't have the words.

"Clever, right?" His voice is pitched too high, almost hysterical.

"Very flarking clever."

He stabilises the ship, as I double check the coordinates.

"Everyone okay back there?" I ask, my gaze half lost in the red and black swirling void that has replaced the star speckled sky.

"Just a little banged up," Alta declares as they step into the cockpit, Nooma supporting them.

Worry and guilt wash over me. There is a gash on their forehead and they're cradling their left arm. I help Nooma settle them in my seat.

"What happened?"

"I didn't have the time to strap in. No big deal, though, it's just a small cut and a bruised arm, could have been worse."

I breathe out in relief even as Nephanie joins us in the cramped space.

"Six hours and forty-five minutes to destination," Akim declares, his attention still entirely on the controls. "Wow, that's a long way."

"Will they be able to follow us?" Alta asks.

"Shinarian engines that size need to warm up before they can jump. We'll have too much of a head start for them to be able to track us," Nephanie explains.

"Glad to hear it," Alta mutters.

"You're a hero," I say, clapping them on their good shoulder. They laugh and shake their head.

"Well, I'd rather not have to do that again."

"So Malek, wanna tell us where we're headed to?" Nooma asks, as focussed as always.

"We're going to Bakula." I'm grinning.

"That's an outlaw colony!" Her expression is a mixture of anger and dread.

"I know," I shrug, giddiness creeping at the edges. I want to laugh, high on freedom. On life. "Which is cool, 'cause so are we."

***

HYPERSPACE
CHARON 63

The hypnotic black and red of hyperspace was the backdrop to so much of my childhood it's hard to believe I'm here again.

In the back, Nooma is distributing food rations she found, but I can't bring myself to move just yet. If this is a dream, I don't want to wake up from it.

I think amma was watching over us today. Maybe she feels the need to make sure I survive our shared recklessness.

It still hurts that she got herself killed in a fight that wasn't hers. But losing her ship had changed her, dimmed the light in her eyes. I remember so many hours alone at the hospital and amma missing, and even when she sat by my side, she was never entirely there.

"Mal, you coming?" Alta calls.

A smile ghosts over my lips.

Amma's crew called her 'captain', but I like this. These people aren't just my crew. They're my friends. On a man-made hell of a planet, against all odds and hope, I forged the beginning of a new family. I love them so fiercely it makes my chest ache.

"Mal, I will eat your share!" Alta is laughing.

Laughing.

Not a tired chuckle at someone's bad joke. Actual laughter.

"I'm coming!"

My friends are settled on the floor, as grimy as I feel. We need new clothes, and shoes. We're going to need so much when we get to Bakula. I'll figure things out when we get there. Things will be fine; I just know it.

I drop down between Alta and Akim, taking a ration from Nooma.

"I can't believe we made it," Alta says. "I mean... I really thought you were going to get us all killed this morning."

"I'm sure Malek had totally planned for the Shinarian attack..." Nooma raises an eyebrow.

"Clearly! *Obviously,* I knew it was the perfect day to escape!"

"What you mean is you were lucky," Nooma chides me.

Nephanie is sitting back against the wall, long legs stretched out, watching us, her eyes a pale lavender. She's nibbling on the edge of her ration, a little hesitant.

"Without Nephanie we wouldn't have made it," Akim points out. He's breaking tiny bits of the bar with his fingers, laying them out on the wrapper he smoothed flat in front of him.

"No, we wouldn't," I admit around a mouthful. It tastes of absolutely nothing, but it *is* better than nothing.

"Why didn't you want to go back with them?" Alta asks.

Nephanie's eyes turn brown as she shakes her head. "Long story."

"I'm sorry about what happened to your people out there," I say, thinking of all the ships we saw fall.

"What are you talking about?" Nephanie asks, eyes turning bronze.

"There were a lot of ships shot out of the sky," Nooma chimes in, shaking her head. "That's a lot of pilots…"

"What? No!" she exclaims, shaking her head. "Divinities, I forget you Humans don't have the same technology we do. None of those ships had pilots *in* them. With the mothership so close, that's probably where they were but not in the attack ships themselves. Those are all remote controlled."

I exchange a look with Nooma that could be summarised to 'huh, didn't know' before turning back to our resident royalty.

"So, what're you gonna do once we get to Bakula?"

"Not a clue. Hadn't planned on escaping."

I glance at Nooma and Alta, the former giving me the slightest nod. Nooma's going to be my second in command; Alta our engineer, and Akim our pilot. The bare bones of a crew.

"You could come with us?" I offer.

"Come do what?" Her voice is almost toneless, Shinarians so hard to read when you can't glean meaning from the colour of their eyes.

"I know a guy on Bakula who owes me a ship and then, well," I shrug, dizzy and giddy at all the possibilities. "We're outlaws now, might as well go raiding or salvaging to our hearts' content. We can pick up some slightly more 'legal' contracts here and there, but nothing that will put us on Berik's radar."

We talked about flying through the endless skies, salvaging lost ships, and raiding the big corporation transports.

"So, you'll be travelling a lot?"

"Yeah."

"Outlaws, huh..." Nooma's voice is quiet, but I hear the doubt, the hesitation laced in that single word.

Fear: sudden, and hot, and burning spears through me. Anger trails in its wake, so overwhelming that it chokes my words. I clench my fist, crushing what's left of my ration. The hope has turned to molten lava scouring me clear of anything but that blinding, unjustified rage.

"Yeah, outlaws, what did you expect us to be after breaking out of prison?" I snap.

Nooma stands up, wiping her hands on her overalls, calm as you like.

"Never really thought about it. But… I don't know. Maybe there's a chance for things to be normal again."

I let out a bitter laugh. "Of course, should have known you'd want *normal*," I spit the word. She glares but I'm standing and riled up. "Do you think they're not going to send people after us? Really?

We're going to be number one wanted criminals as far as Berik is concerned. We made them look bad. We got out. Not one, not two, but *five* of us." My voice is rising in volume with every word. I don't know where the giddy high I was on is gone but this is equally intense. I barely remember how to breathe. "They're going to hunt us and if we try to live normal lives, they *will* find us. Do you get that? I said it back on Helios and I'll say it again, now we're out, there is *no* going back home for anyone."

Apart from me. My home is the stars.

Akim stares at the floor, tapping out a rhythm on his leg. Alta fiddles with a wrapper. I'm the captain, but what if they don't want to be my crew? What if they don't want a ship and space and adventures.

"None of us have done this before, okay?" Nooma says, and she's so calm it makes me feel worse. "You may have done this outlaw and pirate shit but none of us had done anything to deserve ending up on Helios."

The blow shatters my anger to a clear-headedness I don't want. How can *she* say that? She took down half a slave-trafficking ring before she got arrested. She *killed* people. The crushed ration drops to the floor, loud in the sudden silence. The ship, my chest, everything is too small.

All I can hear are the scanner alarms going off when I tried to exit the spaceport of a planet whose name I can't even remember. In that place, cyborgs like me might as well be monsters.

"Mal..." I yank myself away from Alta's touch.

"You know what? Flark off!"

"Mal!" Alta again.

There is only one place to flee and in three steps I'm inside the tiny gunning station, the door closing behind me as I crumple into the seat.

For the first time in two years, tears finally come.

PART 2

TOO FAR TO FADE

Forgetfulness of your real nature is true death; remembrance of it is rebirth.

Ramana Maharshi

CHAPTER 12
MALEK

HYPERSPACE
CHARON 63

"Malek?"

I wish Nooma had waited longer. I wish she hadn't waited at all.

"What?"

She rests a hand on my shoulder. Five minutes ago, I would have shoved her off. Now, I'm too tired.

"I'm sorry." Her words are halting. "I didn't mean—"

"I know." Because of course I do. She knows my only crime is that I'm made of flesh, circuit, and bone.

"How's your hand?" She settles down in front of the chair.

We look at each other's reflections against the swirling red.

"I'll need to get it fixed. Probably need a new one."

"Same with your leg, I imagine."

I tap on it with a knuckle. "Leg's fine."

Nooma scoffs. "I'm not blind, Malek."

"It's expensive, I can make do for now."

"Alta said they could strip the ship. This thing isn't flying again once we land it, but we can sell parts. Especially if you have a guy that can get us another ship."

"Sure but... I got the feeling you guys weren't too keen on coming along with me."

"It's weird, okay? I mean, when I think outlaws, I think people who attack ships and slaughter innocents, so…" She makes an expansive gesture. "But I can't imagine you doing that kind of stuff."

"Amma only went after big Corpo ships. If there were people on board, we just tried to keep them out of the way. All she wanted was to get the goods and leave. We never left a ship permanently disabled or blew one up, not if there were people on it. Not that I remember anyway."

"That still means attacking and boarding ships and there's what, five of us if Nephanie sticks around? How well is that gonna go?"

I let out a soft laugh. "I did think about that, actually. And I mean, Nephanie is like a walking army and we both can fight but... To be honest, boarding other ships was never my favourite part." Truth is I've never done it. "Salvaging and doing odd jobs is gonna be far better for us. Find lost things, sell them, do transport jobs. There are lots of people who don't trust official ships or postal drones, so you can get paid nicely."

"That doesn't sound so bad."

"Beats getting the crap kicked out of you on some junk colony, no?"

"Sometimes I wonder if I should go back there, finish what I started. But I... I don't want to become like my parents. I hate that their first reaction to a problem is to punch it, and now it's my first reaction too."

"A lot of mercs are like that, especially when they see themselves as the 'law'." I make quotation marks in the air and Nooma's reflection smiles sadly at me. "They think it gives them the right to be assholes. But I've seen you, you're better than that, you do what needs doing, you don't use your strength to just impose your will on people."

Her smile falters a little.

"I just want to do what's *right*. I used to think I knew what that was: find somewhere quiet, follow the law, don't cause trouble. But..." She sighs. " I ended up so aware of everything that was *wrong*: of the way people were being mistreated, abused, taken advantage of. And then... When Rish'rinn was taken, I.... I was made, trained to fight, not to just sit around and hope the bad shit doesn't happen to me."

Nooma slumps forward, resting her forehead against the reinforced glass.

"I think you did the right thing back then, for what it matters. I don't know if I'd ever be brave enough to."

Nooma laughs softly and it almost sounds like crying.

"You made a plan, however dubious, to escape Helios, Malek, I think you'd have been brave enough."

"That was to save my own skin. It's not the same."

"You didn't hesitate to take risks for us, either."

"I know but… It was different."

She looks up, her eyes meeting my reflection's gaze. "We've got so much to re-learn. At least I know I do."

"Same. I'm not sure I remember how to live normally after two years in that hell."

"I think if any of us do, it's you."

"How'd you figure that?"

"The fire in your eyes today."

"Yeah, honestly that kinda took me by surprise this morning," I admit. "Not that I've not felt like that before, but it wasn't so intense last time. And last time I had amma to help."

"Help?"

"With this, me," I say, doing a vague gesture at the air around me. "This sudden switch in my emotions. She had bipolar and she knew it was likely I had it too 'cause it's sort of a family trait, so she was always doing her best to help me through mood swings and stuff."

"She cared about you." The way Nooma says that makes my heart ache, as though she can't imagine what it must be like.

"Yeah." My throat is thick suddenly, my eyes blurred by unshed tears.

I wonder if we ever talked about the past with emotion in our voices before.

"I really am sorry about what I said earlier, it came out all wrong," Nooma tells me.

"I know. I get it. Stuff comes all wrong out of my mouth all the time."

She huffs a laugh, standing to face me. There are bags under her eyes I've never noticed before. I probably have some to match.

"We should get some sleep. The cells have padded benches that aren't half bad to lay on," she says.

"I think I'm gonna stay here a bit longer." I'm still afraid this is a dream, and I don't want to wake up. Nooma walks out with a soft smile, squeezing my shoulder on her way.

The hum of the engine is my lullaby. I lean back into the chair, eyelids heavier than I want them to be. I'm tired down to my core. For my first sleep as a free man, drifting off whilst bathed in the glow of hyperspace isn't so bad.

***

KSERAN SOLAR SYSTEM

The jump out of hyperspace is fluid, the red and black replaced by star-strewn darkness and the hulking shape of the Urelhan destroyer: Bakula's silent guardian.

The station is large, ever growing in new jutting sections around the asteroid that housed its very first complex.

"It doesn't even *look* like it should hold together," Nooma mutters. "This place really does look like trouble."

"Don't start again," I warn her playfully.

"I'll take anywhere that isn't this thing," Akim admits. "It's small and cramped and smells of Helios."

I agree. When I woke up the smell was so familiar, I almost thought the whole escape had been a particularly cruel dream.

"Docking is going to be so much fun," Alta declares as they join us in the cockpit, their arm bandaged but otherwise fine.

"I should be able to do it if they have stabilisers," Akim says, staring at the station as we draw near. "They're hailing us."

"Let me handle this," I say, turning our coms on.

My heart is racing. Despite the awkwardness earlier everyone seems willing to let me do the captain stuff. I'm the most experienced but I still feel woefully unprepared. Let's hope I learnt enough watching amma.

"*Charon 63*, Bakula space control speaking: please identify yourselves."

I take a deep breath, a giddy sort of anxiety rising inside me, making my limbs feel tingly. I've been dreaming of this day for so long.

"Bakula space control, this is Malek Sidana, captain of the *Charon 63*. Requesting permission to dock. "

"You're broadcasting Berik codes, *Charon 63*, we don't usually let those dock, surely you know that."

"Malek, they've got some of the station guns trained on us..." Akim whispers.

I expected this. Corpo ships aren't exactly welcomed here.

"We're not affiliated, space control. This is a 'borrowed' vessel. Sending personal ID scans as proof," I add, placing my wrist chip on the console.

We're drawing closer but Akim has slowed the ship, readying for the possibility of escape. Though I don't think the ship will survive if we need to accelerate.

"Where the hell did you pick up that thing?" the space control operator asks, all pretence of formality dropped from his voice. I breathe a sigh of relief.

"Let's just say we needed it to make a quick getaway," I say. There is surprised silence on the other end of the coms.

"What planet you steal it from?" he asks.

"Helios 2," I declare, grinning.

This time the man swears, barking out a laugh. "Good one, kid," he tells me. "Anyone on board need a special bay for boarding?"

"Nah we're good."

"You guys can dock in bay 105. You need stabilising tractors?"

"That'd be helpful," I say even as Akim alters our course, the bay's placement lighting up on our navigation panel. "And we're not joking, we came from Helios 2."

We'll be legends when people realise this is true. The space control officer laughs again, warning us not to cause any trouble. But soon he'll know I'm speaking the truth. Our clothes alone are proof of that.

***

We're greeted by security, who relaxes at the sight of our overalls. The squad's captain lifts her visor, shaking her head in disbelief.

"Well, I'll be a Dpanir with a legal trading manifest, you guys weren't lying."

I beam. "Did say!"

"You guys really were on one of the Helios colonies?" she asks, her accent stretching out every vowel, as Nooma and Nephanie join me. Sparks are flying from underneath the ship. Inside, Alta is swearing.

"Where do you think we got these?" Nephanie asks, words a little clipped as she tugs on her overalls. "Now will you let us on the station? I'm in a hurry to find better clothing."

The captain looks impressed. "Sidana, eh? Well, I never met your mother, but her name certainly made the rounds. I guess you're already living up to her legacy."

I feel warm inside despite the sudden surge of grief.

We check into the station and find our way out of the docking bays' meandering corridors. Beyond lies one of the many trading hubs, a sprawling room with ceilings just about high enough to not feel cramped, noisy with vendors and music played from too many different stalls and filled with the diverse crowds of Bakula.

It's like my first deep breath in years.

"So um, I have enough money to get us a meal, but not clothes, not yet. Sorry about that."

"Me neither," Nooma admits, "The people who caught me emptied my account before handing me to Berik," she spits out the name.

"I have money," Nephanie says, looking daunted by the sight of the crowd. "I can buy clothes. I'm not wearing this a second longer than I need to, and I don't see why anyone else should either. Just point me to a chip reader."

"Are you sure you want to pay for everyone?" Nooma asks.

"I owe you guys. And I have enough."

"Thanks," I flash her a smile, her eyes a bright emerald I wish I could read. "Let's go."

There's a queue in front of the ACR, which isn't surprising given Bakula traders prefer to deal in hard currency, masking transactions from spying eyes.

"So, who's this guy you say can get us a ship?" Nooma asks as we shuffle forward, stuck in between an irritable Vanark whose tentacle hair has nearly hit me in the face twice and a towering Dpanir hunched under the bulk of their back shell.

"Tulain. He's a friend. Owes me a favour."

Nephanie's eyes have gone yellow as she scans the crowd, fingers restlessly knotting and unknotting, the extra knuckle on each finger allowing the strangest of motions.

"A favour? To you?"

"Well, amma was owed a favour. But these things pass down the line, so now she's gone it's mine to claim."

"I'm not sure that's how it works, Malek."

"Trust me, with Tulain, it is," I assure her. She raises an uncertain eyebrow, but I don't think I can explain who Tulain is to me. Not yet, not until I've seen him and made sure everything is alright.

Nephanie steps back out of the ACR with a handful of chips she tries to stuff in her small overall pockets.

"There. I can always get more if we need but er, I didn't think we could carry that much. Anyway, Malek, find us somewhere to eat, will you?"

CHAPTER 13
TRYSTAN

EDEN ONE

"Malfunctioned?"

My eyes open in time to catch the Kundar's gaze.

Their voice is deep and melodic and I'm glad the language programs I downloaded are working. I hope they'll be able to understand me too. A lot of people off Eden One have translator implants fitted but that doesn't mean they recognise all languages.

"No, I..." I, what? Went back to my own body? Not exactly something I can say.

"What do you want from me?"

"Want? I don't want anything."

"Then why are you here?"

That's the question, isn't it? What possessed me to come down here earlier? Curiosity, yes, but more than that. I stare at the alien, almost struggling to take in all the details of how they look: extra limbs and scales and block blue eyes. No, calling them blue is almost insulting: they're something between turquoise and azure, luminescent and magnetic.

"You're an android?"

"Yes," it tastes like a lie even if it's only half of one.

"Did they send you here to monitor me?"

"No. I... They don't know I'm here. I saw what they were doing earlier and…" I look down, their intense gaze unwaveringly on me. "I wanted to see you."

The thin, elegant scales above their eyes draw together in what looks like a frown.

"You're an AI?"

I nod. It's the closest to the truth I dare come. I've never met another species and I have no idea how to read their reactions.

"What's your name?"

"Trystan." A wave of giddiness when I speak it aloud washes over me. "You?"

They cock their head sideways. Is that curiosity?

"Jakoor."

I draw closer to the cell and the alien within, my heart racing.

"Why are you here?" they ask again.

It's still hard to not think of them as a 'he' but their species doesn't have gender, a concept difficult to understand for me.

"I want to help." I'm surprised at the determination in my voice. "They're... I know what they want from you and I... It's wrong, everything they're doing. I want to help you."

Jakoor's luminescent eyes widen, their four arms crossed over their chest. The green of their skin is a sharp contrast with the shimmery black of the scales that curve around their limbs and up their sides. They're distractingly breathtaking.

"Why are you going against your creators? I thought Human AIs were tightly regulated? Because if this is some weird test, don't bother, I won't consent to anything they have in mind."

That's true—especially here, though I'm sure not everywhere—that Human-made AIs are extremely regulated.

"I... It's complicated. But I'm fully autonomous so no, this isn't a test. No-one knows I even came here."

The way their eyes fix me makes me strangely nervous.

"What planet am I on?"

"Eden One. You may not have heard of it; we don't have a lot of contact with outsiders. It's a Human-only planet."

Their eyelids twitch in a way I've only ever seen in movies, for when people check on implants they access mentally.

"It's not somewhere we've come before. What is the nearest planet from here?" They still sound tense and wary.

"Sod- Ishnira. It's in the same solar system as us. We don't have a lot of contact."

Not since the war.

"Could you get me there?"

"What?"

"If you want to help you need to get me there." They're looking straight at me. "Getting me out of this cell won't help if I can't get off the planet."

I chew my lip, both at home and in this body.

"Getting you out of the cell I could do but... I don't know where I could hide you and I don't know how to get a ship," I admit, stomach and morale sinking in unison.

I'm powerless. As always.

Jakoor looks down, passing a hand through their hair, tugging it away from where it snags on their horns.

"They'll hunt me down. I need you to help me disappear if you want to help." A deep breath. "Is there any way you can do that?"

I can tell even admitting they need help is costing them. I've read just enough on the Kundar to know they're a proud and fiercely independent species. Which makes sense after what happened to them.

"I'll find a way." Something inside me is breaking free, floating away from the fear. Looking in those luminescent eyes snapped some tether I didn't even know was there. "But if I do that, could you take me with you?"

In the darkness, the silence stretches. At home, my hands are fists on the sheet beneath me, tears of hope and terror stinging my eyes.

"Why?" Their voice is barely more than a breath, the sound they make hardly a word at all.

"Because I want to be free." There is no hesitation in my voice. No doubt. It is the only thing I have always been certain of.

Their eyes brighten.

"Find a way off this planet, and I'll take you wherever you want to go."

A sob escapes my lips back at home. I want to ask them to take the real me, but I know my parents would never stop hunting us. If I get this me out here, maybe I can find powerful allies. Somehow.

"I'll find a way. Soon. I promise."

They nod, solemn suddenly and extend their lower hands towards me, the other arms still crossed over their naked chest. I mirror Jakoor's gesture until our palms are resting against the glass of their cell, my hands so small compared to theirs, their three fingers and two thumbs impossible to match with my own.

"A promise is a sacred thing to my people. Do not make it lightly, Trystan of Eden One."

"I'm not. I'll find a way, I mean it."

Jakoor nods again, and the next words they speak go untranslated. They sound like magic to my ears, like those binding spells in fantasy novels. Maybe they are, or maybe they're simply something that can only be understood in their language.

"I should go."

I'm afraid but alive with possibilities.

"I will try to wait for you."

Our gazes don't break until I turn in the doorway. I all but run back to my uncle's lab, mind already racing desperately for a plan.

***

I'm starving and parched now that the migraine is gone, and far too awake to attempt sleep. I don't expect anyone to be up, so the voices I hear when I reach the top of the stairs catch me off guard.

I creep down, glad I know which steps to avoid. The door to my father's study is ajar, light spilling out.

If he catches me eavesdropping...

But no, this is too strange not to investigate.

Slowly, heart in my throat, I edge further down the stairs, crouching behind the banister close enough to hear them clearly. They're talking about candidates for the upcoming elections. Then they mention my uncle and I all but hold my breath.

"Your ties with Gideon will work against you, Trent. People will start digging dirt up on him and smear *you* with it. They won't care he's your wife's brother, not yours, the second you gave him that lab you sealed your own fate."

"We can bury it all," father's voice is as cold as the ice I hear dropping in a glass. "We bury his past, and we can use his current research to our advantage. If he actually gets results, we won't even need to spin anything."

"Some will say nothing good comes from aliens," the man replies.

So, my father knows. I bet he coerced my uncle into this.

"What you need first," the man carries on, "is to solidify your ties with your allies. Your daughter is what now? Sixteen? Seventeen? Don't you think it's about time you made her promise to the Pense's son official? You can throw a big party. People are just starting to think about the elections so now's a good time. You present the perfect family, win yourself some easy points with the members. Your wife is a ditz but she's a good hostess. Pense has *a lot* of clout with the electorate, and he's a good orator to have on your side."

I feel dizzy.

"I thought about it but... Tris can be difficult. I don't have the time for her to make a scene."

I hate that I'm sure he's giving me too much credit. I'm too terrified to stand up to him.

The other man laughs. "She's a girl, Trent, what is she going to do? Worse comes to it just say she got a little hysterical. She does take after her mother in looks, you might as well attribute her temperament to the woman. God knows Margaret isn't the most stable woman out there."

My father sighs. "Are any of them?"

The man laughs again. I want to punch them. I know so many amazing girls, like Cat and Shauna. I only wish I was half as brave as them.

"I'll think about it," my father says at last. "It would give Margaret something to focus on. She has been dreaming of organising Tris' wedding for years now."

I know he's just used my wrong name, the one he gave me, but my brain glazes over it, catching only the part of the sound that I can bear. Still, I feel sick at the sound of it.

Sometimes that name is enough to break me.

"If she's any trouble, you know our institution is very good. Her mother did spend a year with us before she married you if you remember," the man carries on.

My stomach drops.

Mom got institutionalised in her teens? I think of her: smiling and docile, a little bird-brained but mostly well-meaning. What could *she* have done to end up there?

"That won't be necessary. I can control my own child," my father snaps.

I'm too terrified to feel any relief.

"If you insist, if you insist," the man says, his tone implying my father is likely to change his mind. "Anyway, I'll look into the accounts tomorrow, see what I can navigate your way."

I can hear a chair creak as he stands. I don't have the time to think about what I just heard, because they're coming out of the study and all I can do is rush back up the stairs, heart racing as I duck into my bedroom. Exhaustion washes over me in place of the anger I'm too scared to muster.

I don't even know what's worse: that my father is doing so many despicable things or that the inevitable engagement I have spent years trying not to think about is going to happen

I need a plan. *Plans.* I can't stay on this planet but before I can leave, I need to make allies who can help me escape.

First, I need to speak to my uncle. I send a message to his office, knowing he'll see it first thing.

I really need to talk to you. Can you wake me up when you get in?

***

A message from my uncle jerks me awake and I slip into my android self. Immediately, a headache blooms, not helped by too little sleep and too much stress.

"Hey."

He whirls, startled.

"You wanted to talk?"

With bags under his eyes and his hair sticking up at all angles, he looks like the cliché scientist from old movies.

To me he's still a hero, the only person to know my secret.

Questions about last night wedge into my throat, I'm too much of a coward to face the truth, to face the fear he might not be the man I need him to be.

"Trystan?"

Back at home mom is calling. I can't move. Can barely think. Tears slip down my cheeks.

"Tris? Sweetie, are you okay?" Mom, in my room.

"My head hurts," I reply out of both mouths.

The migraine is blinding. I feel like I can't breathe enough. I'd felt fine when I got my uncle's message but now it's like I'm being torn in two by the pain.

"Aw, sweetie. Do you need to stay home?" Mom sits next to me, her cool hand on my forehead.

"Have you been splitting yourself more than I advised?" my uncle asks.

"Yeah." It's good I can give them the same answer because I can't tell my bodies apart anymore.

"I'll call school and the doctor, just get some rest."

"I need to run some scans on the chip, maybe do some tweaking."

Their voices mingle, I can't tell what's going on anymore. I'm dizzy, my body at once numb and tingly.

"Tryst, I think the chip is malfunctioning. Just pull back to yourself for now and I'll be over soon."

I don't exactly willingly leave my android self, but I slip away nonetheless, falling into my own body long enough to know I'm safe before my thoughts scatter like leaves on the wind.

CHAPTER 14
LÀHN

KIRILLION

Kode kicks me out of her room as soon as she notices how tough to crack the encryption is going to be. I return to my own bed, turning the star projector on, losing myself in the patterns covering my ceiling.

It's the first gift Zoon ever gave me, on the day he declared to be my birthday. Kode and I spent hours as children curled on my bed, watching the stars. Usually it helps me find peace, but right now there is none to find.

Sleep isn't being forthcoming either.

I should put some music on. Boot up a game. I need to do something, anything, but nothing feels right.

As if the job tonight hadn't been bad enough now Zoon is all I can think about. Did I ever tell him everything he means to me? I can't remember if I ever spoke the words or just took for granted that he knew. What if the hurried goodbye earlier had been our last?

I'm out of my room before the thoughts can go any further, before tears can find their way out. I run, letting my feet do the thinking for me.

They take me to Ashya's, in the way they used to when I was a child running from nightmares.

I hesitate, unsure what I came here seeking. But then I hear voices from inside, and a name.

The name of a police captain I shouldn't be hearing here.

There is no-one in the Guild by that name. Does she mean to take Ashya out after hurting Zoon?

I slam my hand on the door panel, rushing in, already imagining a dozen grim scenarios. But the scene inside is domestic, Ashya and the Shinarian woman sitting on the sofas, at ease, some tea and snacks laid on the low table between them.

Relief wars with confusion and all I can do is stare as they turn to face me.

"Làhn? What's going on?" Ashya asks and I want to run. Only I'm not sure whether to them or away.

"He's the one who was on the job?" the Shinarian woman asks.

"Yes," Ashya motions for me to come closer. "Làhn, come on in. Are you okay?"

"Ashya, what is she doing here?"

The policewoman laughs. "Ah, I take it you know who I am? Or at least part of it," she says, eyes going from auburn to a pale pink that makes my cheeks grow warm. "You want to do the introductions, Ashya, or should I?"

"Làhn, this is Leela Tah Shaa'v, she—"

"She's police!" I interrupt. "What is she doing here? Do you know she was the last person on Zoon's schedule today?"

"How do you know that?" Ashya asks as Leela Tah Shaav's eyes turn magenta. "Did you and Kode go snooping?" Their skin ripples in annoyance but I don't feel the need to explain myself. Not when a member of the Kirillion police sits here as though it was her home.

"Smart kids," Leela says. "I would have done the same at their age." She offers me what I think is supposed to be a smile.

Ashya sighs, rubbing at the bridge of their nose. "Leela is the one who brought Zoon back. She found him injured when she went to meet him."

My frown deepens. "How do we know she's not the one who hurt him?"

I feel like I'm going mad with paranoia, but Leela is part of the police forces and they're nothing but trouble to people like us.

Ashya sighs again. "She didn't hurt him, Làhn... Leela used to be one of us."

I blink. "What?"

"I grew up here," Leela explains. "I wasn't made for this, and when I told Zoon he paid for an education outside of the Guild for me," her eyes turn back to an amused pale pink. "He didn't really approve of my career choices, but I did promise I'd keep the Guild safe no matter what."

"I... That's..."

"Not what you expected?"

"No."

“Come sit down, will you?” Ashya motions for me to settle next to them on the sofa and I do, letting them wrap an arm around my shoulders.

"So, you don't know what happened to him either?" I ask.

"No. I think it had to do with the information he was having you retrieve but I don't have any proof." Her eyes have gone black, focussed solely on me.

"What's the information about?" I ask.

Ashya tenses and Leela's eyes flash amber before turning back to black. There's something she's not saying. The silence stretches as we stare at each other.

"I got shot at tonight," I snap, raising my bandaged arm.

"You were in the shootout at *Purple Gravity*?" Ashya asks, an accusatory note to their tone.

"Yeah, I just… I wanted to tell Zoon but then…" I'm about to make an expansive gesture when they wrap me in a tight hug and refuse to let go.

"You should have told me," they whisper.

"I'm sorry, I wasn't really thinking straight."

They pull back, offering me a small smile. "I get it. But it will be okay, you hear me, Làhn?"

I nod though I still don't know if I believe them.

"The men that attacked *Purple Gravity,*" Leela interrupts. "We believe they're still in the city. Did you happen to see their insignia? They've got blurring tech, so our recordings are all a mess."

"Yeah, I did. It was a yellow circle with red flames around it."

Leela's eyes tip from amber to scarlet and Aysha's skin ripples with a pattern I haven't seen often: fear.

"This is bad I take it?"

"You could say that," Leela mutters.

***

"The Hell Suns?" I repeat. The name means little to me, but Leela and Ashya's reactions tell me all I need to know.

"They don't usually work here," Leela explains. "Divinities know we have enough mercs planet-side as it is. And these aren't known for playing nice." She runs a hand over her knotted hair, cursing under her breath. "If they're looking for that chip... Ashya, you need to put everyone on high alert."

"Why?"

The question answers itself when an explosion rocks the building. The alarm blares as the power goes out and the red emergency lights come on. For a moment that might well last a lifetime the three of us freeze.

To my own surprise I'm the first one to move, bolting away. Kode. She's alone. With the chip.

"Làhn!" Ashya calls but I don't stop.

I can't. If something happens to Kode it will be on me. I hear footsteps after me and still I keep going, throwing myself up the stairs towards her room, even as smoke starts to fill the hallways. Other members of the Guild are staggering out of their room, some already armed, others bleary eyed. I pass Ren, his hair-tentacles flailing, and he tosses a blaster at me.

"Get out of here, kid!" he barks out.

"I need to get Kode!"

If he replies I don't hear him, turning the corner to our rooms only to find Kode, a filter-mask on her lower face and her go-bag in one hand. Of course, she'd manage to react to this with a cool head.

Get your stuff! She signs at me, and I duck in my room. There is so much I'd want to get, all the trinkets and possessions amassed over the years, but I'm going to have to hope they survive the mercs.

My go-bag only has the essentials: clothes, creds, rations, fake ID, and a disposable handset. Against all advice I throw my actual tablet in, refusing to leave behind so much of me. I can't find my filter mask, so I'll have to do without. Guess this is why Zoon is always telling me to tidy my room.

I shove my boots on and grab a jacket and burst back into the corridor to find Captain Leela Tah Shaav and Kode signing quickly at each other.

Ashya sent a message, Kode signs at me. *She's okay, we go with her. Said you'd explain the rest.*

I nod, a strange calm washing over me. There is smoke and cries and distant gunfire but, for a beat, I'm separate from it all.

"We need to go," Leela says, her now sienna eyes going from me to Kode. "Do you have the chip?"

I glance at Kode who just nods. The other one, the copy no-one but Kode knows I have sits in my own pocket.

A second explosion almost sends us to our knees, shattering my calm into slithers of terror.

"Where's Ashya?" I ask.

"Organising the defence. Shey-Roon is getting Zoon out."

Gunfire echoes down the corridor and Leela leads us away, her blaster out. I'm holding mine awkwardly and Kode is putting her stun gloves on.

The smoke stings my eyes, coats the inside of my mouth with a foul taste.

Memories wash over me, flashes of somewhere else, of someone's arms and screaming. No, not now. Not like this. I don't want to remember the nightmares that haunt my sleep.

Kode shakes me. I can hardly focus. The images make little sense: a wide, opulent corridor and fabric fluttering everywhere. Kode pulls me, her hand in mine, my anchor. By the time we're at the lift I've pulled myself together.

"Stairs, now," Leela orders.

"We need to help them!" I protest, although I know all too well that I can do little against the force attacking us.

"Ashya told me to get you both out, so that's what I'm doing!"

I'm about to protest when the woosh of an explosion travels up the lift shaft, shattering the doors. Leela pushes us away and we escape down the stairs with only a few scrapes. They're blocking all our escape routes.

But we must get out, one way or another.

Leela takes point. I can scarcely think as I concentrate on not tripping myself, my heart hammering so loud I can hear little else. The alarm is still screeching, the ear-piercing cacophony slowly making me lose my focus, fear swallowing me whole.

A little over halfway down we're plunged into silent darkness.

My ears ring in the sudden silence. Muffled shouts from upstairs, a light somewhere above us: the Hell Suns on our tail.

Wordlessly, Leela pushes on as I activate my night vision, once more thanking Zoon for all the little augmentations he gifted us over the years.

Kode and I run side by side, boots slamming hard on each step. The Hell Suns are gaining on us, and I don't know how long I can keep going.

I'm about to collapse when we reach the lobby door and crash through it. Four Hell Suns wait on the other side.

Leela takes two out within seconds and Kode punches the one coming at her right in the guts, the shock from her glove enough to send them twitching to the floor. The fourth shoots at me and all I can do is dive to the ground, screaming. I'm not made for this. Leela shoots again and the Hell Sun falls.

She moves quickly, tugging me to my feet and then we're out in the open, the lights of the city bright, the noise of morning traffic rushing over us.

A police car slowly lowers itself in front of the building, but the way Leela tenses tells me this isn't a good thing.

"Move!" she shouts, pushing me and Kode out of the way.

We duck behind a column at the front of the building just in time to escape a hail of lasers from the car's front guns. Debris from the shattered pavement showers us and the noise is deafening. I'm too scared for tears, too scared to scream. But not too scared to move. I grab Kode's hand and together we take off down the street.

I throw one last glance over my shoulder and see Leela fallen to the ground. She got hit. She saved us and now she might die.

I don't know how to live with that.

But all I can do now is run, ducking down the side streets and narrow alleys I know like the back of my hand. I can hear the police car chasing us and with a quick nod, Kode and I duck inside the Shu'a'kash covered market.

CHAPTER 15
MALEK

BAKULA

I'm home.

Nothing has ever felt more real than the chair I sit at, the table on which my elbows rest, the sounds and sights of the food market.

It's two floors above the arrival hall and is possibly the loudest place on the station. Scrolling signs advertise menus in a myriad of alphabets, from elegant scripts to what I think might be sticks hugging each other whilst the vendors hawk their goods in more languages than my translator knows. To top it all, music blares discordantly from everywhere at once. There's no dominant race here: only pirate lieges and mercenary captains vying for power. Only raiders rubbing shoulders with salvagers. Here what matters is the size of your ship and your skills in a fight. Or how much shit you can talk yourself out of.

"What are you feeding me?" Nooma asks, poking the two-pronged fork into the green and red fried balls we purchased.

"Shulash uliot cakes," I declare around a mouthful.

Flavour explodes in my mouth. After two years of Helios' sludge, it's almost too much. It's *so good*. Spicy and sweet, the sticky texture of the dough a perfect accompaniment to the crumbly meat inside.

"What's an uliot?"

Nooma has a lot to learn about the joys of alien foods. And the woes too, I guess.

"It's a type of meat, try it! Completely safe for us. I know we're *very* different from Shulash," I say, glancing at the creature inside its enviro-suit, tentacles and squat body encased in flexible metal. "But a lot of their food is entirely compatible with our metabolism."

"Meat?" Nooma looks dubious. "I thought the Shulash home world was entirely water? Shouldn't it be fish?"

I laugh. "Well, it looks like a fish." A pause. "Kinda. I think. You know, actually I don't know what a fish is supposed to look like. But anyway, trust me when I tell you it tastes like meat."

She takes a bite, closing her eyes, whether to enjoy the taste or because she's scared. Nephanie is already licking her fingers and I'm only two mouthfuls behind her. My stomach grumbles. I could have eaten three times as much.

"I feel bad for Alta and Akim," I admit.

"We can take them something back once we're done. Not that I couldn't eat more *now*," Nooma admits.

I beam at her empty plate.

"Same. But I really need to get to Tulain. I don't want him to hear about my arrival second hand, though he probably has already. Damn, I never thought amma's fame would backfire on me. Anyway, if Nephanie is still cool with paying, you two should see if you can get us some clothes."

Nooma eyes me suspiciously. "You don't want us to come with you?"

"It's… Look, I haven't seen this guy since amma died and we…" I shake my head. "He's kinda the only family I have left, and he probably thought I was dead so..." I shrug. "It's gonna be weird enough as is, so I'd rather do this on my own, okay?"

"What if you get yourself into trouble?" Nephanie asks. "You're not exactly at your best right now."

"I've got my wits, I'll be fine."

"She's got a point, Malek," Nooma insists.

I roll my eyes.

"Look, I've been here before. I know how this place works and I know how to avoid trouble. Please, just trust me with this."

Nephanie's eyes are twin orbs of pale lavender lost on the crowd, but Nooma meets my gaze dead on.

"You still think we can do this?"

I wish that her question didn't give second wind to all the doubts I've been burying.

"Yeah, I do, and then we can track down that friend of yours, find out what really happened to Alta's ship, and maybe even uncover what Akim stumbled upon. So yeah, I think we can be a crew. You, me, Alta, Akim, we can make it work." I glance at Nephanie. "And you too, if you want. We'll be travelling a lot, and well, that should help with running away, right?"

I wish I knew the meaning of her eyes.

"You could have a good portion of the Shinarian fleet coming after you. When they manage to track me again, that is," she points out.

I shrug even as Nooma puts a hand on her shoulder. I don't miss the look they exchange, one that tells me that they stayed up way later than the rest of us yesterday.

"We're all fugitives now," Nooma tells her.

“And either way, it’s not like they’re gonna shoot us with you on board,” I add.

"Okay. For a while. I don't do long term," she adds, and I want to tell her that we’re much too young for long term. But she might be way older than I think. I hold my hand out to her and, after a second of hesitation, she clasps my wrist.

"Welcome on board, Nephanie. Now, I’ll meet you back at the docking bay. You two be careful as well!"

As I limp away, I realise that many eyes are on us. Two Humans and a Shinarian in Helios prison overalls are bound to draw attention. The crowd almost parts for me as I head for the elevator, whispers of awe at my back.

Amma would be proud.

They can no longer say that no-one ever escaped a Helios prison.

***

It’s hard to call anything on Bakula the underbelly, especially when the whole station itself is the underbelly of its galaxy. But even Bakula’s layout follows some form of hierarchy: a power structure Tulain has always carefully kept himself out of. He's a smuggler, a salvager, or a PI depending on what you need. He runs the kind of business that gets people killed and he’s been doing it for longer than I’ve been alive.

He always was a kind of family to me, like an uncle I got to see everytime we made berth on Bakula. Only now my dumb head is wondering if all of that was one sided. No matter how many memories I try to conjure up of our time together, I end up doubting everything.

When I reach the *Shu Fa Rinari* club, there is some comfort in that nothing has changed: same old, battered, mismatched furniture, same old tinny sound system playing high-pitched Hrushan pop. Rows of alcohol—some of which is so illegal it's hard to get even here—line the pillar at the centre of the circular bar.

The barkeep is a species I don't recognise, covered in smooth green scales with eyes on either side of a protruding nose, their mouth parting their face vertically. Which is just as freaky as it sounds.

They say something in a sibilant language my translator doesn't recognise.

I pull an exaggeratedly confused face and tap my ear in the hope they'll get what I mean. It's hard to create a universal sign for *I don't understand* when we all have a varying number of limbs, and ears, and who knows what else.

The bartender flicks up a holographic screen and types something, spinning it to me.

What do you want?

I type my answer: *Tulain still around?*

The letters morph back into their language.

First door at the back. Don't start a fight.

I nod my thanks, realising belatedly that it could be a rude gesture to that species: not the best course of action in a place where fights happen as often as the warnings not to start them

As I limp towards the back, someone shouts something rude my way. I've half a mind to let them know they can do it to themselves until I realise it's a seven-foot-tall Dpanir-Mallak hybrid and self-preservation takes over. I'm sure Nooma would be proud.

Tulain's office door is just as rusted and grimy as I remember, no sign to advertise his services. If you're here, then you know him already. I hit the side panel and the door slides upwards. The place is still wreathed in smoke—I don't even want to imagine his air recycling bill—the two armchairs across the desk still just as shabby.

Tulain is in his big chair, holo-screens hovering above his head, feet resting on the desk, lounging.

He hasn't changed at all: five-foot four, broad, ruddy smooth scales covering his body. His eyes are orange vertical slits, and his forked tongue is hanging slightly at the corner of his mouth with concentration. I'd made a game out of seeing how far I could pull it out when he was asleep. I'd say I was young and needed the money, but really, I was young and needed the fun.

He's wearing Human clothes, tailor-made to fit his frame—a historical costume he's always been fond of: white shirt with rolled up sleeves, a pair of black slacks with black bracers, and a matching neck tie. He gave up on shoes before he met amma, his scaly, clawed feet hard as stones. A black hat sits discarded on the desk, for show as it doesn't fit properly on his long and narrow head.

The cigarette his species favours sits in a full ashtray to the side, smoking up the office. Helios' air was as sterile as the food was bland and my eyes sting, a cough tickling at the back of my throat.

Tulain looks straight at me, shaking his head, mouth splitting into a grin. He's on his feet in seconds, and before I know it, he's wrapped me in a tight, almost crushing, embrace. I let out a choking noise, and he pulls away with that hissing sound that's the equivalent of a laugh, slapping me on the shoulder so hard I almost crumple to the floor.

Furakians are stronger than Humans as standard, and Tulain has years of working out on me.

"Malek Sidana! I didn't believe it when I heard through the tomato-vine that you were back!"

I bite back a laugh at his mistake: Tulain insists on learning as many languages as he can, saying you can't really understand people until you speak their language, but sometimes I'm the one who wonders what the hell he's talking about.

"Hey," I say, smiling a little awkwardly as he takes me by the shoulders, inspecting me.

"Big! So much bigger than last time! But different…" He shoves his face in mine, staring into my eyes. "Ooh, not just the arm and leg then. I had heard bad accident; I didn't know *how* bad."

"Yeah, the ship tried to take me with it," I say, shrugging, pretending it's not something I still have nightmares about.

"New eyes, new limbs... But that hand looks like it's seen better days..."

"Yeah, I got shot at. Not taken the time to find someone to fix it yet."

"That won't be hard here," he nods as though he already has someone in mind. "But where have you been the last few years? I heard of Sabra's death, but you just went missing. Poof! Off the radar!"

I look down. I have no idea how he heard about what happened to us, but I can't imagine it was easy not being able to do anything when I went missing.

"Yeah I..." I wish I still knew how to fall apart and have someone else put me back together. "It was hard after amma died."

Tulain wraps an arm around my shoulder, leading me to an armchair. I plop down as his eight-fingered hand crushes his cigarette.

"You got a long story to tell, don't you?"

"Kinda," I shrug but he sees right through me.

"Tell me, then."

And so, I do.

***

"You're going to be a *legend,*" Tulain muses when I finish. "Not even your mum pulled a stunt like that. I'll get the story out: bunch of teenagers breaking away from Helios, making a valiant dash for freedom, and only just escaping capture by a Shinarian mothership." He lets out his hissing laugh, slapping himself on the chest. "That's going to make one hell of a story! You're going to be famous!"

"*If* people believe it," I point out, though I'm grinning too. "But it won't do me much good if I don't have a ship."

"Ah yes, a ship. Tell me it's not the only reason you came to ol' Tulain first, eh?"

"I gotta admit it was pretty high on the list," I hesitate to say more. "Truth is… I hadn't really let myself think about coming to see you, not in any other term than the ship I mean. I was afraid, after what happened that, you know…" I trail off.

Furakians' emotions aren't so much in their eyes as they are in the motion of their hands and fingers. Even for someone used to them it's not easy to understand.

"You thought I might not want to see you, that it?"

I manage something like a nod, a lump lodging itself firmly in the back of my throat.

"Ay ay ay, silly as your mother! I might not have travelled all over the stars with you and Sabra, but I say to you what I said to her. We're family, Malek. I watched you from when you were this big," he says, demonstrating. "You need anything, you come here. Okay?"

The lump is even bigger now as I nod, eyes stinging.

"But yeah, guess I did owe your mum a ship, eh? She was brilliant at sheyshey, more than anyone has a right to."

There's a fondness in his voice that makes my heart ache. I never really stopped to think who else might miss her and it strikes me suddenly that all those years I wasn't the only one grieving.

"Why did you even bet against her?" I ask and he lets out a long laughing hiss.

"I was very drunk. And so was she. So, I thought, hey, maybe tonight's the night you can beat her! But no, Sabra still won *every* game!" I can't help but laugh. Of course, amma would manage to beat Tulain at his favourite game even when drunk. "The ship I wagered though, rust bucket. It's been docked ages; don't remember last time I flew it. But if your first ship isn't a rust bucket, are you even really from Bakula?" he finishes, with a glint in his eyes.

"That's okay," I say, and I mean it. It doesn't matter how bad of a state it's in because it will be mine. Ours. "We can work on it."

He chuckles. "Ain't cheap fixing a ship. You got any creds left?"

"Enough," I lie, terribly.

"So, you're broke, eh?" I pull a face. "Well," he leans forward, elbows on his desk, claws tapping together. "I might have a job you kids can do for me."

Exhaustion wars with excitement.

"A job?" I hurt; my limbs are busted, but the promise of my first job on Bakula as a free man is enough to push it all aside.

Tulain lights a cigarette, actually smoking it this time. "I'll cover the repair for the ships," he says and I almost leap over the desk to hug him. "Couldn't give Sabra a funeral, but at least I can look after you. But after that, even with the story you're starting off with, you're gonna need capital. You're new to this and people are gonna try to take advantage of that, so you need money in your pockets so you're not desperate for the first crummy job that comes your way."

I look away at the mention of the funeral amma never got. She should have gone to the stars, ashes scattered from her ship into eternity. Instead, I never even got her body back.

Tulain reaches a big hand across his desk and taps my arm gently, a sibilant noise escaping his lips. The grief hits hard. Another wave that I just need to let pass for now.

"Tell me about the job, then I'll talk to my crew. I can't go ahead without talking to them."

"That's what I like to hear," Tulain beams as he brings up his holoscreens. "Let's talk business, then, Captain Sidana."

CHAPTER 16
LÀHN

KIRILLION

The covered market is an old building, ceiling stretching seven floors above our heads, high enough to accommodate anti-grav platforms where small eateries make their business and the mezzanines lined with shops. The bottom is a maze-like food market where the synth-farms come to sell their products.

The police car can't follow, but we spot some uniforms inside and let the thickest parts of the crowd swallow us until we've found somewhere to tuck ourselves.

We need to decide where we're going, I sign, cursing at the Guild's lack of foresight in having no safehouses down here. The emergency protocol cuts us off from making contact for four hours in case we get compromised, meaning I can't see where everyone else is headed. And with people actively looking for us, we're not making it to another district in one piece.

Shuobe doesn't live far from here.

We'll put her in danger! I protest.

I'll message her, tell her everything. She decides, Kode insists.

I worry it's not fair putting that on her girlfriend but it's not exactly as though we have another option.

She says to come over, Kode signs after a couple of minutes. *Her mum is there, we should be safe.*

We take a detour underground, come back up near her building. Easier to make sure we're not being followed.

Kode nods and we get going, all too aware of the growing police presence in the market.

***

We make it to the top of the stairs before a cry of alarm echoes behind us. I resist looking over my shoulder as the door to the underground levels slides open, hitting me with a wave of musty air.

I don't need to look to know it's the police coming for us.

Kode's hand is in mine as we all but throw ourselves down the narrow corridor. I envy her face mask even more down here: the first few moments in the underground are always spent trying not to throw up.

Now not only am I worried about that, but I have to keep running. If we get out of this, I swear I will never let my room be a mess again.

Each thing in its place and a place for each thing, as Zoon always says.

"Stop! We will shoot!" The police's heavy footsteps are gaining, and their voices almost bring me to a dead stop.

But I don't trust them not to gun us down and blame us once we're dead. It's not that the Kirillion police are inherently bad, but when you're dealing with potentially corrupt people, it's hard to judge.

I jerk Kode down an even narrower alleyway as the first shot goes off. It's dark here, and I blink my night vision on, a stitch already threatening at my side. I really should have gone running with Ren more often.

I'm never going to say no to his offers ever again.

We burst out of the metal corridor into a vaster square, this one bordered by misshapen spheres with strangely shaped stairs coiling around the outside, hewn directly into the stone.

For better or worse, the Yoelus market is on, the square bustling with small, squat bodies dressed in scale robes that glint and glimmer in the darkness, chittering at each other in an almost musical cacophony.

Around the edges of the square, feasting on whatever they purchased—none of which looks even remotely appetising—some of the other underground species mill about. Thylens and Gurnips. A Kladok's face is all but split in half as they let out a bellowing sound of delight.

I've got only a second to take it all in before there's another shot behind us and we duck to the side, trying to find somewhere safe.

But the shot has drawn everyone's attention, far too many eyes turning towards us. And almost immediately after, to our pursuers.

There is one rule that anyone who comes down here must follow, one rule that saw me discarding my blaster under a stall before venturing here.

No firearms.

Most of the species that live underground are placid merchants and eccentric scientists, very few if any of their people as fond of violence as the ones they call sky-breathers. When they settled on Kirillion, they negotiated an arrangement that banned anyone from entering the Underground with a firearm. Any who do face their justice, not that of the city above.

And these species might not condone violence, but they can be scary as all hells when they need to be.

I don't want to stay and watch, I have enough nightmare fuel as it is, so even as the chittering turns from musical to chilling, I pull Kode after me.

The passages here are claustrophobic. The cacophony behind us heightens to a dizzying pitch, and I stagger, letting go of Kode to clamp my hands over my ears.

Kode is blessedly unaffected, and she wastes no time in grabbing my t-shirt and giving me no choice but to follow.

We take the stairs back up to the surface two at a time, and I throw myself out into the cooler air, all but slamming into a police grunt.

"You're un—" the guy starts, and I react on instinct, swinging my bag off my shoulder and into his head.

It takes him—and me, if I'm honest—completely by surprise and despite his helmet he staggers, falling entirely when Kode shoves him with all her strength.

We plunge out of the alleyway and into the busy crowd of the main thoroughfare.

We're breathless but we can't stop, pushing through the crowd to the other end of the street where Shuobe waits in front of her building.

She looks more Mallak than Human in a lot of ways but lacks the third Mallak eye in the middle of her face. Instead, she has a small, flat nose only half as efficient as the gills that slash vertically down either side of her long neck. Her skin is a pale purple and isn't as leathery as most Mallak's. Her hair is a vivid green, growing long from her head and her back, and it looks freshly braided and knotted. She's topless, Mallak rarely wearing more than paint and pants, and there is only the barest hint of what could have been Human breasts.

The queue for the nearby restaurant spills onto the street, disguising us until we're nearly in front of her and she must read the desperate panic on our faces because she ushers us in without a word, pushing us into the lift as she steals furtive glances over her shoulder to see if our pursuers are incoming.

I collapse on the floor of the lift, tilting my head back against the cool metal as Shuobe wraps Kode in a tight hug. I'm exhausted, the mostly sleepless night finally catching up with me and it's all I can do to stay awake on the long way up.

A particularly tall, older Mallak greets us in the corridor when we emerge from the lift, and Shuobe introduces her as Nyurae, her mother.

I trip over my own feet as I step into the apartment, and she catches me by the shoulder.

"I think you need some rest."

She leads me to the couch as Shuobe all but carries Kode into the bedroom and I'm out cold before my head even finds a pillow.

CHAPTER 17
TRYSTAN

EDEN ONE

I wake with a jolt, gulping in air to burning lungs as though I'd stopped breathing.

"What—" I start as I register my uncle, his laptop balanced on my bedside table, a handheld scanner hovering above me. A cough silences me until he holds out a glass of water, which I down.

"The chip malfunctioned," he says.

That pierces even through the fog that makes everything feel more dream than reality, sending a shiver of cold dread down my spine.

"What?"

My hands are shaking. Both from whatever happened and the sudden spike of fear.

"Your mind started to...It's hard to describe. Drift, I guess," he tries to explain. "It's always a possible side effect with this kind of tech. It's why I wanted you to take it easy."

I don't know what to say. I don't know how to tell him how much I need to get away from this house, from myself. The things I meant to confront him about tumble away as he wraps an arm around me.

He's the only person who knows. The only person I feel safe with.

"It's okay," he whispers, worry still thick in his voice. "I've re-calibrated the chip; you'll be safe now."

My hand goes to the back of my neck, where my hairline ends, and a small scar sits almost invisible. My uncle used nanomachines to insert and link the chip to my brain.

"You won't be able to control the android for a little bit whilst I finish the adjustments, but after that you shouldn't run into this problem again."

My stomach sinks. Even a few hours trapped in this body, this life, feels like too much. I want to see the city. I want to walk the streets without fear. I want to find somewhere else to call home.

I want to find a way to help Jakoor.

If I can get them off planet, they'll take my other self with them. The tech my uncle used comes from a race that works remotely throughout the universe, meaning I shouldn't lose the connection no matter how far I go.

It sounds so much like magic.

I look up and meet his eyes, so blue like my mother's. I wish I had inherited theirs and not my father's grey: steely on him, washed out on me.

There is so much I want to ask him, to tell him. So much, and nothing comes out.

Because it never does.

"You're going to be okay," he says, standing.

I let out a sharp, mirthless laugh. "I haven't been okay in a while." I wrap my arms around my knees, feeling small and alone suddenly.

"Tryst, come on." He's never been so flippant with me. "It won't be long before you can control the android again, and I promise, you can leave the lab soon."

As though that will fix anything. As though I'm not going to be forced to marry Nathaniel as soon as I turn eighteen, destined to be trapped being someone I'm not.

"Yeah," I mutter, not looking at him. Tears sting my eyes, and I hate myself.

Boys don't cry, my father told Nathaniel when we were children and he'd hurt himself. *Boys don't cry,* as though we're unfeeling machines. *Boys don't cry,* as though I need something else pulling me away from what I know I am.

"You should get some rest; this is going to have taken a toll on you. You've got the day off school?" I nod. "You take it easy then."

"What did you tell mom?" I ask, desperate to keep him here a little longer.

"She didn't see me coming in the back."

"He wants to marry me off," I blurt out.

He freezes, bag halfway to his shoulder. "What are you talking about?"

"Father. I... I heard him talking to someone last night. Heard him say he needed me engaged to Nathaniel for the upcoming campaign." I raise my eyes to him, but I can't read the expression on his face.

"I'm sorry, Tryst."

Something inside me cracks.

"Help me," I breathe out. "I don't want this. I don't want to end up like my mother." I hate how pathetic I sound.

The second he has his arms around me, I bury my face in his shoulder.

"I'm sorry he's being a jerk, Tryst," he whispers. "I wish I could do something to help."

I pull away angrily. No matter how old you are, you always expect your heroes to save you.

"Can't you?" I know it's not as simple as that.

"I'm sorry," he whispers against my hair, pulling me back to him.

I want to hate him. I can't let go of him.

"I hate this life."

He doesn't answer. He never does when I say things like this. I wonder if he thought the android would fix everything, if even the man who gave me the words for what I am doesn't quite get it.

"You should go, you have work to do," I say after the silence stretches uncomfortably. He gives me that look I hate: pity mingled with something I can't read.

My hero won't come to save me. He can't.

***

The last thing I expected when I finally dragged myself out of bed, was for mom to allow me to go and meet Cat. Usually she monitors everything I do, but she just seemed relieved that I was up and functional and actually wanting to socialise.

It's true that I hardly leave the house, Cat normally coming over, and perhaps mom has decided that this new behaviour needs encouraging. God knows she pesters me to socialise more all the time.

She fusses over my hair and clothes though, wanting me to look like a 'proper young lady', and I'm too stressed to fight her on it.

Cat is waiting for me at our favourite dessert house: a small, quaint place off the beaten track.

Powdery blue walls and a black and white tiled floor give it a retro feel, whilst classical Christian rock plays softly in the background, bearable as long as I don't pay attention to the lyrics. I don’t know that I ever had faith, and I’m certainly not about to start now.

Cat is seated at a booth, tapping away on her tablet, gnawing on her bottom lip. She's pulled her hair back in a messy bun, and she’s never looked so much to me like a star waiting to shine.

"Are you going to sit down or just stare at me?" she asks, looking up with a quirked eyebrow.

I laugh softly and slide into the booth.

"Sorry, I'm a little... You know."

"Migraine still?"

"It was bad."

"Given you nearly fainted into your dessert, I imagine so."

I smile. She has a way of making me feel at ease.

"So, what did you want? You *never* ask to come out, especially not after a migraine."

I’m so glad mom doesn’t know me half as well as Cat does.

"I needed someone to talk to," I admit, scrolling through the menu.

Cat pushes her tablet aside, face serious. Usually when I need to talk, I message her, but this felt too big.

"I overheard my father talking to...*someone*, last night. No idea who it was but..." I press my order into the screen, barely paying attention. I like most things here anyway. "They were talking about the upcoming campaign. About father’s chances... And he... He wants to make me and Nathaniel official to secure a political alliance with his father. I knew this was coming but… I’d hoped he would wait until I’d graduated at least."

Cat is staring at me, looking heart broken and I hate putting this on her. Only I have no-one else who will understand how momentous this is.

“Oh Tris, that's awful," she says even as the waitress appears with our orders.

"I don't know how to stop it," I admit as soon as she’s gone.

"No… Especially not when your dad and Pense have been planning this for forever. Shauna only managed to get out of her own betrothal by pissing off her fiancé so much he dumped her."

I snort. "Yeah, but that nearly landed her in trouble."

"I think she didn't care."

Is marrying really worse than being institutionalised? Neither is freedom, no, but at least with Nathaniel I would have a life, wouldn't I? I would still be all of me. Even if being married would mean... No, I’m not going there, shoving a giant bite of cake in my mouth to keep myself distracted.

"I’m scared," I admit.

"I don't blame you."

We're silent for a few moments, digging into our desserts as the reality of our lives washes over us. It doesn’t matter that I know I’m not a girl, this world only cares about the shape of my body, not that of my soul.

“But Nathaniel isn’t all that bad, right?” Cat says and I frown. How can she say that when he is so easily following in his father’s footsteps?

“What do you mean?”

She picks up her tablet, resuming gnawing on her lip though this time I can tell it’s because there’s something she’s not saying.

“Look, I’m due at one of Shauna’s meetings tonight. You know she’d welcome you, so, do you wanna come?”

I blink, the change of topic taking me by surprise. Shauna and her friends have been holding these meetings for a while now, slowly but surely trying to find ways to bring change to our planet. They even organised a protest six months ago and it was only luck and good planning that left no-one dead or arrested when the police descended on them.

Cat had joined them shortly after, but I'd refused, too scared of the consequences. Only now I'm starting to see that the consequences of inaction might be even worse. Since meeting Jakoor there has been this terrible need to do something that has been consuming me from the inside.

"Just tell your parents I'm dragging you out to a movie and that Shauna will be there," she adds, smiling, something new dancing in her eyes.

Can I do this? Can I be more than this scared boy who shrinks away from the world at every chance? Maybe even someone like me can help make a difference, make things better.

Maybe it's time I became my own hero.

***

The apartment we head off to is in a part of town I don't usually frequent, away from the luxury houses of the elites and into a tightly packed residential area. Here, skyscrapers stretch up to dizzying heights, and the parks I'm so used to are fewer and smaller, though trees still line the streets, a break of green amongst the white and steel.

We're shown into an elegant living room, already filled with a half dozen girls lounging on an elegant selection of chairs and settees. I'm so keenly aware of not belonging, of being the stranger that I've half a mind to leave when the woman sitting on a high-backed armchair by the window stands to greet us.

She's in her mid-twenties, with a sharp jaw and light brown skin that makes me question how she manages to exude control and power in a place where people of her skin colour and gender are allowed none. She's striking in a turquoise pant suit, long black hair smooth as silk.

She's the most intimidating woman I have ever met.

I should not be here. I am not brave enough, or special enough, to belong amongst these people.

Cat grabs my hand, flashing me a smile, and I find strength in her presence.

"You must be Cat's friend," the woman greets me, extending a hand I stare at for a second before realising she wants me to shake it.

"Lilac, this is Tris," Cat introduces me and I could kiss her for using my nickname. "Tris, this is Lilac, she's…" Cat hesitates for a beat, and I wonder what she almost says. "She and Shauna run this together."

"Hi," is all I manage, accompanied by an awkward smile. I'm a walking disaster.

Luckily, Shauna chooses that moment to appear, beaming at the both of us. "Tris, I'm glad you could make it!" She says it as though it actually means something that I'm here and I'm too surprised to do more than smile in response. Yep, walking disaster.

Shauna and Cat could be nothing but sisters with their matching brown hair and clever eyes. Shauna's wearing a suit, clearly just back from the secretary job she took to get away from her parents' control. Most girls who work are waitresses or secretaries or any other job considered less skilled or important, and certainly not from wealthy families. It's one of the many things Shauna fights against, wanting more opportunity for her and her sister and all the other girls out there.

"What do you two want to drink?" Shauna asks as she wraps her sister in a big hug.

"Do you have some wine?" Cat asks, a glimmer in her eyes.

Shauna laughs. "Yes, but don't overdo it, okay? You want some too, Tris?"

Honestly, I probably could go in for a little liquid courage but knowing me I'd get drunk on three sips, and it would be a disaster.

"No, thanks, some water will be fine." I hate how my anxiety thins my voice.

As Lilac motions for us to take a seat a new girl walks in. She's around Shauna's age with bright red lips and a platinum bob.

"New blood!" she exclaims when she sees me, beaming. "Welcome to the Suffragettes 2.0!"

"Kaileigh, that is *not* what we are called!" Shauna protests as she returns with our drinks.

"Until we have an actual name, it totally *is*," the girl quips back, making the others laugh.

I crack a smile, wishing for all the world that I could be one of them, so brave in the face of everything.

"Anyone else coming?" Cat asks.

Shauna picks up her phone to check something before she answers. "We've got another three people due, but we can get started without them."

Cat and I settle on a small settee, as Shauna sits next to Lilac. I don't miss the way she takes the other woman's hand or the look they exchange. It's such a small gesture but to do this here, in front of so many, it seems momentous. Only no-one reacts. Because the people here aren't like my parents or so many on this world. They clearly don't care who you love.

“Tris, you okay?” Cat asks in a whisper, and I blink, startled at the tear that suddenly runs down my cheek.

“Yeah,” I whisper back, and suddenly all I want is to tell her everything.

But Shauna is talking now, announcing how they're working on hacking into the big screens that line the buildings all around New Hope Square. They intend to record a message and broadcast on a busy afternoon, and it sounds crazy and wonderful all at once.

I watch her and Lilac talking about their plans with awe, barely able to look away even when a couple comes sheepishly in, the boy's presence strangely reassuring.

Another knock comes a bit later, as Shauna is reading out the draft of the message they want to send, and one of the girls slips away to let in the latecomer. I don't turn to look, entranced by the way Shauna talks about a world where equality isn't just a dream, but a reality.

She pauses as the newcomer walks in.

"Sorry I'm late, my father needed me to finish some things at the office," he says, and I would know that voice anywhere, even if I wish I didn't.

I've never wanted the ground to swallow me more as when I slowly turn around and Nathaniel Pense's eyes land on me.

CHAPTER 18
MALEK

BAKULA

By the time I make it back to bay 105, I'm hyper on a stim patch, and everyone is waiting for me.

"Well, that's better than I expected," I say as I walk in, noticing everyone's new outfits as I toss a bag of candy bars at Alta. "Where did you find all that?"

"I figured if I was gonna use my credits to get us something to wear, I wasn't buying cheap shit—" Nephanie starts.

"Despite me saying second hand would be *fine*," Nooma interjects.

"So, we looked for a printing shop and found one that had decent prices. We had to guestimate people's sizes, but I dare say we didn't do so badly," she adds, eyes flashing red.

"Shit, that must have cost a fortune." I'm shocked she'd be willing to spend that much on us. Printing clothes might be common, but *new* clothes aren't cheap when there are so many second-hand shops around.

"It did," Nooma deadpans.

"It's fine," Nephanie insists.

I want to ask her why she'd so easily spend that much on us, but I'm not about to look a gift-ship in the engine. Speaking of which…

"So, did you get us a ship?" Nooma asks, straight to business.

"Yes, and a job, but I want *my* clothes first. What d'you get me?"

Nephanie glances at Nooma. "We were supposed to get him something?"

I tense at her words, an inexplicable anger suddenly clouding everything. The stim patch was not a good idea, was it?

Nooma shrugs. "Oh, were we? I thought you'd said to get *ourselves* some clothes?"

My chest feels tight. Their words are in sharp contrast with their light tones and part of me knows they're just messing around. But the anger has surged, and I can barely contain my desire to yell.

"Nooma…" I grind out.

"Your clothes are here."

I jump as Akim appears next to me, holding something out.

The anger lessens somewhat as I take the clothes from him.

He turns to the girls, shaking his head. "I told you he wouldn't find it funny. I wouldn't find it funny either."

Nooma shoots me what I think is supposed to be an apologetic look, but I'm too mad and stomp off into the cockpit.

***

On Helios, the world was a grey nothing, my feelings numbed out. Now, everything has been turned up to eleven and I don't know whether I want to punch something or burst into tears. I know Nooma and Nephanie meant no harm, I know it was a joke, but the anger won't leave me. Even though I only believed them for a second, it was enough to kindle this.

I don't know how not to be angry.

I haven't been calm since I woke up with this fire in my soul and I don't know what the opposite of anger is now.

I need amma so badly. I want to hear her say that this is normal and it's okay. That there are things to help. That I'm not wrong or faulty for how my emotions seem to be set at three hundred percent.

I've never felt so much like *me* and at the same time I've never felt so broken. I catch my reflection in the ship's window: lanky, dirty, hair—when did I last wash it? —and a messy stubble. My brown skin is faded by the reflection, as though I'm but a ghost of myself. A ghost with fire in his eyes, striking in my gaunt face.

As I strip the overalls off, I notice how my ribs have started showing under my skin. It's not disastrous yet, but I'm definitely too thin. Growing up in prison for two years with your mental health in the dumps sure makes you miss how your body is changing.

I stare at myself in the bad reflection, stare at what I've become.

Dirty. Thin. Scarred.

I look down at my mangled prosthetic hand, and my wonky knee, and take in a deep breath. Then I look back at my reflection, at this boy who looks like he's about to fall apart. Apart from in his eyes. Bright and full of life, even if they too are prosthetics.

Alive.

I am alive.

I say it out loud, my voice soft. Then louder. I claim it. I stare into my own eyes and own it.

Somewhere along the line the anger simmered down. It's not gone, but I'm not about to yell anymore. Instead, the fire has turned back into what carried me through the last day.

I'm not letting it go, no matter what happens.

***

"So, what's the ship like?" Alta asks, almost too cheerily, as I join my friends.

I don't think I have a calm setting anymore, but I'm learning to embrace it. And now clad in a dark t-shirt, pants, and a pair of sturdy boots I feel more together.

After all, you can *never* beat a good pair of boots.

"It's old and it's gonna take some bringing back to life. But Tulain's gonna pay for the repairs," I say, enthusiastically tearing into the candy bar Alta tosses me.

I haven't had one of these in so long I could cry.

"You serious?" they ask, eyes alive with excitement. "Are you telling me I get to work on fixing up an old ship and *someone else* is going to pay for all the parts?"

I flash them a grin. "That's exactly what I'm saying!"

Alta cheers, punching the air, and like that what was left of the anger turns to a burning, impossible enthusiasm.

"This is the best!" they exclaim, and I've never seen them so animated.

"What about that job?" Nooma asks.

I purposefully don't turn to her. Really, I want to ignore her, so she'll know just how mad I am. Or was.

"It's pretty standard actually, nothing too dangerous."

"How *illegal* is it?" she asks.

Maybe I'm still a little mad.

"Nooma, this is an *outlaw* colony, technically *nothing* is legal here."

I see the emotions crossing her face. I know her story enough to know what she's afraid of, but I really want to snap at her still. Does she really think I would behave like the people who hurt her in the past?

"Bakula doesn't allow slave trade. If a crew partakes in that kind of business, they won't ever find an open dock here. It's one of the only rules ever enforced," I say, my voice a little sharper than intended.

I get that she thinks legality gives her an easy set of rules to follow to avoid trouble, but we all know the world isn't fair enough for that to be the case.

"Fine, what does he want from us?"

I take a long drink of bottled water and the clean taste is a relief after the vitamin-infused stuff we were given on Helios.

"He needs us to retrieve something that was stolen from him."

"Can't he get it back himself?" Akim asks.

"Well, he could *try*, but no-one is gonna let him get close to where the chip is kept. The guy who took it from him has a lot of friends."

Vess has always been the more charismatic of the two, with his Shinarian good looks and his Human charm.

Nephanie lights a smokeless cigarette that brings on a pang of grief. Many members of amma's crew used to have these.

"What kind of chip is it?" she asks.

"An AI chip. Technically on Bakula they have the same rights as organics *but* it's not active so it's a grey area. And given Bador'kerh is in charge right now, Tulain really can't turn to the authorities. Dpanir aren't known for their great love of non-organics," I add.

"A Dpanir?" Alta asks, looking a little bit terrified.

"Yeah, but they're really not all that bad. I mean, they hate synths, but they're hardly the only species like that. Amma worked with Bador'kerh on a couple of jobs and, sure, they're intimidating as hell, but that's mostly bravado. Trust me, okay?"

Alta lets out a breath. "I'm sorry, I just... We have a lot of Dpanir pirates where I'm from, and you hear all sorts of awful stories about them. And now, well I'm in a place where there actually *are* Dpanir pirates and I..." They gesture vaguely, and I offer them a smile.

"I get it. None of you know what this is like. But I was raised with these people. You see outlaws as the villains but, truth is, they aren't the ones that put us on Helios. And yeah, sure, there are some people who are nasty pieces of work, like the people who screwed over Nooma, but they're not in the majority. Most of the people here just want to live their lives in peace."

I look at my friends, all so new and hesitant in the face of this. Akim rubs the end of his sleeve between thumb and forefinger; Alta looks a million lightyears away; Nooma's eyes are fixed on me, an unreadable expression on her face.

Nephanie finishes her cigarette and clears her throat. "Being part of an outlaw crew doesn't sound so bad. I mean, we broke out of jail, so we're outlaws anyway. I need to keep moving, and I imagine we all have huge bounties on our heads now. Berik Corp isn't going to let a bunch of prisoners escape and not show that there are dire consequences to that. So, you can all act as though working with Dpanir or whatever species and professions you don't like is a big deal, but the truth of it is, you don't have much choice." She reminds me of how amma could command attention. I hope I can live up to that part of her legacy too. "I don't know any of you like you know each other, but you must have trusted Malek to follow him into this crazy escape. So, what's changed now? Does being free make you think you can go back to what you had before? Because you can't. You try and they'll pluck you right out of your homes."

I didn't expect Nephanie to take the words out of my mouth—and make them better—but it's pretty awesome.

"I'm sorry," Nooma sighs. "It's hard to… to realise that this is the only choice I have. Not that I have anything to go back to, or that I had plans before but," she shrugs. "I still had choice."

"You still do," I meet her gaze, hold it. "There's always a choice. Sometimes it's a path we can't see yet, sometimes it's just choosing what to make from what we are given. Sometimes it's just choosing how to react. But there's always some kind of choice."

"That's surprisingly wise and deep, coming from you," Alta says and I gasp in mock offence. "But you're right. I can sit here and wallow in the fact that I can't go home, or I can pull myself together and make the best out of this." Their smile is bright enough to light up worlds. "And well, I know which one I'd rather do. None of the people on the *Junya* deserved what happened, and I spent too long wallowing on Helios because I didn't believe there was an after. But this is it, this is the after. And if I ever want to get justice for my old crew, I'd better make this count!"

My smile mirrors theirs. My crew is coming together. I glance at Akim, his eyes skimming my face.

"I'm in as long as all I have to do is pilot. I don't like to handle people I don't know, and I refuse to be blamed for how they can't handle me. And I want a pet."

I blink. "You what?"

"I want a pet. I had a pet back home and it made things better. Not a robotic one either, I want a *real* pet."

I blink again and Alta bursts out laughing, though I'm not sure whether at the request or my reaction. Whatever tension was left dissolves; I even catch Nooma failing to suppress a grin. Nephanie's eyes have gone pale pink, and everything feels lighter.

"Okay, a pet. Sure, we can see about that. We'll need to see what our new ship is like first, though, okay?"

"That sounds reasonable. But I know a lot about ships, so I'll know if you're trying to bullshit me," he says with a completely straight face.

I want to jokingly say something about not talking to his captain like this, but this *is* Akim, and this *is* the way he is, and my joke would probably upset him.

"So, you guys wanna hear about this job?"

"With food," Alta says, pushing to their feet

I laugh, my stomach rumbling in agreement.

"Okay, food and business talk it is. Tulain gave me an advance, so it's on me," I add. "And after that, I say we go check our new ship!"

There is a general cheer and then Akim questioning whether this counts as lunch or dinner, or if we've skipped right round to breakfast.

As we leave bay 105, I'm giddy and overexcited—like a puppy according to Alta. Amma would be proud of me. Of this crew of misfits I'm starting my new life with.

***

We find a Human-run place with food Akim okays; and settle into a booth: Nooma and Akim on one side; me, Alta, and Nephanie crammed on the other. The place is tiny, lit with white ceiling strips accented by multicoloured string lights dangling from the walls amongst a myriad of ad screens and memorabilia from several Thoolat races.

I was very young when we docked on Grull during race season, but I still remember how impossible the maneuvers the pilots pulled looked. I bet Akim would be a match for them.

Sitting around the table, trying to agree on what to order, whether we're sharing dishes, or all getting separates, it feels as though we've done this a million times before.

We're not yet famous enough that people are turning to look, but I'm sure one day that'll be the case.

Maybe one day we'll be the ones running Bakula. I almost laugh at the idea, excited just to be alive.

Nooma talks me down from ordering synth-alcohol, insisting none of us are in good enough health to be drinking. I pout at her for a good ten seconds. She does not relent. I capitulate because I'm too distracted. We're sharing a selection of dishes, save for Akim who is getting his own stuff.

It's strange to finally let ourselves relax. The worst is behind us. In this small, cheap restaurant, surrounded by everything we thought we'd lost forever, we can reclaim our lives.

"Malek?" Alta touches my arm softly.

I wipe the tear I didn't realise had escaped quickly, glad only they saw. Nephanie and Nooma are arguing over dipping sauces and aren't paying us attention.

"I'm okay. Everything just *feels* so much more now. We're here and we're free and... I think some part of me never believed we could pull it off."

"It was *your* idea," they elbow me playfully.

Alta, who had been so quiet and reserved on Helios. Alta, who now smiles as though it is the only shape their mouth knows. So many emotions well inside me and I don't have the words for any of them. I don't know that I ever did. I understand now what amma meant when she said she was too much for her body, for the world.

"Well, I couldn't imagine dying there, in that hell of a prison but..." I shake my head. "Until this it didn't really feel possible."

They smile at me, and again the way it lights their green eyes startles me. "I'm glad you thought we could do it, I'd never have gotten out of there alone." Their eyes take a distant look. "I... It feels like I was there for so long that I… I'm not sure how to be me anymore." I catch them glancing at the others around the table. Nephanie looks unscathed but she's not Human and it's hard to read the flitting colours of her eyes. Nooma is making space on the table for our food, Akim quietly reorganising the condiment bottles. I wonder where their pain is hiding itself. I wonder where my own is.

But I don't want to think about that right now, I just want to be alive.

"We'll be fine," I tell Alta. Their green eyes shine, vivid with life and relief. "I promise," I add, taking their hand and giving it a squeeze. I almost want there to be a spark as skin touches skin, but they just smile back at me.

"Thanks."

I'm about to add something when our food is brought. I hadn't realised how much I missed being around people. Sure, there were people around on Helios, but it wasn't the same. It wasn't warmth and life, and the relaxed intimacy of sharing a meal.

I watch the food being passed around and for a horrible second, nothing feels quite real.

But then Alta is squeezing my hand back and Nooma is pouring me a drink. I cast away the fears, abandon the doubts.

"A toast!" I declare, raising my drink. "To freedom!"

"To freedom!" my friends echo.

"And to being a crew," Nooma adds.

"I'll drink to that!"

Our glasses clink, a crescendo of discordant music. Nephanie joins in, and if she thinks Human customs are weird, she doesn't say anything. Her eyes are that striking deep teal again. Even Akim humours us.

When we've all eaten enough to slow down, Nooma prompts me to explain the job in detail. I do, and as more food is eaten and ordered, we plan and talk, talk and plan, and I don't know that I've ever been happier.

CHAPTER 19
LÀHN

KIRILLION

I'm wanted for murder.

That's the bombshell Zoon drops on us when we make contact. The Hell Suns' crime is being blamed on me, a capture of security footage circulating the city. With our only ally on the police force currently on life support—thank the Stars she's not dead—we have no-one to help us.

I'm a wanted man.

I'm too numb to be relieved at seeing Zoon alive and, if not well, at least on the mend. I'm dazed, unable to process what this means. What I knew it meant even before Zoon said it.

I need to leave.

With my face so clearly captured, my only other option is to change my face completely, to become someone else. But as Zoon points out, there are still risks in staying and when he has a half-brother on a far-off station, it's safer for me to go there.

I can't work out if the worst is that I'm wanted for murder or that Shi'lu'Fan is dead. I can still feel how alive he'd been under me; how warm his hands had been on my hips. No matter who he was or what he had done, no life should have to end so abruptly.

I wish I could just bury myself in sleep and wake to find this was a nightmare. Only my nightmares are never this clear.

“I'm sorry I jeopardised the Guild,” I manage after a long moment.

Zoon tilts his head in his equivalent of a sigh.

"I'm the one who's sorry, Làhn. I never should have sent you on that job."

"You couldn't know."

Another sigh. "Maybe not, but Leela had warned me this was a hot mess. I shouldn't have put you in so much danger."

I want to make some remark like ‘danger is my middle name’ or whatever the heroes of the games and movies Kode and I love would say, but I'm not the guy who welcomes adventure and danger with open arms.

I was happy just living my life, thieving here and there, and spending my time exploring this incredible city, flirting with guys, or hanging out with Kode. But that's over. A line firmly drawn in the timeline of my life, matching the one that marks my arrival here, the one before which I recall so little.

What am I supposed to do? Kode signs as Zoon sends over the details for the flight I'm to take.

Only a few hours before I'm to say goodbye to Kirillion. To my family.

You're safe, Zoon signs back. *You can stay here. We'll find a new HQ and reconvene soon.*

I can see how torn she is as she glances from me to Zoon and then to the kitchen where Shuobe and her mother are cooking. She lifts her hands and then lets them fall down again.

This wasn't how our story was supposed to go.

I'm sorry, I sign. She slaps my hands down with a scowl.

"I'm sorry, kids," Zoon sighs. "I'll send Ashya to pick you up, Làhn. I wish I could see you before but... I can't really move from here."

I wish I could see him too.

"Do you still have the chip?"

"Yeah."

"Give it to Ashya when they come pick you up and we'll take it from there."

"Sure, I will."

I can't tell if being rid of the damned thing will be a blessing or a curse.

Ashya appears on screen, speaking softly to Zoon. He grumbles but he's obviously too tired to argue.

"I need to go, kids."

I swallow hard. This feels more like a farewell than a goodbye.

"I'll come back," I say, stifling a sob.

"No doubt you will, kid," his rumbling voice is a comfort I wish I could bottle and take with me. "My brother will look after you. It'll be fine. We'll get these fuckers off your tail and then you can come right home."

"Yeah."

"Su'lhua noe llitirkiki lhazo demitlleka," he says.

The Furakian saying doesn't translate to anything concise. It's a declaration of platonic love, as well as a wish to meet again, and something about hoping the suns of a thousand worlds watch over the person you are saying it to.

Kode repeats it phonetically and I stammer haltingly through the words. Zoon gives us one last smile and then the connection cuts.

I lean back against the sofa, staring up at the ceiling, startled when Kode flops on me. I run my fingers through her hair for a few minutes, neither of us moving. We both know this might be the last time we get to do this. I don’t want it to be a farewell, not with her, but what choice is there? I wish she could come with me, my hand held out, pulling her with me on this new path. But I can't ask that of her. This is her home too, and she has Shuobe.

I glance down at the tattoo on my wrist, at the curving letters. Coordinates and a simple phrase: *come home*.

If I'm going to leave one home behind, maybe it's time I start thinking about the other. The original.

In the kitchen Shuobe and her mother laugh. Did I have a mother I could have laughed with? Do I still have a family waiting for me?

Come home.

I was seven years old when I got to Kirillion and my memories of before are of crowded ships, and a woman whose face has long since faded.

Come home.

But to who, to where?

I'm about to tap Kode's shoulder to get her attention when the front door is blown off its hinges.

***

Everything happens at once: the blast, Nyurae rushing in, Kode and I leaping to our feet. I grab our bags, both blessedly still resting by the sofa, and then Nyurae bundles us out of the kitchen window and onto the fire escape stairs.

"Quickly!" Shuobe yells.

My heart is hammering as I all but throw myself down the stairs, hands gripping the railings so hard my knuckles turn white.

I should have let Deeno teach me parkour.

Footsteps behind me and I push myself to go faster. They're going to kill us. My bag slips off my shoulder and I almost lose balance, bashing hard against the railing.

So many floors.

I'm dizzy with the spiral of the stairs. I can't breathe enough yet fear keeps me going.

"Left at the bottom!" Nyurae calls.

My feet hit the ground and I turn left, risking a glance over my shoulder. Nyurae is right behind me, Shuobe carrying Kode, her powerful arms cradling her close. Several floors above, the mercs have blown open whatever seal Nyurae had placed on the window.

"RUN!" Shuobe's cry is a roar as she takes off down the street.

The Mallak have powerful legs made for running. There's no way I can keep up. The Hell Suns shout at us to freeze. I scream half in terror, half in despair, as lasers hit all around us, leaving seared marks on the street. Thankfully they're not shooting to kill, yet.

Nyurae scoops me into her arms, bounding down the street so fast my vision blurs even as she activates a shield around us. Seconds later we burst into the crowd of the main street.

By the time we've stopped I've lost any sense of where we are. Shuobe and her mother are hardly out of breath whilst I feel like I could faint.

"I need to speak to Zoon," I gasp.

"No time for that," Nyurae shakes her head. "We're going to the Fleet. Only place you'll be safe. They must have some way to track you: cameras or coms lines or *something,* but you can't risk staying somewhere that isn't technically off planet." Shuobe opens her mouth, but her mother interrupts her. "No, you're coming too. We're all in danger from these people now. "

I should never have come, I'm sorry, Kode signs.

No, this isn't your fault.

I look away from them, back at Nyurae quickly typing something into her wrist computer. "I'm sorry. We endangered you and Shuobe... I don't want them to cause trouble for the Fleet. You should take Kode with you and I'll find somewhere to hide until I can contact Zoon."

"Don’t be stupid," she says, expression serious, pupils narrow in her startlingly violet eyes. "Getting yourself killed isn’t going to help anyone. Least of all you."

Kode looks so scared and worried. It’s all my fault. Ever since the club, everything I touch breaks.

"My friends should be here any minute," Nyurae adds.

I’m hyper vigilant as we wait, every shift of the crowd, every unexpected noise making me jump.

At last, a small Mallak transport lands nearby. We get in without a word and I collapse against the seat as it takes off.

CHAPTER 20
TRYSTAN

EDEN ONE

There's something surreal about sitting here, watching the exchange of ideas that could bring about so much change. The way they all speak so easily, plan and bounce possibilities around is almost dizzying. For a little while, I become lost in their dream. Their talk of acceptance.

I wish I could reveal myself, break down the wall I built to keep myself safe. But there is so much at risk, and in a world that detests people like me so much that we've been erased from history, I daren't take that step.

As the meeting devolves to casual chatter, I become all too aware of the time and, despite both Shauna and Lilac saying they can cover for me, I bid my goodbyes to the group, doing my best—as I did the rest of the night—to not look at Nathaniel.

But it's his voice that stops me at the door. My stomach lurches and I take a deep breath before turning around.

"Nathaniel," I say blandly.

"What's up?"

"Nothing. Just a bit tired, it's been a bad week for migraines," I give a girlish smile, something I've practiced in mirrors as much as strengthening my jaw, but a million times more fake. "I really should be headed home."

"You okay?"

Why does he even care?

"Yes, I..." Words desert me. "My parents think I've gone to see a movie. I can't be gone too late."

He chuckles and for a moment all I see is the boy I spent countless hours playing with.

"You need an excuse that gives you more manoeuvrability. We usually cover for each other," he says, smiling. "So next time we'll cook something up for you."

We. Next time.

"Why are you even here? I thought you were on your father's side," I snap, the accusation slipping out.

He looks wounded, ashamed.

I'm such an ass.

"I have to keep up appearances, otherwise I couldn't help here. I need to get a foot in the door before I can start making changes. It's trying, but if it puts me where I need to be, then so be it. Some days doing nothing kills me, but I have to play the long game."

I don't know what to say, instead staring at him with the words *see me, see me, see me,* going through my head.

"They want us to marry," I blurt out. His eyes go wide.

"So, it's official now, not just a notion?"

"I think so. I heard my dad talking the other night... " Relief floods me when I realise, he doesn't look any happier about this than I am.

"I'm sorry..." he whispers. "My father hasn't said anything yet but... He's been busy. I... I didn't know."

"I'm not supposed to know either."

"Do you... Do you want to talk about it?" he asks.

"No, I... I really need to go. I'm sorry I blurted this on you. I shouldn't have."

I turn to leave, and he gently takes my wrist. It's so unlike how my father grabs for my mother that it makes me wish I was just a girl who could fall in love with the boy she was supposed to marry, like in the corny movies Cat loves to watch.

"I can take you home, it'll give you an excuse for being late."

I should say no. I can't have someone else close who doesn't see me for who I am.

"Sure."

"Great, let me grab my jacket."

***

Nathaniel is still the boy I remember, making me laugh to the point of tears as he imitates the stuffy men both our fathers often entertain. It makes me miss what we had in childhood, his company so easy to keep as we talk about everything and nothing, complaining about terrible vid-shows before he admits in a whisper that he's downloaded some off-world music he thinks I might like.

For a little while we remember that we were friends.

That maybe we still are.

When we begin the descent towards my parents' estate, I fall silent, eyes lost out of the window. Nathaniel rests a hand on mine, not an intimate touch, just an offer of comfort.

"I know things got really awkward in the last few years, what with the games I've got to play and how they all got around us but... If you ever need to talk, you don't just have Cat, you know that, right?"

There's a lump in my throat. I feel that growing need to scream who I am before terror shuts it down. As the car comes to a stop, I face him: his green eyes are intense on me, his dark hair hardly long enough to run fingers through. Perhaps that too is a concession to the games he plays. I wonder how much of what we all do here is only for survival.

I've never really considered that someone like Nathaniel might be trapped too. Not until now.

"Let me walk you to the door," he says, slipping out of the car.

I take in a deep breath against the dread of coming home and push the door open, hitting Nathaniel who's come to open it for me. Despite—or maybe because of—my nerves, I burst out laughing especially as he plays it up.

Things should have been so easy in between us. Marriage might even have been good. But what I am jeopardises both our chances at happiness.

"I'm so sorry," I say as my laughter subsides.

"Dangers of being gallant, I suppose."

I don't want to end this spell. But the sun has set, and the fake stars are alive above us. I am so very late.

Nathaniel extends a hand to me. The spell is fraying, and I wonder what he would be like if he knew the truth of me.

I take his hand, envying the shape of his fingers, letting him lead me to the front door.

"I can tell you're not happy here," he says as we stop in front of the porch steps.

"What are you talking about? I'm fine." I plaster on a smile.

His expression turns sad. "I'm not happy either. But maybe... What we're working on, maybe we can make things better you know? I mean, I know there's not much concrete right now but... We'll find a way out of this mess."

I offer a soft smile back.

"Thank you," I whisper as I slip my hand out of his and hurry to the door.

"Tris?"

I turn around. "What?"

"Look after yourself, okay?"

Before I can ask why he's so concerned, he's turned away. He's slender in his casual clothes. Softer too, somehow. Like the friend I remember. Like the boy I was forced to grow distant from. Before my feelings can get tangled up, I slip inside the house.

***

The entrance hall is dark, the house quiet. Dinner should already be underway: father hates to eat late.

"Mom?"

I half want to run back out and hope Nathaniel isn't gone but I push onward to the living room. The vase from the coffee table lays smashed on the floor, the flowers scattered like so many crushed dreams. Meanwhile a glass waits, forgotten by the open drinks' cabinet, full of melted ice and my father's temper.

"Mom?"

I'm running to their bedroom, terrified of what he might have done to my mother. He always storms out after these episodes, and I'm bolstered by his absence. I find her crying, curled on the bed, facing away from me. It fuels the hatred I hold for him. For all my mother is far from perfect she doesn't deserve to be treated this way. No-one does.

I want to protect her.

When did *she* last protect me?

Does it even matter?

The bedroom is suffocating with its looming furniture and dark walls. The bed is huge, heavy curtains pulled back and tied to the posts feeling like it wants to swallow me as I sit on the edge, reaching for my mother.

"Mom?"

She startles, sitting up and quickly wiping her eyes. She looks exhausted, the dim light of the room doing her no favours.

"Oh, sweetie, you're back."

She hasn't realised I'm late.

"Mom, what happened?"

"Oh, it's nothing, sweetie," she puts her hand on my cheek, as though *she* needs to comfort *me*. "I'm just feeling a little out of it, is all."

"Where's father?"

"At work," she tries to look like everything is fine, but I see straight through it. "He said he had important work to do with Gideon."

"He didn't come home?"

"Just popped by," she gives me a fake smile that breaks my heart. It looks so much like my own. "You know how he is, always so busy."

What did they even argue about?

"Mom... Why is the living room a mess?"

She looks away from me and I hate those secrets that aren't really secrets. You can't pretend the truth isn't there when you leave it shattered on the rug for all to find. This won't be my future with Nathaniel, but what about Cat? What about all the girls I met today?

I'm done doing nothing but I'm so afraid of what could happen if I take a stand.

"I was so horribly clumsy earlier, I told you I'm not feeling so well," again that smile that doesn't reach her eyes. "I ended up tripping and knocking things over. I can get the maid to clear it up, it's no big deal."

So much injustice hidden behind fake smiles. So much pain hidden behind lies.

Eden, they called this planet, but I figure Hell would have been a better name. A place that *looks* perfect but crushes you, tortures your soul until you fit the mould crafted for you. I'm sixteen, and I've felt that crushing pressure my whole life. It broke my mother, whilst men like my father become tyrants, handed so much power when they deserve none of it.

"Can I get you anything?" I ask, desperate to offer her some comfort.

"No, no, I'm fine." Her eyes are elsewhere, sometimes I wonder if it's else*when,* to a time when she wasn't married. "You just look after yourself tonight, sweetie, is that okay?"

I almost laugh. When *don't* I look after myself?

I escape back into the corridor, unable to deal with her acting as though this is nothing.

This damn planet ruins everything.

I throw myself on my bed and out of my body, surprised to find the connection to my android. In a blink I'm lying on my uncle's worktable, immediately able to tell how much smoother everything feels. Controlling both bodies at the same time is so much easier now.

Time to be the hero I need.

CHAPTER 21
TRYSTAN

EDEN ONE

I'm filled with purpose, heading straight for the observation bay where I expect my father and uncle to be. I can't exactly barge in there, but I need to find out what they're up to.

It would be a lie to say I'm not scared, but my anger has burnt itself into a calm, collected determination that pushes me through the barriers my fear has been trapping me behind for my whole life.

I make it to the observation bay without incident, surprised that inside seems silent. I brace myself, pushing the door panel as I stand to the side, the door sliding open to reveal an empty, dark room, lit only by whatever is happening below.

I'm surprised my father is getting his hands dirty, though given how he's wandering around the table on which Jakoor is tied, blood slowly drained from them, dirty is a bit of an exaggeration.

I should have stopped this.

I crouch low in the observation bay, peeking above the controls, finding a way to turn the speakers on so I can eavesdrop. My uncle fusses over readings on his terminal, face gaunt, hair dishevelled.

"I think that's all the blood I can take tonight. They've been refusing to eat so they're getting weaker," he says. I wonder if it's just my imagination that places concern in his voice.

"Let's try and not kill this one, it took an age for them to send it, I don't want to have to wait for another specimen," my father replies, his tone so cold it chills me.

It. A thing. I'm not even surprised that's how he'd see an alien. To him, everyone is a pawn on his chessboard.

"Do you know," my father starts in that way he has when he's enjoying the sound of his own voice, "they were supposed to have been wiped out but instead they mutated to survive the virus. I think that's the only good thing about them, that they became so...resilient."

My uncle grunts in reply.

"If this works," my father's smile is predatory, "we're going to be very famous, and powerful."

"You will be," my uncle says quietly. "Once I've got you what you want, I'm done with this."

"Come now, Gideon, if you pull this research off you will be a very rich man, and a hero to the Human race!"

"Some hero I'd be..."

Watching my uncle so firmly under my father's thumb makes my blood boil, but I suddenly get hit with why he's in that position. Accused of betrayal after the war with Ishnira some twenty years ago, Gideon was only even allowed to return and work on Eden One because his sister's husband vouched for him.

And my father could take that away from him any time. I feel so stupid for not having realised that sooner.

"It should be enough for me to run some more tests," my uncle says, plucking the vials of blood from the machine as it powers down.

"Good, let me know if you can actually make it work this time," my father snaps.

My uncle pales and I see myself in him, controlled by a man we're afraid of.

"I have to run tests before trialling it on the prisoners."

"Don't waste time, Gideon. They've given us a deadline and we need to start testing it on people. You shouldn't care if they die anyway, they're easy to replace."

My uncle stiffens, stooping over his computer as though he can escape my father this way.

"Give me a call when you get some results, I have other matters to see to," my father adds before striding out.

I don't think I've ever hated him so much in my life.

Instead of staying put, I'm too angry to think and I rush to the nearest stairs. I almost want to bump into him, to show him that in this body I never need to be afraid of him again.

But the second I hear his voice something inside of me crumples, my flesh and bone body going numb as a pang of anxiety hits me. Just the sound of him, cold and irritated on the phone, is enough to turn me into a wreck, forcing me to hide inside a nearby server room.

Back on my bed, my chest is so tight I can barely breathe. I try to focus on the room painted in shades of grey by my night vision, pinpoints of light framing the servers and terminals that fill the space.

My father's voice fades down the corridor, but it takes me a good five minutes before I can move again.

If only I was braver.

I all but run to the testing bay, trying to take comfort in how powerful this body feels. When I get there, I open the door without waiting before I lose my courage, eyes snapping straight to Jakoor whose skin looks so wan that for a horrible moment I think they might be dead.

"What are you doing?"

My uncle whirls around, startled by my voice.

"Trystan?" He looks exhausted, eyes rimmed in red.

"What are you doing?" I repeat, voice calmer than I am.

"Trystan you shouldn't be here, I hadn't greenlit you yet."

"It's fine." I don't mean to be this curt.

"Tryst—"

"Answer my question!" My raised voice echoes in my ears, suddenly sounding so much like my father's that I feel sick.

"We're just running some tests, that's all, nothing you need to worry yourself about."

"How many have you killed?"

I don't think I have ever seen my uncle so taken off guard.

"What are you talking about?"

"I heard you two talking," I spit the words out. But my anger is tempered by tears he can't see. "I heard what you said about the alien being a specimen, about testing whatever you are doing on people. What *is* going on here?"

His face shutters and I clench my jaw.

"This is none of your business, Tryst. You wouldn't understand anyway."

He steps towards me, but I step away before he can reach out a hand.

"Then *explain*."

"It's complicated," he starts. "But it is important work and—"

"Is that why you want no part of it when it's done? How can it be 'important' if you want to walk away from it as soon as possible?"

"Tryst, it's not like that. It's just that... I'm not interested in fame..."

"Is that really it? Or is it because you know how *wrong* this is?"

He reels, hurt dancing in his eyes. Once, I would have felt terrible, but with Jakoor still strapped down I can't bring myself to.

"Sometimes we have to do things that seem wrong for the good of the world. Of Humanity," he says but he's not looking at me.

"Who are the people you're testing on?" I feel the sneer painted on my lips even as I speak.

"They're criminals. Sent to us from high security prisons. Really not the kind of people you should worry about."

"Oh, no? What about if they come from places like *here.*" I'm startled by the strength in my words. If only I could muster this conviction in front of my father. "*I* would be a criminal here, for wanting this body, for wanting to be myself. Have you thought about that?"

"Tryst! Enough. These people are criminals and that's the end of it."

Is his own guilt blinding him? Or has he convinced himself of the truth of his words?

"You told me something one day," my voice softens. "You told me that all it takes for evil to triumph is for good men to do nothing. I thought you were one of the good men who would *do* something. You did during the war, didn't you? I thought if anyone had the courage to stand up to this place it was *you*."

The sadness in his eyes is so deep I think I might drown in it.

"Sometimes we don't get a choice," he says softly.

"There is *always* a choice."

"There wasn't."

I don't know what to say. I know it's foolish to believe there is always a choice. But I have to believe there can be, because otherwise what hope do I have left?

I push past him, to Jakoor, brushing their hair away from where it tangled on their horns. Their hair that feels like thin feathers, soft and impossibly light, their horn a cross in between the hard scales I expected and carved wood. Their face is bruised almost as badly as their arms, and I want to weep in horror at what I couldn't prevent.

"Do you even know their name?"

No answer. I want to tell him that I do, that their name is Jakoor and they're a person just like him and me.

"Trystan, please listen to me," he starts, and I refuse to look at him. "I'm doing this for you." I freeze, horror blossoming amidst the anger. "If I didn't do this, your father would have shut down the lab. And then I wouldn't be able to maintain the android."

"You should have talked to me," I breathe. I can't imagine losing this body, but if Jakoor's life is the cost—if the cost is more innocents' lives—is it really worth it? I will not become the selfish monster all the men around me seem to be. "I'm fine now. You can tell father that you quit, that you want nothing to do with this."

I can see on his face he won't.

"I can't, Trystan," he says after a beat of silence. "If I pull away from this project, everything I have spent the last years building will go up in flames. I have to see this through to the end."

"What if it was me you had to test this on? Would you stop then?"

"Trystan, what are you talking about?"

"How do you know there isn't someone whose only crime is the same as mine in that lot of test subjects you have? How would you feel if an alien race kidnapped me to run experiments on me? Did you even stop to think that they could have family?"

"Trystan, I..." He passes a hand through his hair. "I promise you that the people we are sent are true criminals." If only I could believe that. "As for the Kundar they're... Look, as far as I know they don't have families like we do. It's not the same for them."

"So what?" I snap, and I wish he could see the tears in my eyes, but this body can't cry, can't show how deeply I'm hurt by all this.

“They’re still people, they’re still *alive*! Just because they’re different it doesn’t mean they’re lesser!”

“That’s not what I said!”

“Bullshit! It’s what you implied! It’s the same as when our ancestors saw people with darker skin as lesser. Shit, we *still do,* because god forbid this bloody colony ever learns from the past instead of looking at it through rose tinted glasses!" I’m yelling, my temper flying out of control and my uncle just looks startled. At least I don’t sound like my father anymore.

"How—"

"Because I read! Because I stick my nose where it doesn't belong! And thank god I *do* because I can't trust *anyone* on this planet to ever speak the damned truth!"

I need him to say something but all he does is shake his head sadly, as though he expected me to be easily swayed.

"I'm going."

As I pass him, he tries to grab me. But I’m faster than him by far and bolt away, down the corridor and up the stairs until I find a side door and emerge into the night. I run towards the city, its lights like a beacon in the darkness. I run to a place I hate and crave in equal measures.

PART 3

UNITY

If you want to go quickly, go alone. If you want to go far, go together.
African proverb

CHAPTER 22
MALEK

BAKULA

Bay 63 is dusty, but I've eyes only for the ship. It's old and battered, in desperate need of work. But it's a good size, more than big enough for a crew our size.

It's not pretty, nothing like amma's ship was, but it's *ours*. Tulain hadn't lied when he called it a rust bucket; even its name has long since faded. But its potential is plain to see.

"Oh shit, but that needs *so. much. work*," Alta mutters.

"It needs less work than the one we were scrapping earlier," Akim points out.

"That's not bloody difficult," Alta replies, shaking their head. "We blew half the thrusters and damaged the hull and—"

I stop listening, limping to the ramp, sending the codes Tulain gave me to the on-board computer. I'm afraid that might be dead, but after a beat, the ramp lowers. I'm jittery, chewing on my lip as the ramp finishes opening, the lights flickering on. Those that still have working strips, anyway

"Let's take a look, shall we?"

The cargo bay is pretty decent, and as I run my hand along the walls, I find the secret panels I was looking for.

"What are you doing?" Nooma asks as I pry a section of the wall open.

"Uncovering our baby's secrets!" I declare, grinning, revealing more storage space. "In case we ever need to smuggle anything," I add, and her frown is enough to make me roll my eyes.

A catwalk rings the upper part of the bay, narrow, metal stairs the only way up. From the catwalk, there's a ladder to one side, down to the engines, and another door with more stairs up.

"I'm going to take a look at the engines," Alta says. "I wanna see how bad things are. This rust bucket needs some TLC."

"Don't call our ship a rust bucket!" I call after them.

They laugh. "Malek, this *is* a rust bucket. But it's our rust bucket so I'm gonna make sure it's the best rust bucket in the galaxy!"

"It's bigger than I expected," Nooma admits.

Nephanie is shaking her head. "Bigger and... definitely in need of a clean," she says, running her fingers along the dusty walls, pulling a face as a layer of grime comes off on her fingertips.

I raise an eyebrow in her direction. "You're gonna have to join the clean-up crew, princess," I tease but when her eyes flash amber in my direction I decide shutting up is probably wiser.

"There should be some cleaning bots somewhere. All ships are mandated to have some on board at all times," Akim says, and I resist the urge to point out that outlaw ships that have been sitting forgotten in a docking bay for over a decade aren't exactly up to the Intergalactic Union of Planets'—the IUP—regulations.

"We should go see if we can find them. This is gross," Nephanie declares, leading the way up the stairs, followed by Akim, as Nooma tries to get a side door open.

It jams when she presses the panel and I go help her pry it open.

"Well, guess we found med bay." And also, the reason why the cargo bay seemed smaller on the inside than I expected.

It's not a large room but there is an examination table and various devices I recognise from amma's ship as well as a dock for a medical AI, which is definitely going to be a must.

"With a broken door, great," Nooma mutters.

"I'll ask Tulain if he has a medical AI or where's best to buy one. Door should be easy enough to fix."

Nooma nods, glancing around the room, looking half dazed and exhausted.

"What's up?" I ask, laying a hand on her arm.

"I don't know," she admits. "I want to say nothing but you're more observant than most people give you credit for." She lets out a sigh, runs her hand through her curls. "I don't know how to do this."

"This?"

"Being free. I'm not… I was…" She sighs again, drops down on a dusty stool, shoulders sagging. "I never wanted to be a merc and now... Now I just don't know."

"I get it."

I've lost track of the times she's been there for me, and I wish I knew how to help her. Her deep brown eyes meet mine and I give her my best reassuring smile.

"I never thought I'd end up a pirate, either."

"*Outlaw*." I correct. "Really I expect we'll be salvagers more than anything."

A moment of comfortable silence settles over us before Nooma speaks again.

"Thank you, Malek."

"For what?"

"For this. For giving us this chance. I didn't believe escaping Helios was possible, and as much as I give you shit for only pulling this off because of the Shinarian forces, I know we wouldn't have been able to make it if you hadn't already put us on the path to escape."

I beam at her. "Well, a captain's gotta make sure his crew's okay!"

"You're a strange one, you know?"

"Huh, like you can talk," I fire back, nudging her in the shoulder.

She looks impossibly sad suddenly. "I'm scared, to be honest, of this freedom, of all the time ahead of us. Because it means I'm going to have to figure things out that I've never taken the time or space for."

"Like what?"

"Like who I am. What I want."

"We'll have time for that. That's the great thing about being free. No-one else gets to make our choices and with Tulain having our backs for now, we don't need to rush into anything. And I mean, I know this wasn't the life you wanted but—"

"I don't know what life I wanted," she interrupts me. "But I... I always wanted to be free. Maybe this is my chance. *Properly*. I didn't think I'd get another one. But I have and I..." I don't think she has ever looked so soft than as her lips hesitantly find the shape of a real smile. "I'm thinking maybe we can be happy."

***

The ship is a mess.

Cleaning-bots were found and now they scurry all over the place, with years of work to catch up on, being a damn trip hazard as we go about changing what lightstrips we can.

The ship is perfect.

I feel it down to my bones. It's just waiting for us to make it into our new home.

On top of a large quantity of canned food—that Akim has already said he doesn't want to eat—we've also found two discarded tablets that are currently rebooting.

I offered Akim the captain's room—bigger and more private—but one of the other cabins has been painted pleasant shades of blue with silver speckles for stars, and he chose that instead. With six double cabins and the captain's, we have plenty of space.

There's only one shower room, which sucks, but every cabin has a tiny space with a toilet and a sink, which is more luxury than our prison cells had.

We leave all the doors open as the ventilation and air filtering systems reboot but the ship is still pretty musty. I sprawl on an old couch bolted to the floor but quite obviously not intended as ship furniture.

"I wonder what time it is," Nooma says aloud as she comes to flop at the table. To say it's been a long day would be an understatement. Or is it days by now?

"Late. Or early. Maybe even somewhere in between," I reply. Akim has retreated to the cockpit, Alta is still in the engine, and Nephanie has gone outside for some air, so it's just the two of us. "Time is...weird here."

"Place never sleeps?"

"Pretty much, everyone keeps their own hours, and most shops are open round the clock. We can connect to the station's network and decide what routine we want to keep."

"Choice will be nice," Nephanie says, stepping back in.

"We should get some sleep," I say a second before a yawn tries to dislocate my jaw.

"Best idea you've had all day," Nooma replies around a yawn. “The bots might actually be done by the time we wake up.”.

I nod. Tomorrow I can go to the shop Tulain pointed me to and get myself fixed.

"I'll go get Alta and Akim," I say, pushing to my feet. "Get yourselves to bed."

In the engine room, Alta is humming, sitting cross legged at the bottom. I watch them from the upstairs catwalk, their scarred hands moving quick and sure as they work.

"Alta," I call, and they look up, pushing their hair back. The low cut of their tank top is revealing at this angle and if I wasn’t so tired, I might have been embarrassed. "You should get some sleep."

"Probably but I... There's a lot to do."

"It'll be here tomorrow. And we should see to your hands," I add.

They stare down at them, as though realising for the first time how bad they are. Whatever they were doing in the engine has left brand new nicks all along their fingers.

"Can we do that tomorrow? A few hours won't hurt, right?"

I drag myself down the narrow, coiling stairs, mentally cursing my prosthetic. "Sure, but you need sleep." I crouch in front of them as they take a deep breath and let it out. "Afraid of going to sleep only to find out this was just a dream?"

They laugh. "How did you know?"

"Because I’m the same. But we're safe. I promise. Come on," I haul them back to their feet. "Go get some sleep, captain's orders."

They smile and nod before taking themselves up the stairs.

***

When I reach the cockpit, Akim is on the floor, knees pulled to his chest, head tucked in, rocking gently. My first reaction is to reach out, but I check myself. No touching unless he's said it's okay.

"Akim?"

I crouch down, not needing to see his face to feel the emotions rolling off him. I should have come sooner. How overwhelming must Bakula have been for him, with all the noise and colours and people? And given what we'd already been through, that he dealt with it all is admirable.

I feel like an ass. I know Akim can't always verbalise when there's something wrong, but I completely forgot to check on him.

Not a brilliant start for a captain.

"Akim?" I call again and this time he makes a small noise. "You want me to go?"

"No." It's barely a whisper, but I hear it, sitting down across from him.

"You wanna talk about it?"

"I don't know. I don't know *how* to."

I kinda get that. I don't have the right words to express what took over me that last morning on Helios. I have the words amma used, but they feel so flat in practice. How can a word so small as 'manic' even begin to describe the raging fire inside me, the feeling that a sun has been born inside my chest?

"It's okay. Just say whatever comes."

"All of this was..." he pauses. "It's a lot."

"Yeah, that's certainly one way to put it."

"I... I'm scared? I think. It's hard to tell."

"You don't have to be scared here. We'll keep you safe. I promise." The word feels heavy. What if there comes a day I can't protect Akim and the others? I push the thought away, because for now things will be fine. They have to be.

"I just... It's hard to process?" I can't say part of me isn't struggling to come to terms with everything, but at the same time it feels like there is nothing left to process because I'm here, and things are good. "When I close my eyes I... I can still see those ships and... That moment when I thought we would crash into the side of the tear and..." There's a hitch in his voice and it gets so quiet that I miss the end of the sentence.

"Do you want a hug?"

His head shoots up, brown eyes wide. I know that aside from his mums, people weren't always very accommodating. Silent tears trail down his face and I wonder if I've made things worse.

"Hand on shoulder?" he replies, voice surprisingly steady.

I shift to his side, close enough so I can rest my hand on his shoulder, but far enough so that there is no other contact between us. He gives me a grateful smile and leans the side of his face against my hand. It's such a relief that he accepts me this close.

"Malek, do you think this can work out? I mean, being out here, being outlaws?"

I let my head fall back against the wall. "It's all I've ever known, so yes, it kinda has to. I don't know another life."

Akim gives the smallest nod, eyes closed, his fingers playing some complex game together.

"We'll make this work," I say into the quiet settling between us. "For everyone. No-one's getting left behind, no matter what it is they need. You trust me?"

Another small nod. "Yeah. Maybe it can be nice."

"It will be. You know though, we should probably get some sleep if we want to be able to do anything tomorrow."

Akim nods, standing up suddenly. "Yeah. I..." he shakes his head, whatever he was going to say lost. I don't want to push, but I worry about him.

"I'm here whenever you need," I tell him, getting to my feet, a bunch of new aches starting to register.

Akim nods again, not looking at me as he heads out. "Good night, Malek."

"Good night, Akim."

I turn to face the viewing window. Beyond it is only the hangar but soon there will be stars.

Soon I will be exactly where I belong.

CHAPTER 23
LÀHN

KIRILLION SPACEPORT
THE JUKKARI

Reaching Nyurae's ship means passing the main Mallak festivities and cutting around the back of the narrow alleys of stalls that have sprouted all over their corner of the spaceport, offering a variety of trinkets and food and rarer treasures.

I'd give anything to spend more time out here, but safety lies with being aboard the ship, where neither the police nor the mercs can get to us.

The ship is like nothing I could have imagined. Most of the Wandering Fleet is made of modded, patched, and fixed versions of the ships they fled their dying planet in whilst new ships are tweaked to resemble the originals as closely as possible. Smooth metal the colour of the purple night sky lines the walls, with colourful patterns serving as guides. Practical and aesthetic, like a lot of what the Mallak make. Fabric banners hang everywhere, their meaning alien to me.

Kode collapsed into bed as soon as we got here, nestled in thick blankets to combat how cool the Mallak keep their living quarters. I considered doing the same, letting Nyurae take me to my cabin, but no sooner had I been left alone that fear and anxiety set in.

Shi'lu'Fan is dead.

I'm wanted for murder.

I endangered Kode and Shuobe.

I should focus on the positive, like the fact Zoon is fine, and no-one else has been badly injured, but instead my thoughts spiral into darkness.

I need to leave the only home I have.

But no, that's the lie I tell myself. I like to pretend I was born here, a true child of this planet-city.

But I'm not. What *was* there in my life before Kirillion and Zoon? Who was I? Who tattooed coordinates into my skin, asking me to come home?

Before my thoughts can spiral anymore I flee my room, hoping the very act of walking around can help.

"Well, you certainly look lost."

I look up to find a male Mallak standing a few feet away from me, head cocked to the side as he takes me in. His eyes are a swirling jade colour, a paler hue than his hair, pulled back in complex plaits. He's wearing nothing but loose pants hanging low on his hips, the brown skin of his chest covered in colourful paint.

"No, I... Not lost, just wandering."

"You're the boy Nyurae brought back?"

I guess when people live in close-knit communities on a ship, news travels pretty fast.

"Yeah. Sorry if I'm not supposed to be walking around."

I don't mean that. I *want* to be wandering to take my mind off what happened.

The Mallak laughs and shakes his head.

"If Nyurae brought you here then you are welcome aboard. The *shuva* –" my implants don't know that word "– said you're guests, so that means you have pretty much run of the ship."

So Nyurae is important. I make a mental note to ask Shuobe about it. I smile a little awkwardly, passing a hand through my hair.

"Do you want to come to the party?" he asks.

"I'm not supposed to go outside."

Stars, but I want to.

"I didn't say the *show*, I said the *party*," the Mallak grins. "You're not going to find that outside."

I glance back the way I came, towards my room and Kode's, gnawing on my bottom lip. It feels so selfish to walk away now, but the promise of music and company is too much to say no to.

"Sure."

I can think about everything later. Yes, *later* sounds a lot better than *now*.

***

The party is in the cargo bay: flashing lights and loud music drown my thoughts the second I enter. Smoke fills the air, the room so packed I'm swallowed by the motion of dancing bodies immediately, losing the Mallak who brought me here. A raised platform occupies the centre, and two pairs of dancers battle it out to a cheering crowd.

The beat thrums through the floor, overriding my thoughts and I let it.

There are shouts and cheers, half-drowned in the music, and I let myself become nothing more but another body, another silhouette moving in rhythm.

Woven banners drape from the ceiling, some Mallak swaying from them, powerful legs tangled in the fabric, hardly more than shapes in the shifting lights and smoke. The floor panels swirl and flash from pink to blue to red to green; bright and dazzling and as dizzying as the deep beat of the music.

I forget everything but the press of bodies, losing my sense of self in this wonderful crowd.

The song ends, the lights fading for a breath as the new track mounts and then explodes into a flurry of strobe lighting. Two new groups take to the stage, bodies covered in fluorescent paint, hair adorned with similarly glowing jewellery. They are dancers one seconds and swirls of colours the next, a mesmerising display of twirling and spinning.

Surrendering to how the crowd moves is easy with my head so light, my heart pounding to the music's rhythm. The feel of skin against skin is as good as any drug, better than being wreathed in quiet worry in my cabin.

Everything is wonderful until a loud *bang* echoes throughout the room. No-one reacts. I can see no explosion, or gun. *Bang*. I whirl, seeking the source. My head spins with terror. *Bang*. It has to be part of the music. *Bang*. But I'm not here anymore. *Bang*.

There isn't enough air, enough space. I try to escape the crowd, but I can't tell which way I'm going, flashing floor and strobe lights disorienting me, the bodies around me nothing but spectres trying to crush me.

A hand on my shoulder. A voice. Words I can't make out.

I need to get out. I need air.

I need Zoon, and Kode, and home.

The hand tightens. I see men with guns, burning everything. My feet leave the floor. I scream.

The wailing of a child.

Fear tastes like iron and smoke. I'm small in the arms that hold me, my struggles in vain. There is no escape from the grasp. No escape from the fire and the smoke.

Bang.

I can't breathe, can't see, can't hear.

I'm going to die.

Cool air hits my face. I gulp in a breath. Two. Three.

My feet touch the floor and I crumple, gasping.

Slowly, I calm down enough to take in my new surroundings: an observation room bathed in soft blue light, bay windows offering a startling view of the market below, full of people and bright with flashing signs.

Nothing happened. There were no explosions, only my imagination.

The past shapes me into a contradiction. I don't want to remember but I need to. Preferably before fragmented half-memories send me mad.

"You okay?" Someone crouches by my side, deep voice almost like a song.

"I think so," I manage, rubbing a hand over my face, failing to sound convincing.

"You're the one who came with Nyurae?"

I nod.

"Some Humans don't react so well to the herbs we burn, better than other species, yes, but it can still affect you. It's why we always keep this kind of smoke out of our shows."

"I didn't know."

"Most people don't. We don't often have a lot of other species aboard our ships."

I don't respond, finding peace in the crowd beneath, in the stalls and their wares half-disguised beneath tarp and awnings. Behind the glass I'm safe. No loud noises, no memories creeping at the edges. I follow the bright colours of a Hrusha's cloak as they flutter through the crowd, surprised at the tears that sting my eyes.

"Let me get you a drink."

The whisper of the door is the only sign he's left, silence wrapping around me.

I should have just gone to bed. I'm too tired for this. For everything. I bury my face and tears into my hands.

Nothing will ever be right again.

By the time the Mallak returns, I'm balled up on the floor. His large hand finds my shoulder and gives it a tentative squeeze. I can't remember how to move.

I can't remember how to do anything.

"You want to talk?"

"I don't know." My voice is thin and dry, my throat so thick.

"It can be hard, having to leave everything you knew behind. I don't know how my ancestors did it," his voice fills the silence like a melody. "Nyurae said you're having to leave, though nothing else. At the end of the day, it doesn't matter why, only that you do."

I wish I knew what to say. I wish I knew how to pull myself together.

"Some would say that you're alive, and that's all that matters. And sure, if you weren't none of it would matter, but surviving isn't the only thing that's important."

He shifts, sitting cross-legged before taking the cap off the bottle he brought back, placing it next to my hand. The cold radiating from it is almost startling, shattering the spell that kept me motionless. My fingers close around it and I realise I still know how to breathe.

I gulp a drink, eyes closed against the world. I drink until I'm breathless. The Mallak puts his hand on my shoulder again, large and strong, and I lean into it.

"I don't know what to do..." I admit. "I dragged Kode into this and now she has to leave too." And so does Shuobe.

How many lives will I destroy before this is over? And what even is *this*? If only life was a video game, so I could reload my save and make different choices.

"You've got time to figure it out. Don't expect yourself to work out everything in a blink. It sucks that your friend got involved, but it also means you're not alone. And that's powerful. If we'd all left the planet alone, we'd never have survived. But together? That's where you find real strength."

I finally glance at my rescuer. He's got deep brown skin with purple undertones, hair a bright turquoise plaited in with gold thread and accessories. His third eye is closed but the other two are fixed on me, their soft grey gentle and concerned.

"I... I wish I could go back and change the last few days," I say, turning back towards the market where a food cart is moving through the crowd. The sight of it makes my stomach gurgle.

The Mallak laughs. "I think you need some food. Things are always harder on an empty stomach." He stands and holds out a hand to me. His kindness coaxes my lips into the idea of a smile, as he pulls me to my feet. "Let's get you some food."

CHAPTER 24
TRYSTAN

EDEN ONE

Androids aren't built to cry, but at home there is nothing I can do to stop my tears, no matter how much I want to prove to the world that I'm stronger than all this.

The night is nowhere near as dark as it should be and it feels as though I'm centre stage, all the lights pointed at me. I want to scream until my lungs ache and my throat is raw. My uncle was my hero, the man who saved me. But in the end, he's exactly the same coward I am, ground under my father's boot.

I don't know where to go. I can't just abandon the android in the middle of the city but neither home nor the lab are options, and I can't go to Cat's, no matter how much I need her...

What if she rejects me?

Worse, what happens if my secret endangers her?

I find a bench at the entrance of a park and crumple. Maybe I can just spend the night out here, watching the city life passing by me.

Maybe I can find a way to forget everything and carry on like before.

But I can't erase knowledge like I'd delete a faulty line of code.

I can't escape this planet.

I don't know how to stay.

I force myself off my bed, pacing around, pretending to tidy, anything to work out the frustration in my limbs. I turn my music on, desperate to beat back the silence which only invites more anxiety.

Two sets of eyes see a bedroom I detest, and a city that offers nothing but inescapable confinement. Two beautiful, shining, lying prisons.

I thought this body would grant me freedom.

I thought it would make everything better.

I was wrong.

The city is just another place I don't know how to fit into. I flee inside the park, city noises muffled by tall trees and manicured hedges, finding my way to the artificial lake at the centre.

The grass is soft as I sit, eyes lost on the water. St Christina Park is beautiful. It could almost make me forget that here everything hides something terrible. St Christina died for her faith because people have never been capable of just accepting one another. Why has it always mattered so much, who or what we believe in? I can't believe in the god we're told to worship here, not when it would paint me as a monster in my own eyes.

A sound like a scream shatters my thoughts and I'm moving before I can think better of it.

"We told you, you had it coming!" a boy's voice, loud and aggressive, reaches me as I hurry up.

I don't catch anything else. A pit has opened in my stomach, but my self-preservation instincts lie discarded by the guilt that's eating me up. I'm sick of doing *nothing*.

When father turns violent.

When my uncle experiments on aliens.

When the world treats my friends unfairly.

I'm done being passive, done letting this place shape me.

Done. Done. *Done*.

I turn the corner of the hedge, coming up behind a group of three boys standing around another boy with a split lip and fear in his eyes. The kind of fear I see in my mother's eyes whenever father gets angry. Fear I see in my own eyes after an altercation with him. Fear of someone you can't imagine ever not being afraid of, of someone using their power to bend you into submission.

"Come on, you little bitch, just give us the cash and we won't say a word." I suspect it's the ringleader speaking. He hasn't noticed me yet. I hate him already, with his short brown hair and his angry face, his skin even paler than mine in the dim light.

"I... I don't have it..." the boy stammers. He's younger than them, around my age.

For a second, some deep-rooted instinct tells me to run away, that I'm not made for this. But right now, I'm more than myself. More than enough.

"Hey, what's going on here?" My voice is startlingly loud.

In this body, it doesn't tremble.

In this body, I am invincible.

The boys turn, cruelty in their every move. Their victim shoots me a look that pleads with me to run away. Perhaps I should. I've never thrown a punch in my life, never been in a fight. But I don't run.

Who is this person I'm becoming?

"The hell you want?" the leader drawls at me.

He looks a little like the jock who's always harassing Cat and I want to punch his perfectly square jaw more than I expected.

I've never felt so alive.

"I asked a question first."

The boys laugh but I don't feel threatened. Something inside me has snapped.

At last.

"Get out of here," he spits in my direction. "Or you're not gonna have such a pretty face when we're done."

These guys are even lamer than me and I almost laugh.

I take a step forward. "I should call the police on your ass."

I like this new me. Back at home I'm smirking. This should feel like a game but it's more real and empowering than anything I've ever done.

"I wouldn't," the leader warns, and I make to reach for my handset in my pocket. I can't afford to get involved with the police, but they don't know that.

He leaps at me, fists first. I move to the side, surprised at my own speed. My uncle built my body to standard regulations for Eden One which means I'm fast and strong, capable of doing all the tasks Humans no longer want to put up with.

I didn't realise the power it would grant me.

He tries to hit me again and I'm out of his reach in a blink. I close my fingers into a fist—thumb out, I remember hearing that somewhere—and swing. It's a clumsy punch at best, but it's a metal fist that catches him in the shoulder. He gasps, brows knotting in confusion. The other two boys step up, cracking neck and knuckles.

Three on one. So fair. My head spins from the adrenaline.

The two cronies jump me at the same time, and I leap back with ease. My uncle never told me just *how* strong androids were here. I feel like a superhero. I raise my fists in front of me, like they do in movies, and the boys laugh at me.

"Give it up before you get hurt," the leader says.

But I still remember how it felt when my metal fist impacted with his shoulder. I bet he does too.

"You're the only one who'll get hurt," I tell him, trying to remember the way badasses in movies talk.

My opponent cracks his neck and then he's rushing me, swinging a roundhouse at my face. I raise my arm to protect myself, forcing my eyes to stay open, my heart hammering in my chest. His fist impacts with the side of my forearm. I feel no actual pain, but he does.

He swears, eyes growing wide. "What *are* you?"

I expect the question to make me feel sick but instead it makes me feel powerful. It's the 'what *are* you' villains utter when the heroes withstand what they shouldn't be able to.

"Your worst nightmare if you don't leave him alone," I reply, trying for a cocky kind of confidence. At home, I'm grinning. My words remind me of one of my favourite movies, one that Nathaniel and I used to re-enact scenes from all the time when we were younger.

I wish he could see me now.

The older boy spits in my direction. But I don't miss how he's holding his fingers. Bones are no contender for metal. Then he makes a quick motion with his head and his cronies are on me. I take a punch to the side of the head and throw a punch right back, catching one of them in the stomach hard enough to send them reeling. The other has grabbed me by the neck of my t-shirt and I stamp down on his foot. He screams and lets me go.

I am fearless.

The three back up, their victim wide-eyed with awe.

Looking at *me*.

"Don't let me catch you bullying him again," I say, putting on my best authoritative voice, drinking the fear in their eyes as they run off.

"Thanks," the word is barely audible in the deafening silence that follows, filled only by the racing of my heart.

I turn to the boy slumped down in the grass, hugging himself. "You okay?"

"Yeah just... I don't know what would have happened if you hadn't turned up."

I go to him, hold my hand out, and he looks up to me in that way people look at superheroes in movies. Only I'm *not* a superhero. I'm just someone who had the opportunity to make a difference. The boy takes my hand and I gently pull him to his feet.

"I don't know who you are but... Thanks. Really."

He manages half a smile and I respond in kind, giving his shoulder a gentle tap and a squeeze. Like the heroes do, like I have wished a thousand times someone would do for me.

"You'll be okay getting home?" I really sound like someone out of the movies now, checking the victim can make it home before going on to bust another crime.

If only.

"Yeah," he nods, picks up his fallen bag, nods again. He stares at me for a couple more seconds before rushing out of the park.

I watch him go, realisation after realisation slowly dawning on me.

I can make a *difference*.

I can make a difference.

A sense of purpose I've never known crystallises inside me. I know what to do next. I look at my android hands, the ones that have gifted me all this power, and in both bodies, I smile. I will not be idle in the face of evil.

Not anymore.

***

I walk for absolute ages before finding a deserted warehouse to store myself in safely. Despite it being the middle of the night, I'm fully awake and an idea, foolish and terrifying and exciting, presents itself. Mom is probably asleep, and father still out.

I'm as quiet as possible, all but holding my breath as I pause on the landing. I don't know where my father went after he left the lab, but there is no evidence that he came home. Everything is dark but luckily, I know the house well enough.

Downstairs is eerie but where last night I was a quivering mess who hardly dared to breathe, tonight I am someone else.

Someone new.

I am no longer scared of what happens if I act, but instead of what happens if I don't.

The panel by the office door displays a green strip. Unlocked. Luck or trap? I'm being paranoid, he probably just forgot to lock it after he argued with mom. I'm not sure what I'm looking for but there has to be something in there I can use to stop him.

Maybe.

Hopefully.

I have never been in here without my father. Never at all unless I'm being yelled at or pulled apart. The walls are lined with replicas of old-fashioned bookshelves, heavy and dark, the carpet so thick as to be suffocating. It smells of his cologne and alcohol. It smells like all the things that terrify me. I swallow hard, palms clammy.

I push through the fear, almost surprised I'm not struck down for my transgression. I'm in my father's office with only moonlight for company. I've lived in fear of him my whole life. I let him bend me to his will.

No more.

The carpet is soft under my bare feet, not a choking monster. This is just a room. *Just a room*. I repeat the words under my breath as I walk around the heavy desk, lowering myself in his chair. I always thought it would swallow me, find me wanting. But tonight, I fill it just as much as he does, and even though I know this can't possibly last, I delight in the feeling of control that washes over me.

The desk is empty bar the computer and the holo-screens. I turn it on. It asks for a password.

I have no idea what my father's password could be. Nothing so sentimental as my name or birthday or anything to do with mom. I don't know him well enough to guess and I can't risk tripping his security.

More than ever, I know I need to see what he's up to. I should have dug through my uncle's files more, copied them. I'll do that when I go back to the lab. Because I will. I must. In between their computers I should find what I need.

And when I have the documents I need, then what?

I power the computer down and creep out, bolting up the stairs, some foreboding feeling chasing me all the way to my room.

I need to talk to Cat. She's the one person I trust above all. Even if there is still this awkward secret in between us.

I glance at the time and groan. School is going to be so fun tomorrow. I crawl into bed, but sleep is a long time coming, my mind too busy devising plans for the coming days.

CHAPTER 25
LÀHN

KIRILLION SPACEPORT
THE JUKKARI

The dining hall walls are deep red, the room vast and the ceiling low. The atmosphere is friendly and relaxed, soft nature sounds playing in the background. Sitting areas marked by cushions are arranged around small stoves making it easy to forget we're on a ship.

A dozen Mallak are seated around the room, sharing food in hushed company. Refrigerated shelves line one wall, holding many foods I don't recognise, whilst another side of the room offers counters and large cooking implements. I don't imagine many species have ships as homely as the Mallak's.

My companion leaves me to settle by one of the small stoves as he goes to fetch us some food. I know I like Mallak food, but what I really crave is a big bowl of comfort noodle soup from *Chen's*, the tiny restaurant half a block from the Guild.

I wonder if I'll ever eat there again. The synth-meat is always so juicy, the broth just the right mix of salt and spice and savoury. I'm making myself hungrier just thinking about it.

I'm so lost in my noodly-daydream that I startle when my companion returns, bringing with him a board of skewers that he sets up on the stove.

"I was quite rude," he says, leaning back on his hands, taking me in. "I'm Phiros, and you're Làhn, right?" I nod, and he smiles. "I take it Nyurae didn't give you a tour?"

"She said she had things to do and that I should get some rest but... I couldn't stay still. I needed to be..." I shrug. "I needed to forget for a while. Instead, I made everything worse..."

"You didn't know about the incense, and clearly, whoever showed you to the party didn't think."

He leans forward and turns the skewers over before tossing a wayward braid back over his shoulder. The skewers smell like the ones Shuobe made us some months back. Mallak cuisine is a bit of a delicacy: their cultivation and cooking techniques both fiercely kept secrets.

"I think it would have been okay if the music hadn't been so... I don't know. It sounded like gunfire and explosions."

"I don't know what happened to you," Phiros says softly. "But it sounds like you should be taking it easy, not throwing yourself into a party." There's no judgement in his tone, which is refreshing.

"I just couldn't deal with being alone," I admit even as he gives the skewers an experimental poke with a long metal stick. "All I could think about was how I took Kode away from her home too, how I endangered everyone. How I don't know what to do with myself now."

"Are you really responsible for what happened?" He sounds so genuinely interested that I'm a little taken off guard. Most strangers leave people to deal with their own shit.

"I... It feels like it." He gives me a look that says that's not an answer even as he plucks the skewers off and divides them onto two flat plates before liberally covering them in sauce. I accept my share with a grateful smile, taking a bite to save myself from answering.

"Good?" Phiros asks around a mouthful. The twinkle in his eyes tells me he knows the answer.

For a few minutes we just eat, him watching me and me focussing on nothing but the food, but I can tell he hasn't forgotten what he asked me. When there is only one skewer left, I set it down next to me and let out a long breath.

"I took on a job I couldn't know would lead to all this. I thought I could handle it, I thought it was the same thing I've done so many times. But even Zoon hadn't been given all the info because the person he was working with thought the more he knew, the more he'd be in danger. So, no, in many ways it's not my fault but," I hesitate. "I keep wondering if I could have done things differently. If I could have made it easier on everyone. And it's... It's hard because I don't know. Because there isn't an answer to all the 'what ifs' and so I just end up feeling guilty."

"It sounds to me like you did the best you could with what you were given," Phiros' voice is so soothing. "Sometimes it's all you *can* do. Sometimes it's all that matters. Even if things go bad, if you know you did all you could, then that's what's important."

I manage a half smile. "I know but..."

"It's a shock. I get that. I wasn't born in the Wandering Fleet, so when I came on board it was such a change, I didn't think I'd be able to adapt but..." he shrugs. "There are some species that are bad at adapting, like the Dpanir, or even the Shinarians. But Mallak, and

Humans? We're two species that learnt to adapt to whatever life threw at us a long time ago. I don't think either of our species would have survived losing our homeworld otherwise."

Earth.

I know so little about it. Enough to know we pushed our hunk of floating rock until it couldn't cope anymore. We bled it dry and then fled its dying husk. There are some people who talk of going back, rebuilding. There always are. To me, it's just another planet.

"I wonder how good I am at adapting," I muse, letting my head fall back, staring at the ceiling where small pinpoints of light shape constellations. "I... I didn't always live on Kirillion, but I don't really remember anything of *before*."

Before is dust and screams and explosions. Sometimes it's also voices and faded smells, but no memory I can truly recall.

Come home.

"Before?"

"I was seven or so when I was found on Kirillion. Just another orphan but... I know that's not where I was born."

"How are you so sure? Kirillion is a big place."

I sit up, holding out my arm to show him my tattoo.

"It says, *'come home'* and is followed by a set of coordinates. Zoon never managed to find out where to—there's nothing there on our maps—but that's how I know."

He regards me with a mix of curiosity and something I can't read.

"And you have never tried to go?"

Truth is, I never wanted to. I was fine being the boy who pretended he was born and raised on Kirillion. I was fine with my adopted family. But I can't have that anymore. I need to be more than a piece of the Guild.

"It didn't use to matter. I was happy on Kirillion..."

"And now?"

I look up at him. There is a softly knowing smile on his lips.

"Now? Now I don't know."

Whatever he's about to say is interrupted by approaching footsteps and I glance up to see Nyurae, arms folded over her chest, eyes fixed on Phiros.

"So *that*'s what you've been up to," she says.

"Shuva-damaska," he starts. Again, that word neither me nor my translator know.

"You should have talked to me before," Nyurae says. "He isn't one of us, he won't have known what you were doing."

"Doing?" I ask, and they both turn to me.

"Well, I wasn't *doing* anything." Phiros is entirely unapologetic. Nyurae silences him with a gesture.

"Phiros is a shuva-ulriki," she explains. "That means that he is coming into his talent as a shuva. Ah, you probably don't have an equivalent word in your language, do you?"

"No, we don't."

"Shuva are, how to explain in words you will understand," she thinks for a moment. "We can sense emotions in others. We use that to help them come to terms with their feelings, whatever they may be. But we're not supposed to use our talents on people unless they ask. To do so is... It's an invasion of privacy. And especially when you are an ulriki, a trainee, you shouldn't be practising on people who don't know what you are," she adds, turning a stern glance at Phiros.

He shrugs, remorseless.

"It helped," I say. "And I don't think he *meant* to do this. He helped me out and... And we talked. I needed it, so it's not like it was a problem."

Nyurae makes a thoughtful noise and then shrugs. "Fine, but don't make a habit of this, Phiros."

"I won't," he says, but I have a feeling he means it about as much as I meant half the things I ever told Zoon I wouldn't go and do.

"And you should be getting some rest. You've had a tough time and I don't imagine you've had half as much sleep as you need. I've known enough Humans to know how ill your species can make itself by not sleeping enough. Go get some rest. After that, we can talk about getting you and Kode somewhere safe."

I nod, chewing my lip. "Yeah I... Zoon was sending me to his half-brother on Bakula, so I suppose I probably should head there."

"We can see once you've talked to your friend." She turns back to Phiros. "Can I trust you to accompany him back to his cabin?"

"Of course."

Nyurae seems to doubt him for a second and then shrugs. "Làhn, if you need to talk to me, just ask someone on the ship and they'll show you to my quarters, okay?"

I nod, and she turns on her heels, leaving me alone with Phiros. Our eyes meet and we both smile.

"Thank you," I tell him. "I needed this. And whether you were supposed to do whatever you did or not, I'm glad you did. I... I'm not really used to having someone around who knows what to say to help." Kode and I are good at listening but being tangled up in each other's lives means being tangled up in each other's problems.

"I figured," he stands, holding his hand out to me. "Come on, Nyurae will yell at us both if I don't get you back to your cabin."

***

Kode interrupts my brooding just before I can fully sink into misery, and I open the door to her looking concerned, nibbling on her lip-ring, her hair mussed from sleep.

You okay?

Yeah, just had a lot to think about.

Want to talk about it?

Kinda need to... I nod for her to come in and she settles on my bed. She's wearing borrowed loose pants that are too long on her, and her t-shirt. Finding tops to borrow on a Mallak ship is going to be difficult.

What is it? She asks, frowning.

We need to decide what to do. I'm sorry I got you involved in all this but... They've seen you with me now, and I worry what'll happen if you try to go back to the Guild, especially as they don't have somewhere to stay just yet, and-

She stops me, putting her hands on mine, shaking her head vigorously.

This isn't your fault, she starts, staring at me intensely. *I won't say I'm not scared of leaving Kirillion and everything but... This isn't the first home I've lost. And it's not permanent. Zoon said it himself. Let things die down and then we can come back, right?* I nod. *But it's not just scary, it's also a little exciting. Being here? Who can say they got the chance to be aboard a Mallak ship?* She smiles, and I breathe out a laugh. I can't say I've not thought that myself. *I'm with you, and Shuobe is here, so even though I'm scared, I know we can make this okay.*

I let myself smile softly. She's right. Of course, she is.

We should go to Bakula like Zoon said, meet up with his brother, I sign, she nods. *But then...* I look away. Saying this aloud would be impossible. *I was thinking...* I really thought it would be easier to sign but I falter.

You want to try and find a way to get there? She nods towards my tattoo.

Yeah. I'll find a way to make some money on Bakula and then… At least I want to find out more about it. Until today it didn't matter but...

Now we're leaving, might as well do something? She knows me better than I know myself.

Obviously, you don't have to come. I'll make sure you're safe and you could always stay with Shuobe-

Again, she interrupts me. But this time she holds my hands tight in hers. A quiet *I'm here,* the way we've said it countless times. I was there when she tried the aural implants, and her brain couldn't adapt; she was there when nightmares left me screaming myself awake. And she is here now, just as scared as I am, yet offering me support.

I pull her into my arms, and for a long time we just hold each other.

CHAPTER 26
MALEK

BAKULA

My limbs are a mess. For all Huuki—the tech at the place Tulain recommended—was really skilled and friendly, it didn't take away from the agony of having both cybernetics detached. Even anaesthetic couldn't protect me from the mangled mess they were in after Helios. My stumps are painful and not a pretty sight underneath the dressings.

Huuki admitted she was going to need to order new parts for my leg. The connectors in my stump are a rare type she can neither print nor replace without risking further nerve damage. She has what she needs for my arm, but that stump isn't up to it yet.

I'm off balance with half my limbs missing, the phantom sensations back in full force, and I'm having to relearn how to do everything from a hoverchair.

I haven't been back to the ship yet, unsure how to navigate the stairs to the living quarters. Right now, all I want is to meander around the station, familiarising myself with its ever-changing layout. It's the same place I came to with amma, but it's also nothing like it. Five years gave both Bakula and me plenty of space to change.

I thought I'd stopped missing amma, but the truth is I'd just buried it. Despite my bravado, I hadn't really believed we could escape. I spent last night caught in between horrible nightmares and nausea—apparently eating actual food after years of sludge has done a number on everyone's stomachs—and my mood has fluctuated from giddy to terror since then. I even threw up after my prosthetics were removed, a definite low point of the morning.

The chair whizzes around a corner a little faster than intended and I nearly tip myself out. Not advisable. Nooma is there, dutifully waiting for me where we agreed.

The place is a find-all junk shop with more spare parts than anyone can wrap their head around, but it's the best landmark on this level with its modified facade projecting AI faces that spend their day hollering at potential customers. Akim would hate it, Alta needs to see it.

I catch the second Nooma sees me. Sees the chair and the stumps. The damage. The surface damage, anyway: not what's hidden beneath skin grafts on my shoulder, chest, and face. She's not staring at two blind eyes.

The way her gaze lingers on the incomplete parts of me makes my hackles rise immediately.

"Stop staring," I snap. "This isn't why I wanted to hang out." I could have been nicer, sure, but there is a knot of anger in my chest. People are always like this. Even the doctors and the nurses that had never known me before. Staring and staring with pity in their eyes.

Pity I don't need.

"Sorry, I didn't mean—" she interrupts herself as I roll my eyes.

"No-one ever means to stare. But they do. I get it, it's weird to see me in a chair but it's not like you didn't know. And if it's weird for you, imagine how it feels for *me,* alright? I don't even mind the damned chair that much. But what I *do* mind is the way people have been looking at me since the tech took my prosthetics off. I don't need pity and I'm not broken—but what I am is pissed off that people can't keep their eyes to themselves. I'm still me, and that's that."

"Sorry." She looks so upset and my temper flares again. I should have known this would happen. It always does. We see aliens all day long without batting an eye but someone's missing limbs and suddenly people act like it's the weirdest thing they've ever seen.

"Just don't *ever* look at me like that again, okay?" My tone hasn't softened. I don't even care if I'm being an ass.

"I won't," she says, taking a deep breath and rearranging her features in an attempt at normal. It's more than most people do. She actually does a pretty impressive job at it.

It's not like she isn't hurting in her own ways too. The wounds inside us all have started to show at last. Akim silent over the plain breakfast Nooma went to fetch, cutting his food in perfect little squares. Alta staring into space in the engine room. Nooma and I sniping at each other over every little thing. And Nephanie's eyes a strange shade of silver even Akim can't decipher.

I'd been the first one off the ship, half-eager to get fixed, half-running away from the haunted looks.

I need to keep moving. I didn't survive everything just to fail now. But the terror darkens the corners of my vision, and it takes all of my willpower to push it back.

It's okay. I'm okay. Everything is fine. Everything will be fine.

The mantra that carried me through this morning. That kept my head high. It's hard for me to show weakness whilst in the chair when I feel it's what everyone expects. The chair doesn't make me weak. I'm *not* weak, not even with terror clawing at the edges, even with the tears staining my pillow this morning. None of us are weak because we *survived*.

Sometimes that's not easy to remember.

"Do you want to grab something to eat?" I ask, just to break the awkward silence.

I wish amma was here to look after the lot of us. I almost want to run to Tulain, but I can't. If I ever want to be taken seriously, I have to do this by myself. There is no do-over if people find out you have weaknesses. They'll just spend the rest of your life exploiting them.

"Yeah, just, let's go for something plain. My stomach is still recovering."

I laugh. "Same, same. I think we all forgot we needed to get used to food again."

"It sucks," she mutters as we set off, my chair cutting a path through the crowd.

"You can say that again. How was everyone else doing when you left?"

She shrugs, hands shoved deep in the pockets of her baggy fatigues. "I don't know. It's hard to tell even how *I*'m doing, let alone anyone else. Akim's locked himself in the cockpit to study the controls and Alta said they wanted to do an inventory of what we'd need but they didn't seem to be getting anywhere."

"And the princess?"

"Nephanie?" There is the slightest hint of a smile in her eyes. "She seemed to shake things off a bit after you left, got me to help with the knots in her hair. They were too tight for her to undo by herself."

"So, no more creepy silver stare?"

Hearing Nooma laugh is startling. "No, no. She walked me to our meeting spot and then went on her way, said she needed to stretch her legs. She... I don't think she's been to many crowded places before."

"I guess royalty doesn't usually mingle with us commoners." I navigate my chair around a stall and curse as a Hrusha child flies over my head instead of changing their course.

We've reached a busy corridor and manoeuvring is getting harder so Nooma steps in front, a glare from her even shifting a tall, brooding Kundar.

"I think it's more complicated than her just being royalty," she says over her shoulder.

"I get that feeling too," I admit. "Here, that place looks good."

Nooma's face scrunches up. "Stars, what is..." she hesitates, likely bringing up a translation for the curling script on the sign above the door. I don't know if she'll have full translation for alien scripts but then again, most mercs I ever knew about had some of the best translator implants around. "*Chuapa?*"

"Simple, plain meat. Sperool find it a delicacy but then their taste buds are weird."

"My parents only went to Human-only stations, so I'm a bit lost with all this alien food," she admits.

"I feel so sorry for you."

She shrugs. "Synth food can be pretty great. But teach me the way of all the alien food I've been missing out on, why don't you?"

"Sounds good!" I grin up at her and she shakes her head as though she's baffled by my enthusiasm. "Let me order: it might be a plain meal, but we might as well make it as good as we can!"

***

Sharing lunch with Nooma, hunched over our tiny table, is everything I needed. Company. A friend. I've never done well left to myself.

We were tentative at first, but soon the walls fell away, and we were talking about games and music and all the things we'd done and loved before Helios. We laugh and eat and talk, just two friends out for a meal, free of the ghosts looming at our backs.

When we return, the ship is a little too quiet, making me wish we'd stayed out longer. But I'm too tired, like I have years of sleep to make up for. Nooma lets me go ahead when the cargo ramp jams, and I stop at the base of the stairs. I didn't even think of asking for a chair suitable for ship-life but Huuki might not even have one laying around.

"Do you need a hand?"

I want to say no. Maybe once I could have managed the awkward hop up the stairs, but I'm out of practice.

"Probably but... You should get the bags in the kitchen first."

She nods and hurries up the stairs. They're a taunt, a challenge that I'm bowing out of. I know it's best to wait for Nooma, but something inside is egging me on. I think of the pity in her eyes earlier.

Before I can think better of it, I push myself upright, my hand gripping the handrail. I look up at the stairs, heart already hammering. I swear they have multiplied since yesterday. Nooma is only going to be a couple of minutes, so I can't hesitate. I cling onto the handrail and bend my knee, pushing myself to jump onto the first step. I wobble badly, my right-hand clinging to the railing. My wounds throb at the sudden motion.

But I can do this.

I'm not even halfway up when Nooma comes back, sweat dripping down my brow, knuckles white on the handrail.

"Mal..." she doesn't sound scolding, not even surprised.

I force a smile as I look up at her.

"I figured it was only a few stairs."

"Well, now that you've made the point that you *can* do it, do you want a hand the rest of the way?"

"Actually, that'd be really great," I admit, smile tight.

She comes to wrap an arm around my waist, bracing me against her. She feels strong, reliable. I can loosen my grip. I'm sure she could pick me up and carry me, but she doesn't. I'm infinitely grateful

The rest of the way up is still tricky, but she takes most of my weight, supporting me. There isn't the space for the chair up in the living areas and I didn't even think of getting crutches. I want to kick myself. How did I not think? I've been through all this before, but it was so easy to forget.

"You okay?" Nooma asks, brows furrowed.

I don't know so I ask for a drink instead and she disappears into the kitchen as I flop on the sofa. I could sleep for a week.

Emotions tangle inside me, exploding like fireworks in my chest, leaving a burning trail of passion and sorrow behind. I miss amma but I have a new family, and the two don't have the space to co-exist inside me.

"Malek?"

Akim is standing in the doorway, his brown skin ashen, his eyes red.

"Hey, Akim, how you holdin' up?"

He looks past me, chewing his lip. The look in his eyes, the way he stands, everything tells me he doesn't know. Perhaps it wasn't a fair question when even I'm not sure. I catch him glancing at me, taking in the stumps, but he doesn't say anything, his eyes don't linger. I relax a little as he sits cross-legged on the floor by the sofa.

"Good to see you out of the cockpit," Nooma reappears, handing me a soda.

I shove the bottle in between leg and stump and twist the cap off.

"I heard you coming back. I thought you might have food."

"Haven't you eaten yet?" Nooma asks.

"I don't know the things you brought back this morning. And Alta is still in the engine room, and I didn't want to bother them."

"Do you want to go check on them?" I ask Nooma in between long sips. The soda tastes like crap: not a brand anyone with sense would have bought. That's what I get for letting Nooma do some groceries this morning.

"I'll take them some food." She hands one of the boxes to Akim before heading off with another. She looks worried. Tired.

Akim opens the box, poking tentatively at the food.

"I promise it tastes good."

"You ate some?"

"Yeah, we figured you guys might have eaten some of the stuff Nooma brought back."

"I didn't know what it was. Or if it was okay," Akim says around a tentative mouthful.

"You should have messaged."

"I didn't want to bother you."

"How are you feeling?" I try again.

"Tired. It's weird being...free. I got used to the routine. And before that I had a routine at the academy. I liked that, the routine part. It made... It just makes things easier. And so, today I..."

"You didn't know what to do?"

He takes a bite of the fries and nods.

"I'm sorry I left without thinking. I was in such a hurry to get to the tech shop. I should have checked you guys were okay before I left."

He shrugs as though it's no big deal, but I know better. I feel bad. I ran away because I couldn't deal, but in the end, I abandoned my friends. That's not what a good captain does. Or a good friend.

"The ship's pretty big," I start, shifting until I'm comfortable. My stumps itch like crazy. Cleaning them later is going to be ten shades of hell. "So, I was thinking, after we've finished this job and gotten the cash from Tulain..." I trail off, watching him from the corner of my eye, seeing the moment the realisation dawns on him and his eyes almost meet mine.

"I can get a pet? Really?"

"Well, you did make it a condition, and it wouldn't be right for me to go back on my word."

He's beaming a little awkwardly, eyes closer to meeting mine than they have ever been.

"I can't wait to go pick one!"

"We need to wait till the job is done first, okay? So, we know exactly what we're working with."

He nods, but the light in his eyes doesn't fade.

I wonder how Nooma, and Alta are doing, how Nephanie is finding the station. What can I do to help them through this? To help myself? Everything feels distant: like the fear and the pain and the two years of awful aren't quite real. What happens when that stops? What happens when it all crashes down on me?

"What are we doing for the rest of today?" Akim asks.

"Not sure yet. First, I'm going to take a nap."

I settle further down on the couch, staring at the ceiling above. Akim is fiddling with the box of food.

"You can do whatever you want," I tell him.

"I think I'll go ask Alta if they've got a tablet working yet. I used to read comics back at home and I wonder if I can get hold of them here. I bet I have loads of catching up to do."

He gets to his feet, smiling in my direction.

"Malek... Thanks. For this, for getting us out."

"I promised you guys I would. Though I think you really need to thank Nephanie for bringing half the Shinarian fleet down on the place."

He ponders that for an instant. "Then I'll thank her too. I'm not good with change but this... This is good. Even if it's hard to adjust, I'm really glad it happened."

"Me too."

I hear his footsteps down the corridor as I throw my arm over my eyes, blocking out the light.

Sleep does not take long to claim me.

CHAPTER 27
TRYSTAN

EDEN ONE

Cat and I slip inside the VR booth, relieved for a break from the world. It's been a long day at school and we're both in desperate need to take out some tension. We slide the headsets and gloves on, loading into the game.

We're freer here than at home and the soundproofing makes it a safe place to talk.

I pick my usual male avatar, as Cat selects a particularly unclad lady, her outfit nothing suitable for fighting a horde of zombies.

"Cat, why?" I despair.

"Because she's hot," she replies, selecting the biggest gun she can. I opt for a pair of pistols. Duel-wield all the way. "And what about you? You *always* pick Leon."

Her character is looking directly at me, mimicking her motions. Luckily, *House of Satan* was never made to be an emotional experience, so the facial animations are basic and don't register my cringe.

"I like to look at him," I reply, echoing her answer.

I guess he is fairly cute: floppy blond hair to his cheekbones, just the right level of toned, and a pair of pretty blue eyes.

"Sure, you do..." My stomach sinks at the thought she might suspect something, but then she's equipping her rocket launcher—better her than me—and that's that. "You ready?"

I grab some medkits before the screen fades to black, the cut-scene kicking in. We skip it in unison: we've watched it too many times as it is. When the gameplay starts, we're by the gates of the mansion, the horde already heading for us.

"I'm going to imagine that every single of these rotting bastards is Michael," she says, which given the way he was today is not surprising.

She levels the grenade launcher and fires, leaving a gaping hole at the centre of the oncoming horde. I duck behind cover to shoot because I'm nowhere near as reckless.

"I'm going to imagine they're my father."

"Still mad about the engagement thing?"

"Wouldn't *you* be?"

"Well, I'd rather be engaged to a pretty face with some sense than to all the idiots out there."

Point.

Still.

"I'm just not ready for it, you know? I was hoping he wouldn't try to marry me off as soon as school was over. And... It's not just that anyway."

Talking about Nathaniel is only going to complicate everything.

The music picks up as the action accelerates and I'm already starting to feel better. Cat backflips to safety as a rain of magic explodes across our vision.

"A necromancer this early?"

They don't usually spawn until we're inside.

"I felt like a challenge today." I can hear the smirk in her voice.

"Did you put us on *hard*?"

"Damn straight I did!"

"We're so gonna die..."

I unleash another hail of bullets. The guns are old fashioned, like the decor, the whole game an homage to a genre popular on Earth long before my ancestors ever left.

"More shooting, less complaining, Leon."

Hearing her call me by a boy's name gives me a renewed desire to kick some ass.

"So, what else has your father done?"

Grenades explode in rapid fire as Cat glows with the infinite ammo bonus, and we rush forward, my guns already trained on the necromancer at the back, who's flinging out spells we're having to dodge.

"He's involved in some really..." I hesitate. How to say this? I meant to rehearse but falling asleep in history class messed with that plan. "Dodgy stuff."

"Dodgy st—Left!"

I whirl around just in time to blast a zombie in the head.

Counter headshot, flashes across my vision in obnoxiously bright yellow. *Invincibility 10s!!*

"Get the necromancer!"

I bolt forward, emptying both my guns into the necromancer as soon as he is in my line of sight.

3, 2.

Shit, shit, shit. My invincibility will run out before he's dead.

"Right, ice cream truck!"

1.

The necromancer targets me as I duck behind the ice cream truck, the spell rattling the vehicle as it hits. I'd be dead without Cat.

I glance out of cover: she's picked up another power-up and is now emptying the contents of a flamethrower on the horde. She's viciously good at this.

"As I was saying, what kind of dodgy stuff?" she asks whilst burning another dozen zombies to dust.

I peek through the truck's window, spotting a power-up. I break the window and drop inside, picking up a better pair of pistols as well as a magic shield.

"The kind he's got my uncle involved in." The new pistols glow with holy magic. This is beyond lucky.

"Seriously? I thought your uncle had stopped doing stuff he shouldn't?" Cat knows nearly everything about my family. I find the door of the van as she yells. "Back up!"

"Coming!" I kick the door open, stepping out, guns blazing. The magic shield protects me from the first blast the necromancer throws at me as I empty the barrels of both pistols into the lines of enemies rushing Cat. Her health is low, so I toss her a medkit as my guns go on cool down.

"Nice one! Now down!"

I drop to the ground as she cackles, stepping onto the pile of corpses and firing the grenade launcher at the necromancer. He lets off a spell at the same time. Her health is still too damned low. I leap in the way, taking it to the chest, as the grenade goes off right in his face. My magic shield shatters and I lose a little health but we're both still alive and the necromancer is down.

VICTORY! Scrawls across the screen and Cat whoops as I get back to my feet.

"Okay, next time you put us on hard, *warn* me."

She laughs. "You did fine, Tris."

"We would have been screwed if I hadn't picked up those power-ups."

"But you did, and we won. Come on, let's move to level 2!"

I shake my head and follow her inside the mansion. It's a mess architecturally, designed solely for gameplay: too-long corridors stretch from the hallway, lined with numerous rooms as likely to be filled with enemies as they are bonuses. I let her pick the path and walk a few steps behind.

"Spill the details," she orders as the eerie music envelops us. I'm just waiting for all the doors to burst open and the zombies to rush us. So far, they've been locked and that's exactly why I'm on edge.

"Experiments on aliens. And people from other planets," I blurt, and Cat stops in her tracks. I can feel her tense up next to me.

"You're sure?"

I know her enough to know she'll care but I'm still anxious. "Yeah."

"Shit." She takes a breath and then curses again. "Do you know why?"

"Not really," I can't bring myself to tell her everything I've read yet. Mostly because, honestly, even I wouldn't believe it if I hadn't seen it. "I only overheard some stuff. But I saw... I saw the alien."

"You... Whoa. Okay that's... And they're sentient?"

"Yeah. Yeah, they are. Like you and me."

"No wonder you're so freaked out."

"Yeah. And last night I tried to get onto my father's computer but it's password locked. I figured maybe if I could find all the details I could... I don't know what I could do. But I have to try, don't I?"

Neither of us is moving anymore, the empty corridor with its peeling wallpaper forgotten.

"I could speak to Shauna but... She doesn't know how to bypass systems either. Lilac does but... She'd have to be there, and she's not going to get invited to your house any time soon." I shake my head in agreement. "I know some of the girls have been learning how to hack but... You don't know them, and they don't go to our school so you coming back home with them out of the blue would be weird. Nathaniel however..."

Oh, of course it had to be Nathaniel. Not like his very existence doesn't mess with me.

"You haven't been learning?"

"I'm crap at it. I thought it'd be like a game, but it really isn't."

"Nathaniel would be easy to get at my house." Why did I say that? He makes me smile and laugh and he makes everything hurt. But I need to know what my father is hiding.

"We can talk to him later."

"I have a party to go to tonight," I say, scowling under my headset. Just thinking about it makes me feel nauseous. "Father is dragging us to this 'charity' event to make himself look good."

And also, I might be a bit distracted because I'm going to try and bust out the alien my uncle is experimenting on.

"We *all* have a party tonight. Do you really think you're the only one being dragged there?"

"Oh, yeah, I didn't really think. Guess we can try and talk to him then."

"Want to shoot more stuff in the meantime?"

"Hell. Yes."

Cat's avatar takes a step back away from mine and all the doors burst open, vomiting a horde of brain-eating monsters on us. I swear, she laughs, and we start shooting.

CHAPTER 28
LÀHN

THE JUKKARI

The *Jukkari* has taken off and it's time to start making plans. First, get to Bakula. Second, well, that's more nebulous. I told Kode I wanted to go look for my home planet, but I've changed my mind fifteen times since. Now I hesitate in front of Nyurae's quarters, taking in the details etched into the door: curling vines and flowers around intricate symbols.

The doors slide open to reveal her smiling face, the swirling colour of her third eye almost hypnotic.

"Come in, we have much to talk about."

The room is large, with drawn curtains hinting at another, more private space beyond. In the centre sits a small pond, rivulets of water winding between the metal tiles, encased in glass, glowing a soft blue. Piles of cushions sit around a small table with a tea service waiting. Where the walls aren't covered in tapestries, greenery tumbles from a planter to skim the top of a sort of altar. Herbs burn inside a decorative bowl, filling the room with a gentle scent.

The scent of homesickness.

I don't realise tears are streaming down my face until one tickles the side of my mouth.

My hands are shaking as I reach up to wipe them.

Only now do I hear the soft music playing in the background, accompanied by the natural sounds that echo everywhere throughout the ship. Birdsong, wind rustling leaves, gurgling brooks I only recognise from docu-shows.

The sounds of homesickness.

In this alien room, surrounded by smells and sounds that should be unfamiliar to me, an ache spreads through my chest. Memories unfurl like the coiling smoke of incense, rising far above all the walls I ever built.

Nyurae did not call me here by accident.

The water at my feet is a fountain in a forgotten courtyard I once played in, small and laughing, chasing a face lost to time.

I cry for the faces I no longer remember, for the place that should have been my home. Only the fountain is a clear memory, soothing and inviting. Around it shadows move like so many faceless ghosts, all as distant as they are familiar.

The hollow parts of my soul have never been so alive, so awake, filling themselves on half remembered sights: a flash of brightly coloured sleeve, a ring of red-leafed trees, a mountain capped in purple clouds.

A hand on my shoulder brings me back to reality.

"I..."

"You carry a lot inside your soul. A lot of hurt hidden even from yourself," she says, taking me to settle on the cushions.

I lean back against the wall and notice a painting framed by tapestries: a beautiful, alien landscape of deep purple leaves, black and pink flowers, and grass in a riot of reds and oranges.

"We try our best not to forget home," Nyurae says wistfully. "We have photos of our planet, of course, but some of us like to recreate it by hand, as though we can breathe new life into a world long since gone."

"It's beautiful." Beauty is everywhere on the Mallak ship. I considered staying here, joining the Wandering Fleet if they would have me, shedding the me from Kirillion and becoming someone new.

"There is a lot locked inside of you," Nyurae says, pouring us tea.

"I thought it was lost."

"Memories are a hard thing to truly lose."

I meet her kind, violet eyes. "Humans lose them all the time."

"Buried more than lost. I have worked with a few Humans as a shuva and they are always startled to see how much more they recall than they thought they would."

"Do you remember differently to us?"

"Yes and no. We recall very strongly through our senses, smell especially. We may forget what someone looked like, but we will never forget their scent. But we do not... We are not so good at burying memories the way Humans do. We can set them aside, but we are aware that they exist, and we have to be very careful not to touch them. It is better, if you ask me, though it can be difficult. Still, I would not want to have the perfect memories of the Shinarians, that cannot be easy to deal with."

I shake my head. "No, no that can't." But then I would know who I was. I would remember every moment of joy Kode and I shared. Would that be worth also remembering all the bad?

"You are going to look for answers, aren't you?" Nyurae asks, handing me a cup.

"How do you know?"

She gives me a smile, part mystery, part motherly kindness. "I am a shuva, Làhn. It is my purpose to know such things."

"I'm scared of what I'll find."

"And are you also scared of never finding out?"

I let out a startled laugh, distracting myself by sipping at the tea, fruity and light and soothing as it is.

"I don't know. But since the attack on the Guild, I've been remembering more. I think whatever happened on my home planet it wasn't pretty, and it makes me wonder if there is anything worth me heading back. What if there is nothing left?"

A few beats of silence follow. I drain my cup. Nyurae fills it up.

"What if there is everything left?"

The flipside to the question that haunts me. Will I find answers if I head there, or just more questions?

"I'm worried that it... That I won't be *me* anymore if I go there."

"And why is that?"

"Because maybe knowing who I was, who I could have been, it won't be something I can reconcile with who I am now."

It would help if I knew who I was before all this happened, but only now do I realise I never knew. I was Làhn of the Guild, a charming thief, always a smile on his lips. But that's not who I am inside, that's the mask I wore whilst my insides tangled into impossible knots.

"Only you can stitch together all the pieces of who you are."

Only me.

It would be so much easier if I could just let someone else do it. Like I always have, letting other people decide what I would do with myself, letting the flow carry me.

"I don't think I know how to do that."

"That's okay," Nyurae says softly. "It is not an easy skill to learn, but it is necessary. You won't learn it overnight, but trust me, if you keep running from your past, you will never truly move forward."

Her words frighten and bolster me both.

"First, we need to head to Bakula," I say, because I'm not ready to tackle any more of that conversation. "I guess you can just drop us off somewhere and Kode and I will get a shuttle there."

"And what will you do after that?"

I look away, staring at the painting once more, fingers finding my tattoo. "I guess I'll try and find someone who can take us all the way. Or at least part of the way."

"We can take you there," Nyurae says, and I blink.

"It's really far!"

"No, no, I didn't mean to that planet lost off the map," she clarifies. "That would be so far out of our planned course that I would have to ask the Council permission, but to Bakula. We make regular enough stops in the area that it won't be an issue to make one jump there."

I'm startled by the offer. I looked at the coordinates and Bakula is nowhere near Kirillion even with the fantastic hyperspace engines the Mallak have.

"What would you want in exchange?"

Kirillion taught me that nothing good ever comes free, but Nyurae shakes her head.

"Nothing. But I do get to spend more time with my daughter this way. She is everything I was at her age and that means I hardly get to see her anymore."

"You think Shuobe will come with us?"

"I would have," Nyurae shrugs. "She and Kode are very close, she talks about her all the time. And Shuobe can fend for herself, so I would be surprised if she didn't jump at the opportunity."

"And you'd let her come to a place like Bakula?"

She lets out a startled laugh. "I don't tell Shuobe what she can or can't do. I'll be here to help if she ever needs, but she is free to do as she likes. I am her mother, not her puppeteer. And either way, Bakula is no better or worse than Kirillion. I'm not worried about her getting into trouble. Well, trouble she can't handle in any case. If she wants to get into trouble she can handle, then that's perfectly acceptable."

There is a small, jolting pang of jealousy at the idea I'll have to share Kode with someone else on this journey and I immediately kick myself. Kode has never put me or Shuobe over the other, always there to reassure me when I thought her having a girlfriend would diminish our bond.

"Thank you. For everything."

"I'll check with the duvaj but I imagine it will take a couple of days before we can make a direct jump. In the meantime, feel free to enjoy the ship. How have you been finding it so far?"

Magical. Wonderful. Overwhelming.

"It's been great. People have been lovely."

The way she smiles makes me wonder if she can read my mind.

"Good. Then you should go and enjoy it some more. I will update you when I have an ETA."

I nod and push to my feet. I'm not ready to leave, yet I've never been more ready either. Nyurae pulls me into a tight embrace. I return it, hands tangling in her masses of hair. I close my eyes against the tears, fight back against the ache in my chest. Eventually she pulls away and nods towards the door.

"Go. And remember to look after yourself."

I can barely speak but before I step through the door, I manage a quiet 'thank you'.

CHAPTER 29
MALEK

BAKULA

I wake up to Nooma and Nephanie talking in low voices in the kitchen, the rest of the ship quiet. Note to self: do not fall asleep in the communal area, it's rude. I rub my face, sleep quickly replaced by my new normal energy.

I want to go out and have some fun and not waste a second of my freedom.

I'm going to treat everyone to a night out. We can let our hair down, relax and have some well-deserved fun.

Stars, but is it evening already? Further note to self: set an alarm when going for a nap.

"Nooma!" I call, loudly. "I'd totally come to you girls, but I can't, mind coming in here?"

Nooma mutters something before striding out of the kitchen, Nephanie a few steps behind her. There's no sign of Alta or Akim, I hope they're both doing okay.

"I didn't think he was going to wake up today," Nephanie says to Nooma. "Guess you win that bet."

I scowl half-heartedly. "I had a very long morning."

"You feeling better?" Nooma asks.

"Yeah, much. I was thinking maybe we could do something?" I offer her my best smile. It doesn't seem to have much of an effect.

"Something like what?"

Why does Nooma always sound like she doesn't trust my ideas?

"Go out? You know, *live* for a bit."

"Shouldn't you be resting?" Nephanie asks, leaning back against the wall.

"I just did that. Now I want to *do* something. Come on, don't tell me you two are happy staying cooped up on the ship?"

They exchange a glance and Nephanie shrugs.

"Well, I certainly could do with a change of scenery," Alta's voice startles us. "But you will need to let me get changed first, I'm not going out looking like I've been bathing in grease all day."

I stare at them. So do Nooma and Nephanie. They're covered in grease all the way up to their elbows, face smeared with it, obvious tear tracks cutting through the grime. Their shirt is tied around their waist, revealing more of their tanned olive skin which is also splattered in oil.

"What happened to you?" Nooma asks, aghast.

"Oh, I found a leak. By, you know, getting leaked on."

"Are you okay? That can't be good for your skin," Nephanie asks.

"I've seen worse actually, once had an entire tank empty on my head when I was a kid. Joked for days I should have gotten superpowers. I didn't, but I got lots of presents for having to stay in hospital, so I guess it evened out," they laugh. Their eyes are brighter than they were this morning.

"So yeah, out sounds good but let me get a shower."

"Since when do we have running water?" Nooma asks.

"Since about five minutes ago. I cleaned the filters and flushed the tank and it's just done refilling itself. And I am going to be the first to take advantage of that. Where're we going anyway?"

Nooma shrugs.

"Karaoke?" I pipe up. Alta grins, Nooma looks mortified. Clearly the sign of a good idea.

"Oh, that sounds like fun. Someone should see if Akim wants to come, and also let him know there is running water." Alta drags a greasy hand through their hair and scowls. "This is gonna take some work to get out. See you guys in a bit." They give us a wave and vanish towards the bathroom.

Nooma rounds on me. "Karaoke?"

"You got a problem with that?" I grin at her.

"Do *not* make me sing, Malek. Don't even think about it."

I've never wanted something quite so badly.

***

The karaoke club is flashy in all the ways Bakula loves to be. Androids greet us at the front: androgynous with features from different species, dressed in neon clothes and flashing LED jewellery, synth voices singsong as they show us to a private room and take our orders. Nooma is a complete spoilsport, again, and insists we abstain from synth-alcohol, but as soon as I'm relaxing in the plush seats, with our food laid out in front of us, I stop minding so much.

The U-shaped seating faces the small stage and I'm itching to get up there.

Akim has withdrawn to the back, tablet in hand, but he looks the most relaxed I've seen. Watching him catch up on his comic makes me desperate to get my hands on the new games and music that came out whilst I was locked up.

Blue LEDs ring the ceiling, and the table is lit from beneath in blue and green neon, painting our snacks in strange and intriguing shades. After a wash and with our new clothes, we look surprisingly like a bunch of normal teens.

"So, who's going to give it a go first?" Alta asks before shoving too many fries at once in their mouth.

"Not me," Nooma replies, sipping at her drink: a tall, pink construction of fruit and whipped cream.

"I might give it a go. *If* they have Shinarian music. Otherwise, screw it," Nephanie says, eyes flashing turquoise. She stands up, all but climbing over Nooma. The fact Nooma clearly doesn't mind when she'd punch most everyone else for invading her personal space is telling me I haven't been dreaming this thing between them.

Being here, with my friends, feels almost surreal.

We are free.

We are alive.

A few days ago, all of this was nothing but an impossible dream and now, it's my reality.

"Found anything?" Alta asks as Nephanie scrolls through the selection.

"Yes!" Nephanie's eyes are a bright, happy red. "I love this place already," she adds, selecting the song. The screen behind her comes to life, displaying the title.

The Shinarian alphabet is a swirling, curving script that reminds me of their markings. My Neurolink offers the translation of 'The Green Petal' but comes with a note that it is a literal translation and might hold a more complex meaning in the original language.

"What is it?" Nooma asks. I'm distracted by the way her straw flashes every time she takes a drink.

Why didn't I get a cool straw with my drink? I mean, granted, mine is a rainbow in motion, the syrups and juices reacting with each other so that they are moving around the glass. But still, my drink isn't *flashing*, and I feel cheated.

"It's a song from my childhood," Nephanie replies, eyes turning silver for a moment. I don't need to know the meaning of that colour to sense the melancholy in her words. "My father always wanted me to learn," she hesitates. "*Proper* songs, but this one was one of my favourites."

"What's it about?" Alta asks, stretching over the table to try and take one of Akim's seafood chips, but the bowl is on the seat by his side in the blink of an eye. Alta laughs. "Okay, okay, no touchy those. But they look so goooood, let me have one."

"No. I'm not interested in what you guys got. These are mine."

Alta pouts and then relents. Nephanie is still looking at the screen longingly.

"And this one is…?" Nooma prompts Nephanie.

"It's a war song," she admits. "But not... Not the war songs Shinarians sing anymore. It's... This song knows how hard and ugly it all is. But it's not...sad. I don't know, there's hope in it, because it sees how things are. If that makes sense." She looks almost embarrassed, her eyes shifting colours too fast for me to keep track.

"Let's hear it then," Nooma encourages her. I don't think I've ever seen so soft a smile on her lips.

Nephanie pulls herself taller.

The ambient music dies down as the song begins. There is no denying the beauty in how it flows, a deeper beat woven into the melody. It's not slow, but heavy and deep, and I can feel it thrumming deep inside me. My Neurolink doesn't translate songs, so when Nephanie starts singing, I hear the Shinarian words, alien and mysterious. She's good, her eyes closed, her whole body still, hands fisted at her side.

Even Akim looks up from his comic. I can feel how the song touches her soul from how she sings. She was right: the music, the way her voice carries, isn't sad. Heavy, yes, but there is something about it that reaches into my very core.

I'm going to get us a sound system for the ship. A home should have music.

Nooma is riveted, eyes never leaving Nephanie's face.

Something about this song feels like it suits all of us, though I'd be hard pressed to put it into words.

Everyone is silent when she finishes. A single tear rolls down her cheek, but her eyes are still red, her head held high. I understand this impossible mix of feelings more than I care to admit.

"That was beautiful," I say. "Like, seriously, you have some skills."

She laughs. "I had a teacher when I was younger, she was very good even though I was very stubborn," she shrugs. "I guess it paid off?"

"Definitely!" Nooma is beaming at her, cocktail raised. "A toast to Nephanie for her singing skills!"

Alta raises their glass, I answer in kind, and no-one is surprised when Akim mimics our gestures with a slightly confused look.

"Guys, please, you're embarrassing me," Nephanie laughs, scooting back to her spot.

"That is going to be *so hard* to top," Alta points out.

"This isn't a competition," Nooma scolds them. "Just have fun if you want to have a wrestle with that infernal device."

"What do you have against karaoke?" I ask her. "It's just fun even if you can't sing well or you don't know the song. I bet there are plenty of people here who can't sing and are still having a blast."

"That doesn't mean *I* want to be one of them."

"Well, I do," Alta chirps up, doing their best to not jostle into me as they make their way to the stage.

"What are you going to sing?" I ask them as they ponder over the selection screen.

"It's going to be a surprise, Mal, just wait."

Alta's choice of song is some poppy monstrosity that is definitely not to my taste. Their language sounds a little like what Enry—a gunner on amma's ship—spoke. But it's hard to tell how similar when Alta is slaughtering the song. Nooma is laughing, a hand over her mouth, as Alta hits some really high notes completely off-key.

I make a show of covering one ear. Alta sticks their tongue out, stumbling to catch up with the words. They mess up so royally that I burst out laughing. Nooma follows suit and then Alta can't sing from laughing. Laughter pours out from the three of us as though we're broken androids looping through a program.

By the time I'm able to wipe the tears away, Akim and Nephanie are staring at us as though we've gone mad. Alta is on the floor, bursts of giggles escaping them every time they mutter 'I'm calm, I'm calm'. Nooma has sobered up though she's still grinning. Nephanie mutters 'Humans' just about loud enough for me to hear even as Akim slowly picks up the tablet, half hiding behind it.

"Okay, I give," Alta manages between bursts of laughter. "I can't sing. I can't even *try* now." In the background the cheerful tune carries on. "I hadn't tried this since I left home, that was awesome." They slide past me and grab their drink. "I need to try again but first I need to stop laughing. And next time, you *all* have to behave," they add, shooting me a glare. "Clearly only Akim and Nephanie are kind enough to appreciate my art!"

"Alta, that wasn't art. That was... I don't know. But not art." Akim's deadpan has me bursting out laughing again as Alta's mouth drops open.

"Let's see you guys do any better! Nephanie has an excuse, she's royalty and they always get taught useless shit like singing. *Fun*, but useless. Well unless you make a career out of it."

"A lot of Shinarians can sing," Nephanie says, setting down the long flute that holds her bubbly purple drink. "All prayers to the Divinities are songs, so we all tend to have a basic knowledge on how not to sound awful. Humans however... I wonder if you people have ears sometimes."

"Oh, I'll show you we have ears," I declare. Nooma mutters something that sounds awfully like 'Stars, please no', as I scoot out from the seat and into the chair. The screen lowers to my height as I manoeuvre onto the stage. I know what I want to sing. I'm elated when I see the elegant font of the title and band name, neither needing translating.

This song, this language, is more home than perhaps even a ship and the star-speckled darkness of space. It's the one thing amma gave me that can never be taken away.

It's been years since I last sang anything, let alone this, and I'm a bit nervous. Amma and I sang it all the time: it had been her favourite song long before it became mine. I'll probably find new favourite songs, now that I'm free and older, but this one will always have a special place in my heart.

My friends are chatting, Alta already teasing me, and for a second, I marvel that I'm here, alive, surrounded by my friends.

I told you I'd be like you, amma. I hope you'll be proud of us. We'll do good, I promise.

The track starts: heavy guitars and drums. I close my eyes. I don't need to see the lyrics. I don't need to hear them. They're written into my very soul. I start singing, nervous despite myself, my voice a little thin until the first line is out—amma usually sang that one—

pand then I find my feet, my rhythm. Eyes closed, the world falling away, I pour out all the excess of feelings into the song.

It's marvellous.

It's the goodbye I never got to say, the perfect song for a new beginning, for finding strength in everything that makes me who I am.

I'm a little breathless when I finish. Alta is gaping, Nooma laughing at them as Nephanie offers me an approving nod. Akim grins up from his comic and I don't care if he's smiling at me or what he's reading.

"Okay, I need to have another go. Not losing to you at this," Alta declares, joining me on the stage. "Shoo, I'll show you what I'm capable of."

I don't budge. "What about a duet?"

"I have no idea what language you speak, Mal, that's going to be hard."

I shrug. "Doesn't matter, pick a song in your language, I bet I can keep up if I get a phonetic translation."

"You just want to show off," Alta plants their hands on their hips. "And I am going to enjoy watching you fall."

"Stars save us all," Nooma mutters even as Nephanie leans closer to her.

And then Alta has picked a song and the best night of my life kicks off into full gear.

PART 4

TO THE OTHER SIDE

The future depends on what you do today.
Gandhi

CHAPTER 30
TRYSTAN

EDEN ONE

I think the next time Cat tells me I look lovely I'm going to murder her. Or rip the damned dress off. It's not that I don't think I look good in it, it's that I can't *stand* what it implies about me.

As soon as my mother finishes parading me around her friends, I join Cat who has abandoned the gaggle of girls that always gravitate towards her. I used to want to be one of them so much and spent a lot of my childhood wondering why I never fit in.

The top floor of the Golden Tower—with its glass roof and walls—offers an impressive view of the city twinkling in the night, and the fake stars above. I've not spent much time stargazing at my parents' countryside home, but I can tell the difference. This is just another lie everyone pretends is a truth.

"Stop glaring at the stars," Cat laughs, nudging me with her elbow.

"I'm not!"

She raises an eyebrow in a 'oh, really?' that looks like Shauna's face every time she found us trying to hide something we weren't supposed to be doing.

"Okay, okay, maybe I was," I admit, brushing a loose strand of hair from my face. My pearl bracelet catches the light, and I can't help imagining how good it would feel to tear it off and watch the pearls scatter to the floor.

"Why *are* you glaring at the stars?" She's more amused than serious but I'm not sure I'm ready for all the truths loaded in the answer.

"They're not real... They're a lie we use to cover the darkness we create," I say, slowly, quietly.

I doubt everyone over-thinks the way I do, but to me the fake stars are like the masks we put on everything so we can pretend that this is the Heaven our ancestors claimed they deserved.

If this place is Heaven, I'd rather be in Hell.

"I suppose," Cat muses. "But I like them. I think it would be lonely if we didn't get to see them."

I glance at her, at her face turned towards the sky. She's radiant with her hair artfully tumbling in soft waves. Her dress is on the cusp of provocative, and I thought her father was going to have a fit when she shed her shawl earlier. There is even the slightest hint of glitter at her lips. I envy all the little ways in which she can thrive. I know her life is far from easy but at least she doesn't have to hate what she sees in the mirror.

"I prefer the stars you can see from the country house," I admit, frightened of the silence.

"I'll admit the sky is nicer outside the city," she says, turning back to me. There is a hint of nervousness in her eyes, the same I feel. Though mine is two-fold, what with the rescue I'm going to be attempting.

The walk back from the city had been strange: people's eyes on me felt different. They saw a boy, not a girl and I had discovered the power of being seen as who you truly are.

I've only got the roughest plan. Ideally, I would need longer, but Jakoor's life is at stake here.

"Stargazing in the middle of a party, that's new," Nathaniel's voice startles me so much I almost drop my glass.

I don't want him to see me like this, but I steel myself and turn to greet him.

He's dressed impeccably in a dark blue suit with a bowtie. With his hands in his pockets, he looks less like his father and more like the boy I remember. When he smiles my grasp on my feelings scatter to the wind.

Back at the lab, my uncle finally walks out, shoulders slumped under his lab coat. He looks worn. I know he was forced into this, but it's hard to forget how he acted in front of me.

"You two wanted to talk to me?" Nathaniel asks, eyes sliding from Cat to me.

"Can we go somewhere more private?" I ask, heart pounding with nerves, the familiar ache of a migraine inching at the corners. I took some pills, but preventative meds aren't always that efficient.

Nathaniel frowns, concern etched into his handsome features, and leads us to an empty cluster of tables. In the wide expanse of the restaurant nowhere is private, but we're unlikely to be overhead here.

I walk up to my uncle.

"Trystan?" He speaks first, relieved.

If he was that worried, he could have found me, or even just messaged.

I answer by stepping into the light.

"I'm so glad you're back." He makes to hug me, and I take a step back.

Cat settles between me and Nathaniel as a waiter appears, asking for our order. We quickly pick something from the menu, eager to be left alone.

"You could have come after me," I tell my uncle. He blanches.

"Trystan, I... I figured you needed space."

"Sure. Needed space in a city I can hardly navigate, alone in a body that could get us both killed. Isn't this why you didn't want me to go out before we were ready?"

He swallows hard. Nathaniel asks me how school is. I give a vague answer.

"You should come inside," my uncle says.

"What she means," Cat pipes up, "Is that she hates school because everyone there is a sexist douchebag."

"Cat!" I hiss as Nathaniel barks out a laugh.

"I can't imagine it's easy for either of you," he admits, shaking his head.

It's so rare to hear someone actually agree.

My uncle leads me back inside, silence hanging thickly between us. I hate it. He's not apologised. I refuse to speak first, refuse to be the one apologising when I've done nothing wrong.

"Trystan I..." he hesitates as we wait for the lift. It's hard to keep my android face stony when Cat cracks a joke and Nathaniel nearly chokes on his drink, but I'm mad enough to manage it, crossing my arms over my chest.

"What?"

Cat is making small talk with an ease I envy.

"I just... I know you don't agree with what I'm doing," my uncle says, stepping into the lift.

"No, I don't."

We're quiet all the way to his lab where I take position by the wall, watching him intently.

"You have to understand that part of being an adult, part of being able to survive here, means doing things you're not on board with."

"How can you justify working on this to yourself?" There's an angry buzzing in my ears.

"Your father would have taken the lab from me. I wouldn't have had the freedom to do this for you," he gestures at the android.

I refuse to feel guilty or responsible. It isn't *my* fault. I didn't ask for any of this. If this place wasn't so messed up none of this would be needed.

"There could have been another way." I need to believe that.

The waiter brings our food, I wish I were hungry.

"So, what did you want to talk about?" Nathaniel asks.

I look down at my plate. This is scary.

"And what other way would there have been? You were miserable," my uncle pushes back.

I close my android eyes against tears of frustration that cannot fall in that body. My uncle doesn't understand that a body of wires and metal was never a long-term fix.

"My father is involved in…questionable stuff," I say to Nathaniel, stealing a look at Cat who gives my leg an encouraging squeeze under the table. To my uncle I say: "You could have taken me away. You've left this place behind before. You ran away for yourself, but you never considered doing it for me. And this," I motion at my body. "Was never going to fix *everything*. It doesn't fix the rest of the life I have to live."

Nathaniel is frowning. "What stuff?" The tension in his voice echoes how I feel.

"Trystan, your parents would have come after us if I'd taken you," my uncle argues. I turn away. It might be the truth, but it doesn't excuse anything.

"You could have *tried*. But instead… Instead, you seemed to think that this," I motion at myself, "would solve everything. As though I didn't have to still *exist* here, where people would treat me like you treat the aliens if they knew the truth! Do you see me like that too? Am I just an experiment?"

His face falls.

"He and my uncle are carrying out experiments on aliens." A pause. "And Humans too," I finish in a whisper. Nathaniel's eyes are wide, forkful forgotten halfway to his mouth. "I don't know all the details," the same half-lie I told Cat. "Both aliens and Humans have died to this. The Kundar, they're being brought here by someone who can't carry out that research elsewhere." Few places are as lax with their laws regarding aliens as Eden One.

"Trystan, you know that's not true," my uncle's tone sharpens with defensiveness.

"Have you got any proof of that, anything we could use?" Nathaniel asks. My eyes go to my uncle's computer.

"Only what I saw. But I should be able to get something off my uncle's computer. Though that's not where most of the info is stored, from what I know. That's where you come in."

"You don't understand," my uncle starts, and I throw my arms up in frustration.

"Where I come in?"

"We need you to hack into her father's computer," Cat finishes for me. "Tris tried to get on it but it's password locked."

"Trystan..." my uncle speaks my name almost like a prayer, breaking a silence I don't know how to fill. I long for a time when his arms were the safest place in the world. "I'm sorry I couldn't do more for you. I really am. I tried to help but I... I knew your parents would do anything to get you back. I thought maybe when you got older, we could do something more and, in the meantime, you could have the android."

"Older? What, once I was married? Once I'm someone's *wife*?" I didn't mean to yell. I miss whatever Nathaniel says. I blink. I've dropped my fork and Cat is by my side.

"Tris? Hey, Tris, you okay?"

I put a hand to my head, forcing myself to refocus.

"Sorry I just... Headache came on suddenly." It's the easiest lie, the closest to any truth I can tell them.

"You need to go lie down?" she asks, and I shake my head slowly.

My uncle hasn't moved, just staring at me. He starts to speak, and I raise my hand to silence him, even as a waiter rushes over to replace my fork. I hate the fuss.

"I need you to do something for me," I tell my uncle abruptly.

He frowns. I already know what he'll say, but I need to give him the benefit of the doubt. I have to hope I can reason with him.

"What?"

"Lend me your shuttle."

He blinks. "Excuse me?"

I clench my jaw.

"Lend me your shuttle. I'm leaving."

"What?"

I've taken him completely off guard but now I can't read the look on his face.

"Are you sure you're okay?" Nathaniel asks.

"I'm leaving and I'm taking the Kundar with me. I'm not letting you carry on with this. And once I'm gone you don't have to agree to anything father wants for my sake." It's hard to keep my tone steely at one end and reassure Nathaniel on the other.

I watch something come apart in my uncle, like a piece of a wall falling loose and letting light shine through. His eyes glisten with tears and the smile on his lips is sad and proud all at once.

"Do you know what model the computer is?" Nathaniel asks, still sounding worried.

My uncle's voice is barely a whisper. "You realise how dangerous this is, don't you?"

"I do. But I have to do this," I tell him, admitting to Nathaniel I can't remember what computer my father has.

"If you could check that would be great, some brands have inbuilt protection I need to watch out for."

My uncle takes a deep breath. "I don't know exactly how far the chip will reach, not in a Human brain, as it's never been tested, but the alien race who created it go very far from home with this technology."

I nod, swallowing hard. It would be a lie to say I am unafraid.

"I'll try and get into his office again," I say as Cat finds my hand under the table.

"How are you going to explain me being in your house?"

For once, I have a solution. "I overheard father saying there's gonna be a party in a couple of days. He sprung it on mom today. Your father will be invited, like always, and so will you."

Nathaniel nods.

"When did you decide to do this?" My uncle asks.

"After I spoke to the alien." He blinks and I see the question in his eyes. "I went to see them after I walked in the observation bay the other day. I needed to understand."

"If you two play the lovebirds everyone wants you to be, that'll alleviate suspicions when you go to talk in private," Cat adds, winking. I blush, and Nathaniel looks positively aghast, eyes looking at everything but me.

"You're braver than I gave you credit for," my uncle says and a lump forms in my throat, stealing the words from both of my mouths.

"If we do that my mother is going to chaperon us all evening. It'll be easier if we just sneak to your dad's office separately," Nathaniel replies.

I am so relieved; I don't think I'd know how to play lovebirds as Cat puts it.

"Will you give me the shuttle?"

My uncle passes his hands through his hair, leaving it sticking up at odd angles. He looks so tired, so old in that moment, remaining silent for so long I wonder if he'll ever speak again.

At the party Cat changes the subject with grace and ease as a waiter comes to check on us.

"Why do you want to do this?" he asks me at last.

"Because of what you told me. Because I believed you when you said that all it took for evil to win was for good men to do nothing. And I don't want to let evil win, not any more than it already has here. So, I'm doing something. Will you help me?"

There is a light in his eyes I thought I'd never see again.

"If you're sure you're ready for this."

As if I could be sure of such a thing. But I have to be ready because the alternative isn't acceptable.

"Tris, you okay?" Cat clutches my leg and I blink, snapping the party back into focus: I'm zoning out too much. I need to stay focussed.

I'm taken by the sudden need to tell them, to pour out all my secrets. Only here is the least safe place to speak about this shit. Not that I know anywhere that would be a hundred percent safe.

"I am," I tell my uncle with all the confidence I can muster as I reassure my friends.

"I can always cover for you two if needed," Cat adds, wiggling her eyebrows suggestively.

We're all risking so much. My friends, my uncle, me. But it's worth it, to do what's right. To do what needs doing in the face of injustice and corruption. It has to be.

"Okay," my uncle takes a deep breath. "But you're going to have to do something for me too," he says, turning to his computer.

Keeping a smile on my face at the party is tricky, let alone as my mother comes to fetch me.

"What do you need?" I ask, trying to keep my fears at bay.

"I need you to take all this data, and as soon as you get the chance, get it in the hands of people who will care. If you can get any more info on Berik Corp. once you're away, do, you're going to need all you can to take them down."

I stare at the datastick he hands me as Cat tries to convince my mother that I need to take it easy, but she informs my friends their own parents are looking for them.

"I won't let them get away with what they're doing," I assure my uncle.

CHAPTER 31
TRYSTAN

EDEN ONE

My uncle takes the lead, assuring me there should be no-one else left in the building. We make a quick stop by the security office, so he can create a looping feed for the lab and side exit cameras.

At least all I have to do at the party is keep a vapid smile on my face and nod at appropriate intervals. No-one wants to know what a sixteen-year-old girl has to say anyway.

Once he has the loops in place, we hurry down to the cells where Jakoor is kept.

They're on their cot, asleep or unconscious—I can't tell—with nothing but a sheet about them for clothing. I'm still angry at my uncle for ever accepting to do this.

"Open the cell!"

He's already at the console.

The door slides open, and I rush inside. I can see all the bruises mottling Jakoor's body. Very gently, I lay my hand on their shoulder. One of their hands shoots up and grabs my wrist. Their grip is so strong I have to hold back a squeak of surprise. Their eyes open, luminescent blue staring into my soul.

"Trystan."

It sounds like a prayer and the whisper of a dream. They move slowly as they sit up, eyes snapping to my uncle.

"Why is he here?"

"Because he's getting us out of here." I catch what I think must be distrust in the way Jakoor moves. "I convinced him," I add. Then I turn to my uncle. "Do you have clothes for them?"

My uncle pulls a face. "No, they didn't exactly send us their stuff."

"I can use this." Jakoor is on their feet, tearing the sheet in half so they can wrap it around their waist. "Now let's go, clothes can wait."

I turn to my uncle. "Back door?"

"Follow me."

"What about the cameras?" Jakoor asks.

"I created a looping feed, we're safe for the next thirty minutes."

I'm so relieved to find the man I thought my uncle was back at the surface, so glad that I could trust him.

We slip out through the fire exit, up a short flight of stairs, and out in the cool night air. From the party I glance at the spaceport towers.

Freedom.

For half of me.

What would happen if my organic body died? Would I find a new, permanent home in metal and wires or would I fade away altogether? I doubt even my uncle would have the answer. But if I did survive, then it could be freedom for *all* of me. Only, would it be the freedom I want?

"Get in the car," my uncle hisses as footsteps suddenly draw close. I slip in the front seat and Jakoor lays down in the back just before someone comes around the back of the large van parked in the next space.

At the party, the migraine isn't a lie anymore, and I barely manage to reply to my mother before she digs out a painkilling patch from her purse, placing it on the inside of my wrist. I hear the silent 'don't you dare make a fuss' she never voices.

"Gideon, I thought you'd gone home already."

I don't know the voice, but there is an edge to it that makes me afraid.

"Forgot something and then I got caught up checking some results that came in," my uncle lies so naturally it's almost impressive.

"You know we're supposed to scan everyone that comes in and out, right?" the man asks, and I risk a glance in the rear-view mirror.

Shit.

Security.

"Come on, I was only in there for what, half an hour at most since you last checked me," my uncle sounds so calm. "Is there really a need to go through all this fuss again?"

The security officer sighs, I can feel him hesitate. Procedure versus the fact he seems to be on good terms with my uncle. On the backseat, Jakoor looks ready to launch themself out of the car. I hope it won't be necessary.

"Fine, fine, but don't let me find out you snuck something out to study at home, eh? You know the rules."

"You know I do," my uncle replies, and the security guard gives him a sharp nod before returning to his station.

My uncle slips inside the car.

"Heads down, both of you," he says as he starts the car.

I all but vanish beneath the dashboard, as we flee the carpark, crawling back in my seat only when the car takes off.

***

"Care to dance?"

My head snaps up, I'd been lost in watching the city pass us by in the car, expecting to be left alone. Only now, Nathaniel is looking at me with his bright green eyes and his lopsided smile, a hand held out to me.

"Tris?"

My cheeks flush as I realise, I've been staring, and I completely forget how to speak. He pulls up a chair and sits down close. I wish the heat would leave my face.

"You okay?"

"Just the headache, and..." I glance towards the window, looking for something to say.

"Not the greatest party, is it?"

"Are any? Though you usually seem to thrive at them."

"You've been watching me?"

A new rush of heat floods my cheeks. "No, I... It's just..." *Get a grip!*

"I'm teasing, I'm sorry. You're usually so hard to spot, is all."

My laugh is a little too high and brittle from nerves. "Guess I hate them that much."

He slants me a look and I stare down, fussing with my dress.

"This one is pretty dull, but usually I have to play political games around my father," Nathaniel admits, and I'm not sure if he's talking to me or filling the silence.

"At least you have more to do than just look pretty," the bitterness in my voice is so sharp he startles.

"Sorry."

If I look at him, I'm going to start wishing I wasn't who I am again.

"My mother had a chat before we came here, about you and me," he says. "About how they're going to make the engagement official, and I should really be seen around you more."

"I suppose that's handy for what we need to do." My hands are bunched up in my skirts, the music drowned out by the beating of my heart. I want to flee this place, this world, this everything.

"Did I do something wrong?" he asks softly.

"What?"

"I thought maybe you and I were okay, that we could be friends again. I know things suck but... I thought maybe we'd started mending things. But now you won't even look at me… Was I wrong?"

I turn to him faster than I meant, catching the sadness and worry fleeting on his face.

"No, I... It's not you, really." I really do make a mess of everything I touch. "Tonight's just been really hard on me, is all. And I've had days of a headache that won't go away which really doesn't help me be social." I try to make my smile as genuine as possible.

"Sorry, I can leave you alone if you'd rather."

I should say yes. But our knees are almost touching, the presence of him reassuring, the closeness surprisingly pleasant.

"You look really upset." His words catch me by surprise. Nobody bar Cat ever notices how I'm feeling. Not since he was forced out of my life by our parents' stupid thought that boys and girls can never be something so simple as friends.

"I... It's really complicated." I expect him to push but he just gives me a smile that seems to say, 'I know what that's like'.

A bunch of boys are edging our way and Nathaniel pulls a face.

"Not friends of yours?"

"Not exactly, but I have to play nice around them."

"That sucks."

"Yeah. Tris, you know that dance I offered? Would you be willing?"

He's standing with his hand out again. If I go with him, I'll save him from those boys, but I will be *dancing* with him. It's something I want but it's the wrong way and he's looking at the wrong me, and God, but I wish this wasn't so complicated.

"Sure." My hand is in his.

"I warn you though, I'm a terrible dancer."

I laugh. "Well, I always try to lead so we're off to a good start." I sound like an idiot. My heart is racing.

"Lead away!"

I blink as he pulls me onto the dancefloor. It's just crowded enough to disguise our terrible dancing, but not so much that we're a liability. I can't remember the last time I've done this. Our hands are intertwined, his other hand resting very lightly on my waist and mine on his elbow because I'm too stiff to reach for his shoulder.

I have to nudge us into the first steps. The song hasn't long started and it's not hard to find the rhythm. Nathaniel is as terrible as he warned and, before long, we're laughing softly as he trips, and I try to keep us on course. I like this. His laughter so close to my ears, my steps guiding us. It lets the rest of the world fall away for a while.

The music ends as the car begins its descent towards the spaceport, and the spell shatters. Unlike Cinderella, though, I'm still standing here in my beautiful gown.

"Tris?" Nathaniel looks so worried suddenly.

"I'm sorry," I manage before fleeing the party. I don't care if people stare, if my parents are furious, I just rush to the bathroom, tears choking me as soon as I collapse in a stall.

#

The lights come on as my uncle parks in his private hangar, revealing his small shuttle.

"Do you have security in here?" Jakoor asks. "Cameras or guards?"

My uncle shakes his head.

"Cameras yes—but there's no-one to monitor so I can doctor the footage—just alarms in the event someone broke in."

"So, they'll know you let us in here," Jakoor points out as I step out of the car, eyes fixed on the shuttle. Even I can tell it's an old model, but it doesn't matter, because as far as I'm concerned, it's the freedom model.

"I'll say you forced me. No offence, but with the way Humans see Kundar, they'll buy it pretty easily."

"Not if you're unhurt," Jakoor replies, and I step up to the two of them ready to interpose.

But the sad smile on my uncle's face says he's already thought ahead.

"That's why I expect you to knock me out and tie me up before you get on that shuttle."

I gasp. "No! I don't want you getting hurt!" I thought I could have hurt him earlier but now I know I couldn't. Not with everything he means to me.

"It'll be okay, Tryst," he turns to me. "It won't be the first time I've taken a punch to the face."

I throw myself at him, wrapping my arms around him, letting him do the same. I know I'm not *really* leaving, that I will still be able to see him and speak to him, but it still feels like a strange kind of goodbye.

"I'm sorry," I whisper into his shoulder.

"Don't be sorry, Tryst, be proud of yourself." He pushes me back so he can look in my eyes. "I'm proud of your strength. This can't be easy, but I believe in you."

I'm so glad I can't cry in this body.

"Did you really accept to do this only for me?"

"Yes, and no," he admits, shame tainting his voice. "I won't lie, Tryst. Your father is a very influential man, and I didn't want to lose what I'd built since I came back. But you're right, *nothing* should be worth what I was doing."

He pulls me back and I hold onto him tightly.

"I'll make this right," I tell him. "I promise. I'll find a way." I look up at him. He looks taller, stronger, than he has in a long time. "I want to make this place *better*."

He smiles again, his eyes shining with tears as he leans down to place a kiss on my forehead. His strength bolsters mine. How many more people are there on this colony like him? Like Lilac and Shauna and me. People who want to make a difference. Can there be enough of us to change this world?

I have to believe there is.

"Go," he tells me. "Get on that shuttle. I'll see you soon."

Pulling away is hard but I don't want to watch what's next any more than he wants me to see it, so I hurry to the shuttle.

It doesn't take long for Jakoor to join me in the cockpit, immediately settling in the pilot seat and starting the take-off sequence.

"You know how to pilot this?"

"I'm Kundar, we can pilot pretty much anything," they say, the sparkle in their eyes comforting.

"Good, 'cause I don't," I say, buckling myself in my seat.

Jakoor presses something and the viewing window becomes clear. I can see my uncle's car below, imagine him stuffed in the back seat and I hope he's okay.

Luckily, the take-off sequence is automated. Jakoor cheers as we clear the open roof.

We're silent all the way up, as we pass on the other side of the fake stars and then punch out of the atmosphere, the viewing window turning red for a breath before space reveals itself, breathtakingly beautiful.

A twisting nebula in pinks and blues twirls in blackness painted with a thousand dots of silver. Too many stars to count, to even dream about.

"You're not *just* an android, are you?" Jakoor asks as they steady the ship.

"No," I whisper, though my attention is on the nebula, and the stars, and the outline of Ishnira far in the distance. "No, I'm not."

CHAPTER 32
TRYSTAN

JOVAR SOLAR SYSTEM
PRIVATE SHUTTLE

I tell Jakoor *everything*. Even as mom lectures me and father drags me to the car, his grip so tight it'll leave bruises, Jakoor listens to me, accepts me, and I'm not scared as father slams the car door to send me home early. In fact, I never felt so brave as when I snatched myself from his grasp and entered the car myself, risking everything for a defiant look his way.

The distance in between Eden One and Ishnira is only three quarters of an hour, just long enough to tell my story and lock myself in my room, dropping face first onto my bed.

Jakoor handles the coms when we get hailed and then we're descending through the atmosphere and I'm crying as a whole new world reveals itself to me. It's nothing like Eden One, the spaceport city ringed by a sea the colour of sapphires and beyond a forest of dark, almost black, trees.

The city is a maze of buildings and multi-tiered roads clustered around the gigantic tower that stretches miles above the ground and forms the central complex of the spaceport. Everywhere I look I spot billboards and holographic ads.

It's nothing like the squeaky-clean facade of Eden One, not with the light of dawn—or dusk, I'm not sure—highlighting where grime and age has made its mark. Yet it's breathtaking. I'm aching to lose myself in those streets.

As we pull into the docking bay, I'm almost giddy with both nerves and excitement. Everything here is so different to what my home is like, and I need to explore every corner of it I can.

A floating drone waits for us in the antechamber between docking bay and spaceport. Jakoor goes first, stepping into a scanning chamber and following the drone's instructions. It takes a handful of seconds and then they step out and it's my turn.

My heart races as a series of bleeps go off and the light dims slightly.

"My apologies," the drone states in its robotic voice. I'm so glad I downloaded a giant language patch for this body. "I did not realise you were an android. Please state your model and serial number so I can create your temporary ID."

I freeze. "I... I don't know it."

The drone pauses. "Are you an artificial intelligence or limited intelligence model?"

"Artificial intelligence." That, at least, is easy to answer.

Another pause. "Given name?"

"Trystan."

"Are you part of a series or the only one of your name?"

"Only one."

"Very well, I will leave your serial number blank for the moment, please have it added as soon as possible. You will need it to access automated workshops. You can find a manned one on the ground floor where you can have the serial number retrieved. Use any administrative booth to register it." A pause. "Please have a pleasant stay on Ishnira. If you seek to venture outside the city limits, please do acquire the proper documentation."

The door slides open, and I hurry out to where another drone is waiting, holding out an ID chip.

"Ishnira has special ID chips, please allow me to put it under your skin."

I glance at Jakoor, and they show me the tiniest cut on their wrist.

"Er, sure, not like it's going to hurt anyway."

The chip is so small I can hardly see the incision left behind after my synth skin is knitted back together with a spray.

"You are now temporary citizens of the Ishnira Space Tower. You may download any further information from the terminals available here and in the city. Have a nice day."

I download far more than I need from said terminal as Jakoor studies the map, still in nothing but the sheet around their waist. They're rocking it with so much confidence, you'd think it had been a choice. The scales peeking along their sides are also strangely enticing. Isn't it good androids can't blush?

"What do we do now?" I ask.

"There should be a Kundar cache not far from here, I just need to work out where. It'd be easier if they hadn't taken all of my stuff."

"I'm sorry."

Jakoor turns to me with a tilt to their head I'm starting to think is the equivalent of a raised eyebrow.

"What for? You are not the one who captured me. Quite the contrary, you are the one who freed me, despite the dangers to yourself."

"Yeah, I don't think I could have done that without, well, this," I motion at my body. "I'm not exactly very brave," I admit with an embarrassed laugh.

Jakoor puts their hand on my shoulder, turquoise eyes boring into mine.

"We do what we must to survive, to keep living until we can overcome what holds us down. I know that. I come from a planet that lives by that mentality. For generations we lived underground and then under domes before we were ready to venture out. But just because we put our safety first didn't make us cowards. You're doing the same. And with this body you have the tools to do more, but that doesn't take away from what you do."

Despite all my doubts I smile, thinking of my uncle telling me he's proud of me. I feel stronger than I ever thought possible.

"You want to stick with me for now?"

"Yeah, I don't really know my way around."

"Alright then, let's go find this cache and then some food, I need something solid to eat."

***

ISHNIRA

The Kundar's history has left them with a mistrust of other species and a tradition of leaving caches for each other wherever they travel. We traipse around for a good half-hour before finally finding it. The panel reads Jakoor's DNA code, and the cache opens, revealing a small storeroom.

As they get ready, I linger by one of the large windows, watching the city. Everything is foreign and strange, yet achingly alluring all the same.

"Do you want to go have a walk around?"

It's hard to reconcile the person standing in front of me with who I rescued. They're clad in deep purple synth-leather pants and a tight tank, their hair pulled back in a bun at the top of their head, showing off their horns. Twin pistols sit at their back, twin blades at their hips.

Their turquoise eyes are full of something new I wish I understood as they linger on me, self-conscious in my standard issue android uniform I changed into because the clothes I'd worn before were too grimy.

"I..."

"It's okay if you do. I need some food anyway, and everyone knows spaceport food is never the best you can get."

I manage a mumble of agreement and then I'm following them, grateful when they take my hand to lead me through the thickening crowd after they acquire city passes for the rest of the day, lying by way of claiming they're my owner to save on awkward questions regarding my lack of ID.

Buildings of glass and dark metal stretch above and below the street on which we emerge, the ground too far down to see. Walkways interconnect levels, flying cars and small shuttles navigating between. Everywhere I look, holographic and 3D ads catch my attention, a cacophony of music and voices emanating from them.

In the last remnants of the setting sun, the city feels dreamlike, especially with all the species walking around us, none of which I have names for.

No-one glances our way, but instead of feeling invisible, I feel safe. Blending in is magical, the energy of the crowd becoming mine.

It doesn't take long for Jakoor to find somewhere to eat: a street cart with greasy food with such a potent smell that my organic stomach turns, reminding me painfully that this escape is only half of my life, the rest still trapped back in a world that hates me.

To distract myself, I go to look at an ad-pod offering cybernetic limbs and body mods.

"Be the best you, today! Just drop into one of our workshops and ask to speak to our specialists who will be delighted to help you. Most parts can be printed within seventeen hours, and you could be fitted with your new modifications in under a solar cycle!"

"Thinking of changing something?" Jakoor asks, joining me.

"No, I was just… This is like nothing I've ever seen."

"I didn't see much of your planet but…" They shrug. "This is pretty common if I'm honest. Plenty more places like it out there."

"I'd like to see them," I admit quietly.

"Maybe you will. You get to decide what you do now."

"I guess." My hand finds the datachip in my pocket. I have yet to look at exactly what my uncle gave me. "I'm not sure what to do. I promised my uncle I would try to find more info on Berik…and try and get some help."

"Any idea where to find some?"

"I was thinking of heading for the United Planet space-station but… Like my uncle said, Berik is powerful, and I need all the proof I can against them," I sigh. "What about you? What are you going to do?"

"There's someone I need to find."

"Who?"

"A Kundar scientist. They… They were my mentor. One day they left without a word, all their research gone with them. I tried to recreate it by myself but…" They shake their head. "I need to find them. I had a lead before I got captured: someone I'd paid to do some digging. I never got to find out what they'd found as I never made it to the meeting."

"You're going to find them, then?"

They nod. "My contact works from Bakula, so I'll be heading there. It shouldn't be that long through hyperspace."

"Can I come with you?"

They seem a little taken aback.

"Are you sure? I don't know if an outlaw hub is exactly where you'll find what you need."

For a second, I agree, and then, I realise that outlaws might be exactly the people who can help me. After all, who is more likely to amass dirt on big corporations but the very people whose interests are at odds with the rich and powerful.

"It might be exactly what I need, actually," I say, with a renewed sense of purpose. "So as long as you'll have me, I'm coming."

"The company's definitely welcome."

I smile, wide and bright and genuine. There is so much at stake, and yet I am undeniably happy to be here, on this journey.

Jakoor disposes of his food wrapper and pulls something out of his pocket. "Found a shuttle access card in the cache, so we can leave your uncle's behind. It'll be better. Before we go check it out, though, wanna have a look around?"

"I'd love that."

CHAPTER 33
LÀHN

BAKULA

Bakula juts out of its asteroid, its uneven shape like a blemish on the beautiful landscape of purple nebulae and a thousand stars.

But what truly steals the show is the Urelhan destroyer Nyurae told us about, its hull shimmering, its very presence unnerving and I'm glad when we dock and it's no longer hovering at the edge of my awareness.

Inside, Bakula might well be the most confusing place I have ever seen. Kirillion is a sprawling, overpopulated metropolis, but there is logic to it: quarters and districts and zones, all—mostly—labelled and signposted. Chaos seems to be Bakula's very essence.

By the time we find the exit and cross what passes as boarding control—a bored Zuulaat who doesn't even check our IDs—I'm ready to call it a day. Beyond the corridor we're greeted by a large open area crammed full of people, stalls, and so much noise. It's even worse than market nights in Shu'a'kash.

This place is amazing. Kode signs and I pull a face. She laughs. *Grumpy*.

Not! But how are we supposed to find our way?

"We ask," Shuobe interjects.

"Ask who, though?"

"We buy some food, and we ask, you have his address, right?"

I nod and Shuobe gives me a look of 'well, then', before setting off.

Unlike Kirillion, where races have carved out some spaces mostly to themselves, everyone mingles here, and navigating around enviro-suits has never seemed so hard.

Shuobe leads us to a food stall and slides up to the front. The cook isn't full blood Mallak, but they definitely have some of the Wandering People's genes in them and are delighted to see Shuobe.

They exchange pleasantries as I take in the crowd. Kode signs some particularly cutting comments about the fashion going around. I laugh despite myself. The cook gives us directions, but we have to get them to repeat three times, taking notes all the while.

When we pull away, Shuobe hands us each a drink.

"I'm still lost," I admit.

Shuobe laughs. "Lucky you have a Mallak with you, then."

***

We had to ask for directions five more times, almost stepped into a gang dispute, and ended up in three dead ends before finding the *Shu Fa Rinari* club.

The bar looks part junkyard, part high-tech disco, only without the correct sound system to properly play the Hrusha pop currently being slaughtered.

I take the lead, determined to not have to rely on the girls for everything.

The alien behind the bar is a surprising sight: the Zezzjri don't often leave their hives. Their big, bulbous eyes are fixed on me, the twin antennas on their head quivering as they let out a clicking, hissing sound. I've little experience with this species but know enough to bring up my holo-screen; Zezzjri don't communicate with words, but at least their written language can be approximately translated.

They point over their shoulder with a spindly arm, pincers clicking twice to draw my attention to the list of alcohols. I type my question and flick it from my screen to theirs. More clicking noises and something like a hiss and they're pointing at a door. I nod for the girls to join me.

The corridor beyond is short, the first unmarked door the place we′re after.

″Stars, we made it." I press the buzzer and it slides up.

Tulain is reclining in his chair, bare clawed feet on the desk. He′s a ruddy colour, and looks nothing like Zoon, save for his build—broad and muscled—although he is considerably shorter.

"I'm going to bet my collection of hats that you're Làhn, right?" he declares as a greeting. "Come in, come in. I *have* been expecting you. I mean, I was expecting two! Brother didn't say a Mallak′d be gracing my office. I'd have dressed better."

Tulain takes his feet off the desk and offers us a smile that makes me want to run away. No species should be allowed to have this many razor-sharp teeth.

"Don't look so terrified. I mean I know Zoon doesn't have the teeth, but still, he's a giant!"

I let out a nervous laugh. "Sorry we're... We had trouble finding you."

"Ah, first time on the station?" I nod. "Figures, really. Even people who know, if you're gone a while, you're still likely to turn yourself around five times. Like those pets that chase their tails, eh? But no matter, no matter, you're here now, and I promised Brother I'd look after you. I don't have accommodation set up, was waiting till you got here, but for tonight you can crash at my pad. Now, I suppose you'd like me to show you the way instead of just sending you there alone, right?"

Shuobe laughs in a way that says, 'what do you think'.

"Come on then." The Furakian stands up, claws clicking on the floor. "How long d'you intend on staying? It'll be easier to find a place if we have a time frame."

"Not that long hopefully," I manage, Kode signing encouragement. I'm still a little nervous about our plan.

"Oh?" Tulain stops, a ridiculous hat half-way to his head.

"There's somewhere I need to go. So, we're going to try and find a ship to take us there."

Tulain's vertically slit eyes narrow. "Brother didn't tell me anything about this."

"That's because I hadn't told him yet, it's—" I'm about to say complicated, but I pause. It's not so much complicated as difficult to talk about.

Before I can speak again, the door slides open, and a boy in a hoverchair all but comes flying in.

"Tulain, we need to talk!" he exclaims. Only then does he notice the three of us standing there. "Oh, you're busy. Sorry. Anyway, we *do* need to talk, like *now* preferably."

He sounds a little angry, but mostly agitated. His eyes are a stunning mix of teal and turquoise, and his skin a pleasant, warm brown. He's good looking, with a strong, wide nose, hair tumbling in unruly waves around his face. It takes me a second to notice his missing limbs.

"Excuse me," I say before Tulain's recovered. "But we were here first."

The boy turns his chair to me. His eyes trace up and down more than is polite, a smirk quirking up one side of his mouth.

"Sure you were, pretty boy," he replies and I open my mouth for a retort I don't have. "But I've got important business with Tulain. I'll only borrow him for five minutes. Well okay, maybe ten. Or fifteen. But then he's all yours. How does that sound?" He offers me a grin I want to slap off his face.

"Enough, Malek, enough. Whatever you've got to talk about is going to have to wait, Zoon sent me people to look after so I've got to take them to mine for now. We can talk when that's done," Tulain says, trying to step to the door, but the boy—Malek—blocks his way.

"Since when does anyone trust you with looking after people? And either way, this is important. This is about the stuff you *didn't* tell me."

Tulain freezes, glancing from me to Malek and back.

"What do you mean?" he asks.

"Oh, you want me to do this in front of strangers? You think that's gonna stop me? Okay, you know, whatever, I don't care who they are. I want to know why the blasted stars you didn't tell me Vess is working with what's left of amma's crew. Why did you keep that from me? What *really* happened between you and Vess, Tul?"

Tulain sighs. "It's a long story."

"I have time."

"Well, that's great but we don't. It took us hours to find this stupid place, and I'd like to get somewhere I can get comfortable," I snap and Malek turns my way, scowling.

He's kinda cute. Stars, why am I noticing how cute this rude idiot is? Focus, Làhn, head in the game.

"We can talk once we get to my flat, does that sound okay?"

"Fine," Malek snaps and turns his chair around with so much speed I'm surprised it doesn't tip over. Kode and I exchange a look. All we can do for now is follow Tulain.

CHAPTER 34
MALEK

BAKULA
TWO HOURS EARLIER

Two days of resting and lazing about, eating too many snacks—and making myself sick twice—have me desperate to be active.

As soon as we could, we got everyone's augmentations reactivated—all the cool tech that comes with my cybernetic eyes is back on and Nooma is back to being superhumanly strong instead of just stupidly strong.

She and I head off to the club where Vess carries out his business, expecting to find the same dingy bar full of shady types that I remember. What greets us instead is a pleasant, clean place, cleverly lit in blues and purples, with comfortable seating suited to a multitude of species; the circular bar is manned by an attractive pair: a half-naked Kundar and a Hrusha in a dazzling tunic.

I order a light synth-cocktail, whilst Nooma gets something fizzy and green like some biohazardous poison.

We settle at the back to people-watch. Nooma is acting relaxed, but I can tell just how alert she is, recognising her manners from back in the mines. Just thinking about Helios makes me want to throw up.

We're out, we're fine, we're free.

Nooma takes a long sip, eyes scanning the room discreetly.

"So, go over what you know about Vess again?"

"He's Tulain's ex-partner. And ex-boyfriend. But then, they're on and off more often than a light switch. Vess's part human, part Shinarian. I was never as close to him. If what Tulain said is true, he owns half the level around this bar."

"Is that why Tulain couldn't come and take back what he stole? Couldn't he have reported it?"

"Like I said, their relationship is complicated. Tulain says no-one will let him within twenty metres of this place, but neither does he want to drag the authorities into what is, essentially, a lovers' tiff."

"A lover's tiff? Really?"

"Yeah, they're off at the moment, but when Vess paid Tulain a visit they spoke and drank and one thing led to another. When Tulain woke up Vess was gone, and so was the chip."

"What's so special about the AI on that chip?"

"Beats me. Tulain only said he really needed it back. I didn't ask more."

"Might have been wise."

"I trust him."

"And I'm sure once upon a time he trusted this Vess. You gotta be more careful, Mal."

I roll my eyes but drop it. She's about five times as stubborn as me. And probably five times more likely to be right.

"Anyway, I said we'd do the job. Remember, Tulain is the one covering everything we need for the repairs, *and* he's going to pay us for this. Without him, no ship, no sound system!"

"You have a very skewed sense of priorities..."

"What? We *need* a sound system."

"Need is not the word I'd use."

"Let's face it, even you had fun at the karaoke."

"I did not."

"Well okay, you had fun watching Nephanie sing at least," I tease, gasping when she kicks me under the table. "Ow, what was that for?"

"You know exactly what it was for, Mal. Now *focus*, we need to figure out how to get to Vess' office."

I look around. Three doors: one for the bathroom, two unmarked. We can't risk asking and making our intentions obvious—especially if someone recognises me. Tulain was adamant on us being discreet. Sure, I've changed since I was fourteen, but I've taken more than a little after amma.

"His office's at the back, like Tulain's, so it's gotta be one of those doors."

Nooma nods. "So, we sit, and we sip, and we watch. Send me the picture you showed me earlier."

The picture is the most recent Tulain could find: Vess relaxing against a doorway, his Human eyes in their disquieting purple hue dancing with the hint of a smile. His hair is all done up in the Shinarian fashion, his features sharp with high cheekbones, his skin a warm brown devoid of markings.

"Getting into his office is gonna be tricky. Can't exactly burst in there," I say, taking another sip. It's almost like that one cocktail I used to share with amma all the time. Stars but I miss her.

"We could just make an appointment to scope the place," Nooma points out. "I go in there," she taps the side of her eye. "Record looking around the place, and we can see if there's another way in from there."

"Like the air vent?" I ask, half joking. Nooma rolls her eyes.

"None of us are small enough to fit in air vents, Mal. Even you should know that."

"I'm kidding!"

"Can you not, for like, five minutes? Working a job is serious. We also need to learn Vess' routine."

"We should've started earlier," I mutter and Nooma glares. At least I don't get kicked this time.

"We needed rest. I don't know how you've been going nonstop, but not everyone can do that."

I look away, feeling like I've been an ass again. It's not like I'm not tired, especially with the lack of accessibility on the ship. But the fire in my soul just won't let me stop.

"I just..." I falter. "I'm sorry. Stopping scares me."

I'm surprised when she reaches a hand to rest on top of mine.

"It's okay, Malek," she reassures me. "Nothing bad is going to happen if we take a break."

I manage a small smile.

Our heart-to-heart is interrupted when a tall man wearing expensive black pants, and an off-the-shoulder top showing off copious amounts of smooth brown skin strides out of the back. Dark green eyeliner frames violet eyes and jewels glint amongst the knots in his hair.

Vess.

I had never realised how attractive Vess was until now. Many of the patrons are greeting him as he stops here and there to exchange some friendly chit-chat. He's nothing like I remember, but I wonder how much of him was tainted by how jealous I was that Tulain had chosen him over me and amma.

"That's our man?" Nooma double checks.

"Yeah," I sound a little startled. "He, um, isn't quite what I remember." I rub my face and am reminded that I haven't shaved since we escaped. I'm going to tip from rugged to scruffy in a day or so.

"Now at least we've confirmed where the office is. Only need to figure out if—Malek are you listening?"

"I wonder what he's up to..." I follow him with my eyes as he leaves the bar.

She raises an eyebrow at me. "Don't even think about it. We're not prepped for that."

"For what?"

"Following him."

I break into a grin. "That's a great idea actually!"

Nooma smacks her forehead, groaning. "No, Malek, it really isn't."

***

BAKULA
NOW

I should have listened to Nooma.

I'm glad I didn't.

The silence is heavy as we ride the lift down, anger throbbing through my veins. There are some things I wasn't ready for. Like losing the sense of security I felt around Tulain. But I can't erase what I saw.

I can scarcely deal with the tension. Pretty boy and the two girls to one side, me and Tulain on the other. Silent. I hate silence.

"So," I start, my fake cheer grating even to me. "Where're you guys from?"

"Kirillion," the boy replies sharply. Well, this is off to a good start. I glance up at him and allow myself to drink him in. Golden brown skin, high cheekbones, softly curving eyes pointedly looking away from me. His hair is pulled back in a messy bun, some loose strands framing his face. The girls with him are cute too, the human one smiling a little hesitantly at me, then waving her hands in a way I don't understand.

"She's asking if you're from here," the part Mallak girl—her girlfriend if I'm reading the body language right—translates.

"Not really, I'm a captain, so I guess I'm from my ship," I reply. Just saying those words is enough to put a genuine grin on my face.

The girl beams back. She must have read my lips, which is impressive, especially when we don't speak the same language. The boy scowls.

"Everyone is from *somewhere,*" he says.

"I was born in space." I shrug, sparing him a glance. "Nothing else ever really mattered."

The boy scoffs and turns away, crossing his arms over his chest almost defensively. The girl signs again.

"What kind of ship do you have?" The Mallak girl translates.

"For now, just a small cargo freighter. It's a bit shabby but it's about to get some awesome renovations!"

The girl's smile is lovely. I catch Tulain muttering something that sounds awfully like 'what in the stars are you doing to that ship?' but I ignore him.

Finally, the lift stops, and Tulain leads us down a couple of narrow corridors with so much junk littering the floor that my chair struggles. He stops in front of a rusted door that reminds me of the place amma rented when all her cash had to go to my hospital bills.

I feel the ache of her absence so keenly now, even as I follow Tulain inside. It's small and messy, cluttered with random junk. One room with a bed, a tiny table by a landscape display, the kitchen area nothing more than a workstation and a bio-grade printer, a narrow door to the bathroom at the back. He used to make a fortune, from what he told amma, so how did he end up down here?

"It's not much but you can relax in here whilst I find you somewhere with enough beds for the lot of you," he tells his guests.

"Now can I get my answers?" I snap, the words biting.

Tulain sighs but doesn't reply. "If any of you need a wash, there's a shower. With real water, only luxury I got in here, but chemicals make my scales itch."

No-one takes him up on the offer.

The deaf girl collapses on the bed, the boy settling in one of the chairs, as the Mallak girl declares she needs to buy stuff and walks right back out.

Tulain busies himself around the room, piling things in an attempt to create the impression of tidiness. Even by my—admittedly low—standards, he's failing.

"Tulain," my tone softens despite myself. I just want the truth. I wish I'd let Nooma come but I knew I had to do this by myself.

Tulain sighs and faces me. Pretty boy pulls out a tablet from his bag whilst his friend buries her face under the pillow to block out the light.

"It's complicated, kid."

"Why didn't you tell me?"

"I didn't think you were going to sneak around following Vess. I mean, you never liked him, so I figured you'd just sneak into his office, grab the chip and get out," Tulain shrugs. "I didn't think there was any need for you to know anything else."

"Huh, is that so?" My temper slips out of control again. "Figured I didn't need to know that some of amma's crew had survived, did you? How d'you figure that, eh?" He opens his mouth to reply but I steamroll on. "You always give so little info to people when you pay them for a job? Or is it just me? You give me the ship and you send me money but telling me all the details, no need for that, right? The hell's going on?"

For a moment I wonder if all he's going to do is sigh again and I want to scream. I thought I could trust him.

"A lot happened since your mother's ship got blown to pieces," he starts. Pretty boy's making a poor attempt at looking like he's not listening. "After I heard she got killed I tried to find you, but I couldn't. You'd vanished off the grid." He shakes his scaly head, looking at the floor. "I didn't know what had killed her and I worried you'd died too. So, I came back here only to find a message from her dated from before she died. She... There were things in there she asked me not to talk about. Things about the chip."

My eyes go wide as my chest goes tight.

"What things? Tulain, what the hell is going on?"

"Like I told you, there's an AI on the chip. When your mother rescued it, it was operational. It came from a world that had been invaded by some corporate goons, and they'd sent the AI out like a message in a bottle. But when your mother activated it, she got tracked by the corporation and they blew you all out of the sky without questions. Your mother escaped with the chip, and I imagine she sent it to me when you landed on that rock where you got seen to. Only it took a long time to get here, and by the time I had it, it was too late to help her."

He runs a hand over his face, the sound of claws on scales startlingly familiar. I'd loved having him on board. When amma was alive. When things were simpler

I push the memories away and let out a long breath. I didn't know why we'd been attacked, amma had always been cagey about it. I always thought knowing might make things better, my rage finally having a target, but instead I'm just exhausted.

"Why do you want the damn chip back, then?"

"Because your amma's old crew got some stupid idea in their head to get their own back on the jackasses who blew them up. A lot of them lost friends and limbs in that attack. La'min got them together, and then they came to me. I told them what to do with their idea, that I didn't care how much they were willing to pay or how ready they thought they were for the fight, I wasn't letting them have it. They got pissy, but they didn't make a scene and I thought that was that. They went to Vess behind my back. So Vess turned up at my office out of the blue, all smiles and I thought, hey, maybe we can make things work again. And well," he clears his throat. "You know what happened. Which is probably my bad for not changing the safe code since he left me."

I mostly stopped listening after he said *La'min.*

La'min, amma's second. Uncle La'min, who had been far too patient when child-me was dangling from his tail. La'min, who taught me so much about ships, about how a crew works. I thought he'd died. I thought all of them had died. I remember his voice urging amma into the escape pod as my body burnt and I screamed. I remember hearing his voice before another explosion, my ears ringing and the pain dragging me under.

La'min lives.

I want to shake Tulain for not telling me, but I'm frozen, breath coming ragged as I swallow my tears.

"I've been trying to get the chip back from Vess for weeks now, but he's well-loved, has made a name for himself as one of the good guys. So, when you turned up, so ready and willing, I figured this was a good way to get it back. And once you had it, I could tell you what it was, and you never had to get embroiled with this ridiculous plan they have going."

I open my mouth and close it again. I'm barely keeping my tears at bay.

"Who was it?" I ask in a breath. "Who was it who attacked us?"

Tulain shakes his head, not answering even as I yell the question again. I need the truth.

"They're a big company, mostly Human from what I know..."

"WHO?"

He relents, and it looks like it breaks him. "Berik Corporation."

The room goes out of focus, my stomach plummeting.

Berik.

The same people who own the Helios prisons, the same people who control so many mercenary groups, including the one Nooma's parents work with. Berik Corp who has, one way or another, destroyed the lives of all my friends.

"Do you know where amma's old crew is?"

"No, after my initial refusal they made it clear they didn't want to talk to me. And Vess won't listen to reason either."

"He'll talk to me."

"Malek, don't—"

"Don't what? Don't go talk to the people you grew up around? Don't go try to understand why they think they can get their own back on one of the biggest corporations in Human history? Because I think I have the right to know what the hell is going on. See you later, Tulain."

He tries to get in my way but I'm faster in the chair and seconds later I'm out the door. He doesn't come after me and I don't know whether to be grateful or hurt.

I hurtle around a corner too quickly and the chair tips, sending me rolling to the floor, frustrated tears escaping my control.

CHAPTER 35
LÀHN

BAKULA

Something about watching Malek rush out of the room spurs me into action. It's reckless, foolish, but his pain echoes mine and for the first time since *Purple Gravity* I don't hesitate.

I find him on the floor, staring up at the ceiling, hoverchair toppled to the side. Tear tracks run down his face, and I can feel the weight of his soul from just looking at him.

"You alright?" Malek lets out a strangled laugh. I feel so stupid for asking.

"Not…really. It's been a bit of a day... *Days*. Months. Years, actually." He sits up with another brittle laugh. "What do you want?"

"I heard what you and Tulain were talking about."

"Yeah. And?"

His tone is a little sharp, his teal eyes fixed on me, the intensity of his gaze almost derailing my thoughts.

"You said you were a captain, right?" He nods, a proud light returning to his eyes as the idea of a smirk quirks up the right side of his full lips. "Well, I'm looking for a ship to head…somewhere. Wondered if you could help."

I had such a great spiel prepared for this, but Malek's eyes and growing smirk have completely disarmed me. I should be the one turning on the charm to catch his attention but instead his mere existence has sent my thoughts tumbling away.

"Why me?"

"Because you're here, now, and..." The Guild taught me to not trust too easily, to keep my cards close to my chest. But looking at this boy, at the earnest look in his eyes, I can't help but speak the truth. "And you sound like you can handle the trouble I might bring."

"And what kind of trouble is that?" His smirk has blossomed.

"There's a bunch of mercs after me." He quirks up an infuriatingly handsome eyebrow. "Not any mercs, though: they're the Hell Suns. They're Berik Corp."

The light in his eyes turns to steel and suddenly he's as dangerous as he is good looking.

"Berik, eh? What about you and I go and grab a drink and have a chat. Let me message my crew and… hmmm… Can you pick my chair up, please?"

As easily as breathing, he's just a boy my age again, the smirk turning to a sheepish grin as he wipes the traces of his tears away.

"Sure. Are you okay, after falling I mean?"

"Oh yeah, just, um, help me back up?"

Note for the future: helping someone back in a hoverchair is seriously not easy. It doesn't help that I'm not the strongest person around and he's not exactly good at moving with me either, but he somehow seems to find the whole thing far more amusing than I do.

I just hope that has nothing to do with the heat that rises to my cheek after he—I suspect purposefully—falls against me.

"Let me send Kode a message and then we can go," I mutter as he finishes sorting himself out.

***

"So, you want to get to that planet of yours even though you've no idea what's waiting for you there?" Malek asks when I'm done giving him a breakdown.

He leans back in his chair, eyes focused on me, holding all the control in a situation where I can usually use my charm and wits to stay on top. But I'm definitely the one under his spell here.

"Yeah. I can't go back to Kirillion yet, and there's no point going to the IUP, not with Berik on our tail and not enough evidence on our side."

Malek scoffs at the mention of the Intergalactic Union of Planets. "The IUP won't do jack against Berik. Big corpos like that are practically untouchable. Amma always talked about how corrupt all those systems were, and that's why she'd chosen to live outside of them."

His words are so jaded, but I can't help wondering if he's right. I've seen first-hand the corruption that runs through the ranks of the rich and powerful. But the IUP is supposed to be above that, isn't it?

"There's gotta be something I can do against them," I say, carefully. "If I don't, I won't be able to go home." Sure, Zoon might find a way to bury all this, but I'll always feel as though I need to keep looking over my shoulder. "And I've got to believe that with enough proof we can take them down."

“Maybe, maybe not,” Malek shrugs, but I can see that steely anger in his eyes. “Anyway, the real question is, what’s in it for me and my crew if we take you guys on?”

I feel like he knows full well I don’t have enough to buy passage for a journey of that length. I have no convincing lie to offer, and neither do I want to ask Zoon for help when I don’t know if he’d agree with me going.

My silence is answer enough for Malek.

"Look, I can't make any promises, but when this job of ours is done, we don't exactly have plans."

"Anything I can help with?"

"Well, I'm supposed to get an AI chip back for Tulain but... I guess that got rather awkward, didn't it?" He lets out a brittle laugh. "Either way, I need to find out what's going on with mum's old crew. Given Tulain won't talk to me, that means I need to find another way to track them down. And, no, I can’t just call them because my old data got flarked a few years back. I only caught a glimpse of a couple of them earlier and I was too shocked to act. Which, in retrospect, was pretty dumb."

"People register when they get on the station," I point out.

"Yeah, but those records aren't publicly accessible."

"Kode can probably get them. I don't imagine the security here is a match for the stuff on Kirillion." Malek's eyes light up with interest. "I can ask her. Give me your details, so I can let you know what she says. I’d rather ask her in person," I add, wanting to run this by her and Shuobe before I make any more decisions.

"Sounds like a plan!" Malek exclaims as we link up through the station’s network. "You go have a word with her and, well, let's just say that if you get me the info I want, I'll be more inclined to consider taking you on board."

He starts to pull away, then hesitates, eyes suddenly serious.

"Do you think the mercs will come after you?"

"I don't know. But they seemed dead set on getting the chip back."

Malek's eyes are full of dangerous promises.

"Good. I've got some scores to settle. You see what you can find, and I'll have a word with my crew. "

I watch him leave, wondering if the girls will tell me I'm being an idiot.

***

They do not, in fact, call me an idiot as I recount my meeting with Malek, and we're already talking as though we'll be leaving with his crew and what we might need to go on a long-haul trip.

Kode doesn't need asking twice to get her kit together and before long she's complaining about how bad Bakula's security system is. As she does her thing, Shuobe and I take stock of what her mother gifted us before we left. Mostly the essentials we left Kirillion without, stuff I'm grateful we don't need to spend our credits on.

Kode tracks down the three names Malek gave me: *They're on the Urelhan destroyer,* she signs. *You have to register to dock on there, maybe get special permission, it's why I can see where they are. It's sort of under Bakula control, I think.*

Sort of? Shuobe asks.

Kode shrugs. *Don't ask me, I'm just going by what I saw on here.*

Thinking of the monstrously large ship makes a shudder run down my spine. I don't like the look of it at all.

I should tell Malek.

I pace to the other end of the tiny apartment and dial him, trying my best not to lean on anything with how grimy the whole place is. I don't think Tulain spends a lot of time here.

"Hey pretty boy, you got anything for me?" I'm going to slap him for this damn nickname.

"Yeah, I do, can we talk?"

"Sure!" He hisses in pain.

"Are you okay?"

"Yes, totally fi-OW!"

"Malek?"

"We're good, *shit,* fine, really, carry-OW!-on."

"You don't sound okay…"

"Just getting my arm reattached. Gotta have the nerves live to make sure it's done right but—" He swears so colourfully my translator gives up. "It's fine, I'm fine, it's nearly done. My nerves were a little… fried."

"Oh, I... I see," I stammer, not knowing what to say. *Well, that must suck,* doesn't seem to quite cut it. "Well, Kode found out that your guys aren't on Bakula anym—"

"What? Where the hell are they?" he interrupts, and I hold back a sigh. If he'd waited two seconds he'd know.

"They checked in on the Urelhan destroyer. From what Kode saw, there's quite a few people gathered there."

"Oh shit. *Shit.* The Urelhan destroyer? Stars, La'min hasn't changed one bit." He takes a deep breath. "Okay, okay, thanks for the info. *Shit,* though. Flark this scrambled Neurolink, I really need to speak to him."

"I told Kode about that and she said she might have a way to get the data back for you." I hate how useless *I* have been so far.

"Seriously?"

"She said she could give it a go, at least."

"Alright, cool. Sure. I'll be over as soon as I can." A pause. "Thanks, Làhn."

I shouldn't care that he said my name, but I can't ignore the little flip my stomach just did.

CHAPTER 36
MALEK

BAKULA

Kode is every bit the tech-whizz Làhn said she was, running a gazillion checks on my Neurolink, various menus I'd never even seen flashing across my eyes.

I don't understand how, but my Neurolink is whole again. Everything is within reach, save a few files that had to be sacrificed.

Old photos of me and amma, songs I loved, memories locked away after the accident when my storage chip got corrupted. My contacts list makes me wonder who's still alive.

I can't wait until I'm back to ring La'min, instead tucking myself in a corner on the way.

He can't believe his ears and I almost burst into tears. They'd thought me dead when they could track neither me nor amma down and I can't help but wonder if amma's own Neurolink got messed up during the accident. That would explain why they couldn't find either of us.

The signal is crackly, the Urelhan destroyer causing interferences, but I give him a brief summary of what happened, and he invites me to join them, asking if I could bring along my whizz of a hacker.

My friends are eager for the plan La'min and the others have set into motion.

Berik Corp—the name that marked the end of our previous lives: a Berik affiliated ship for Alta, Berik law enforcement for Nooma, and strange information about a Berik facility that Akim stumbled upon.

As we get the ship ready, we really start to move like a crew and more than ever I'm sure of the path I'm on.

I have my arm back, but my leg still needs time to heal. But I don't care, not when I'm going to reunite with amma's crew. The promise of answers and bringing Berik down a peg or two is definitely motivating.

We'll teach them that their actions have consequences.

I head to Tulain's place to speak to Làhn. He opens the door with wet hair and a hastily thrown-on t-shirt clinging to him. Not calling ahead was clearly the right decision.

"Malek, hi," he seems startled. "I thought it was going to be Tulain as he forgot his keycard."

I laugh. "If I know him, he's sulking in his office right now."

Làhn chuckles before stepping out of the way. "Sorry, come in. Can I help?"

The girls are sitting cross legged on the bed, playing a game on their tablets. I'm itching to see what it is. Going to the arcade with Alta the other night was a good reminder of all the games I have to catch up on. Though Nooma might kill me if I buy a gaming rig as well as the sound system.

"Yeah, I do kinda need a hand, actually. I spoke to amma's old crew and well, their hacker's in need of a new perspective on something she's trying to crack. Figured maybe Kode could help."

"Gimme a sec." Làhn taps the girl on the shoulder. She ignores him at first, tapping rapidly on her screen, until the Mallak girl lets out a wail of despair, smacking her forehead in disbelief. No need to guess who won.

Làhn signs and I hover to the side, resisting the temptation to go through Tulain's things. Knowing my luck if I open a cupboard a ton of crap is going to fall on my face.

"Kode's asking what you need." I open my mouth to reply to Làhn, but he shakes his head. "You can talk to her; she's got software that can read lips."

I'm left feeling a little rude as I turn to her. "They're asking if you could come take a look at the AI chip they've been trying to decode? The hacker working on it wouldn't mind a pair of fresh eyes."

Kode stares at me, chewing her lip-ring thoughtfully before turning to Làhn and signing quickly.

"She's asking if she'll get paid for it."

I like her. She's got her wits about her considerably more than pretty boy.

"We can work something out, La'min's never been the stingy type."

I'm going to have to learn sign language if they come along so I don't always need someone to translate, aren't I?

"What happens if he doesn't want to pay?"

"Then I'll cover it," I say, without thinking. "I know you guys are looking to head somewhere. Now, I'm not saying we'd make a beeline there, but if you'd be willing to also pull your weight on the ship, we could head that way. How does that sound?"

I glance from one to the other as they exchange a quick-fire conversation the Mallak joins in on.

"Deal, as long as it's for the three of us," Làhn says, and I flash him a grin.

"Sounds good to me, long as no-one on my crew's got a problem with it. If La'min doesn't wanna pay, I'll take you on board."

The Mallak girl stands up. "I guess he does seem reasonable. Be careful on the Urelhan ship, you two; those things are bad luck whichever way you look at them. I'll stay here and get what we need ready, there's no way I'm setting foot on that ship."

"Even for adventure?" Làhn asks and she laughs.

"There is adventure and then there is following Human stupidity. I'm not stepping on a Urelhan ship if you pay me."

"When do we need to leave?" Làhn asks me, looking both excited and anxious.

"Taking off in about two hours, you cool with that?"

He nods. "Where do we meet?"

I give him the bay number as well as a quick explanation on how to get there so they don't get lost.

"We'll be there. But remember what you said about payment, okay?"

"I wouldn't dream of forgetting," I tell him with a wink before setting off back to the ship.

***

Làhn and Kode join us as we're finishing preparations. Alta worked their magic, and I was roped in to help with a last-minute leak, leaving me with a face streaked in grease. Làhn stares at me, then the ship, then back at me.

"Can this fly?" he asks even as Alta appears at the top of the ramp, their mechanic's overalls in need of a wash as much as my face.

"Damn straight this baby can fly, I haven't been working my ass off on it for three days for nothing," they say before glancing my way. "How's the work we did on the outer shield holding up?"

"We're all good, another miracle!"

They beam proudly.

"I'm Alta, and you gotta be Làhn, right?" He nods. "Malek was right, you *are* pretty!" Làhn opens his mouth to respond but Alta turns to me. "Didn't think we'd have matching taste! Clearly, it's only the music you like that's dodgy," they laugh before moving their hands at Kode. The girl squints; replies a little hesitantly. "You read lips too?" Kode nods. "Had to learn sign language when I was a kid. Didn't know if you'd be able to understand but I guess some things are still close enough. Let me show you the ship!" The entire time their hands move carefully.

Kode rushes up the ramp with a grin, motioning for Làhn to follow. He lingers behind.

"Having second thoughts?" I ask. "Because if the ship bothers you, I dare you to find someone else willing to help you for basically nothing." I'm failing at keeping the irritation from my voice. But it feels like he's judging me as well as the ship. If one of us isn't good enough, then neither's the other.

Làhn looks away. Good, no-one looks at my ship like that.

"I... It looks old, is all. And battered."

I roll my eyes. People who live planet-side don't get that slick hulls don't necessarily make for a better ship.

"It's a good ship, but if you've got doubts…" I shrug, heading up the ramp.

"I'm sorry. I just want to make sure we'll stay in one piece during the flight," he mutters, following me to Nooma waiting inside.

"We've got permission for take-off, Captain."

"Let's get going. Take Làhn to strap in and make sure Alta hasn't kidnapped his friend, please."

She nods, Làhn gives me one last almost dubious look, then follows her.

With my crutch and my new arm, the stairs are no challenge. The arm is both stronger and lighter than the old one, far more balanced.

Akim is already settled in the cockpit, waiting for my orders.

I slide into my seat next to him. No captain chair like on amma's ship here, but I think I prefer it this way. "Alright, let's give this baby their test flight."

***

The Urelhan destroyer never looked so big as now that we're heading for it. Its golden hull ripples as though breathing. Amma boarded two Urelhan destroyers in her youth to scavenge them. She came back empty handed, things turning so bad the second time she's never talked about it. There are things best left alone in the vastness of space. Even I know that.

"It's alive," Akim whispers, awed.

"I think it's just how it looks. Something alive would have moved its ass away from Bakula a long time ago." I try to make light of it.

"I feel like we shouldn't be here," Akim's voice is quiet, almost reverent.

"It's gonna be fine, we're not the first to set foot on this destroyer, trust me. Some people spent weeks on there, setting up the oxygen filters I was telling you all about yesterday, and nothing bad happened to them!" I turn to flash Akim a smile, but his eyes are fixed on the readings.

Or more accurately the lack of readings.

The ship takes up the entirety of the viewing window now but doesn't show on our radars. Urelhan ships are invisible to most species' scanners. Shinarian navigation systems can see them—and a bunch of other things we can't, making them one of the best—which is why a lot of long-haul ships go to the expense of buying a Shinarian navigation system and hiring a Shinarian navigator to go with it.

The docking bay is a yawning maw kept sealed by a translucent film, a few ships visible beyond, all of them dwarfed by the size of the hangar.

"So, we just go through, right?" Akim checks.

"Yep!"

The membrane all but pulls us in as soon as we come in contact with it and the transition is so smooth, I barely notice it. Akim lands to the side, away from the other ships, in the way he'd settle himself in a crowded room.

"Is it okay if I stay on the ship?"

"You don't want to look around?"

"No. I've got a bad feeling, Mal, so be quick, okay? I know we want to get back at Berik and all, but...be careful. Please."

Akim holds my gaze and I know by that alone how serious he's being.

"We will be. Message if there's a problem, okay?"

With our Neurolinks synced through the ship, coms have never been easier.

Alta stays behind too, wanting to monitor the engine as it cools down, so I head to the cargo bay to meet up with the others. The metallic-looking ground of the hangar feels more like some weird carpet with too much give, adding to the overwhelmingly *other* feel of the place, made all the worse by the gigantic proportions of the hangar and its doors.

I can see why thrill seekers and treasure hunters come to these ships. We know nothing about this race, and little more about the ships they left dead in space. Even Urelhan isn't their name, it means *Lost Ones* in the tongue of the aliens who first discovered these ships, the Gurpa. And even that species is mysterious, long since withdrawn unto itself, all but forgotten.

The gigantic doors slide open, silent as though they had been oiled yesterday.

Whatever dread had reared its head vanishes when I see who's in the doorway, a broad grin on his face, elongated canines standing out in that way that made me giggle and try to poke them when I was younger.

"La'min!"

I'm speeding to him, tears already in my eyes. He was the other constant of my childhood—always up for playing and mischief. His fur is longer than I remember on one side, the other shaved in intricate patterns and dyed bright blue. One of his ears—ears that sit on the top of his head, large and pointed—is cybernetic now, but still, they both perk up when he sees me. He runs, tail swishing behind him and I'm reminded of all the times I tried to catch him by it.

We collide half-way, me hopping out of the chair and him wrapping his arms around me. He's crying, and I'm crying, and this is everything I didn't know I needed.

He's alive. I've not lost all my family. He pulls away, looking at me as though I'm a miracle and I manage a half smile through my tears.

"La'min," I say, voice thick. "Meet my crew."

CHAPTER 37
TRYSTAN

KUNDAR SHUTTLE

Father and I had words. Well, he had words whilst I stared at my toes, wishing the vastness of hyperspace would just swallow me. He was furious I'd made a scene, though, really, it's everybody else who made a scene by reacting to something that had nothing to do with them.

I've been grounded, attending school online and monitored too closely to be able to speak openly to Cat.

Mom hired help to prepare for the party tonight and I'm only allowed out of my room if I watch and learn how to be a proper lady and in a pointless act of rebellion I refused.

I've become better at keeping myself split, but I'm taking a break until Jakoor lets me know we're leaving hyperspace.

I've not been able to see or speak to my uncle either, though I heard him drop by and argue with father yesterday. It was awful not being able to go to him, but I couldn't risk blowing our cover.

Hopefully after tonight I can start moving against my father. I don't exactly know how yet, but I hope Nathaniel and Cat will help me.

I need to make sure I'm presentable for the party. I don't want to. But I don't have a choice, do I? Fear keeps me in the closet. Jakoor called it my survival instinct and I wish I could see it as that, so I'd feel less like a coward.

I wish I could still pretend this is some long-term undercover mission and that my team will come get me. It's how I survived the onset of puberty. But the lie is starting to wear thin.

I sigh, set aside my tablet, wondering why I thought it was clever to sit in silence. But I don't want to listen to music when it might help. Feeling better is like a betrayal of everything. Which is absolutely ridiculous, but I don't think I'm winning any competitions for rationality today.

When something shakes android me, I slip into the escape gratefully.

"We're coming out of hyperspace."

I open my eyes, first to Jakoor's handsome face, so much healthier since they've been able to look after themselves, and then to the sky beyond the viewing window.

I always thought the nebulas around Eden One were beautiful, but the sky here is something else altogether.

The stars seem to cluster tighter, shine brighter. They're so different from the ones I know. The pinks and reds and purples of the nebulae are so vivid and breathtaking. Then the station comes into view. I can make out the asteroid where the station started before spiralling out, the hull made of a thousand materials and ship parts, like some giant chimera.

Beside it sits a giant ship, bigger than anything I've seen, like a winged beast slumbering in the middle of space.

"What is that?"

"An Urelhan destroyer," Jakoor says, which doesn't actually answer my question. I have so much to learn. "It's where we're headed. My contact is there and he's not going back to Bakula for a couple of days. I've no interest in waiting around when I'm so close to getting the info I want."

Jakoor told me about the scientist they're looking for: someone who believed there had to be a cure for the poisoning of their whole world, not only their species. Someone who disappeared without a word or hint of where they'd gone.

Jakoor has been away from their people for five years and where I'd call being away from home that long a blessing, it clearly pains them in ways I can't understand. Sure, I'd miss Cat and Nathaniel and some of the small things: the dessert house, the sunset catching at the top of the forest, the endless summer afternoons Cat and I spent together. But I could never miss Eden One itself.

At home, I slip into a bath with loads of bubbles to disappear under. I can't concentrate on anything else, and I don't want to miss a beat of our arrival on this strange alien ship.

"What are the Urelhan?" I ask, eyes glued to the ship we're approaching.

"We don't know," Jakoor replies, a little distractedly. "It means the *Lost Ones*, and all that remains of them are their ships, just sitting around in the weirdest places, deserted. Most people don't really like to set foot on them, there's a lot of superstitions going around, and a couple of species see them as the empty vessels their gods have left behind and have been trying to get them to move for centuries, convinced that when their technology is advanced enough, they will get to join their creators in a better life. Personally, I think that whatever happened to that species made them abandon their warship and run away. I've been on one, once, when I was much younger: there's one not far from Helhiaid. It was a stupid dare to go there and bring something back."

"What did you bring back?" I ask, trying not to notice how much this place is suddenly giving me the creeps. This is not so slowly edging into horror movie territory, and I usually watch those from behind my hands.

"Not much, just this tiny little coin-like thing I found lying on the floor. Got an earful and a half from my *doolma* for bringing something back to the surface without proper decontamination. At least it turned out to be harmless and I won double food rations for two weeks!"

"Your food is rationed?"

I wish I could read the way they tilt their head at my question.

"Of course, our world still has limited resources; even after all this time there is a lot working against us. We can produce synth food, of course, but that requires a lot of energy, and materials, which we need to keep other facilities going. We've gone back to cultivating where the soil is safe but we're never swimming in food. Better than the first generation of pod-grown Kundar had it, though, as they needed shots of stimulants to keep their muscles growing properly."

I can't imagine not having enough food to eat whenever you're hungry. I've never realised how much of a privilege it is. I wonder if on Eden One too, people go hungry. I feel so guilty for how much I've taken for granted, and complained about, without ever thinking of what it must be like for other people.

"It's not that big a deal, I never went hungry. But it was just nice to win yourself something extra once in a while," they add, and I can't tell if it's just for my benefit.

"Sorry," I mutter, looking back at the ship. We've reached a translucent film, with something like a giant hangar behind. "Aren't we going to hit that?" I ask as we get really close to the membrane.

"Don't worry about it," Jakoor chuckles even as they push the ship forwards, the membrane pulling us inside.

Jakoor lands and moves quickly, eager to get their information. I follow them, a little nervous, but not keen on being left alone.

The floor is soft, not at all like the metal it looks to be made of, more like a carpet on sand.

"Do you know where your contact is?"

"Somewhere on the ship. But there are other people here, so we just need to find someone."

I look around the hangar, its ceiling lost in the darkness. The place is badly lit, just some orbs that give a glow far dimmer than I'd like. The walls are pale grey, but the texture seems weirdly organic, and I stay at a safe distance.

I blame Cat for all the horror movies she made me watch now coming back to haunt me.

"You okay?" Jakoor asks over their shoulder. I swear they can feel my nerves.

"Yeah, just... This place creeps me out."

"It's fine, I promise. Come on, all these ships have the same layout, so I've got an idea where to start looking."

***

I'm thinking back on all the terrifying movies I've watched and regretting every single one, only able to relax when we start to hear the sounds of people.

We step into a wide and open room not unlike an atrium, bathed in fake sunlight dancing on the purple water of the enormous fountain at the centre.

People turn to us: Humans and aliens alike. Uncertain of how to act I keep my eyes down and follow Jakoor, which feels awfully like meeting my father's business partners. The thought alone makes me force my chin up.

"And who do you think you are, waltzing in here?"

The alien approaching is so startling it's hard not to stare. His face could almost be Human. But only almost. His nose is too small and a little squashed, pupils vertical slashes set in too-large eyes. His long ears—one fluffy, the other cybernetic—are perched on top of his head like a cat's or fox's would be. Then I notice the thick, bushy tail swishing angrily behind him. He doesn't really look *that* much like a cat, but the resemblance is all I can see.

"I'm here to see Vess," Jakoor replies. "He told me he was here. We don't mean any trouble." They're holding their hands out, demonstrating peaceful intent despite the blades and guns strapped about their person.

"Flark, of course he did." The alien turns around, motioning at someone. "Get that idiot here! We can have a word about him inviting strangers. Stars, honestly." He turns back to us. "And the pair of you decided it was fine to wander around inside a flarking Urelhan ship as though it's nothing?"

Jakoor shrugs. "It's not like it's my first time. It's not going to eat us."

Something about the alien's eyes harden, his fangs showing, ears swivelling back on his head.

"You tell me about what these ships are capable of, *kid,* when you've run a proper expedition on one of them, okay? Knowing you Kundar you probably just went for a walk on one of the ships as though it would hand you its secrets. You've never tried to figure out what really makes these things tick."

"We're not reckless enough for that."

The alien bursts out laughing, tail flitting about. "Oh, that's a good one. Kundar, not reckless? You're cute."

I see Jakoor's fists tighten at their side, mouth opening for a retort when someone else walks up to us.

"La'min, I see your lack of tact is still an inherent part of your character." The voice is smooth, elegant; the newcomer tall, handsome in a strange kind of way. His purple eyes go from Jakoor to me and back to Jakoor. "I'm surprised you brought company. Anyway, that's none of my business. La'min, before you offend our guests any further, this is Jakoor, one of my clients. Given I'm tolerating your foolish idea, you are going to tolerate me doing my business here. Berik hasn't turned up yet, so I don't see the problem."

"Berik? Why is Berik coming here?" I speak before thinking, terror seizing me.

"That's none of your business," La'min spits.

"It is very much so our business," Jakoor retorts.

They tower over La'min who lets out a hiss, ears flat to their head and it's really hard not to think of the stray cat that lives at the back of our garden. Vess steps between the two, his sheer height making up for his slimness.

"Enough, both of you. La'min is right, technically what is happening here is none of your business. You're here to see me and then you can be on your way, so let's keep it at that."

"Berik is very much so my business," Jakoor repeats.

"Jakoor, whatever your sudden beef with Berik is, they're not going to get in the way of us carrying out our business. Now do you want this information or not?"

My companion stiffens before turning to me, pressing something into my palm, leaning in. For a brief, startling second, I wonder if they're going to kiss me, but their lips only brush my ear as they whisper: "Hang around here, if they start acting strange, press the button and I'll get us out."

When did I start considering kissing Jakoor a possibility? I'm at once grateful and disappointed that their lips did not find mine, and definitely relieved that I can't blush as they set off after Vess.

La'min hasn't moved, eyes on me.

"And who are you? You smell funny for a Human," he snaps, sniffing in my direction.

"I'm an android," my voice is small. I really need to build some confidence. Or acting skills at least.

"That'll explain it. You're theirs?"

"No, no," I shake my head emphatically. "We're just travelling together."

"Oh, an AI! Shiny!" He grins, and I feel the urge to step back. "Not seen many Human AI models. I was pretty convinced they were worried their own creations were gonna destroy them or something," he laughs as though he's said something hilarious. He's strange and loud and the swishing tail is very distracting.

"La'min, who are you harassing?"

A boy in a hoverchair pulls up, too-bright teal eyes on me. I notice the missing leg and it's all I can do not to stare. I don't think I've ever met someone with a visibly missing limb. I force my eyes back to his intense gaze, but everything about him is startling. You don't often see people with warm brown skin like his on Eden One.

"Vess brought some blasted guests without asking if it was okay. Client of his and—" he pauses, glances at me. "What's your name?"

"Trystan."

"Did I hear right and you're an AI?" the boy asks, and I nod. "Nice! Only Human AI I ever met didn't have a body. They were on mom's ship and monitored pretty much everything. They were really cool to talk to, though. So, what's your thing?"

"I... Um..." I wrack my brain for the little I know about AIs. I don't want to say something I can't follow through with, but my mind's gone blank. "I'm a companion type," I blurt out.

At home I sink fully under the water, groaning in disbelief. *Companion type? Really?* I've been reading too much fanfic lately.

"Oh, nice," the boy comments, and I swear his smirk grows.

"What are you people all doing here? Isn't this ship dangerous?" I ask, hoping to deflect the attention away from me.

"If you don't know your way around, it can be," La'min replies with a notable hint of pride. "But if you know what not to do, it's not a bad place to lay an ambush."

"You're *ambushing* Berik?"

"Damn straight we are," the boy replies with worrying enthusiasm. "They're gonna come in here thinking they can grab this thing easily and get a nasty surprise instead."

"Do you know when they're due?" I ask, hoping that Jakoor and I will be long gone when that happens.

La'min reassures me that Berik isn't due for a while, but the boy has paled.

"Min, get everyone ready. Berik's boarding."

CHAPTER 38
MALEK

URELHAN DESTROYER

La'min swears.

"Akim, take off and hide!" I order.

"Already on it," Akim replies, his voice crackling through the coms as though the signal is being interfered with.

"How did they get here? I thought you hadn't sent the signal yet!" I ask La'min as he starts yelling orders.

"We hadn't!"

"Well, someone sure did," I snap back even as Nooma and Nephanie come running.

"We need to get out of here."

"No shit," I turn my coms with the ship on full time so they can follow what's going on. "Alta, Akim, how many have we got?"

"Two large ones," Alta replies. "Akim's taken us far above so I can't really see but I think they're disabling the ships. I'd suggest we blow them to pieces but I'm not sure our weapons are fully operational yet and I don't really think a field test is wise."

"We need the ship in one piece to get out. You two stay out of the way, we'll get back to you." By my side, Nooma looks ready for battle, and Nephanie's eyes are one shade away from gold.

I pause for a moment, expecting an answer from Làhn who should be hearing this on the coms, but nothing comes through. Nadine—a hacker amma took on board when I was about ten—took him and Kode to the room she'd set up her stuff, and I have no idea where that might be.

"Min, where did Nadine take the others?"

He's handing blasters around, passing me a small one and Nooma a rifle as he joins us.

"First room on the left in the corridor at the back." He's solemnly looking at me in a way I really don't like. "Get them, kid, and then get yourself off this ship."

"No! Like hell I'm leaving you now. I'll get them, and we'll come help you fight I—"

"Malek, no, thought I'd lost you once, so now you do me a favour and get your ass out of this mess, okay? I'm not mourning you a second time."

With that he turns around, cocking the large gun he's carrying, bellowing for the barricades to go up faster. How can I run away from this fight? How can I abandon him?

"We need to move. We don't have long before they swarm this place."

How is Nooma so calm?

"I can't..."

"Can you abandon Làhn and Kode? Can you abandon Akim and Alta? You're *our* captain now."

That shakes something loose inside me and I blink hard, reopening my eyes to a different perspective. "You're right, let's go."

I speed out of the atrium and down a short corridor, bursting into the room where everyone should be, throwing myself out of the chair the second I see Nadine's body in the corner, a hole in her chest, and Làhn on the floor, blood seeping from his temple.

Nooma rushes to Kode huddled in a corner as I fall next to Làhn, heart in my throat.

This is my fault.

Coming here was my call. Yes, everyone agreed but I'm the one who made the first call to take this risk. Now everything's gone to hell, and it falls on me to make sure they're safe. No time for hesitation, no time to let my doubts creep in. Act now, wallow later.

"Làhn, wake up, come on," I shake him gently. A quick scan reveals his wound isn't too bad. I spent enough of my childhood running headfirst into things to know how much head injuries bleed.

"We need to move," Nephanie says. "They've started shooting."

I heard the blasters go off too. My past waits for me with La'min and the others, whilst my future stands around me in the form of my crew.

It's not a fair choice but there's only one right answer.

"Làhn, come on, nobody's gonna carry you!" I shake him again, and this time he groans, eyelids fluttering open.

"What happened?" he blinks when he sees me and then Kode is by his side, signing rapidly. "The tech," he starts, groaning as I help him sit up. He's probably got a monster of a headache. "He did something on the computer and Nadine flipped at him. She called him a traitor and he... He..." Làhn swallows hard, Kode wrapping him in a hug. "He took the chip," Làhn adds, "When I tried to stop him, he hit me in the head and I... I don't remember after that."

"There should be a back way to the hangar. If we hurry, we might be able to catch this guy," Nephanie says as though she can read my burning desire to end him.

A traitor.

Someone La'min trusted enough to have here and who sent the signal too early. Nadine is dead and I hardly had the time to give her a hug. We should have had so much time to catch up. Like I should have with La'min but might never get.

Because someone betrayed them.

To Berik.

Always Berik.

"Let's find him." I push myself back into the chair. "Can you walk?" I ask Làhn.

"I'll keep up, don't worry."

I glance one last time at Nadine's body despite myself. She didn't deserve to die like this.

None of us deserve what Berik keeps putting us through.

"Let's find this asshole and get the chip back. Berik isn't winning this."

***

An explosion vibrates through the ship, walls, and floor growing rigid all at once, like muscles tensing.

Absolutely not unsettling at all. Nope.

Nephanie skids to a halt and we stop beside her, waiting. Nothing moves, nothing shifts, nothing else changes.

"What's going on?" Nooma asks in a whisper.

"They've woken it up." Nephanie's answer sends a shudder down my spine.

I have a feeling she knows way more about these ships than she ever said.

"What do we do?" Làhn asks, still wiping some blood from his temple with his sleeve. He looks like he needs to sit down and take it easy, which isn't exactly possible right now. If I had a better chair, we probably could have ridden together but this one would just tip over.

"We get back to the ship," Nephanie's tone brooks no argument. "I don't care where that other guy has gone, we need to get out now. With some luck he'll be going the same way as us. If not, well, we really don't want to hang around."

I want to argue that we need to get the chip and that I'm the captain and it's my choice but… I know she's right: what matters most is getting everyone off this ship with minimal damage.

"You know the way?" I ask.

"Roughly."

"Good enough."

Nephanie forces a more sedate pace, marching at the front whilst Nooma holds the rear. The floor rumbles under our feet, echoes of more explosions. Maybe of something else altogether.

We're almost to an intersection when a small group of Berik droids rounds the corner. I have the time to take in their shape—skinny arms and legs with only the idea of a head—before they start firing.

I scream, throwing my hands up in a vain attempt to protect myself but the blasts never hit.

"Take them down! Shield's one way!" Nephanie orders as I open my eyes to see the dome of golden energy protecting us.

I fumble to get the safety off my blaster—it's been too many years since I've handled one—and by the time I'm done Nooma has already blasted two down. Làhn fires a shot with Nadine's old pistol but his aim is worse than mine. At least I hit the droid I'm aiming at. Another second goes by and Nooma shoots down the two remaining droids, hitting the cool-down mode almost as an instinct when she lowers her rifle.

"Thanks," I breathe to Nephanie as she lets go of the shield.

"They're here to kill, not about to let myself be cornered by a pile of junk." She kicks one of the fallen droids.

There's a white noise in my ears. I knew they were here to kill but hearing it said aloud makes it worse, especially with La'min and the others left behind.

"How far to the hangar?" I ask

"Not far now, but there's going to be a lot more of them."

"I know."

She turns to face me. "If I run ahead, I can divert their attention long enough for Akim to pick you up—"

"No. No-one stays behind or runs ahead. We do this together."

I swear her gold eyes grow brighter. "Why? Why risk your life for me?"

Because Nooma likes you, you imbecile, I want to say. "Because you're part of the crew."

She nods once, turning away, and I feel like I passed some kind of test. "Okay then, let's go show them what we're made of."

CHAPTER 39
TRYSTAN

URELHAN DESTROYER

Mom comes to do my hair and pick a dress whilst, lightyears away, I'm huddled behind cover, hardly able to think over the sound of gunfire. I'm trapped between silk and Berik, curls and blasters.

Jakoor slides to my side as mom settles me in front of the mirror. An explosion shudders through the floor as she picks up the brush.

"Vess has a way back to the ships. We can sneak past most of the fighting," Jakoor says, taking my hand.

In my normal body I'd be out of breath trying to keep up with them. But as it is, it's far easier to run than it is to ignore mom styling my hair.

Especially when I'm facing the kind of danger that would see my stint of freedom away from Eden One come to an all too sudden stop.

"The hangar is just ahead!" Vess calls as an opening in a smooth wall widens enough to let us through.

Beyond, chaos awaits. Several of the ships are damaged, smoke and sparks filling the air with the scent of broken things. The droids are currently rushing to another side of the hangar.

Jakoor flattens us against the wall before we can be seen, pulling out their blasters and handing me one.

"I don't know how to use it."

"Point and shoot. It's not hard."

Easy for them to say. I'm focussing so hard on my body here that my head droops and mom's cold anger lashes out, leaving me to bite my lip not to snap back at her. I hate how small she can make me feel.

"You really need to start putting more effort into your appearance," my mother says as Jakoor unsheathes their long knives. Vess has pulled out a blaster that looks far too small to be of any use. I wish I felt as confident as they look.

"Did they disable our ship?" I whisper.

My mother tugs on my hair a little harder than needed.

"Do not just sit here ignoring me. I do so much for you, but you have to be stubborn and get yourself in trouble. You cannot behave like this when we're nearing election season; you have to be seen supporting your father in all things."

I clench my jaw. The 'yes, mother' I have relied on for so many years won't pass my lips. I am being shot at, people's lives endangered because of a corrupt corporation, and all my mother can think about is my father's career.

"I don't know, we'll need to go check." Jakoor crouches by the mouth of the corridor. They glance at Vess. "You're coming with us?" The man nods, his eyes an eerie, shifting violet. "On my—" But a droid finds us first, opening fire as soon as it sees us.

I let out a cry, flattening myself to the floor as my mother demands my attention. Jakoor rolls into the hangar, taking the droid down so fast I scarcely understand what happened.

"Hurry!"

I rush towards them even as more droids converge on us.

"Stop this behaviour this instant!" my mother snaps.

I don't have the time to answer her when I need to run and figure out how to shoot at the same time.

"I don't know what ridiculous notions your uncle has been drilling into your head, but this is *not* how proper young ladies behave!"

I'm not a young lady!

If only I had the guts to say it.

A laser misses me by an inch as Jakoor yanks me down behind cover. They're hurt, bleeding from a wound in between their arms, face twisted in pain.

"Are you okay?" I ask, worry choking me. I can't lose them. At home, I find enough of a voice to tell my mother I'm just not feeling very well.

"I'll be fine," they say through gritted teeth. "I'm tougher than this."

Vess slides next to us, clothes still somehow immaculate, even as another hail of lasers pummel our cover.

"We really ought to get out of here soon," he points out, fiddling with the settings on his blaster.

"Well, you'd better not make a scene tonight. Everybody will be delighted to hear about you and Nathaniel being engaged and it will do *wonders* for your father's career," mom carries on as though I hadn't spoken. Which is fine because I'm not listening.

"Our ship's the next one over. How many droids?" Jakoor asks, taking the blaster back from me.

"Coming for us? About a dozen. And about twice as many engaged with another group."

"Tryst, you stay back here and—"

"No, you're already injured, and you can die. I'll draw their fire first and then you two can follow."

All the courage I wish I could wield at my mother, at my father, surges in me now. I glance at the distance in between us and the ship. Jakoor will be able to unlock it from here and I know how fast I can run.

I'm not Human.

I'm more.

Stronger. Faster.

Like a superhero.

"You sure?"

The droids batter our cover with lasers, getting closer by the second.

"Yes."

My mother admires her handy work before turning to my closet. My attention is hardly on the monstrosities she presents me with.

I bolt, faster even than before. The lasers whizz past me but luck is on my side. Seconds later I'm leaping up the lowering steps, my body so powerful in that second that it steals my breath away. Mom thinks my gasp has to do with the dress.

She has no idea.

I land hard and roll into the ship, straight into a cloud of smoke coming from the engine room. Even without looking I know we're not taking off. I run back to the door, spotting Jakoor cornered behind cover, Vess nowhere to be seen.

I need to do something.

A droid appears from the side, blaster pointed at me. I move as it fires, ignoring the sensation that goes through my upper arm as I swing a clumsy punch at its head. It staggers back, lifting the blaster again and I realise I'm screwed.

A shot goes off and the droid collapses, revealing the boy in the hoverchair, a wide grin painted on his face as he twirls his blaster.

"Need a hand?" he asks, just as another three droids descend on us.

CHAPTER 40
LÀHN

URELHAN DESTROYER

"Get back! Get back!"

Nooma pushes me and Kode out of the way as Malek and Nephanie rush into the fray. I'm terrified for them, the odds we're getting out intact diminishing by the second.

"Can you shoot?"

I shake my head, manage a sound approximating a no. This is a thousand times worse than what happened at the Guild.

"Then get out of the way, find somewhere to tuck yourselves!"

"But—"

"If you can't help, move before you get shot! Both of you!" Nooma's voice brooks no argument and as a laser hits the wall inches above my head, I decide discretion really is the best part of valour.

Kode and I exchange a glance, then we're running back, ducking around the nearest corner, taking a second to figure out what to do.

My head is sluggish and throbbing, the blow I took finally catching up with me, but I refuse to sit here doing nothing. Only I can't even focus on Kode's hands as she signs something to me.

How bad is your head? She signs slower this time.

It hurts, but I'll live. Could I have a concussion? *We need to do something.*

Something different shudders through the ship, dread washing over me. Kode doesn't pay it any mind, her face lighting up with an idea.

We need to get on the ship!

What?

The Berik ship, with the droids, we need to get on it!

What? I repeat, certain I've misunderstood.

If I can get to the terminal on the ship, I should be able to disable them!

It's the craziest idea I've ever heard.

We'd need to find a way around the fight, I say, trying my best to bury my fear.

We sneak round. Stay low. Like when dealing with security at home.

Only most security on Kirillion would ask questions before shooting. The Berik droids? Not so much.

But she's right, this is our best shot, so we move back to the mouth of the corridor. Nooma has moved and I can't see anyone else, only catching glimpses of moving shapes. The Berik droid ships stand out as two sleek giants.

At least there is plenty of cover on the way.

I'm about to step out from behind our first cover when all the lights go out. It's only for a couple of seconds but we freeze. A breath, and they're back on. We exchange a look, Kode's resolve hardening before mine as she takes the lead.

The lights turn off again, no longer than the first time, but that's when I see it: something easily three times my height and somewhat Humanoid, body shimmering silver in the dark. Then the lights come back, and it vanishes.

Something about the ship is awake. It doesn't feel like a positive, at all, and I can see the same thought in Kode's eyes.

The creature is silent, only visible when the lights are off, every time a little closer to us, marching from the edge of the hangar.

I clamp a hand over my mouth as it reappears, standing a foot or so away, long arms dangling down, its legs too long compared to its torso. Before I can see anymore the light is back.

Lights off, it's moved past us, carrying on down the side of the hangar, the edge of the ship it touches disintegrating into nothing.

I had never truly known fear before

We need to move! Kode signs but I'm rooted to the spot.

She grabs my wrist, pulling me after her. I stumble when we spring out of cover as the lights go dark, the sound of a ship falling apart echoing behind us.

I'm too scared to look, to watch it half reduced to nothing as the creature carries on its destructive walk. We sprint, moving from cover to cover, using the bouts of darkness to our advantage, the droids distracted by the creature and our companions.

At last, one of the Berik ships is near. The large bay houses more droids unfolding from storage. So many more coming to eradicate everyone.

I let Kode lead, keeping an eye out as I follow her to a side door, one in case a Human crew is needed I suspect. Hopefully, there's no-one in there.

The door is shut but Kode takes all of thirty seconds to prise the side panel off and hot-wire it open. We slip inside a dimly lit, narrow corridor leading to the cockpit and another room beyond. Hopefully, the control room we need.

Moving quietly, we creep past the cockpit, towards the room where the control terminals should be located. Of course, it's locked. Kode struggles more with this panel and when I join in to help pry it open, it slips from our grip and clanks loudly to the floor.

Someone moves in the cockpit.

Stop them! I sign before rushing at the door even as it opens, throwing myself at the person.

I can't let them see Kode. She's our best chance. Only as I bodily collide with the other, do I realise it's the traitor we were running after in the first place. The guy who's already knocked me out once. At least, this time, I'm the one with the element of surprise.

From outside the ship comes a blood-curdling wail and I find I'd rather not know what that was.

CHAPTER 41
MALEK

URELHAN DESTROYER

I don't even have the time to think we're screwed before Nephanie appears out of nowhere, slamming into the back of two of the droids whilst I manage to blast the third.

But this isn't going as well as I'd want, not with so many of the flarking things still coming from the ships. There just aren't enough of us.

Nephanie reaches my side just as a fourth droid comes out of cover, blaster pointed at us. I whirl to aim.

Too slow.

I'm a dead man. The thought doesn't really process before the shot goes wild, the Kundar crashing knives first into the droid. My head is so light with adrenaline, I could start laughing.

"Do you have a weapon?" I ask the android boy, who looks definitely out of his depth.

"I don't know how to shoot."

"Can't you download how to?" I ask even as I level my blaster and fire down another droid. The Kundar is by our side, their twin blasters raised and ready. Vess joins us, shaking dust off his clothes.

"Can I advise we take cover?" he says, reloading his handgun. "I personally am getting rather sick of being shot at."

"The ship's not going anywhere," the android says. "We're grounded."

I'm about to say that we're not when the lights go out. For a second, I think my eyes are playing a trick on me, but then the light comes back on and, judging by everybody else's expression, I didn't just dream up the giant creature stepping through a wall into the hangar. I wonder if amma ever encountered them. If La'min knows something that might help.

It strikes the kind of terror in my soul that tells me Humans were never meant to exist alongside these beings, let alone fight one.

"What the hell is that?" the android asks, the Kundar already dragging them into the ship, Vess hot on their heels.

I'm staring at the creature when it reappears. A long arm curls around one of the smaller ships, reducing it to nothing in seconds, the creature wailing in answer.

"Malek, down!" I duck as Nooma joins us, blasting a droid behind me. "There's just too many of them!" She wipes sweat from her brow. "And Làhn and Kode have vanished. Get Akim to come pick us up."

"If he lands before we've taken care of the droids, they're going to blow the ship apart!" I protest even as we take shelter behind some debris.

"If we stay, we die!" she snaps, and I grit my teeth.

She's right, but at least for now the creature—creatures, actually, as a second shambles into view as the lights turn off—is buying us some time. I can't endanger Akim and Alta when they have the highest chance of survival right now.

I link to La'min, the signal crackly.

"Mal, kid, how's it going? You out of here yet?"

"Too many droids. How's it going at your end?"

"Badly, we've got one of the Urelhan wrecking the place and the droids on the other side." A pause. "Leave the blasted doors! Set the charges and get out!" La'min shouting orders feels all too familiar. "You need to get out of here, Mal!"

"Not as easy as that!"

"We're trying to get to you guys. Are any of the ships still operational?"

Lasers blast our cover, and it would crumple if not for Nephanie rallying her power.

"Ours is."

"Then what are you waiting for?"

"My pilot can't land it! And I'm not leaving anyone behind," I snap. Nephanie can't keep us safe forever. We need to move, but every time the lights turn off, I see the Urelhans making their deadly way around the hangar.

I wish I had a clever plan like amma always had, wish I could be half the captain she had been. She wouldn't be cowering in terror. Not amma.

"I don't know if we can make it out, Mal," La'min admits quietly. My ears are ringing again, my heart is my throat. I can't lose him again. I dig my nails into my palm hard, trying so hard to not let the past wash over me.

But it's no use. The connection with La'min cuts and I'm back in the escape pod with amma and La'min's face disappearing as the airlock seals.

When Nooma yanks me out of the chair and throws me away I've no idea what's happening, landing in a dizzy heap behind the low cargo bay of another ship, screaming as my stump hits the ground. I turn to my friends and wish I could stop time.

The lights go out, the ship behind them catching fire, the explosion lighting up the hangar a beat later.

I scream. In grief, in rage. I scream at the pain of losing everything once already. Phantom pain throbs through my absent leg as I flatten myself, face down to the ground as debris turns into a scalding rain.

I don't know by what miracle the ship above me doesn't blow too. A newer model. A better engine. Some kind of failsafe.

I can barely hear anything over the persistent whooshing in my ears, but I know the droids are coming for us.

For me.

The girls aren't by my side.

Nooma chose to save me, and I don't want to turn, don't want to see their bodies. But I need to know. I need to see.

I should find my blaster, ready myself for a shootout, but Nooma is gone, and I can't muster the strength to. Still, I owe her to look, to honour her death by fighting.

I turn and a noise half-sob, half-laughter escapes me. Instead of charred bodies, I see Nephanie a foot above the ground, holding Nooma tightly within her golden shield.

They're alive.

"Flark you, Berik!" I bellow, filled with renewed energy. I find my blaster, not caring that the grip is too hot and burns my palm.

The droids are coming, their weapons at the ready. There's too many of them. We can't win this. I don't have a body force-shield yet, but I'm not going down alone.

The Kundar leaps into the fray, blades slicing at the droids, the android next to them, fists caving in metal heads, screaming his rage as I empty the charge of my blaster.

The droids start shooting.

A laser hits me in the arm, another sears a path through my side. I scream. In desperation. In defiance. Because of the pain and because I don't want to die. Every second feels like a minute. Blasters fire to kill and I refuse to close my eyes.

Nothing hits, bouncing off a glimmering shield instead. Nephanie kneels beside me, one hand on my shoulder, one on Nooma's thigh as she stands, rifle in hand, mowing down the droids. The Kundar and the android are still fighting, Vess firing from cover. I have never felt so alive. Despite the fear. Despite the pain.

If this is to be my last stand, then I will make it with my eyes open and my head held high. I slap a new battery inside my blaster, sitting up as best I can, and resume shooting.

CHAPTER 42
LÀHN

URELHAN DESTROYER

If I get out of this alive, I need combat training.

I wasted my element of surprise in a clumsy rush, and now the traitor has me slammed against the wall, pinned by my throat, his grip like a vice.

"Bad move, kid."

I can't breathe. My head is spinning. Clawing at his arm is getting me nowhere.

I go limp, blinking as though fighting to stay conscious. I'm lucky he buys it, letting go.

I should pretend to be out cold. Bide my time to flee. But I'm done with that. I can't be the only person here not helping. Not anymore.

I make myself fall against him, startling him so he's not looking at my hands. By the time he's pushing me away, my fingers have already closed on the chip, my instincts correct as to where he'd put it.

I let myself drop so I can slip the chip in my own pocket unseen.

Only now he's pulled out his blaster, his eyes the unfocused gaze of someone checking their Neurolink implants.

"Well, guess I hit jackpot," he grins. "Knew I'd seen your face somewhere. My boss is gonna be thrilled when I bring you back as bonus."

Shit.

He flicks his blaster to stun

I don't think, going against all my instincts, and lunge at his legs. His shot goes wide as he falls, and within the next seconds we're scuffling on the ground. I try to get the blaster from him but in less than a heartbeat he's on top of me, pinning me down. All I can do is throw my arms over my face as he strikes.

If they're bigger than me, I'll just hit them where it hurts most!

I remember Kode saying this what feels like a lifetime ago. I can't even remember what we were doing but she'd been so confident.

I need to beat this guy for her. Because with everything we've both lost I can't let us be separated. I can't be weak and afraid anymore.

I keep my arms up even as he punches me in the ribs, yanking my leg up into his crotch. He makes a stupid noise and I roll, finding my feet and stumbling into the corridor. I need to get out to where there'll be the chance for backup.

He tackles me as I'm about to make it and we land on the alien floor, which isn't half as hard as it should be.

He's back on his feet before I've even caught my breath and I glance up in time to see his blaster levelled at me.

The lights go out.

The Urelhan is inches from us, its arm sweeping down. It misses me and passes right through the traitor. I hear a scream—mine?—as his body vaporises, the arm holding his gun thudding to the floor in a spray of blood as the lights come back.

Kode appears in the doorway, triumph on her face for all of a beat before she sees what just happened.

She's done it. The droids are down.

I offer her an attempt at a smile before lurching to the side and emptying the contents of my stomach.

CHAPTER 43
MALEK

URELHAN DESTROYER

The second the droids go down, the Urelhans appear to calm down, though their wails are enough to keep my nerves on edge.

Nooma moves like she's done this all her life, calling Akim down even as she gathers together everyone she can see. Vess rushes over to get La'min, and all I can do is sit there, trying to breathe through all the pain.

But we're alive.

Kode, it turns out, is our saviour, or so Làhn tells us as they return, also proudly declaring he has the chip. I have so many questions, but La'min is here and we're hugging and then boarding our respective ships: Vess flying the remaining Berik vessel with La'min and crew, and ours taking everyone else.

Nooma carries me to the cockpit and for once I'm not too proud to let her.

I've sent everyone else to the infirmary or to buckle down, but I'm not budging from this chair until I know we're safely on our way home.

Nooma grips the back of my seat as the ship lifts off, and I'm already moving all shield power to the front so we can ram through the membrane trying to keep us in. I feel the moment Akim starts to break through.

"Hold onto something!"

It's almost as bad as atmosphere entry, but nowhere near as bad as what greets us on the other side.

I swear. Nooma swears. Akim stabilises us with the calm of a seasoned pilot.

We're in hyperspace.

"Well, isn't this brilliant! Akim, how's the pull of the destroyer on us?" I ask because nothing I look at makes sense anymore. I'm three seconds away from freaking out.

"Too much. It's pulling us after it even with the engines at max. We need to jump out now." He hits the coms to the engine room. "Alta, are we ready to jump?"

"Stars, no! We'll blow ourselves up!"

"Then we need more power to the engines!" I order.

"Mal, this is all the ship can give!"

"We need something, Alta, or I don't know how this is gonna end!"

"I'll see what I can-Nephanie what-?" Alta cuts off as a burst of noise fills the coms.

"Now!" the Shinarian girl shouts. "All power to main engines, NOW!"

I'm slammed into my seat as Nooma is thrown to the back of the cockpit. I squeeze my eyes shut against the sudden pressure and pain, only daring to move when I hear Akim speak again.

"We're clear. We're away from its pull, we can—"

A blast sends the ship rolling.

"What was that?" Nooma yells, clinging to the safety handles.

"Shields down twenty-five percent! What hit us?"

"Must be a cloaked Berik ship," Akim replies, calm as anything.

"Guess we're testing the weapons!" I say, reaching for the controls.

"I said that was a—" Alta's protestations are interrupted as we're hit again.

Shields at zero percent.

A defiant determination washes over me. We didn't make it this far to fail *now.* I re-route power from everything but the oxygen to the shields on the side we're being hit.

Starboard shields at thirty-six percent.

Another blast takes them out almost immediately a breath before something out there blows up, the camouflage winking out as the ship falls apart. The coms crackle to life.

"You kids in one piece?" La'min's voice rings in the cockpit.

Neither Berik ship was showing on the radar. We're gonna need better kit.

"Stars, thanks for that, Min," I manage, teetering between maniacal laughter and tears. I didn't need to stare death in the face a second time today. Or is it a third time by now? I'm losing count. "We're okay, I think. Meet you guys back on Bakula?"

"You in a state to jump?"

I patch the question to Alta to confirm we should just about be ready to, and I let La'min know. "Alright then! First one to figure out the route home gets a free drink!" La'min challenges.

I take a deep breath, focussing on nothing but now. Everything else can wait. "Akim, can you get us back?"

"Huh huh. Especially if you're not here to distract me."

La'min laughs. "You're like your mom, always in the way of the important work," he jokes, and I'd pull his tail if I could.

"That's fine," Nooma speaks over me. "Means I can look after him."

"You do that, kid," La'min replies. "Com us when you figure out a good path home and we'll do the same if we get there first. Cool?"

"I can do that," Akim says, even as his hand flicks over the navigation tools with the confidence of a seasoned Shinarian navigator.

Nooma puts a hand on my shoulder. "Come on."

I restore the ship's gravity power and let her take me away.

PART 5

TOGETHER

Coming together is the beginning.
Keeping together is progress.
Working together is success.
Henry Ford

CHAPTER 44
TRYSTAN

EDEN-ONE/HYPERSPACE

I survived a firefight; I can survive this party.

I can survive whatever comes next, no matter how scared I am.

In a blink everything has gone from chaos to being safe on a ship, Jakoor's arms strong and comforting around me.

"Tris, what's up?" Cat asks, worriedly taking my hand. I keep missing what she's saying, zoning away from this body to the one I feel at home in.

"Tris?" She tugs at my arm. I blink, forcing myself to even out my focus. I can't afford to screw up tonight.

"Sorry I..."

There is so much she doesn't know. Too much.

"You know you can talk to me, right?" I admire her body language, so casual for the onlookers whilst her voice sounds so worried. "You nervous about tonight?"

I was, but then I survived a gun fight, escaped an alien ship full of monstrous ghosts, and now I'm flying through hyperspace, back to a station of pirates and outlaws. Nervous went out of the window at some point.

"A little." Cat looks at me as though she can read the lies on my face. "I'll be fine, I just... I'll be glad when it's done, you know."

"Did something happen that you're not telling me?"

I feel bad for worrying her. She squeezes my hand, letting me know she'll be here no matter what.

I don't deserve her.

"Not really."

"It'll be okay."

I wish I believed her. I wish tonight didn't mark the beginning of the rest of my life. The announcement of the engagement. An engagement party in a few weeks. A marriage too few years down the line.

I wrap my arms around myself, nauseous at the thought of it all. Why had I ever thought someone like me could dream of studying like my uncle had?

"Hey, you alright?" A girl with chin-length hair and brown skin joins me where I lean against medbay's wall. "I'm Alta, you?" she adds as mom comes to drag me away to meet father's newest business partner.

"Tryst. And I'm fine, thanks. Just a bit... Overwhelmed."

"You're the AI Mal mentioned?"

I nod, wishing Jakoor was here but they're in medbay with those that needed seeing to.

"We have lots of AIs on my home planet. Most are inside homes or ships, but a few have bodies, if they want them," she adds, voice filled with a homesickness I can't understand.

"We're...rare where I come from." I look down, aching to tell the truth. "I ran away."

"Was it a bad place?" The kindness in her eyes almost breaks me.

"Yeah," I whisper, even as mom introduces me.

I never saw the man's face that fateful night in my father's office. Never heard his name. But as he greets my mother and turns to me, I know his voice like I know my nightmares. Terror floods me. Just the thought of ending up institutionalised is almost enough to make me abort tonight's plan. Alta puts a hand on my shoulder, welcoming me to the ship. And in that touch, thousands of light years away, I find the strength to keep myself together.

"It's a pleasure to meet you, Mr Telloney," I say in my most polite voice. "I hear you'll be helping papa in the upcoming campaign?"

"Indeed, I am. Your father and I have worked very closely on several projects in the past and I'm pleased to contribute this election season." He takes my hand and lays a kiss on it, and I want to snatch it back and slap him, but I keep my smile frozen in place.

"We're very grateful for your help," I sound so lame but around this man it doesn't matter. "Can I get you a drink?"

"That would be lovely."

"What were you doing on the destroyer?" Alta asks, leaning next to me. Inside medbay Nooma sounds like she's telling everyone off. Even the medical equipment.

"I was with Jakoor. They needed to talk to Vess. We weren't expecting everything to go to hell."

"You can say that again!" The girl's laugh is brittle. "Are you hurt? Do you need anything?"

"I'll need some new skin, and a wash, but that's about it."

I'm pouring the drink for Telloney when Nathaniel and his father are ushered in, aware of how every single one of my motions feel stiff and staged as I force myself not to glance towards him. I'm handing Telloney his drink when Malek comes hobbling out of medbay, leaning heavily on a crutch, top off, revealing far more skin than I'm used to seeing.

I feel my cheeks growing warm at home and wish I'd put some make up on to keep my reactions to the other half of my life hidden.

"Alright, well that was a thing," he says, hovering in the doorway so he can address everyone. "I think Nephanie deserves a medal and— Where is she?"

"In her room, said she needed some rest," Alta replies.

"I'll go see if she needs anything," Nooma says, pausing to look at Malek. "You gonna be okay with the stairs?"

"Don't worry, *mom,* I'm not that badly injured."

Mr Telloney is making pointless conversation and I'm struggling to keep from just tuning him out.

"Your arm would disagree," Nooma fires back.

"Well, isn't it good the cybernetic one is in one piece and strong as ever. I'm *fine,* go see to your girlfriend."

"She is not my—!"

"Yeah, yeah, and I'm not a wanted fugitive."

Nooma makes an exasperated noise and storms off.

Malek grins. "Anyway, let's get back to the lounge, shall we?"

I'm replying meaningless pleasantries to Telloney, doing my best to act like Cat and father looks pleased as he joins us.

Back on the ship I sit on the floor next to Jakoor as they stiffly settle on a chair, keen to be close to someone I feel safe with.

"Okay, pretty boy," Malek starts as the two I don't know walk in, looking worse for wear. The boy scowls at Malek.

"Do you mean me?" he asks with the kind of attitude that says he knows the answer already.

"Do you see any others around here?"

"He's pretty," Alta says, pointing at me.

I almost stumble over my words in front of my father. The *he* part never gets old, but back on Eden One no-one would call a boy 'pretty' without meaning it as an insult. But then I guess the boy is kinda pretty, with his long hair and golden-brown skin, and the elegant up-tilt of his eyes.

Malek glances at me, purses his lips, then shrugs. "Guess he is. But not *as* pretty." He adjusts his stance on his crutches, flashing the other boy a wide smile, before pressing the coms unit on the wall. "Akim, do we have a path to Bakula yet?"

"What do you think?"

"That I don't know and that's why I'm asking."

Akim groans audibly. "Of course we do, what do you take me for?"

"A very skilled pilot who is also a very skilled navigator. How long before we're back home?"

"Around half an hour. Give or take. Maybe closer to forty-five minutes. The destroyer's engines must have been something *else* because we went really far given when it must have made the jump. It doesn't help that the engines aren't at their best since Nephanie decided to superpower us away."

"I told you this was a rust bucket," the 'pretty boy' mutters and Malek's smile falters.

"Watch it."

"Malek, Làhn's right. But it's our rust bucket so remember, that makes it the best rust bucket the galaxy has ever seen," Alta interjects and Malek perks up.

I don't think I've ever met someone who acts so much like a puppy.

Làhn smirks. "See, listen to Alta. They're the engineer after all."

They. Oh. They must be non-binary then. I wish I could catch a moment alone with them, maybe ask some questions. Knowing someone else who didn't fit their assigned gender is so exciting and also a little nerve wracking.

"Alright, *alright."* Malek tries to regain control of the situation. "What about we try and see what's on that chip?"

I'm about to ask what chip when someone touches my elbow. I whirl, and when I catch Nathaniel's eyes, I can't help but smile. Oh boy but I wish everything wasn't so complicated.

"Good evening," he says, then greets my mother with a smile. "May I borrow Tris for a little while?"

CHAPTER 45
MALEK

HYPERSPACE

Time to see if the AI terminal on this 'rust bucket', as everyone is calling *my* ship, works. The thing is decades old and probably going to croak it, especially given I didn't manage to scrape all of the blood off the chip. But I need to know what got amma killed. I need to know what is on here that Berik would slaughter so many people for.

Nooma and Nephanie join us just as the screen turns on, revealing a beautiful, androgynous face.

"DNA recognition complete, emergency shut down protocol terminating, systems rebooting."

Everyone stares at the face on the screen as it blinks once, twice, and then its eyes focus on the room.

"I am Anh Giang, guardian of knowledge and servant to the Chuan royal family. Prince Làhn, I am pleased to find you well, it has been a long time since we last saw each other."

Silence falls, heavy and shocked. The AI has soft features paired with angular eyes, their hair up in an elaborate style dripping with decoration. There is something of Làhn in the face, and the skin tone.

Prince Làhn. I turn to him, slowly. Làhn's eyes are on the AI, wide and startled, all but terrified.

"Well, that's unexpected, *your majesty*," I say jokingly.

"I'm not a prince," Làhn's voice is no louder than a breath.

"Well, Anh Giang, guardian of knowledge seems to think you are!"

I realise I'm being an ass the second the words are out of my mouth and his face shutters.

"Is this some dumb prank?" he asks. "Kode couldn't even get the damn thing to boot up earlier."

"I was in emergency shutdown after the ship I previously resided on came under attack. It was the only thing I could do to protect the information I possess. After such a shutdown only a DNA scan would allow me to reboot fully."

"I didn't do a DNA scan!"

Kode gets his attention, her hands a blur to me. Làhn slumps, something like defeat washing over him.

"It's not possible," he murmurs, passing a hand through his hair.

"Your blood…" I realise.

"Yeah. My hand was still sticky with it when I grabbed the chip. I… I don't understand what's going on."

Anh Giang's voice is soft. "You appear to have come a very long way from home." They pause. "Prince Làhn?"

"No!" Làhn's voice is sharp, startling. "I'm not a prince. I don't know who you think I am, but you're mistaken!" His hand is fastened around his wrist, around the tattoo I spotted earlier.

"I understand this might be difficult for you to believe, Prince Làhn; you were barely six-years-old when the attack occurred, and you were not to be told anything until you were older. Your parents did not expect to lose the war. That is why I was sent away, not only to track you down but also to get word out of what had happened on Chuan."

"Back up, back up," I turn back to the AI. "Where exactly are you from?"

"Chuan," they repeat. "If you give me access to your maps, I would be able to mark its location."

Kode beats me to the console and honestly, it's good because I barely have a clue how to operate the thing.

Another stretch of silence as the projector turns on, revealing a star map so zoomed out I can't tell what's what. Eventually it focuses on an area I'm unfamiliar with, outlining a planet surrounded by three small moons, its coordinates highlighted underneath. It's far away from anywhere I've ever been, far from any other Human settlements from what I can guess.

Làhn takes in a sharp breath, running fingers over the coordinates.

"They match," he whispers, signing to Kode. "When I told you we had somewhere to go, that was it. This planet. These coordinates."

"I know those coordinates too," the Kundar speaks up. "Those are the ones Vess gave me."

"What do you want with the place?" I ask.

"Someone I'm looking for went there."

"Prince Làhn?" Anh Giang calls out. There are tears dancing in his eyes as he turns back to the screen.

"I think I remember you. You had a body back home, right? I remember you walking around the courtyard. I... What... what happened the day of the attack?"

I put my hand on his arm, because I'd have to be blind to miss how upset he looks.

"Days prior to the attack your father received a message asking that we peacefully surrender the planet. We thought we were well prepared to defend and, either way, the people had nowhere else to go. We had no contact with other planets, knew little about the rest of the universe. We were alone, but we thought we were strong enough."

"Only you weren't," Nooma isn't asking.

"The force that attacked was like nothing we had expected. They were not people, but machines of war. No matter how many we killed, more always came. The Emperor and the Empress entrusted their only son to his nurse and had them flee. Until now I was not sure either had survived."

"What happened after?" Làhn asks as Kode moves to take his hand in hers.

"We lost. Everyone they could find; they took prisoner to work in mines they drilled into our sacred mountains."

"How did you get here?" I ask.

"The Empress survived. She managed to escape her captors long enough to bring me out of emergency shutdown. She transferred what she could of my consciousness onto a chip and flew me out of the planet's gravity before launching a capsule with me in it into space."

"A message in a bottle," Alta whispers.

"What happened to her?" Làhn's voice is a rasp.

Anh Giang looks at him, eyes a little too wide in their perfect face. "I do not know, my prince."

Làhn's chest constricts, and I watch him struggle to hold everything inside.

"If Berik's chasing after you..." Nooma starts, eyes hard and flat. "Does that mean they're the ones who attacked your planet?"

"We did not know their name then, but after doing some research with Captain Sidana's help, I believe they are."

"I don't think amma ever told anyone about you," I say, aiming for flippant but my voice cracks. Trust her to keep something like this to herself.

"Captain Sidana thought she could keep her crew safe, but unfortunately Berik was able to track me as soon as I connected to her ship's system."

A wave of grief washes over me. I want to be angry with amma for everything to do with this, but the truth is that I get it. She wanted to help. Wanted to do what was right and... And I'm standing here, not even half the age she was then, already sailing through the same stars.

"Are Berik *still* tracking you?" Nooma asks and the AI nods. "So that means they're going to come for us now, right?"

Kode signs something quickly.

"I think she's saying we should be able to block the AI tracker," Alta says as Làhn just stands there, staring at Anh Giang. "For now, we just need to keep them offline, so Berik can't tag them when we pop out of hyperspace."

Kode nods approvingly.

"I can turn off until you have found a way to keep them from tracking me," the AI says.

"Okay, but they knew where the chip was, what stops them following from there?" I ask.

"Their ship tracker will show there was a hyperspace jump," Nephanie declares. "If your friends disable their tracker before we jump out, Berik is gonna have hell figuring out where the destroyer took their ships and droids."

“Oh, I think I can tell them how to disable the tracker!” Alta declares. “Kode, do you think you can help me a sec?” They add, signing partially, and the girl nods, the two of them heading off.

"I... I need some space," Làhn suddenly declares. I try to take his hand, but he bolts out. I'm half considering going after him when Akim's voice echoes over the coms.

"Captain, you might want to come up, we're jumping out in less than ten minutes, and I'd rather not have to do the talking. They're gonna want to know what we did with the destroyer."

CHAPTER 46
TRYSTAN

EDEN ONE

Nathaniel's hand is gentle on my elbow as he leads me to a safe corner to talk. My eyes catch on Cat, engaged with my mother, who looks delighted. I'm sure she'd prefer having her as a child.

"I've got something for you," Nathaniel says, and I hate how much his smile works on me.

"What is it?" I ask, my heart suddenly beating faster.

"Take a look," he says, pulling out a box from inside his jacket.

I almost drop it when he hands it to me—*smooth, Tryst, so smooth*. It's thin and long and I know it holds something I won't want. Inside is a delicate silver chain with three small teardrops of semi-precious stones dropping down.

"Let me put it on for you," he offers.

This is unknown territory, far more dangerous than it should be. I go through the motions I know are needed, lifting my hair out of the way, turning my back to him, though I hardly feel like I'm controlling my body anymore. He slips the pendant around my throat, leaning in, so close I can feel his breath on my ear.

"It's a skeleton key to both our fathers' offices," he whispers and I almost gasp. It's a struggle to keep my face neutral, but when I turn back his expression hasn't changed at all. "The pendant is lovely on you."

Despite myself I run my fingers over the three little stones.

"Thank you." My words are quiet, hesitant. "When should we... you know?"

His smile turns into a smirk that lights up his eyes.

"In about half an hour, excuse yourself to the bathroom. I'll follow. We meet *inside* the office, okay?"

I'm about to reply when my mother sidles up to us, a slightly harried looking Cat in tow. Nathaniel doesn't miss a beat.

"Mrs Wright, a pleasure to be hosted at your wonderful house. The buffet looks particularly excellent tonight, my mother will definitely want to find out which caterer you used, she's had such dreadful luck lately."

My mother fawns all over him. It's painful to watch.

"Nathaniel, it's so wonderful to see you here. I was worried after what happened at the charity ball that, well... I know my daughter is terribly sorry for how she behaved, and we're incredibly grateful you're not holding it against her."

I clasp my hands tightly in front of me, trying to not roll my eyes out of my head.

"Oh, that was nothing, Mrs Wright. It's a very emotional time for me and Tris. You have to understand, we were such good friends in childhood, but being as we are now it…changes things, so I suppose it was a little much, especially with the engagement upcoming."

How does he manage to sound so insufferable?

"My husband is so excited to make the announcement! Your father and he have been friends for so long it seems only right for you and Tris to be married."

What kind of backwards logic is this? Not to mention it's the biggest damned lie. This is just another political move.

"I look forward to it all being made official," his smile is still perfectly in place.

Cat slips her hand in mine. I don't know what I'd do without her.

"Anyway, Mrs Wright, I'll talk to you later if you don't mind, but I see Senator Rubens over there and I must have a word with him regarding the work experience my course requires."

And with that Nathaniel excuses himself, leaving my mother smiling beatifically.

"He'll make a wonderful husband for you, Tris," she tells me. "Truly wonderful. And he's so handsome too."

I roll my eyes so hard; Cat nearly bursts out laughing.

***

Jakoor and I are left alone, settled on the sofa whilst I do some pointless meet-and-greet with mom.

"Are you sure those are the same coordinates Vess gave you?"

"Yes," their voice is a little rough, their head in two of their hands.

"Can I do anything to help?"

"No. It's... This Chuan is so far, and... If it's under Berik control, I fear what it might mean for them."

I lay a hand on one of their arms, their scales smooth under my fingers. I don't know if the gesture is strange to them, but they don't pull away.

"They might have managed to hide, or even escape."

They nod, but we both know that things might not be so easy.

"What do you want to do?" they ask.

"Now? Rest. I have *stuff* going on at home."

They nod. It's reassuring that they know; that they just accept me.

"Feel free to power down a little, I'll look after you."

I frown. "Will you be okay by yourself?"

"Don't worry, I've seen worse than this. And I could do with some rest and time to process all this."

"Are we safe here?" I ask them before I fully close my eyes.

"Yeah, I think we're good." They touch my arm, mimicking my gesture. I smile, almost surprised at the soft wave of quiet happiness I feel by their side.

I glance at the clock, nerves creeping back in, the fake wood more offensive than usual. I have stared at it so much in my life—usually whilst being lectured—that I know its curves by heart and hate every single one of them. But at last, it's time to make my exit.

My mother is engrossed in conversation with a woman whose daughter, a couple of years my junior, is the perfect doll at her side. I feel a pang of mixed pity and envy as I make my excuse. Every step I take, I'm terrified someone is going to stop me, that my parents are going to realise I'm up to something.

When the door finally shuts behind me, I let out a long breath. The maid rushes over, asking if I'm alright. I manage to brush her off and wait until she's gone back to the kitchen to sneak inside my father's office.

Time to wait for Nathaniel.

Every noise from the corridor makes me jump until I hear footsteps. Fear clouds everything and I throw myself under the desk, curling into a ball. This is stupid. This is the worst idea ever. I should never have taken this risk.

"Tris?" Nathaniel's voice is a whisper but it's enough to make me squeak in surprise.

I crawl out from under the desk, looking up at him.

"I thought you might be my father," I hiss as he raises an eyebrow, holding out his hand to help me up.

"Sorry," he says, but he does look a little amused.

I swallow a retort as he pulls out his kit and gets to work.

"How long will it take? " I ask, barely talking above a whisper.

"I don't know, depends how deep the encryption is and whether it's different to my father's," Nathaniel explains. "We should be fine though; I doubt they'll come looking for us in here."

"If they start looking for us at all we're in trouble," I snap. "And keep your voice lower, I don't want someone passing by hearing us."

"We can say we got nervous about the announcement and needed some time to talk," he says, nonchalantly, only slightly lowering his voice.

"My mother is *never* going to buy that. She *knows* I'm unhappy with this."

He glances at me, and I look away because I can't read his expression.

"I'm not exactly thrilled either," he mutters.

His tone brushes me up the wrong way. I try to hold back the words. Really. Well, maybe I could have tried harder. But it's been so long since I've wanted to say something, and Nathaniel is the only person it's safe to be angry at.

"Oh yeah, I'm sure this is *so bad* for you, right? You'll get more political power from it, just like our fathers, and you're basically guaranteed someone to look after your house the second you leave home. I mean, *really,* it won't even change things for you that much will it? You'll still be able to go to university and have a career and..." I stop as I take in the tightness in his jaw.

"Yeah, sure, what would being forced into marriage change for me, right?"

My own jaw tightens. I want out of here. Out of this conversation, out of my skin, out of my anger. But I'm stuck. I'm always stuck.

"What *does* it change? I'm not exactly going to make your life hell!"

"Well for a start I don't even *like* girls!"

The words look like they were out of his mouth before he could think better. And as though we're both under a spell, I hear myself speak before I can stop.

"Well, that's great, because I'm *not* a girl!"

Silence falls as we stare at each other.

Then something bleeps, and we both jump.

"We're in," he says, though we're still looking at each other. "You're...not a girl?"

"We're not having this conversation now," my voice is small but firm. This was not how I planned on coming out.

"No, good idea. Maybe..." he hesitates. "Tomorrow?"

All I can do is nod as we turn our attention to our work.

"There!" I call when a file with the Berik logo comes up.

"Okay, I'll copy everything across, we can take a look at it later."

My heart is still racing by the time he's finished and now there are footsteps outside. We wait for them to disappear but not a second after the door shuts behind us, we hear his mother. Nathaniel moves quickly, pulling me away from the office and pushing me against the wall, kissing me.

I squeal in surprise as his mother comes into view. His lips are gentle against mine. I want to push him away. I want to draw him close.

"Nathaniel!" his mother sounds disgusted.

He whirls around, feigning shock. "Mother, I can explain—"

"No explanation needed," she snaps. "Hot blood like your father. But I'd better *not* find you like this until you've married her. You hear me?" She looks at me and shakes her head. "I'm sorry, sweetheart, but don't worry, Nathaniel won't go spreading any rumours, I'll make sure of it." She is so much more in control than my mother. She's always been scary but at the same time I've always secretly admired the way she holds herself in a world that wants nothing but to crush her.

"I'm sorry, mother." Nathaniel acts chastised, but the look he slides me is the true apology.

"Go be sorry in there, just tell your father you had to take a call. Go!"

He slinks off, and she turns to me, softening. I'm not going to be blamed for something I had no control over, and the relief is startling.

"Before you two get married, you and I are going to have a long chat, sweetheart. We don't get to make a lot of decisions in this life of ours, but there are many ways to be in control of your household, trust me." She pauses for a second, looking after Nathaniel. "And if he thinks he can behave however he wants... Well, I'll give you a few tips to keep him in line. Now, come on, let's get back to that wonderful party your mother is hosting," she adds, holding out her hand to me.

I take it gingerly but the smile she gives me is genuine.

CHAPTER 47
LÀHN

BAKULA

Prince Nguyen Van Làhn.

What a strange turn for everything to take. Of course, I'd always known I'd had a life before Kirillion, but this is beyond anything I could have imagined.

I'm strangely numb, not even startling when Kode lays behind me on the bunk, wrapping an arm around me.

We lie like that for a while

Talk to me. She messages, sitting up and I follow suit.

I don't know how I feel. Or what to do. I don't know whether to turn around and go back to Tulain and stay there until it's safe to go home or... I falter.

What do you want?

I don't know.

I have so few memories, so little tethering me to that place. Truly, I have no reason to return to a planet most likely still under Berik control. Yet there lies the whole of my reason.

Berik.

It's because of them I ended up on Kirillion and because of them I had to flee again. Without them, I don't think any of us would be here.

It's almost ironic that the people who have destroyed my life, not once, but twice, would be the very reason I'd want to return home. Because even if it's foolish, I don't mind the idea of taking some revenge.

For what they did to me. To the Guild. To Zoon.

For all the pain Malek and his friends went through.

Berik deserves us to try and find our way to Chuan and see if we can help.

I don't think I can go home yet, I admit.

Kode gives me a knowing smile. *So, we're still going?*

If Malek is, then yes. I won't let Berik get away with everything they're doing. I don't know what we can do, if we even can do anything, but at the very least we can get proof of what we're doing, and then see if anyone on the IUP or something will hear us.

She nods and her presence by my side is invaluable. This is such a foolish decision, a risk that could lead us to our deaths, and yet, here she is, willing to take it by my side.

I wish I could ask Anh Giang if they had any proof of what happened, I add.

It won't take that long to work out a way to block their signal, I did something similar on a job couple of months back. But either way, I think if they'd had anything to show you when you asked about the attack, they would have. They did say only part of their processing was transferred to the chip which tells me it's gonna have been core processes and personality stuff. The rest is going to have been left behind.

I nod. Really, the Empress would have been better off sending Anh Giang with videos of what had happened instead of as they are. No-one is going to listen to an AI's word without proof, not when going against Berik. But then I don't imagine she had a lot of time to sort any of this.

I pass a hand through my hair and glance at Kode.

I always did want to go on an adventure, she signs, and I let out a short, startled laugh.

It's true, though, she was always the one dreaming of adventures and doing something big, ever since we were children. Instead, adventure came to find me, and she followed, same as I'd have followed her.

Do you think Shuobe will be okay to come? I don't want to come in between them, not if Shuobe doesn't want to take this risk.

Pretty sure she will, Kode signs, and the light in her eyes tugs my lips into a smile.

And like that I realise that the part of me who wanted to remain small, hidden, lost in the banality of everyday life has been left behind, lost somewhere in between leaving the Guild and surviving the Urelhan destroyer. I'm surprised to find that a part of me is eager for what is to come.

I guess I should go talk to Malek, I sign, and at that thought, a little bit of my apprehension returns.

What if he says no?

***

Malek's in the cockpit, sprawled in the co-pilot seat, tipping his head back to look at me as I slip to his side, fighting to keep my eyes off of his bare chest. He's almost distracting to look at: warm brown skin, thick black hair, a smattering of stubble around his jaw. But he's also a little too thin, and the dressings and constellation of scars he sports worry me. Not for the first time I wonder about his and his crew's story.

"What can I do for you, pretty boy," he asks, smirking, and I groan.

"You can start by calling me Làhn."

I don't trust his smirk for one second.

"Sorry." He doesn't sound it. I've never known someone I've wanted to both smack but also kiss. "Would you prefer *Prince* Làhn?"

Perhaps I will just hit him.

"No, just Làhn is fine," I grind out. But it's hard to be really angry at someone who's looking at me like this. His eyes are promising things I'd lie if I said I hadn't thought about myself.

"Alright, *just* Làhn, what can I do for you?"

"Malek!" I smack his prosthetic arm.

He laughs, eyes twinkling with mischief. He's a wildfire of a boy: beautiful, fascinating, and dangerous. I'm drawn to him, like he's a planet whose gravity I don't really want to pull away from.

The shape of his lips is making me want to forget everything I came to talk about.

"Sorry, sorry," that twinkle in his eyes again. "So, *Làhn*." He purrs my name in a way I'm not sure anyone else ever has. "What can I help you with?"

For a brief instant I consider kissing him, just to see his reaction. To know what he'd taste like.

Focus, Làhn, focus.

I let out a long breath, passing a hand through my hair. His eyes trail my every move.

"What's your plan now?" I ask, buying time.

He shrugs. "Not sure yet. Tulain might threaten to not pay us—he won't mean it though, and if he does, La'min will threaten to make a pair of boots out of his scales. Then Tulain will probably threaten to make mittens out of La'min's tail, and La'min would—Never mind. Guess we need a new gig. We're a small crew so we can't take on something too big, but we'll make it work. We've already got a bit of a reputation."

"What if you had more crew?" I'm hedging, scared he'll turn me down.

"Why? Thinking of joining?" I look away from him, afraid he can read my every thought in my eyes. "What can *you* do anyway? Kode's one hell of a hacker but what about you?"

"I'm a thief," I turn back to face him. "And I'm pretty good at seducing my way to what I want."

His smirk widens, an eyebrow lifting in appreciation.

I should not have said that.

"Oh, is that so?" He all but drawls.

"Yeah, it is."

"You'll have to demonstrate."

I really do want to smack him. And kiss him.

"Maybe I will," I shrug. "But it'd come with a condition."

"And what's that?"

My heart is racing so fast I feel like I can't breathe. "You take us to Chuan. I need to get records of what happened there so I can take this to the IUP."

Malek makes a ponderous noise, lips pursing a little as he looks down at the console. My throat tightens with every second that passes. When he turns back to me, his teal eyes are dancing with dangerous mischief.

"Funny you'd say that, given I've thought about giving Chuan a little visit myself." I blink. "I mean, given that Berik are being shitheads over there, and that's the reason why amma died and I spent a couple of years on Helios and all," he carries on as what he just said hits me. He *escaped* a Helios prison. That's impossible. "I figured we could go to where it all started, maybe mess up whatever they've got going on, and then," a shrug. "Move onto the next paying gig I guess?"

This was not how I pictured this conversation going and my words fail me.

"Even Nooma agreed it sounded like a solid idea," he grins. "She's got her own beef with them, and whilst we're travelling, we can pick up jobs and make some money, let Nooma punch some assholes she's been dying to catch up with, that kind of thing."

I blink again. "You serious?"

"I wouldn't joke about this. Certainly not when you had that super serious expression on your face a second ago. I mean, it would have been funny to see what you did if I said no, but," he smirks. "We've just been through hell, so I figured you deserved a break."

I let out a nervous laugh. "Will you let Shuobe come too?"

"She's the Mallak girl I saw with you guys, right?"

"Yeah."

"I believe we've got the space on the ship. But she'll have to earn her keep, like everyone else, okay?"

"Sounds fair."

Malek grins, eyes twinkling. "Maybe I have a condition, too."

My stomach drops. "What?"

"Seal the deal with a kiss?"

Smack him. I am definitely going to smack him. He's laughing and I'm on my feet.

"I'm going, I need to let the girls know," I say, but before I can leave, he grabs my hand.

I whirl around, glowering and he just winks at me.

"You're an ass." I snatch my hand free, but the feel of his fingers lingers on my skin, warm and inviting. I can only imagine how warm and good his lips would feel against mine.

"I know. But I'm not dreaming this spark between us, am I?"

Heat rushes to my face and I turn away, storming out of the cockpit without another word.

CHAPTER 48
TRYSTAN

EDEN ONE

The night is surprisingly mild: the air cool, the breeze soft. Everything feels a little lighter, as though now the secret is out, there is no longer a band constricting my chest.

Cat's head rests on my shoulder as we sit on the wall overlooking the pond glittering in the garden lights. Our shoes are discarded, our dresses getting grass-stained, but it doesn't matter. For a moment I'm worriless, leaning against her.

"Tryst suits you," she speaks, her voice soft.

"I thought of picking something else but... to start with it was easier. Now I'm kinda attached to it."

I feel her smile. Telling her had been both easier and harder than expected. I'd dragged her away as soon as I could and blurted everything out: a tangle of words she'd somehow made sense of. When all had been said, she'd just pulled me into her arms and held me close.

Now we've snuck out, like we've done so many times before.

"I still can't believe Nathaniel and you snapped all this at each other," she all but giggles and I playfully poke her.

"Don't, just don't. I thought I was going to die of embarrassment," I mutter, my eyes on the stars.

Tonight, they feel a little less fake.

"It's okay," Cat tells me, shifting so that she's got her head in my lap. I dread to think what state her dress will be in, but she's far more capable of getting out of a scolding than I am. "Nathaniel's on our side. He's like us, Tryst, he sees everything broken about this place. He's not going to think there's something wrong with you."

"I hope you're right."

"You know I am. You two always used to get along so well, you just need to reconnect now that you're actually allowed to."

"But this... This is *weird,* isn't it?"

She taps me on the nose like she does her dog when he acts silly.

"It's not *weird,* Tryst. We both know it only seems that because we live on some backwater planet that tries to keep all this knowledge from us. The problem is, they *can't.*"

She's right. As long as the internet exists, there will always be ways to get information about all the things the people in charge want to keep from you. I feel guilty for not trusting her before now. I should have known Cat would accept me no matter what.

"What's that look for?" she asks.

"I feel bad for not trusting you sooner. I know you said you don't blame me but—"

Her finger comes to rest against my lips.

"I knew there was *something* up with you, I just didn't know what. And I never asked you outright, never gave you that opening. So, I get it. I'm not mad, I promise. I'm happy you told me now."

I smile at her, tears barely held back. Good tears. She accepts me. She *sees* me.

"Our mothers are going to freak out we got grass on our dresses," I say, to stop myself from actually starting to cry.

"I think it's good we came out here given you looked one congratulation away from murdering someone."

"I was more thinking of killing myself, actually," I mean the words in jest, but she grabs my hand, squeezing it tight.

"Don't joke about that, okay. Just…don't." There's something in her eyes I can't read, sudden and new and raw. "Tryst, I'm serious," she places one hand on my cheek. "One of Shauna's friends, she... She wasn't just joking one day. And she was a bit like you, quiet and withdrawn, and nobody realised when she stopped being okay. I don't know what her deal was, I don't know why she did it, but I'll never forget the look in Shauna's eyes. So please, please don't do that to me. I know it's selfish but, please…"

She's squeezing my hand so tight it almost hurts. I wonder if she's worried about me before, during the nights spent in secret at my uncle's lab not responding to her messages.

"I know I didn't reach out to you before, and that was shit of me, but I'm here. I promise. I'm done letting you fight alone," she tells me, and I clasp her hand back.

I've never felt so strong.

"I promise you I won't," my voice is a little hoarser than I expected. "I..." I think of Jakoor, asleep, sprawled on Vess' bed—we relocated to his apartment as soon as we could—with two arms over their eyes to block out the light. I think of Nathaniel and the way my heart races when I see him. Of Cat, who knows *everything,* laying on my lap as though nothing has changed. "I have too much to live for to do that," I whisper, and I believe it so much more than I ever have.

Not so long ago despair almost engulfed me, but I won't let it win. Not when there are many wonderful people around me.

"Damn straight you do," her voice is thick too, her eyes moist. "You're my best friend, Tryst, and you might get to run around the universe kicking butt as an android, but I want to keep *this* you safe, you hear me? So, you and me, and Nathaniel, we're going to find a way to help you. And hey, given you're a guy and he's into guys—"

"Don't." I can't hold that hope.

Cat turns back to me with mischief in her eyes, and that brightness that has always lit up my world. "Don't what? Tease you because I know you have a crush on him? No way I'm passing that opportunity!" She laughs as I poke her in the ribs. "Best friend prerogative!" she claims, and I laugh too.

Everything feels so normal. A real sort of normal I've craved for years.

"I'll admit he's cute," I say, leaning back, fingers splayed in the soft grass. "But his hair sucks."

"What's wrong with his hair?"

"Too short, he looked way better when it was longer."

She laughs. Then silence falls, comfortable and soothing. Clearly our parents are too busy to notice our disappearance. Either that or Nathaniel is charming everyone to cover for us.

"We'll find a way," Cat repeats. "We'll find a way to make this work. Together."

My hand finds hers. "Together."

***

"Are you sure you want to come?" Jakoor asks, still sprawled on the bed, in a position not so dissimilar to how I am at home.

"Why wouldn't I?"

Jakoor went to have a word with Malek, and he agreed to take both of us on board if we work on the ship. And as Jakoor needs to head to Chuan to find their mentor, they accepted, as it's safer than heading there alone.

"You don't know how dangerous this might be. War isn't pretty, occupation even less." They push themselves up, hair like a black-green waterfall. They're bare chested and, at home, I flush a little. It's hard not to drink in the sight of their powerful muscles, the nip of their waist and the scales peeking out above their trousers. They're hot and there's no denying it.

"Berik are after you and forced my uncle into all this through working with my father. But no-one in power is going to take our word against theirs. We're too small, too insignificant against a corporation like Berik. But if we find an entire planet of proof..." It's strange to feel such determination. To claim the power of deciding what to do with myself. "I want to stop them: what they're doing there, and what they're doing to your people and... I just want them to be stopped. I can't do that by myself but… I can help."

I like this me willing to fight. To take a stand.

"You've already helped," Jakoor points out. "Without you I couldn't have escaped. I didn't even know *where* I was and..." They tilt their head in that way I still don't understand. "What they did to me, it weakened me. I'm still not at full strength." I gawk a little at that given how they were fighting on the destroyer. "But my race heals fast, and I'll be back to normal soon. But if they had been allowed to carry on..." They make a sound like a sigh. "Shorter-lived races are jealous of how long we live. They don't understand that's just who we are. We grow up slower, we age slower. It's a balance. But people just take from us, as though we're some science experiment all theirs to examine." A bitter laugh. "I think it's all we've been for a long time. Just a science experiment gone wrong. Or right. Who knows what those who attacked us *really* wanted? We don't even know who they were."

I've never seen Jakoor like this, head thrown back against the wall, voice thick and fists clenched. I move closer, offer the comfort of a friend, a hand on their arm.

"Do you know we weren't always this long lived? That *this*," they motion at their body, "Isn't always what we looked like? We've been changed, so profoundly it changed everything about us. About our culture and how we think and… And sometimes I hope we can find a way to turn back time… But then I just want to move on from it all. I want us and our planet to *heal*."

I squeeze their arm gently, moving to thread my fingers through theirs the way Cat has done a thousand times for me.

"I know I can't do much but… I'm here, okay? I want to help."

Their eyes meet mine, the block colour so luminous in the dim light.

"Why?"

"Because it's the right thing to do. On Eden One, if I didn't do something, who would? It had to be me, there and then, or it might have been never." I glance at the fake window that displays an alien cityscape gilded in eternal sunset. "I was done being powerless. For the first time in my life, I could make a difference. So, I did. Maybe it was selfish, so I could feel like the hero, so I could feel like I mattered."

"Does it matter?"

I look back at them, heart catching a little at the intensity in their stunning eyes.

"What do you mean?"

"Does it matter if it was a little bit selfish when you did the right thing, when you helped?"

"Being selfish is never good, I mean, I'm pretty sure it's what made my home world so bad. They're all so selfish and so self-serving and just..." I let out a frustrated sound. "I don't want to become like them."

"I don't think you're at risk there," they say with something like a chuckle. "I don't know much about your world but... You didn't expect anything in exchange for saving me. We both know you would have let me go even if I hadn't taken you with me. So maybe it was selfish but..." A pause. "Sometimes we need to be, to survive. I was selfish when I left home. My peers certainly think that there are better things I should be doing. And I guess it is selfish that I want to find my mentor but... I believe in them; in the change their research can bring. So even if I'm a little selfish, that's not all I am. Same as you, right?"

I nod, smiling softly. I think of the Suffragettes, how some would call them selfish, saying they're only looking out for themselves. But I know the truth. I know everything that they could change. I suppose, sometimes, to break away from a life of quiet oppression, to make things better, we need to be capable of being selfish. Of wanting something better for ourselves too.

"I mean it, I want to come. I might not be that useful but..." I shrug. "At least I'm strong. I can find ways to help."

"I'm glad you're coming," Jakoor admits. "You make for good company." I almost laugh. Almost cry. "I'll teach you how to fight, though," they add. "Because you cannot throw a punch to save your life. Being made of metal isn't always going to save you," they tease, playfully punching me in the arm, which barely registers. This no pain receptor thing is pretty cool.

"Teach me how to fight? Seriously?" It's an exciting, terrifying prospect. It's everything I never dreamt of.

"Yes," they make an amused sound. "We'll need to get something for you to train on, there is no way I'm letting an android punch me, especially when he can't do it properly."

"I can!" I protest.

"You *think* you can, but there is a hell of a lot more to it than throwing your arm out and hoping your fist connects."

I scowl playfully at them.

There is a moment where we just look at each other, everything else falling away. For a breath I wish time could stop, that we could stay here, close and quiet and safe. But that's not *really* what I want. Not anymore.

"I look forward to you teaching me."

CHAPTER 49
MALEK

BAKULA

"Please tell me this did not come out of a can," Akim mutters as Nooma sets a bowl down in front of him.

"We cleaned the cans before cooking," she assures him, sliding another bowl to me. "We made sure everything was clean before we used it to cook too."

"Really?" Akim peers suspiciously at his food. Then he looks up at Nooma, avoiding her gaze. "Tell me Malek didn't clean them."

"He didn't, I did," Alta pipes up from the other side of the table.

"Why am I being singled out?" I ask, a forkful halfway to my lips. The spicy, savoury smell is so appetising.

"Because you would only *pretend* to clean them," Akim points out, poking the food with his fork, looking put out.

"I would not!" I protest as both Nooma, and Alta burst out laughing. "I *begrudge* that, greatly."

"Begrudge it all you want," Nooma replies, settling next to Nephanie. "But he's got a point."

"He does not, and you should all show me a little more respect. I *am* the captain here after all." I pull myself up as tall as I can. More snickers and Nooma rolls her eyes, though she's clearly amused.

How could I be mad though, when these people are so much more than my crew and me so much more than their captain? We're family, first and foremost. We found each other and through the horrors of Helios we built something lasting.

We're the only ones staying on the ship, preparing for our trip to Chuan. La'min and his crew are helping with the repairs and Tulain paid us, as promised, although we're keeping Anh Giang. I need to find a job sending us in the right direction whilst Alta tweaks the engine, Nooma decides what upgrades we need, and Akim customises the cockpit.

We've got five more people due on board, and the ship is just about big enough to accommodate everyone.

For now, the atmosphere is cosy, music playing from the tablet, everyone now agreeing a sound system is a must, and I know we're going to bicker over what music to play. I like knowing things like this are in our future. It makes me feel alive.

"You Humans have strange taste buds if this is supposed to be edible," Nephanie says, wrinkling her nose.

"This isn't the best, is it?" Nooma admits around a mouthful.

They're right. It's bland and horrible, the spicy smell definitely not delivering on the taste, and some chunks have a really weird texture.

"This is almost as bad as being back on Helios," Alta complains.

Akim is studying a piece of would-be meat up closely.

"I did what I could!" Nooma grumbles. "Didn't see any of you offering to cook up something."

"I *did* offer to get some take-away," I point out, swallowing a mouthful almost whole. It's better than chewing at this point.

"We need to save money for the trip ahead of us," Nooma points out.

"Well, I can't fix anything on an empty stomach, and I'm not eating this," Alta pushes the bowl away from them.

Akim's bowl joins theirs in the middle of the table to a frustrated noise from Nooma. Nephanie laughs.

"Oh, shut up," Nooma nudges her in the ribs which only makes Nephanie laugh more, eyes a gleeful turquoise.

Now I'm laughing, because Nooma looks so mad and Nephanie's laugh is stupidly contagious. Nooma turns her glare on me. I try to stop but, as I push my lips shut, I can hold the laughter in even less.

"Fine, fine, you ungrateful bastards, I'll go get something from out. But I'm *not* paying," she adds, jabbing a finger in my direction. "You are not taking this meal off our cut of the job."

"I won't," I half-giggle, tears stinging the corner of my eyes. "I won't. I'll come with you, we can buy too much food and eat ourselves silly."

"That doesn't sound like a very pleasant plan," Akim declares, looking quite concerned. Alta giggles.

"You sure you want to come?" Nooma asks. "You shouldn't be hopping around just yet."

"First of all, I don't hop, and secondly, you did a beautiful job sealing me up and filling me with painkillers, so I think I'll be fine." She shrugs and gives me a 'on your head be it' look.

"Please bring back something edible," Akim pleads. "I want something safe and not too greasy."

I nearly pat him on the shoulder but stop myself at the last second.

"Don't worry, we'll find more of that stuff you had at the karaoke. Alta, want any—"

I don't finish. One second, I'm upright and the next there's blinding pain and I'm on the floor. Nooma appears above me, shaking her head. Did she just accept to let me come just to watch me fall over? Well, I can't argue now. Guess I'm not ready to crutch it anywhere. Damn. Tonight's dinner really is in somebody else's hands. I need to get a new hoverchair.

"You alright?" Alta asks, sounding somewhat worried.

"He'll be fine if he stops being an idiot," Nooma replies, all but plucking me off the floor, depositing me back in my chair. She is far too strong for my own good.

I dust myself, scowling a little.

"I'm fine, changed my mind, Nooma can go fetch us dinner. I'll wire you some credits. I just don't feel like going out, too tired," I add, feigning a yawn and a stretch, immediately regretting the latter. Alta snickers. "Oh shush."

"I'll go with you," Nephanie stands up with that Shinarian fluid grace.

"Are you sure you're up to it? You pushed yourself really hard earlier." This time Nooma sounds concerned. I see favouritism is starting to show.

Nephanie's eyes shift to a colour I don't recognise as she lays her hand against Nooma's cheek.

"I'll be fine. Come, teach me what is safe for you strange creatures to eat," she speaks in a tone that should be reserved for private spaces and certainly not for food talk. Then she's heading down the stairs, leaving Nooma rooted to the spot.

I let out a whistle. "Don't take *too* long, eh?"

She glowers and then she's gone. Alta is giggling, Akim looking at us with a puzzled expression and all I can do is laugh.

Because I'm happy.

Because I have my crew. My family.

***

"This station plays *awful* music," I lament from where I'm sprawled on the sofa, too full to move.

"Hey, I like this!" Alta protests as they bop their way from the table over to me. How are they still moving? They ate almost as much as I did. They plop themselves down, bouncing to the music. "I can't wait to have a sound system, so I can get some tracks from home."

"It had better not be pop," I mutter, pretending to stick my fingers in my ears.

"If it is, you will have to *deal*."

"Nu-uh, I'm the captain, I should get to have final choice on what music plays!"

Akim looks up from what he's reading, shaking his head. "Being the captain doesn't make you all powerful. A crew like ours is more like a democracy than a dictatorship." Alta snorts and I just stare at him, mouth half-open in a retort I don't have. "So really it's more like we should get to *vote* on what we listen to. But that's messy, especially if people only vote for their stuff, so a rota would be easier."

"I'm not making a sound system rota," I grumble.

"I will!" Akim seems rather happy at the idea.

From the kitchen I can hear Nephanie and Nooma 'tidying up', though I think they just wanted some alone time. They did make it very clear they didn't need help—although Nooma had to pretty much hand Akim the tablet to stop him from joining in the cleaning up.

It makes me realise I'm kinda pining for Làhn. I probably pissed him off in the cockpit. I think I was a bit of a jerk, but it wasn't as though I'd dreamt up the way his eyes kept going to my lips. Maybe in the context it wasn't the best thing to say. I'm going to need flirting practice.

"How are you feeling?" Alta asks. "You gave me a scare when Nooma brought you back, you know."

I shrug, all too keen to not think of how many times I thought I would die back on the destroyer.

"I'm okay. Painkillers are fading a bit, but I'll be good as new soon enough." They give me a soft, gentle smile. There's a vulnerability that runs deep inside them, hidden behind the masks we all wear. But we're family now, and that means we get to see behind those masks. "I'll sort out some way for you to send a message back home, same for Akim. I figured it's something you'd want. Tulain and La'min probably know people that can do it in ways that can't be tracked, so you won't have to worry about Berik."

Alta looks away, and I catch the glint of tears in their eyes. Berik took everything from us. One way or another they stole our lives. Our dreams. But we'll make them pay.

"Thanks," they whisper. "I wonder if they think I'm dead. I wonder what people back home think happened... I just... I feel bad I couldn't help anyone else when we escaped." I glance at them as they lean back, staring at the ceiling. "I didn't let myself think about it until now because I was just so glad to have made it out but... There are still people I know there, people who have done nothing wrong."

"It wasn't your responsibility," Alta glowers, but not at me. "They kept you separated from each other, so they didn't run the risk of you all moving as a unit. It's likely some of your people weren't even there, you know."

"Still, I—"

"You'll be able to help them, not just *now*. But we're going to bring Berik down and when that happens, we can bust the doors down on their prisons!"

They smile. "I like the sound of that."

"Like the sound of what?" Nooma asks as she walks back into the room.

"Blowing the doors of the Helios prisons wide open when we've brought Berik low," Alta replies enthusiastically.

Nooma just shakes her head. "Let's do things one at a time, shall we? We need to find a job before we even leave this place. A job heading in the right direction and not requiring a return trip, at that."

"There are always delivery jobs to be done, and we have a nice cargo bay so that won't be a problem, trust me." Nooma raises an eyebrow. "Hey, you *should* trust me with this. I did get us a ship like I said I would, didn't I?"

"I guess you did," Nooma concedes. "But still, we don't want to do anything too illegal. We'll have enough trouble with Berik chasing us as it is."

She'll learn, one day, that things aren't as simple as legal versus illegal. I know what she means though: there's no point in getting on people's bad sides when we've got this long trip ahead of us. And an entire corporation on our tail.

"How long do you think the engine will take to fix?" I ask Alta.

"After what Nephanie did to it? Not a clue." They twist into their seat as the Shinarian girl joins us. "What *did* you do to the engine?"

Nephanie's eyes flash orange. "Gave it a bit of a boost. Sorry your Human tech couldn't handle it."

Alta's eyes narrow playfully. "La'min did say he'd send some of his people to help, so it shouldn't take that long," they add.

"Good." Nephanie leans on the wall near Nooma. "The Shinarian military will eventually figure out where I ended up, and I'd like to be far away when they do."

"What do they want with you?" I can't help but ask. For a second, I think she's gonna shut us out, but then her eyes catch Nooma's.

"They want what I can do. Only a handful of Shinarians are born with the capacity to control their telekinetic and kinetic abilities. If you have that skill, you're trained as a soldier from childhood. We're meant to be the best the Shinarian army has. I told them where to stick it as soon as I got old enough to understand. Been running ever since."

"Wow, that's…messed up," Alta whispers.

Nephanie shrugs. "It is. But that's what happens when you're at war for hundreds of years, it messes everyone up. I let myself be thrown into Helios hoping they wouldn't find me. But when they did, and you guys came along, I figured joining up would be a nice change of pace."

"And has it been?"

Her eyes flash another colour I can't read. "Well, this time I rather enjoyed using my powers. So yeah, guess it has been."

I beam at her and Nooma shakes her head, a small smile curving her lips.

"I'm going to go read in bed," Akim declares suddenly, getting up and walking off.

Bed sounds like heaven right now.

"Akim has the best plans," Alta stands, stretching. "I'm gonna call it a night. Tomorrow, me and the engine can start our face off," they declare, cracking their knuckles.

Nephanie takes her leave after giving Nooma a long, lingering look.

"You're better in a fight than I thought you'd be," Nooma says, settling next to me on the sofa. "But try and be a little less reckless in the future, okay?"

I chuckle. "I'll try, but reckless might as well have been amma's middle name, and I think I inherited it."

"Just don't get yourself killed. You might not be a military captain barking orders at everyone, or a specialist at anything but... Without you we wouldn't be here. So, remember that next time you feel like throwing yourself in the line of fire. You're the one who pulled us together."

I wish I could tell Nooma how much hearing this from her means.

"I'll remember," I say, throat strangely thick. "Thanks, Nooma, for everything."

She smiles, a simple, bright smile that touches her eyes and fuels the swelling in my chest.

"Anything for a friend."

"Anything for a friend," I echo. “For family.”

EPILOGUE

NEW BEGINNINGS

A home isn't always the house we live in. It's also the people we choose to surround ourselves with.

T.J. Klune

CHAPTER 50
LÀHN

BAKULA

Shuobe managed to find a Mallak restaurant tucked away in a small alley, packed almost to bursting. Most of the waiters are bizarre looking droids that whizz back and forth, the decor mimicking Mallak ships with banners, tapestries, and fake plants.

It's noisy and busy: a happy place, like *Chen's*. I ache for Kirillion, for the streets and sights that I knew by heart, for the dizzying sunsets and the rain pelting my window. But Kirillion was just a place, and I'm starting to realise that I don't belong to a place, but with the people around me. With my friends.

Ordering food is chaos: Mallak dishes are made for sharing and Kode is so excited with what's on offer that I'm happy enough to let her pick.

Ever since the decision I made after discovering the truth, everything has been lighter. The power of having a course set ahead of you, I suppose.

It might take months to reach Chuan, depending on what jobs we do on the way, but right now I don't care. Right now, having a goal and people to head towards it with is enough.

I'm going home. I don't know if I'll stay, if I'll be the Prince some might want me to be. But I'll go there, and we'll do our best to help.

The girls have ordered enough food for an army, and we have to reorganise the table several times as one mouth-watering dish after the other is brought. There is a light in Kode's eyes I worried I'd never see again.

Làhn, stop daydreaming and eat! Kode signs after poking me in the forehead with one of the long chopstick-like instruments the Mallak use.

I laugh. It comes easily. When we left the Guild and Kirillion, I wasn't sure I'd ever laugh again.

"Is your mother going to mind you coming with us?" I ask Shuobe.

She shakes her head. "Nah, I sent her a message, but this is normal. Most Mallak go journeying by themselves at one point or another, usually bringing back something of value. And hey, I'm not ruling out finding some treasure I can bring back."

I don't think Malek and his crew are after treasure... Kode signs. *They don't give treasure hunter vibes,* she adds. *More like justice-bringers!*

I try not to laugh imagining the grin on Malek's face if he heard that.

"Yeah, he's not as tough as he tries to look," Shuobe says around a mouthful. Kode giggles as a bit of food flies off her chopstick as she signs. I once flicked a noodle in my own face signing whilst eating; I've learnt to be careful since. "I think Malek likes to make himself sound dangerous, but they're freelancer outlaws, not space pirates, which is good 'cause those aren't the kind of people you want to deal with."

Làhn is a thief, so I'm sure he would have done fine! Kode signs enthusiastically and I fake glower.

Says the hacker who once emptied a politician's bank account! I retort. *You've stolen way more than I have.*

One, it was a job, and two, I didn't get to keep that money. If I had, we would all be living on a resort planet right now, she retorts.

I didn't keep anything either! She raises an eyebrow and I laugh. *Okay, okay, maybe I did keep some creds every now and again. But then I'd buy you something with it too, so don't complain!*

We laugh and Kode ends up smearing sauce on my face by trying to feed me, proceeding to do a far less messy job when she feeds Shuobe.

We eat ourselves silly—obviously, the sensible thing to do at an all you can eat—and an hour later we're stumbling out, giddy on too much food and good company. Kode's holding her stomach and dragging her feet, making a show of how exhausted she is. Around us Bakula is as bustling as ever, reminding me of Kirillion.

"You wanna come back to the room?" Shuobe asks and I startle, having drifted ahead, turning to find Kode snuggled on her back, a soft smile on her face.

Sometimes there is nothing like seeing the people you love happy.

"Nah, I'm gonna walk around a bit, need to digest!"

Shuobe laughs. "Let us know when you're on your way back, okay?"

I assure her I will, and I can't help but think of Malek as I watch them leaving together. I hate how much he's wormed his way into my heart. It's that damned smirk, the way his eyes catch mine whenever they can. The way his hand felt on mine.

I let my feet carry me around the station, avoiding anywhere that seems too empty or dark. Malek and Nooma warned us about the dangers, but I've been street-savvy for long enough to not have needed the lesson.

I like the strange group of misfits we've somehow fallen in with. I want to trust them. No, I *do* trust them. Zoon would tell me I'm being too quick but something in my gut tells me I'm right.

Bakula is a maze of corridors devoid of continuity and logic, yet I find myself drawn to it. The crowd is thick and jostling as I turn into a marketplace, vendors hawking their wares over loud adverts and live music. It's life as I like it: chaotic and busy and loud. I let the flow of the crowd move me along stalls laden with parts and gadgets and many other things. Everything here seems geared towards cyborgs, androids, or races who rely heavily on enviro-suits. A stall has a selection of pre-made limbs for 'Cyborgs in a rush', next to a set of 'build your own face' parts. A little further down, I watch someone take off their mouth, exposing silicone and wires beneath before trying on a different plate, turning this way and that as the vendor holds up a mirror.

It reminds me of the place I overheard Malek talking about, the body-mod 'district' Alta was asking about. I don't know my feet are taking me there until the lights switch from neutral white to purple and the corridor opens onto a series of hole-in-the-wall workshops. The crowd is thinner here, music pouring out of the shops and mixing in questionable ways as holo-ads offer a variety of services. I walk past a few stalls, assailed by offers to have my ears elongated, or have various parts of my body pierced whilst digital tattoos are displayed on lifelike mannequins.

I didn't know why I came here until now.

I find a quiet tattoo shop and slip inside. An old woman, only part Human, looks up from her computer, squinting at me.

"Do you know what you want?" she asks, a little brusquely, her accent so clipped as to be sharp.

I nod, a little hesitant.

"Well show me then, can't get started if you don't and there's a Thoolat race starting in an hour I don't want to miss!"

I show her, we haggle on the price—she wins—and then I settle in the chair. I don't want a digital tattoo which softens her to me. She is covered in traditional, static tattoos. She doesn't talk as she works, doesn't ask me questions. I'm grateful for the quiet.

Less than an hour later, I'm done, my right wrist stinging. I look down at it, at the symbol of the Guild etched into my skin above the coordinates for Kirillion and smile, bringing my other wrist up, both tattoos side by side. Both my pasts, written forever into my skin. Because as much as I am Nguyen van Làhn, I am also Làhn the thief from Kirillion.

When I set back towards the room, sending the girls a quick message, I feel at peace with myself for the first time in a long while.

CHAPTER 51
TRYSTAN

EDEN ONE

Mom was almost more excited than me that I made plans with Nathaniel. She's thrilled that I'm trying harder, doing what is right. Little does she know the truth. But I suppose in appearance alone this works in my favour. She's insisted I wear a skirt and I gave up arguing, stuffing a pair of pants at the bottom of my bag when she wasn't looking.

"You have to look *proper,*" she repeats for the thousandth time as she fastens the top button of my blouse, half strangling me in the process. At least it's not the original frilly monstrosity. "You two are only engaged. You must project the right image of modesty."

It's all I can do not to roll my eyes, instead glancing at the message Cat just sent.

Good luck!! With a line of crossed fingers emoji.

A second message appears, with a throbbing emoji of kissing lips above the text: *Tell me if this happens!*

I am going to murder her.

Finally, mom deems me ready, and I don't even look in the mirror as I hurry into the waiting car. I need to be early, so I can get changed. And calm down. Which doesn't feel possible.

I message Cat back to give myself something to focus on, but she is zero help. She is convinced everything will be fine but I'm so worried I can't bring myself to believe it. No matter how many deep breaths I take, there isn't enough air. Telling Cat had been a spur of the moment thing, but this is planned, *orchestrated*. It's a terrible idea. I should run home and hide, pretend I never said anything. Only I can't. What was said can never be taken back.

The cinema complex is sprawling, and the driver drops me off at the nearest entrance to where we're meeting. We didn't decide where to go eat before the movie. We didn't even agree on what we would go see. Maybe that means he's as nervous as me. Is that good or bad?

I rush inside, to the women's bathroom—definitely not my favourite place—but I need to change. I slip into a cubicle and into my pants. It's not great, but the best I can do.

I step out and head to the mirror, tidying my loose hair. The young woman who is reapplying her lipstick gives me a compassionate smile and I frown slightly.

"Never a good time to come on, is there?" she asks, and it takes me a second to realise what she means.

I suppose rushing into a toilet stall and coming out in different bottoms could look like my period crept up on me at an inopportune time.

"Yeah," I mutter, feeling my cheeks heat up. I'm seriously bad at unexpected conversations.

In the mirror our eyes meet as I wash my hands.

"You got everything you need?"

I nod. I don't want to be talking about this. I don't want to be talking at all. I'm so nervous I feel like I'm going to be sick.

"I need to go," I blurt, feeling as though just walking out would be rude, and awkward, and oh god please, someone get me out of here.

"Good luck," the woman replies with a slight wink, and I wonder if it's *that* obvious what I'm here for.

I spot Nathaniel almost immediately despite the crowd, as though he's a magnet for my eyes. Like in the stories. He's got his back to me, and if we were in a movie he'd turn around and smile, and maybe, depending on when this was taking place, we'd run towards each other and... I close my eyes. If Cat knew what I was thinking I would never live it down.

He doesn't turn—I don't know if I'm grateful or disappointed—as I walk up to him.

"Hey!" I manage to sound mostly normal.

He's wearing tailored pants and a shirt opened at the collar that is far less roguish on him than he probably thinks. But it suits him so much more than the suits he wears around his father.

"Tris, hey, you're early."

I forget how to speak so we just end up looking at each other, awkwardly frozen in place.

"We should, um, maybe move?" I manage to say, keenly aware that we're standing in the middle of the lobby.

"Um? Yeah. Yeah, moving. Where do you want to eat?"

I don't know. I don't know if it matters.

"Frankie's has private booths?" Right now, I can't even remember what food they serve. I just know I want to be somewhere quiet.

"That sounds good," he says, but doesn't move. He's staring at me as though he doesn't recognise me or is trying to see something beyond the face I wear every day. I don't know how to do this, so I grab his hand and turn, leading him towards the restaurant. I expect some resistance, but he follows, hand clasping mine.

I tell myself he's doing it to keep up appearances.

I want him to *really* hold my hand.

We're seated in a private booth at the back and left to look at the menu. But neither of us are scrolling through it.

"I guess I owe you an explanation," I blurt out in the tense silence at the same time as he says, "I'm sorry I'm being so awkward!"

We stare at each other, silent once more before both trying to speak at the same time. He cracks an awkward smile and I have to bite my bottom lip not to laugh. We're *so bad* at this. He must see the fear on my face because he reaches out across the table, laying his hand on mine, unaware of what it does to me.

"It's okay, Tris, you can talk to me."

"Tryst," I blurt, eyes not meeting his.

"What?"

"I prefer Tryst. Short for Trystan." My cheeks are burning. This was by far easier with Cat but then I don't want to *kiss* Cat. Since when do I want to kiss Nathaniel? I'm being ridiculous.

"So, you're…transgender? That's the right word?"

Oh. He looked this up. He *looked this up*. I wish the booth would swallow me. I was so prepared for my big speech and explanation and instead… Instead, this. Why is it that no matter what, Nathaniel always manages to surprise me?

"Yeah," I manage, still not daring to look up. "I don't want it to be a problem." My voice is getting smaller by the second.

"It won't be." I like how he says it. Not, *why would it be?* which always makes me wonder if there is something that's not being said. No, he states it. I look up, meeting his green eyes. He's smiling. "Plus, it's not like you don't know my little secret," he adds, and although he says it flippantly, I wonder if he's as worried as me.

"That's not a problem either," I say, and I swear I see something light in his eyes. "Actually, I'm sort of relieved you don't like girls." Why did I say that? Why do I do this to myself?

"Oh?"

I swear I must be the colour of a beetroot by now. "I don't exactly like them either," I mumble, almost wishing my hand wasn't still under his, that his eyes weren't pinning me to my seat.

"Well then," he says. "I guess that might make the whole getting married easier, eh?"

I let out a breathy laugh. I feel like I could cry with relief.

"Guess you must be happy you're not marrying a girl."

He smiles, a little bit of that old mischief in his eyes. "Definitely."

And like that, just like that, I wonder if everything *can* be okay. If I can be happy. Because I'm not alone. A few days ago, I had no-one but my uncle, and now I have friends both here and out in space. Now I feel stronger, confident.

Now, I'm even happy.

CHAPTER 52
MALEK

BAKULA

The *Altayih* sits proudly in the hangar, hull repainted a deep midnight blue.

It's been three weeks since the events on the destroyer. Three weeks since my crew of five became a crew of ten. We've renamed the ship: the letters bright silver along the hull, and my throat tightens just looking at them. It's what amma called us. *Wanderers*. She used to say we had space in our blood. She was right.

My boots feel good and solid, brand new, trousers tucked in, synth-leather jacket thrown over a tank top. I'm becoming who I'm meant to be.

Around me everyone is finishing the last preparations: Jakoor affixing a training dummy to the side of the cargo bay not overtaken by the crates for the job we picked up, whilst Nooma checks everything is securely in place.

Akim is already in the cockpit, his new pet undoubtedly curled in my seat whilst he argues with Nephanie as to which route is best. We're headed to a small mining colony and getting paid generously for it. Alta is doing the last engine checks, reassuring themselves that everything is in order. Last I knew Làhn was helping Shuobe and Kode settle into the cabin the three of them are sharing. Tryst sits on the stairs watching everything unfold with stunned wonder.

"Malek!" Nooma calls.

My new leg is so good I'm excited at just walking. The synth skin on my arm has been replaced and I've bought some patching-gel in case I get myself hurt again. Not that I plan to, but rather safe than sorry and all that.

"What is it?" I ask, still half admiring the ship.

"Get your ass up here and *help*, will you?"

I chuckle. I might be the captain, but Nooma is going to make damn sure I never get a big head from it. The title of captain is really just a formality here anyway.

I jog up the ramp, the sound of my own footsteps music to my ears. I only got the leg yesterday and it took some adjusting, so I stayed at the tech shop. Today is the first day I get to walk onto my ship.

"Can you double check all the crates scanned right?" Nooma asks, tossing me the scanner. "This is a pain to use."

"We're all good," I announce after a quick scan. "How many times have you checked this?"

"Better safe than sorry," she mutters.

She's more stressed than anyone else, having spent last night and this morning triple checking everything and driving us nuts. I feel like there's something she's not saying, but I've let her know she can talk to me, and that's all I can do.

"Tryst," Jakoor calls and the android perks up. "Can you come give me a hand?"

"You already have four," he points out. I chuckle as I turn back to Nooma.

"We'll be fine, I promise. We calculated what we need for the food printer, and we've got spare. We've got spare parts, the engine is fine, the weapons and shields are fine, and we have every crate we're supposed to have."

Her hands fall away from the cable ties.

"I just... I... We're going a long way. I mean, not to Chuan, but even just to Jhost, it's still far. Over a week and a half in hyperspace, that's a huge distance."

"We have breaks planned in between so we don't get hyperspace sickness. You and Nephanie helped me plan it, remember?"

She nods. "How do you never worry about anything?"

I shrug. "I don't know. Sometimes all I can do is worry, and sometimes I just feel that everything will go right no matter what."

Nooma laughs softly. "I almost envy you that."

"Almost. You wouldn't want what else it comes with."

"No, I wouldn't."

Over the ship's coms, Akim lets me know we're ready to go. My excitement is alive inside my skin. "Go ahead," I tell Nooma, "Make sure everyone is ready for take-off."

I turn back to the docking bay. This is it; we're leaving.

My ship.

My crew.

At last.

"Hey kid, were you gonna leave without saying goodbye?" La'min appears in the hangar doorway, and I grin. I knew he'd come. Vess and Tulain follow him as I rush to greet them.

La'min pulls me in a tight hug, and I fuss his furry ear just to hear his noise of protest. I could have gone with him: off to a job that doesn't involve Berik. But that's not my path. Vess and Tulain step forward, clapping me on the back as I pull away from La'min.

"You better make it back safely," Tulain mutters, his orange eyes intense on me.

"I will," I say, and he hugs me tight.

I don't pull away for a long time.

Fifteen minutes later the docking bay doors are sliding open, Akim and I settled in the cockpit, his pet secured in his cabin whilst everyone else straps in. The music is quiet up here, so we can concentrate. Behind the doors, space reveals itself in all its glory of twisting nebulae and shining stars. Once, the Urelhan destroyer would have dwarfed everything, but now it's gone. I don't think anyone will miss its looming presence.

"Ready to go, captain," Akim declares.

"Bakula control, this is the *Altayih*," I speak slowly, over-compensating for how fast my heart is beating. "We're ready for take-off."

"You're free to go, *Altayih*," the harsh voice of a Dpanir responds. "Have a safe trip."

Akim lifts off gently. Then with one, smooth motion we're into the open. There is a tangle of hope, and happiness, and so many wordless things in my chest.

"Time to hyperspace jump, forty seconds," Akim tells me.

I hit the ship's coms. "Everyone, get ready for the jump." The screen shows us how far we are from our jump spot. I watch the countdown with bated breath. Akim hits the button sequence so fast I can hardly follow his hands. It's the smoothest transition into hyperspace I've ever seen.

And like that, our journey officially begins.

ACKNOWLEDGEMENTS

First, I want to thank my partner—Leontiy—for the years of support he's given me while working on this novel. A bottomless font of encouragement, pushing me to keep going even when self-doubt made me think nothing would ever be good enough.

My parents—for raising me with a great love of books and stories. Dad, for that infuriating, but invaluable ever-critical eye (useful for editing and the killing of darlings!); Maman for giving me the final push, and the means to get this off the ground. Without her, I'd probably still be endlessly trudging in the trad-pub trenches.

Lily—best friend and webmaster—for her excitement and support, for being an enthusiastic cheerleader and coding angel (without her, I would not have the awesome website I do!).

A big thank you to Adrian/Ria, my copyeditor and far-more than merely a self-professed typo-hunter. You certainly did more than just catch a few typos, and we had some good laughs over the differences between British and American English along the way.

And finally, a giant thank you to the booksta community—especially my Street Team—for coming on this wild adventure of self-publishing with me, and having done so much to support me. Without you, *Breakout* wouldn't have reached as many people as it has. You have all contributed to this book being out there, through your hype and your kind words, which bolstered me through even the toughest day.

Special thank yous go to:

Amanda, for all her wonderful words about my work, for being probably my biggest fan (Leo not counting) from day one, and for understanding my work in ways I worried it never would be.

Tia, a fellow self-publishing writer of all things queer, for her support and guidance as I threw myself headfirst into this industry.

RunRun and Anna-Ruth, for their beautiful reviews that I'm so pleased I get to feature on the dust jacket.

And honorary mention to Klayton, aka Celldweller. Thank you, for *Breakout,* for the line "my only crime is that I'm made of flesh, circuit, and bone". Without this song, Malek would still be in Helios, and the Altiyah would never have launched.